What was locked in shadow stirs, and where darkness has laid dormant, evil awakes.

This is not some mythical land, nor the distant past. Our own world, our own time, will face malice not seen since ancient times.

Once, when the world was new, the Fallen battled the Light over the destiny of humankind.

Civilization was left in flames, the Scourges turned back by the Watchers in the last hour. The Darkness, though, was not defeated. Retreating to the shadows, they waited for a time when the world slept unaware.

Standing before them are six that will decide the fate of us all. A new generation of Watchers, gifted by the Light with abilities few among us wield.

Those they face, the Dark One's Followers, are also gifted, but with power forged by blackness and terror.

The depraved seek lost relics infused with unimaginable power. Through portals of time they will raise an army of nightmarish creatures once lost to myth and legend. Collapse and ruin they will bring.

A war of the worst sort has begun. The six Watchers must stem the tide, or will they be drowned by the flood of darkness that ends the age of man?

Among the Shadows

Watchers of the Light
Book 1

DARRICK DEAN

Sword and Shadow Press

"There are no ordinary people. You have never talked to a mere mortal."

- C.S. Lewis

Historical Notes

The Mayans built their city of Uxmal on the Yucatán Peninsula, an area populated by numerous underground caverns. There, some believed, the entrance to Xibalba, the Place of Fright, could be found.

The initial earthworks of what would become Stonehenge were raised around 3000 B.C. Humans had first shown interest in the site 5000 years earlier. Why men went to such lengths to raise the monoliths, and fashion other sites on the surrounding landscape, is still not completely understood.

The Vikings attempted establishing settlements in Canada beginning around 1000 A.D. The sites are not believed to have survived long, but the intrepid mariners continued to sail to the North American continent until the mid 14th Century. The extent of their explorations, and who may have followed, is unclear.

Between the Second and Third Crusades, on the 4th of July 1187, the Sultan Saladin won the battle at the Horns of Hattin against the Kingdom of Jerusalem. The Crusaders had carried a fragment of the True Cross into battle and lost it to the Saracen army. Its fate is not recorded by history.

On the 11th of September 1275, St. Michael's church on Glastonbury Tor in Somerset, England was destroyed by an earthquake. The hilltop site has long been the rumored hiding place of various sacred relics. Some things are best left lost.

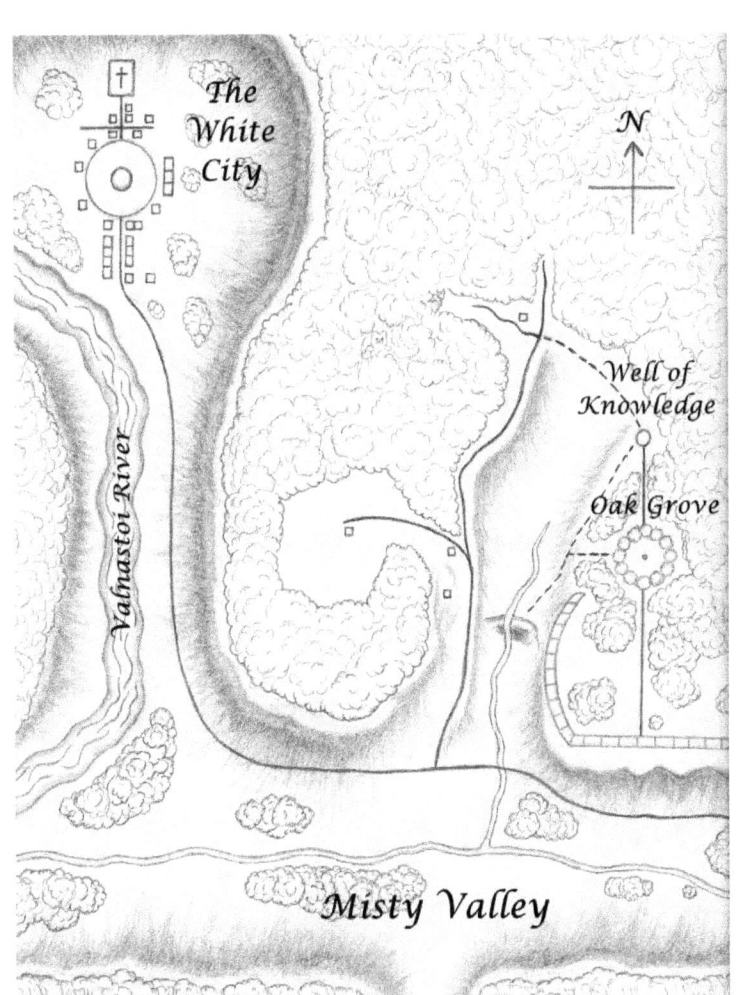

PROLOGUE

*M*ake no mistake, this is a war. One of the worst
sort.

It had been years since Grayson Kirby had last spoken those words. Now they came intruding in between Ethan Dietrich's thoughts at the worst possible time. Standing among the shadows of a sandy alleyway watching and listening, he couldn't afford to lose focus on the mission at hand. Midnight had passed an hour before and most of the town finally slept as the heat of the day gave way to a cool breeze off the ocean, making the smells of trash and human waste a bit more tolerable. Wandering out at night often meant never returning home — nothing ever good happened between 10 p.m. and 5 a.m. — so there was little chance of running into any of the locals. Not that Ethan had much cause to fear them, which the power simmering in him attested to, but no need to invite unnecessary trouble.

An errant bark of a dog broke the quiet of the early morning as it scrounged for scraps of food. In a way, a strange sound to hear, not because dogs were unheard of in this corner of the world, but as a reminder of normalcy. No one cared that the dusty, ramshackle slum on the Horn of Africa existed. A haven for terrorists and pirates, their law written by whomever killed the most people. It was no wonder that if one of the warships beyond the horizon reduced their fiefdom to rubble, few would notice its passing. Perhaps that was why, every so often, this apocalyptic backwater of civilization did something requiring attention. Or maybe it was here they believed their work would go unnoticed. The battle down the coast at the ancient port city of Mogadishu had made the world a bit hesitant for awhile. That was years ago, before Ethan's time, but now his attention — and that of others — had certainly been aroused. He had every intention of leaving a glimmer of hope to these oppressed people. The evil living among them would be found and eliminated. A war it had been, but what else was the old-timer hinting at? Too many secrets he had kept.

The bark again. This time closer. The emaciated animal stopped and looked into the darkness, but didn't see Ethan. Lucky dog. It wasn't the only one having a good night. After this there would be no more operations into the lairs of those who would see the world collapse and burn. Ethan's employers — they weren't exactly his bosses, no one was — had been quite perplexed by his announcement. No one was better than him. He lost no sleep over what he had seen and done. That was precisely one reason why he was moving on.

Not that he was callous, he just understood how men were. Some killed out of malice. Others used death to end the terror of the depraved when all other options evaporated. Many would never get it. Still, he feared he'd become numb to the wickedness and death and become detached from the world and all that was good would turn distant and dim. Was there a point of no return? He wouldn't have to find out, but he couldn't shake the sense of something unfinished. His gifts from the Light couldn't only be for this. There had to be more. It wasn't a mystery to him why people feared what the shadows concealed. He had seen more than he cared to remember. All so others didn't have to. Yet, even after being dead all these years, Grayson's voice was still there reminding him that he hadn't seen it all. The fear in his eyes had been unsettling. Afraid of who and of what? Ethan pushed the old man from his mind. Dawn was approaching quickly.

He took one last look around. His situational awareness was acute, but carelessness killed many operatives. Impatience never bode well on a mission like this, but time was short. There had been no reason to engage any of the guards. They were out front, barely awake and not even close to a sober state. Even had they been aware, when Ethan merged with the shadows, he might as well been invisible. The bizarre secret government programs could never create people who could wield the energy that flowed in and around them. People who could disappear. So they didn't care how Ethan could infiltrate impossible situations and always come out like it was a trip to the grocery store. The fact he did it, and did it again, made him invaluable. None of that would soon matter. He and Milena had grown tired of the politicians who meddled and stumbled about stupidly in the affairs of the world. They also wanted a family and normalcy. "Imagine us wanting to settle down?" Milena had asked.

First, the Shadow had one final task.

The mission was a simple one. Neutralize a man that had orchestrated deaths of hundreds of innocents around the world. Neutralize. Now there was a politically correct term for what was about to happen. The Righteous One, the terrorist had named himself. He thought no one could find nor touch him.

Ethan stood right outside his door.

An unlocked door at that. The Righteous One obviously didn't think anyone so bold to simply stroll into his compound. Ethan entered silently into the darkened hall, taking note of the faint light coming from a room to his left. He sensed one person inside, but it wasn't evil that he felt. Quite the opposite. Lingering in the blackness, he slowly opened the door without touching it. In the dim light of a lamp sitting on the floor of the otherwise empty, windowless room, a hostage sat in the center, strapped to a chair. The woman had a dirty rag in her mouth, tied tight around her head. A mess of black hair tumbled past her shoulders. Around her neck hung a small, Coptic gold cross. Deep, expressive brown eyes with a glint of green, and a face with a hint of something Middle Eastern. A striking woman; who was she? No one was supposed to be here. Ethan detected no trickery from her. Whoever she was, she was far from home and he couldn't leave her to some unspeakable fate.

He separated from the shadows.

The woman startled. She had seen the door open, but no one had been there. Ethan held his finger to his mouth and removed the gag.

"Who are you?" he whispered.

"I was going to ask you the same thing." She wasn't hurt and her English was perfect. American, in fact. "Are you some spook here to knock off the psychopath down the hall? I almost beat you to it. Never been caught before, so this is a bit embarrassing."

She finally took a breath.

Ethan knew all the operatives and freelancers. At least

he thought he did. "What's your name? Who do you work for?"

"Solana. I'm self-employed. I guess you can call me a free spirit, a world traveler type."

"This isn't exactly a vacation hot spot, missy."

"Well, you showed up, didn't you?" She laughed. "I see something in the news that needs taken care of and I go do it. Spur of the moment, that's me. Always in a rush."

"This place is going to be history in about ten minutes." He sensed the energy that surged in her. She was different, like him. "I don't know how you got here, but I can get you home."

She looked at him carefully. "You know what I am, don't you? No wonder I didn't see you coming. Then again, I didn't see this either." She nodded toward the rope. "How about a hand? I'm really not this kind of girl."

Ethan almost cracked a smile and began to untie her. She didn't seem overly distraught about her situation. Some people excelled at hiding fear, or perhaps her strength came from elsewhere.

"What happened?"

"I don't know." She rubbed her wrists. "A gang of goons came out of nowhere and it was like their leader was draining the life from me. The evil was overpowering. This isn't your average fanatic. I had never felt something like that before. I thought I was prepared for anything." She looked down and shook her head. "Obviously I'm not. I can't believe I wasn't tortured or raped. I figured that would come soon enough. Every few hours they have been forcing water down my throat laced with something. Keeps me nearly knocked out, but no one has showed up for awhile."

Ethan had caught an essence of Solana when he touched her. An untapped power simmered within her.

He wasn't sure what her abilities were. What they could become was a different story.

"Whatever is inside you, it isn't fully realized. Coming here was foolish, perhaps a trap to lure you or someone else."

"You are most correct, infidel." The voice came from behind. The Righteous One, his face hidden beneath a black shemagh, almost laughed with pleasure. "It is indeed a trap and instead of one, two I have ensnared." His ragged men, armed with barely functional AKs, surrounded them. Probably recruited from the poverty stricken streets, the eight unlikely had any idea who or what they were fighting for. Their eyes, unfocused and bloodshot from hours of chewing *khat,* were awash in one purpose.

Killing.

"Didn't see them coming?" Solana asked.

"Oh, but I did," Ethan said quietly. He also knew what Solana had said about the Righteous One to be true. The Darkness had taken hold deep in his soul. The mission planners had no knowledge of this, nor would they understand if told. Ethan knew, that's why he had came to this forsaken place. "Get ready to dive to your right."

Her nod was barely perceptible as he grabbed the back of the metal chair with his right hand. His blue eyes brightened, and for a moment she focused on his unshaven face. Then a faint shimmer around his body separated him from the surrounding space.

"Now!"

As Solana threw herself to the ground, Ethan propelled the chair at two of the derelicts closest to him. The impact to both their heads dropped them to the floor, but not before Ethan grabbed the rife muzzle of a third and landed an elbow strike to his neck. He swung the gun around and clubbed another as the addict tried to aim his gun without shooting his comrades. Ethan turned to face the others, aiming the weapon. Its visual state didn't convey confidence of its functionality. In fact, the lack of a clip told him one important thing. The gun had no bullets. The hesitation of the remaining four men proved that they didn't share this knowledge.

"Death to him! What are you waiting for?" The Righteous One unsheathed a blackened dagger that Solana swore had a subtle red glow. This wasn't time to sit by like a distressed princess. These men had almost killed her and still intended to do so. No time like the present to stir things up a bit.

Their drug had all but left her body as she drew the ripples of energy through her body to her fingertips. Dust began to spin on the floor beneath each hand, rising to them in a swirling column. Soon torrents of air tore through the doorway, forming a cyclone around her body. Her hair whirled; her eyes burned green. One man fired his rifle as Solana approached them, only to have the bullets sent back into his chest by the blasts of air she commanded. Her opponents had never experienced such terror as they shouted and cursed in their native tongue. They turned to run, but the vortexes of air she threw reached them first, lifting each off the ground and crushing them against the wall. Falling into a crumpled heap, they didn't move.

The Righteous One charged Ethan with a cry of foreign words as the woman of wind engaged the men. The dagger swung toward his head, but Ethan caught it with the rifle, sending the blade flying into the wall. A foot to the chest flipped his adversary over, tracing a circle through the air, before slamming into the ground. The Righteous One clutched his chest as the damage to his internal organs began to take his life. Ethan looked at Solana. She appeared to be fine and her cyclone had dissipated.

"Neat tricks you have there," Ethan said. "Thanks."

"Don't mention it." Her heart raced. "I've never taken it to that level before."

"Sometimes evil brings out the best in people like us." Not the best time to be funny, but nonetheless true. "Your control is strong, but don't take it for granted. Don't let anger provoke your abilities or you may lose that control."

"I know. I won't be doing this again for awhile, but I'm not the only one who can do a cool thing or two." He shrugged at the comment. Ethan had moved in a speed, and with a strength, she had never thought possible. "What about him?" Solana nodded at the Righteous One. He had moved like the wind, but even that had been too slow against Ethan. "His reign of terror appears to be at an end."

"It certainly does." Ethan attached an octagonal beacon to the wall and pressed a button on the device. A red light began to flash. He looked at the man on the floor. His breathing was labored. "A little something to hurry you on your way to the Dark One."

The final moments of his life were about to slip away. No inkling of remorse could be found in the dying man's eyes, no longer veiled. In a final moment of clarity, he spoke carefully and slowly.

"The worst evil you can imagine is but a shadow of what lies conspiring, hidden and unseen, waiting patiently to emerge and spread its suffocating malice. I am nothing compared to what is to come." His eyes froze, vacant and still, and the last breath left him.

Darkness fled from the room.

"That was a bit disconcerting," Solana said, with a shiver. The weight of oppression had vanished. A crossing through the veil.

"Time to get out of here before any more of his friends show up," Ethan said to her. He couldn't help to think that the dead terrorist, like Grayson, knew something he didn't. Something more terrible existed out there, but what?

"Don't have to tell me twice."

Five minutes later they were speeding through the desert to the exfil location in a rusted-out pickup truck. Ethan had explained they would be extracted to the U.S.S. Seawolf a few miles off shore. He wasn't keen on the claustrophobic sub, but Solana agreed it would be superior to her previous accommodations. Now he was quiet; his gaze didn't flinch from the vaguely outlined road. What he had done — what they had done — no doubt ran through his mind. In hers, it made her feel alive, but would it always? She could see that Ethan had been through so much more.

"Here it comes," he said in a whisper.

Solana looked through the broken rear window of the truck. A streak of fire fell from above. An explosion reached into the sky and a rumble moved across the desert. Poetic justice it was.

No one could hide from the Light.

CHAPTER ONE

The autumn day had arrived cloudy and damp during its early hours. Now the late afternoon Sun finally began to part the stubborn clouds. Rays of red light broke through the openings in the sky and imparted a ruddy glow to the sandstone buildings of the college campus. For the first time since the season began, the trees shading the brick sidewalks radiated their colors. The hillside across the river valley, high above the small-town college, blazed as if touched by fire. And yet the wind refused to move and the leaves stood still. The few whom noticed the dead calm overseen by the crimson Sun, briefly wondered if it was warm or ominous before forgetting the thought and returning to other matters.

Ethan noticed and wouldn't hastily discard nature's signs. The light wasn't quite right, just a few shades off, and the calm wasn't restful. He tried to clear his mind as he stopped at the center of the campus, surrounded at its borders by solid and imposing stone buildings. They could have been remnants of a forgotten hilltop keep, had no one known better. The founder of the college had said he chose the site overlooking the river after he discovered a strange stone that washed out of the ground during a storm. It had a worn script of some sort on it, witnesses had claimed. No records even suggested what may have been carved on it and the faded photos were of no help. This was of little concern to the generations of students that had since passed through the lecture halls and dorm rooms. Nor was it to Ethan. Duties called. Fifteen years ago he had been a student here; now he was a professor of physics. Ahead, among the trees of the northern end of campus, its bell tower rising among the leaves, sat what appeared to be a medieval church. This, though, was the college library, not built in such a distant age.

The light found its way through the stained glass windows of the library, shimmering as errant clouds passed in front of the Sun. Inside the vaulted reading room, Ethan set his backpack on one of the long wooden tables. Instead of sitting, he stood in front of the arch that framed the bayed windows as the colorful panels illustrating scenes from John Milton's *Paradise Lost* were awash in the warm glow. He had stared at them hundreds of times and more than once wondered how many people caught the subtle irony. Among the floors overflowing with books, the brilliant windows revealed what happened when the thirst for knowledge, and the power that often came with it, abandoned wisdom. A warning, perhaps.

Ethan took a quarter-sized, round stone from his pocket and turned it in the light. The calendar glyphs on the miniature Aztec Sun Stone circled a fierce solar deity. An overpriced trinket, but its buyer made it priceless. Milena had been an archaeology major and it hadn't taken much convincing to join her on digs in Mexico every summer break. She had given him the stone on the first trip, bought in some tourist-trap marketplace. He had been a physics major, but what better excuse to spend those months with his girlfriend in an exotic land than in a college-sponsored semester abroad? One tended to forget the hot, backbreaking work those days really were. They were young and he hadn't cared about those difficulties. Milena had left him speechless when they met at orientation. Yes, she was gorgeous, but it wasn't only that. Their first meeting years earlier had been in a fashion they could not readily explain to anyone. That was then. Anxiety tried to form in the pit of his stomach.

Ethan focused on an antique globe hanging in front of the stained glass. It usually went unnoticed, but it had a subtle glow in the reddish light. Only two other people were in the room and both had their heads buried in books. With another glance, the globe began to spin slowly. A smile almost appeared on his mouth. He had to be careful using his abilities openly, not that anyone would know it was him. At least the control had been returning, considerably more every month.

The ticking of the multiple dials on his watch broke the quiet. Almost time to go and Dr. Ransom had yet to appear. He had some of Milena's papers to give to Ethan. Thanks to his semi-retirement after decades of teaching, Milena had been hired to replace him, the college pleased to have an alumni and another accomplished archaeologist. She was certainly not an eccentric like the illustrious Ransom, but respected no less. Their years of traveling for her digs and his jobs were behind them. They planned it that way, which paved the way for Kyra's entry into the world. All the planning in the world hadn't prepared them for the past year. For all that he was, he could still barely stay focused. He blinked his eyes. Something else was wrong.

The light had shifted, the windows no longer brilliant. Shades and shadows enveloped the room and he looked behind him. The tables were empty except for a man sitting in the back. Perhaps only fifty-something, he wore a tailored black suit and smiled at Ethan. Certainly not a smile of happiness — evil hung thickly around the man. The Light began to build in Ethan, his body tensed.

"Well now, it is a pleasure to finally meet you, Ethan Dietrich. Or is it the Shadow, the bane of the Darkness?" The man stood and walked around the table. "What, nothing to say?"

"Who are you?" Ethan had encountered many within whom the Darkness had taken hold, but not like this. His humanity was a disguise or, perhaps, all but gone. What lived beyond the veil had stayed away from Ethan in such form. No longer.

"Who am I? Ah, that is not important. I am a messenger, here to make you an offer." He sat on the table. His gray and black hair was short; penetrating eyes lacked any color within the white. "I have been told the Darkness had come close, the cliff's edge only a hairsbreadth away. Anxiety constantly threatens. Your girl...well, you know." His voice was low and deep. Malice clung to it.

"What do you know of her?" Ethan stepped closer, his hands now fists. Other presences entered the room. He looked to his sides. Nothing visible. The attempt to raise fear inside him would fail.

"I didn't come here alone. Not stupid, am I, and no, I know nothing of your wife." He stood and approached Ethan. "I have no doubt you have felt the subtle shift in the fabric of existence. Light has grown stronger. So has Darkness. Two powerful armies arrayed against each other on the verge of battle. Is it the End that the charlatans constantly divine?"

This had been pressing upon Ethan's mind since autumn began. Was it because of what day approached? Partly, but there was something more. He had joked with his classes that the world was overdue for an "old-fashioned cataclysm." This was no longer a joke. "Speak your message before I take away your opportunity."

"Distressed, I see. Very well, listen carefully. The histories of man are full of dark times, many preceded by natural disaster. Volcanoes, earthquakes, or the occasional celestial demon of death have all precipitated pestilence and war. Of course, not all those events were natural. Soon those floodgates will open again." He paused. "This is the last chance you will have to choose sides."

Ethan started to laugh. "Is this what it has come to? Desperation? You think I would turn to the Darkness? What, because my life is a wreck?" He stepped closer. "I don't know how many like me are out there, but your kind fears us, always has. You're worried someone like me will interrupt whatever scheme you are conjuring." Ethan didn't add that he wasn't completely sure what he was other than the Light had gifted him.

"Listen human — you are still only human, by the way — what is coming will far eclipse anything you have seen." His words spit through his teeth. "Think of the greatest evils you have faced or history has recorded. Hundred-fold of those will be unleashed upon humanity. You or no one else can stand against them."

"We shall see," Ethan said as he raised his hand. He didn't have to do that, but he was, like the possessed being said, only human. The invisible energy poured out of Ethan, throwing the man across the table and into the bookshelves. "Weren't expecting that, were you?" He hid his own surprise as he turned to face whatever hid in the shadows, but whatever they were, they fled back into the ether. The man was already coming to his feet, straightening his clothes.

"Apparently your abilities are returning." The smile returned and he shrugged. "I had to try." Light returned through the windows and the man faded into nothingness. His evil face lingering for a moment too long. Something inhuman seethed behind the eyes.

Ethan looked around. The reading room had already emptied and a lone librarian sat at the counter in the lobby. The sunlight touched his brown hair, reddening it as he looked at the stained glass. What had that been about? A test? Never had he been approached so brazenly. He always suspected what lurked beyond the senses, felt them. He knew what they were and how easily they could fool people. That was the thing, though. They stayed behind the veil, whispering and pretending to the unwary. If they would openly reveal themselves to him, what was coming? Ethan shook his mind clear, grabbed his backpack and left the reading room. When he opened the creaking oak door, he noticed how the stone stairs had been physically worn from decades of footsteps. Sometimes nature did yield to man, but what if cataclysm had been used as a weapon? What if it had been created in the Darkness? He breathed deeply. For anyone else, this would have been cause for a mental breakdown. The anxiousness grew even in him.

The students were hurrying to their evening classes. They were so young and unaware. It wasn't that long ago, was it? Ethan didn't feel old in his late thirties, but once Kyra was born he began thinking about all those years past. So much experienced and nearly forgotten. When he was her age, he couldn't begin to fathom life decades away, all impossibly distant. Time would never stop, but he would give it a fight it wouldn't forget. A student bumped into him and mumbled an "excuse me." No one could even fathom sneaking up on him when the Light had coursed through his body unfettered. That worried him. He couldn't be falling into daydreams. Next time it might not be a hurried student.

He waited as the sidewalks cleared; the light faded slowly as the Sun dropped behind the hills. There it was again. Something in the air. In the living things that usually went about unseen, there were subtle changes in patterns and behavior. The campus squirrels were noticeably absent. Nearly at the end of October and the trees had yet to give up any of their leaves. Quiet had crept over the land and all life except the people knew it.

Across campus, he stopped to open the door to the science building. Leaves rustled behind him. Strange, it was the first time he heard that sound since the leaves turned. His hearing would hone in on sounds like an eye focused on a light in the darkest night. His ears had always been exceptional in their ability, regardless of what Milena might say to the contrary. The air went still and at that moment he knew the quiet was the calm before the storm. He didn't know what the storm would bring.

As the door closed behind him, he thought he heard the wind come again as it swept through the decaying light.

CHAPTER TWO

E than stopped on the sidewalk, breathing in the cool air. The stars were visible, moving slowly and quietly through the crisp sky. He always encouraged his students to look up and see what their ancestors had seen. The stars connected them with the generations that had come and gone since antiquity. The heavens also ensured life existed at all.

Any one of hundreds of minor changes out there would imperil life on Earth. Life balanced on a knife edge and, in the vast voids of space, this was tenuous at best. The blue orb shouldn't even be as it is, but here it was, and they were all visitors on its surface for a brief time while the universe ticked along in impossible precision. The students liked to discuss and debate the big questions of existence, but now the campus was empty.

Ethan half-expected something or someone to be there waiting for him. Instead, vacant walkways bathed in the orange-yellow light of scattered lamps greeted him. It almost felt like autumn. Almost.

The parking lot the professors used had been full, so he had parked a few blocks north along the road that ran into the campus. It wasn't unusual for him to park there at any rate, because he enjoyed the relaxing stroll. Walking past the homes where people were ending their days, the smells of late dinners wafted into the street. A flicker of a television behind the curtains, or a shadow passing a window, all subtle signs of someone's world. In the dim light of the faintly buzzing street lamps, he wondered what went on in those homes. Who were the people that lived there? What was their story? Would he be surprised at what he found if invited in for a bite to eat? His pedestrian walks were a mystery he enjoyed to let be.

Ethan stopped to cross a road and jumped ever so slightly, being a bit disturbed that he hadn't seen the old man standing next to the telephone pole earlier. The man stepped out of the shadow; his fedora hat silhouetted in the dim light. He looked toward the eastern sky and then back to something in his left hand. Under his other arm, the handle of a cane glinted in the light. Ethan sensed no danger. He stepped off the curb and crossed the street toward the odd fellow intending to speak some polite pleasantries in passing, but the old man spoke first.

"Good evening, young man. Do you have the time?" The voice was steady, slow in purpose. Definitely a man advanced in years with a distinct sense of antiquity.

Ethan tried to make out the man's shadowed features in the dim light. He could see gray hair underneath the hat. "It's 9:11."

The man looked toward the East again quizzically. "I can't figure out where the Moon is. It should be out by now. The Hunter's Moon is supposed to rise tonight, you know."

Ethan did know. "This is a bad area to view the Moon,

at least this early in the night. The hills hide it. By the time it rises it won't be large anymore and will have lost most of its color. Not many still know of the Hunter's Moon." A relic of a bygone era, the October Moon had given extra light to hunters. He too had hunted under the Moon's light. His prey had not been animals.

"Yes, that makes sense," the man nodded. "Much is hidden this time of year. Especially now."

Ethan's eyes adjusted to the light and the man's features came into focus. Slightly wrinkled, yet distinguished, he resembled an old man who had lived in the house across this very street many years ago. The house was always hidden behind a yard full of exotic plants. Ethan hadn't seen that man for years. He couldn't still be alive, could he? This fellow's eyes were dark, but not sinister. His battered raincoat had seen better days. "What do you mean? What's hidden?"

"It's not only the seasons changing this year, young man. Something much greater is about to occur. I can feel it."

"You're not the only one." Interesting. Was he just making small talk? No, the old man had the signature. That's what Milena called it. Someone who gave off the barely perceptible energy revealing they were not entirely part of the natural order of things — as most people knew it. They had control over the part of them that crossed the veil. People like themselves. This was becoming quite the night. "What do think is going to happen?"

"I think you know as well as I do the answer to that question. You have felt changes in the wind all your life and always knew when a storm was coming. You knew when you were walking on ground that held ancient history. You couldn't always put your finger on what exactly you were seeing, but you knew it was there.

Something most people no longer notice. Most wouldn't see or feel of what I speak if it were pointed out to them, if it could be pointed out." The man paused for a moment, shifting on his cane, continuing before Ethan could interrupt.

"You've had a gift from birth, a connection to parts of this broader existence many people deny exists. We all live divided between two worlds, living simultaneously in this temporal world and our place of origin. A place where time has no meaning. Few people — very few indeed — can cross those boundaries in this lifetime even if they know they exist."

Ethan opened his mouth, to ask him who he was, but everything the man said was true. He had once wanted it all to be more than barely tangible whispers. Indeed, it had become so many years ago. In a similar way with Milena. Always in Kyra from birth, but when they had needed understanding in their greatest time of need, it wasn't there. For a while he had lost all of his connections and nearly destroyed himself. It wasn't some sort of magical power or fanciful dream. He simply had a door that was slightly open to the unseen around him, and while he had opened it farther than anyone could imagine possible, now the door was nearly shut. The interference had decreased in recent months, but regaining complete control over his mind and physical being had proven difficult. He had surprised himself in the library. Granted, he hadn't appeared to have injured the creature that had come to lure him. Ethan had conquered mountains standing in his way before. He would do it again.

"Why do I have the feeling that I'm about to find a lot of answers?"

"Ah, that's not just a feeling, my friend. You know it to be true. Of course, there will always be more questions.

Obstacles to overcome; choices to be made. Choices are placed before everyone throughout their lives. What we choose becomes our destiny, our destiny is ours to define. It will be up to you what part you play, whether a greater role or lesser one. If you are compelled to take up the role that will soon be before you, it won't be because of what you have always felt. It's not simply the logical ends to a lifetime of senseless decisions. It will be because..."

Ethan, nearly entranced by the words of the old man, noticed again the stranger's cane, which the man had begun pointing slightly at Ethan as he talked. Attached to the top of the cane was an object he knew well. It was an exact replica of something that he had found years ago. Then the man's last words entered Ethan's mind: "...long ago you decided to enter the shadows fashioned from Light and Darkness, to ensure the fate of the world would be decided on the side of Light." Ethan stared at the ground for a fleeting moment.

Something else the old Tower Keeper might say?

When he looked up, the man was gone, the streets empty. Leaves rustled from a warm wind as the moonlight moved silently through the trees. Like an ancient sentinel, the old man had delivered one last message before moving on into the Light.

Ethan took a breath and left the street corner to find his car. All anxiety from the demon messenger in the library evaporated, now replaced by a different anxiousness. The energy burned inside him like it hadn't for many months. He would soon learn what he had been gifted to accomplish, the purpose that had alluded him. In this, he was certain.

The day of answers had arrived.

CHAPTER THREE

Death was in the air.

Ethan ran toward the shadows looming on the crest of the hill as arrows cut through the air inches from his head. The heavy footfalls and clanging weapons of his pursuers followed close behind. Their terrifying cries could empty villages, but now they chased one man. He hadn't come this far to fail moments before escaping through the portal. Only a few more feet and he would be safe. The monoliths of Stonehenge were beginning to take shape in the moonlight. There he would find his way back home.

That place was thousands of miles away — or perhaps thousands of years was more appropriate. Cradled in his left arm, the jeweled reliquary sparkled in the moonlight. The real treasure lay inside and the Darkness hoped the relic could be used to raise armies and conquer nations. Either wield it as a weapon or use it as a key to hidden realms of the universe known only to a few. The shadowmancer would assemble his legions and lead them on a reign of terror. A new Scourge that would bring destruction not seen since antiquity.

Only these armies wouldn't be entirely made of men.

Legend and myth were full of creatures that mankind had forgotten. Time had turned fact to fable, but Ethan had seen them. *Fomorii*, the Irish called them. Hideously mutated monstrosities of man and beast. Many were not completely of the world of men, at least the existence most people knew. As they were conquered and destroyed, and man lost his ability to peer into the eternal, the nightmares evanesced into history. Unfortunately, they were never completely spent so long as evil thrived on Earth. Some people still looked to the shadows for belief and power and used what they found there for mayhem. The simple minded wanted wealth. Others dreamed of much more. To march across the world unopposed and the enslavement of all humanity. People like Ethan stood in their way.

An arrow clipped his boot, catapulting Ethan into the ground like a boulder. As he rolled over and tried to ignore the pain of impact, he stood and realized he had made it through the outer monoliths. A bluish mist swirled at the center of the ancient monument. It surged upward, forming a rotating helix, hovering over the ground. Its height reached only slightly above the towering stones. At its edges, the coil of light blurred the surroundings, pulling at the fabric of space. Before Ethan could run toward it, an unnerving, guttural roar tore through the darkness. His heart jumped.

Searbhan.

If this beast from the beyond was anything like Balor, Ethan didn't want to be standing in this spot when it reached Stonehenge. The other pursuers ceased their chase a few dozen yards out, fearing entering the sacred grounds. Searbhan would have no such fear. Ethan stepped toward the swirling mist. It was time to go home.

Before he reached the portal, two people separated from the shadows of a fallen monolith. They had weapons in their hands. One raised his bow toward Ethan and let an arrow loose.

Ethan awoke, his heart racing and clothes drenched with sweat. All his life he had vivid dreams, but nothing like this. Normally he had control of them, but these were different, like memories. No, he was experiencing actual events as they happened, events he had no power over. There were none of the subtle disconnections of dreamworlds. Instead, these were windows into the stream of time itself.

The sunlight slipped through the slats of the cherry wood blinds, chasing the darkness from the room. Ethan threw the tangled sheets aside and raised the blinds. The Sun tried using all its energy to burn away the unusual late-autumn fog. The mist stubbornly held onto its occupied land as the Sun bathed the stone walls of the house with color and radiance. This day was the beginning. The beginning of what, Ethan didn't fully understand.

He remembered it was Friday, and the start of fall break, so there were no classes to be taught. Just as well, because there was much to accomplish. He rubbed the sleep from his eyes one last time before heading downstairs to the library. In the doorway he stopped to view the room aglow in the morning sunlight. He had designed the house with the windows of this room facing east and south, so the room would be well lit for most of the day, but particularly for the mornings. Books lined the wood-paneled walls and shelf stacks, some of which reached the ceiling. The old maps and artifacts throughout the room alluded to Ethan's antiquarian interests and Milena's profession. In the center of the room was a small table finished with an antique world map motif. At each side of the table sat a couch for reading, and an antique brass ceiling fan moved the aromas of old books around the room. Here, one could easily disappear for hours into the past or other worlds.

Indeed, ever since Kyra could move around on her own as a toddler, they would find her in the library. She would spin the antique globes and randomly pick places to ask her father about. Much time spent imagining fanciful adventures to the strange places of the world when she wasn't lost in fairy tale books. Surprisingly, she wasn't up yet. It wouldn't be unusual for her to already be sitting on the couch with Scout curled up next to her.

Ethan picked up a picture of his family sitting on the shelf among the books. Taken at the lake two summers ago, they had been swimming in the crystal clear, spring-fed waters. It was the last time they were there, where he and Milena had first met, a story they had never completely told everyone. Kyra was six years old now, but she had grown a few inches since the photo was taken. Her dark brown hair grew long and curly, with a little blonde streak on the right side that appeared when she was a toddler. The deep blue of her eyes radiated the reflection of the perfect sky of that sunny August day. Ethan had never seen someone with that hue of blue. No one had.

In the days after her birth, it wasn't long before a personality began to emerge. So much of a person is shaped by their environment and the people around them, but there was something already in Kyra. Somewhere inside, an adult tried to fight her way out. Watching Kyra,

Ethan would think about his own youth. There were many flashes of adulthood scattered among the actions and thinking of a child. He never realized this until she was born. Many people believed in having a soul, but for the first time Ethan truly began to understand what that meant.

In the photo, Ethan stood behind Kyra, and the sunlight of the hot summer had lightened his brown hair. He didn't tan well, which was no concern as he couldn't sit next to the water very long. He had to be exploring in or around it. Next to him was Milena, who proved yearly she had no problem tanning, her long, black hair pulled up into a ponytail. Ethan could almost see her brown eyes behind the sunglasses and her smile was infectious as always. She was nearly as tall as him, not that he was a giant at two inches under six foot. He could never take his eyes off her, and that day was no different with her toned and fit in shorts and a tank-top over her swimsuit. Gorgeous and lethal. Who could look at her and know of her reach through the veil? Milena was an intense sparring partner, and the thought unleashed a whole other set of memories in Ethan for the woman he loved. They quickly ended, interrupted by a faint disturbance and then a low growling.

Ethan turned and found Scout standing behind him. He had entered the room soundlessly and could have hid in the shadows indefinitely as he sometimes did. Scout was a huge cat, not large in the fat sense, but muscular, and about the size of a small dog. His stubby tail and ruffs of fur around his cheeks signaled his half-bobcat ancestry. Many people didn't make the connection, and once told, they suddenly became a bit cautious around Scout. The cat rubbed against Ethan's legs, purring.

"What's up? Out all night hunting, I bet." Ethan didn't talk to the cat very much, not like the girls who spoke to him like a person. Scout would give his look of indifference as if his masters were loony. Ethan and Scout were males and they had an understanding. They didn't need to fill the air with constant talking. Besides, it was silly speaking to animals.

Ethan raised his head. A door had opened upstairs and footsteps creaked across the hardwood floors. Ethan set the picture on the desk, under the window, and scanned the bookshelves, stopping upon finding a particular book. In his mind he heard, *Dad, it's me. I'm up.* He looked down at the cat and said, "Go get you sister." Scout sprinted out of the room, not making a sound.

A few moments later, Krya walked into the room carrying Scout in her arms, his front paws standing on her shoulder. He liked being off the ground in a position of power, even if it was only a few feet. "Hey, Kyra. You're up early." There was much of his wife in her. The smile, the confident walk.

"Good morning, Daddy." She walked to her father and he bent over to kiss her on the cheek. "Scout wouldn't leave me alone. What are you reading?"

"Ancient mythology." He pointed at a picture of over a dozen misshapen, vaguely human creatures. "These are the fomorii and this is their leader, Balor. He is the Irish Cyclops."

"That's creepy." The massive, grayish creature repulsed her. She read the caption under the picture. "This claims it supposedly could paralyze people who looked into its eye. Are you teaching a class on myths or something?"

"No. I had another dream. This time I knew names and could remember some images. Look at this one." Ethan turned a few pages and pointed at a more hideous creature, the one-eyed, one armed Searbhan. "In my dream I hadn't seen this creature yet, but I knew it was coming. I could clearly remember seeing Balor, even though I never saw it in this dream. He was far more hideous than the artwork in here. I remembered seeing him in battle, but couldn't remember any details of the battle other than he actually had two arms, not one. These weren't products of my imagination, they felt like memories." Ethan paused then added, "I wonder how much of mythology is history that man has chosen to forget."

Scout, restless, jumped to the floor and left the room. Kyra's arms were tired of holding him at any rate. She flipped through a few pages. "I had a dream last night, too. We were at the White City. It's been awhile since we've been in town."

"That's where we are going today. We'll stop at Kane's place before we go to the Tower library. The rest of the guys are arriving tomorrow morning." He had already planned a "Man Weekend" with his friends, which meant, among other things, some exploring in the Old Wood. Now that was about to take on a new purpose. Ethan told Kyra about his encounter with the old man. He rarely had to speak to her as a child, but he did leave out the incident in the library. She read through more of the book as his mind wandered. That day he brought her home from the hospital, so small and helpless, felt like it had been only moments earlier.

⏳   ⏳   ⏳

Outside, Kyra would see and feel what others could not. Too young to describe in detail what she was experiencing, Ethan and Milena would shield her, and if necessary, ward the invisible away. Centuries adrift from their origins had distanced most people from the universe they lived in — especially what was just beyond the senses. The uncluttered minds of children were a different story. With Kyra this had been constant and persistent, and became stronger as she grew.

The ability of animals to sense coming danger or approaching storms is often pondered over by scientists. Some people could do the same. Kyra knew before other people. Before the animals. Ethan didn't find this terribly unusual, because Milena always had a connection with nature and animals. It was her gift. The animals understood her and would do whatever she wished. Kyra had Milena's gift and then some. It went far beyond reading life around her. Sometimes it was frighteningly obvious. Once, after visiting an elderly relative, Kyra had told them matter-of-factly, "Auntie is going to die soon."

"Don't say things like that," Milena told her daughter. She shot a look at Ethan, *She's right, isn't she?* Three days later, Kyra's aunt died, but she wasn't upset so her parents weren't troubled either. Kyra was indeed the farsighted one, something her parents hadn't achieved. At least not at her level.

⏳   ⏳   ⏳

"Dad, you're drifting off again."

She was right, he frequently lost himself in thought.

"Sorry, just thinking how old you are now. It seems like yesterday when you were crawling around chasing after Scout when he was a kitten." The two of them had practically grown up together. "No matter how much I know everything will work out, I still worry. We'll know soon what all of this means."

"You always tell me to let tomorrow worry about itself."

"True enough," Ethan said. *Easier said then done.*

"You know what tomorrow is, don't you? Does that have anything to do with this happening now?" Kyra asked.

"I have never believed in coincidences. Especially not now." Ethan picked up the antique dial calendar on the desk. He aligned the brass dials to view the correct day. Tomorrow would mark one year.

One year since Milena disappeared.

CHAPTER FOUR

Ethan paused a moment before getting into his vintage '79 Landcruiser, after making sure Kyra was buckled in. To the south, past an old farm, began the Old Wood. They would take the shortcut through there. It was also where Milena had last gone.

The neglected dirt road hid under the trees, creeping alongside a ravine while dropping steeply toward the Misty Valley. Kyra quietly peered deep into the woods as it passed. Ridges rose over the ravine and on the opposite side of the road. It wasn't much more than a dirt path, rutted by storm water and barely passable. Once used by miners and loggers, and before that, it probably had its start as an animal or native trail. Through the ravine flowed a small stream that emerged from a hidden underground source. Shortly after the streambed became polished limestone, the water flowed over a cave and continued into the valley. Kyra tried to find the cave through the trees, while her dad kept a firm grip on the wheel as they descended the narrow road. It had been two years since they last explored there. She sensed that much more had transpired along the bubbling stream. The forest quietly hid its past, a history that had long passed from the memory of men. It wasn't a dark forest. Even before a number of ageless trees were logged, light still found its way through the canopy. They had often hiked and camped among the towering guardians.

Where the crumbling path met the Misty Valley, a modern road ran its length along another stream. They drove through the green valley to the west. Years had slowed to a crawl among the ridges, the old farms preserved from an era barely remembered. The southern ridge rose high above, its crest flat, but quickly dropping to the south among valleys, old forests, and forgotten homes. A small hollow cut the ridge in half and a road followed it into a decaying wood. The Indians called the area Gothgol, though some of the old books named it Goathgol. There were those that believed this translated into Valley of Foreboding. Others thought it meant Land of Skulls.

Sparsely populated, the area's few residents never appreciated the stigma bestowed upon their valley by native myths. Nor did they care for the teenagers that came searching for lost cemeteries in the dark of night. Or when they spent the night in abandoned homes deep in the woods on a dare. Kyra had heard older kids tell the stories, thinking their silliness misplaced. As each generation passed, fewer remembered the old folk tales, and all that kids knew, or what they thought they knew of dark places, came from movies. Something hid in those woods, wanting to be ignored. She knew it wasn't fiction. Only a handful had heard it called the Dark Hollow. Even her father had only explored its outskirts.

The road turned right at the Valnastoi River and Kyra strained to see the town that sat to the north. The river flowed from the west between two ridges, before sharply turning south. Above the river's bend sat an elongated, bowl-shaped valley, which sheltered the town. For many years, from a distance, the end of the valley looked white almost like it was covered with light snow. Once in the town, the many white colonial-era homes lining the hillsides would reveal the illusion. This was why the small hamlet of Haydburg had forever been known as the White City. Most of those homes had since disappeared, or had been painted different colors, but the name remained.

While not far from larger cities, Haydburg's isolation had the feel of a distant country. The hills and river kept the town from growing outward, so little had changed since its founding. Its cobblestone roads and old homes — especially the Victorians perched on the shaded hillsides — made Haydburg a window into past days usually only read about. Kyra almost expected horse drawn carriages on the streets or steamboats to come puffing down the river.

They followed the main street through the White City, passing brick-faced shops and businesses before circling the town square in a roundabout. A shaded park filled the square and, in the distance, the street ended near the base of the northern ridge. There, on a small rise, sat a small stone church. Surrounded by green yards and aged trees, its grayish stone had darkened with time, making it stand out against the buildings in the streets below. It had little ornate decoration other than the small stained-glass windows lining its sides, while larger ones in the bell tower glimmered brilliantly in the sunlight.

Ethan turned right after the town square, up a side street that climbed halfway up the slope. He turned right again and parked along a shaded road in front of a Victorian home. Largely hidden by massive maple trees, the house was built from the same dark gray stone as the church. The only stone home in the hillside neighborhoods, its turret on the third floor peaked through the turning trees. In the White City, autumn had emerged and the Sun illuminated the colorful hardwood trees that lined the hills and streets. Fragrant fallen leaves scented the breeze. The gathering storm had not entered the valley.

Kyra quickly exited the car and ran up to the porch. Kane O'Neil was already opening the front door. "Hi, Kyra, how are you?"

Shaking his hand quickly, she said, "I'm fine. Can I go upstairs?"

"Sure, go ahead."

Seconds after Kyra scrambled up the stairs, Ethan saw her in the turret window with a pair of binoculars looking over the valley. She no doubt thought she was a princess looking over her kingdom.

"Hey, Ethan. She sure has a lot of energy." Kane's brownish hair was a bit disheveled, as usual. His near six-foot height and solid appearance didn't fit the stereotype of a doctor. He could have built a successful practice anywhere, but not one to be forced into anyone's mold, he and Anna moved to tiny, hidden Haydburg. Three years had passed, and he now ran a small medical center in town.

"You'll be finding out soon enough." Kane's wife Anna was two months pregnant. They hadn't even known until two weeks earlier when Krya had asked Anna if she was expecting. He laughed, remembering Anna saying, "Do I look pregnant?" Sure enough, when she took a test the next day, she was. Never a dull moment with Kyra.

"Yeah, I guess we will. Anna is at work. I'm not sure what her and the girls have planned for tomorrow. They don't want to be around for Man Weekend." The tradition had started during college when he and Ethan, Duncan and Conrad would set off into the woods adventuring and camping. It was one of many things that left their girlfriends wondering what they had gotten themselves into. A couple, though, stuck around to become wives.

Ethan looked over the valley toward the church. "I need to find something in the Tower library." He told Kane of his encounter with the old man near the college. "The last thing he said was something to the effect of 'long ago you decided to enter the shadows fashioned from Light and Darkness to ensure the fate of the world would be decided on the side of light.' Who does that sound like?"

"Sounds like something from Grayson's journals. He was always going on about conflict hidden in plain sight, good versus evil. Remember we read through some of those back in our college days?"

"They looked like they were unearthed under the pyramids. Maybe they'll have some clues to what is going on around here. Grayson wasn't quite telling us everything he knew." Ethan paused and looked up at the turret. Kyra was still there. "There is one other thing."

"What's that?"

"Remember the small Celtic cross I said I found near the ruins of the old foundation, where we eventually built our house?"

"You mean near where you planted that apple tree in your front yard? Didn't you give it to Grayson?" Kane remembered seeing the photo of the hand-sized cross made from blue-tinged silver. Carved with intricate knotwork, a ring circled where the crossbeams intersected. In the center it had a purple gemstone, an amethyst.

"Grayson said he didn't know how it got there, but he thought it was an authentic artifact. In any case, it apparently isn't one of a kind."

"What do you mean?"

"The top of the old man's cane had an exact replica of the cross."

Kane thought about it and said, "There are thousands of copies of that cross. It's not an unusual design. I bought something like that for Anna. She said the circle represents time unending. Not necessarily the time that began at the beginning of the universe, but an existence with no beginning or ending. Celtic symbols are a popular fashion fad these days, though I suspect many don't attribute much meaning to them."

"Probably not, but how many have gemstones that glow in the dark? I don't think that old man would have some cheap trinket. Grayson could never figure out why the amethyst gave off light in the dark. Gemstones typically don't give off any appreciable energy, let alone visible light," Ethan said.

"That's interesting. Well, there's no better place to go than the Tower and we can dig up Grayson's journals. Maybe we'll find where he stashed that cross. It's not a bad day, we can walk over. It will be like old times," Kane said. Exploring old buildings had become a bit of a hobby for him. Anna thought his collection of antiques and collectibles was becoming a bit too extensive. Only a few steps from being a hoarder.

"There's something strange going on beyond this valley, but maybe the answer is right here." Haydburg was a monument from the past, Ethan always believed that. "A history hides beneath the surface here that we don't know about."

"Ever since I first came here with you, I could sense that, too," Kane said. "That's partly why I became caretaker of the old church. I can't believe it's been six years since Grayson died." He had been the pastor for decades and had left no children. His wife had passed eight years before. The church now only had visiting pastors from local churches on any given Sunday. "Grayson Kirby, the Tower Keeper always up in his keep, researching and writing. The townspeople thought of him as their guardian keeping an eye on their little town."

Kane looked out over the town he had adopted as his home and spotted the church.

"What the White City can tell us is right down there."

CHAPTER FIVE

The southern sky had been growing dark.

"Normally there is a glow in the southern sky at night from the next city over," Kane explained as they walked to the church. "At first I didn't notice, but you can't see it anymore. Obviously the city is still there, but the darkness is coming from somewhere in between the city and us. I should have told you."

"The Dark Hollow," Ethan casually suggested. He had been occupied with other matters and had paid little attention to the night sky at home, but now the answer immediately entered his mind. He had never explored those lands, though it wasn't the ghost stories and spooky legends that kept him away. There was simply no reason to go there, almost like the place innately repelled people like him. Kind of strange considering the places where he had followed perpetrators of evil. At any rate, he should have sensed the change. "Troubling, to say the least. So close to us." Very troubling.

"Yes, but surprising?" Kane asked. He didn't think so.

Years ago, this would have all been unusual to him. Dark Hollows. Strangers on dark streets. The White City and its church out of antiquity. Granted, he had always felt pulled to parts of the unseen world around him since he was a child. For the longest time, he blamed it on reading too many strange books. Or was it his parents who said that? Then his unusual ability became apparent and brought with it a whole new set of anxieties. If people knew about it, would he be an outcast? Would he be secreted away to some undisclosed location for experimentation? It wasn't until college that he completely came to terms with who he was.

"I've learned a lot about what lies hidden in this world. Remember when we first talked about time and energy and all that?" Kane asked.

"Yes, seems like a long time ago. Little did we know what that would turn into," Ethan said. He looked over at Kyra. Life sure had changed, but he would never want to go back to the way it was. "I'm sure we've seen nothing yet."

"That's what I'm afraid of," Kane said.

Their destination was only a few blocks away and the church's stone steeple rose against the skyline. Something would be revealed there today, Kane was certain of it, but he wasn't sure if he would like everything they found. "The old days sure were simpler." He laughed. He couldn't believe he was already calling them the old days.

⧗   ⧗   ⧗

"Senior year should have a little more time for fun. Isn't it mandatory?" Kane asked over lunch in the dining hall. His course work never ceased coming and he didn't have much time to do anything else. Or perhaps his roommates weren't studying enough. He also wondered why he was trying to eat the pizza with the super-thick layer of rubbery cheese.

"Well," Ethan began, "we all have the same amount of time. We're just not good at using what we have." Ethan had opted for the hamburger. Not like the ones they grilled back at the apartment, but at least it wasn't encased in the plastic cheese. "We overburden our days, but we blame time. Then again, I guess time does limit us in some ways."

"How's that?" Kane asked. He knew this was leading to a scientific discussion. He enjoyed science, but physics wasn't his favorite. Ethan, on the other hand, liked working it into the conversation whenever he could. What was college without some deep discussions? Wasn't that the point?

"Oh, here we go." Milena looked up from her laptop, teasingly rolling her eyes. "I think I need something else to eat." She stood up and Ethan returned her smile and watched her as she walked away, never missing a moment to see her move in those jeans. How she could eat as much as them, he could never figure out.

Kane laughed with a shake of his head. Those two were nearly inseparable.

"Okay, where are we going with this?" he asked.

"Well, here it is: We measure time to organize our life, but time is part of the fabric of the universe." Ethan tapped his watch. "That is different from clock-time. Space-time intersects with the three dimensions of space that define our existence, but if we are more than our physical selves, then are we completely bound by space-time? Our physical bodies are our limitation, but what about our nonphysical self?"

"Some argue that we are only physical, nothing

more." Not that Kane agreed with that, he had experienced otherwise, but playing devil's advocate was not an opportunity to be missed. He had been the star of the debate team in high school after all. Ethan smiled skeptically at the suggestion.

"Most of mankind has always believed there is something more to the universe. That isn't proof in and of itself, but the existence of human consciousness defies chance. Science has revealed the independence of the mind and the physical brain. So were our ancestors simply primitives making myths, or will our history become the myth?"

"Some people try to stave off reality as long as they can," Kane said. "People too easily believe everything they hear or read. It's the age of seven-step plans to try until the next expert comes along on the afternoon talk show."

"Someone said something like: 'There are many views about everything until you know the answer. Then there is only one correct view,'" Milena said as she sat back down with a bowl of tropical fruit.

"Who said that?" asked Kane.

"Don't remember," Milena shrugged. "Read it somewhere. It may sound harsh to some people, and finding answers isn't always easy, but I think the point was that there are answers to be found."

"Some people don't even try," Kane replied. "There is one great mystery that probably can't be solved."

"What might that be?" Milena asked, eyebrow raised.

"Can science explain this food?" Kane asked.

"It can't," Ethan said, laughing. "Hey, are we still on for that project at the school tomorrow?"

"Yeah, you know how much I like to paint." They had volunteered to help at a local school. Many of the rooms in the old building needed stripped and painted. "Toxic fumes and lead paint, here we come."

The next morning, Kane was alone in one room painting the walls, standing on the ladder, wondering where his mask had gone. One spot at the limit of his reach didn't yet have the yellowish color. He stretched his hand to the unpainted corner and he knew, even as he did it, it was a stupid idea.

The ladder began to tip.

His mind began to react instantaneously and, with some surprise, motion began to slow. He almost laughed, hanging there in a moment of time, considering his discussion the day before, but he still had to try to save himself. Fortunately, the new ceiling tiles hadn't been installed, exposing steel girders above. He twisted around, upward, and grabbed the metal beam and then caught the falling ladder with his foot. Time started to move again. He steadied the ladder back on its feet and stood on one of its rungs. He climbed down and nearly collapsed with a sudden wave of exhaustion. Every bit of energy had been drained from him.

Expended in a flash, like an exploding weapon.

He looked up at the ladder and the ceiling. It was physically impossible to reverse one's self from a state of falling acceleration in midair. Yet that was exactly what had happened, and it occurred in an instant. No, it wasn't even an instant, because even that can be counted.

But when time stops, there is nothing to measure.

When Kane and Ethan were driving home that afternoon, Kane told him what happened. The fatigue had given way to mild euphoria as his energy returned.

"So what do you think?"

Ethan had listened as Kane talked and didn't say anything at first. Then he suggested, "Maybe time did stop in some fashion."

"Is that possible? Maybe it happened too fast."

"No, when you began to fall, it was like a jolt to your mind. You were able to function separately from your body, outside of time, so time felt like it stopped. Then you were able to direct your body to cease falling. Your exhaustion was probably from the energy expended to propel yourself in another direction. Think about it. There is a fantastic amount of energy contained in the body at the molecular level. Atomic, quantum, zero-point, whatever. There has to be a way to access that energy and use it. I think you did just that."

"It was by accident. Controlling or using this 'energy' on demand is a whole different proposition. That would be nice."

"It takes practice." Ethan stopped. He wasn't ready to go down that road yet. He had known something surged through Kane since they had met, but Kane had only begun to grasp what was inside him.

"Practice?" Kane wondered what Ethan wasn't telling him. It wasn't the first time.

"Well, I guess learning to see the signs around us would be the first step." Ethan hoped Kane would forget the practice comment. "I think we cross the boundaries of space-time more than we realize. Or at least encounter the places where the boundaries are thin."

"I'm afraid to ask what would actually cause said 'encounters.'"

"Say someone dies violently in a battle. That death is going to cause a tremendous release of energy as the spirit is separated from the body. Even if one doesn't believe in souls, maybe the body undergoes some release in a traumatic situation. This leaves a fault in space-time where it happened, and some people feel presences or sense visual apparitions at that spot. They aren't dynamic and don't talk to you like ghosts in movies because they aren't people. They're simply a fingerprint of some material event on a physical level we barely understand."

"And what if the ghosts do talk to you?"

"A whole different category. Sometimes quite dangerous."

Kane considered asking for clarification, but decided to save it for another time. Darkness underlined Ethan's tone. What had he seen? "Still, if this energy can be controlled and used without draining the body, that could lead to some amazing possibilities."

"I believe it can, but that's a story for another day," Ethan smiled. "Besides we're home and it's eating time. It looks like Conrad is grilling some slabs of meat."

Ethan was definitely leaving out something that he knew or experienced, but so was Kane. When he had caught hold of the girder, he had cut his hand on the steel. He sat down and held his fingers to stop the bleeding. When he took his hand off his fingers and wiped away the blood, the cut had vanished.

Kane was a Healer.

⧗   ⧗   ⧗

As if cued from his thoughts, Kyra looked at Kane and asked, "You're like us, aren't you? Can you do something?"

He stood speechless for a moment and then looked at Ethan who smiled and nodded.

"Want to hear a story?"

"Of course! Tell me."

"Well, I had been quite the daredevil. More than once

my horrified mother came running after seeing me fall or jump off something, only to see me sit up, brush myself off, and return to roughhousing. It never occurred to me that I was different. Kids are flexible and heal quickly. Then there was the day I finally figured out I wasn't entirely like other kids.

"We had built a small tree fort, and I was up there waiting for my friends. Then I heard them at the neighbor's house in the pool. I had forgotten that we were meeting there that day. I climbed down the stairs so fast that I missed one and went flying backwards. The fall knocked the air out of me and I'm not sure how long I laid there before sitting up. That's when I noticed the pain in my side where a stick had impaled me. I pulled it out, which wasn't pleasant, but once the pain began to subside, I wiped the blood away and the wound was gone."

"Cool. I always thought there was something different about you." Only to Kyra would such a story not seem out of the ordinary.

"I guess I'll take that in a good way," Kane laughed. "Here we are."

The first thing he always noticed at the stone church was being immersed in calm. The subdued music of unseen birds and an occasional flutter of leaves almost went unnoticed. An unusually quiet Kyra took her father's hand as they walked with Kane toward the church. The gray stone structure stood out from its green surroundings with a barely perceptible shimmer. One of the blocks near the foundation had the year 1706 carved into it.

Kane walked up the stone stairs and pulled open one of the weathered oak doors. The heavy, iron-covered door opened easily. Inside, the foyer's stone walls were trimmed with oak and the polished marble floor was inlaid with a granite Celtic cross. Tiny quartz crystals in the granite shimmered in the colored light that poured through the stained glass windows above the doors and to its sides. Two candelabras hung from the copper-plated ceiling, their candles long ago replaced with electric bulbs. Craftsmanship like this was expected in a cathedral, not inside a countryside church. Kane had seen it many times and opened a door to the right with a silver skeleton key. A staircase went up and to the left above their heads. At the top of the stone stairs he opened an identical door, and the three stopped for a moment when they entered Grayson's tower.

The midmorning Sun flooded through the stained glass windows on all four walls, welcoming the visitors. Unlike the windows below, these depicted brilliant scenes. The window overlooking the city was lit with a Celtic cross. Knights with swords raised over a jeweled white reliquary overlooked the church in the opposite wall. The sight took Ethan by surprise, he had forgotten the scene.

The reliquary was the same as the one in his dream. How could that be?

The eastern window depicted an empty tomb hewn out of rock flanked by an angel and two women. In the west, a knight held his sword across two hands in front of him. Over his armor he wore a white surcoat with an eight-pointed red cross — the *croix pattée* — centered on his chest. The same cross was on the reliquary in the northern window.

The room at first appeared circular from the bookshelves that lined the walls in an octagonal fashion. At the center of the southern shelf a small stained glass window overlooked the city, its hand crank busted from age and use. The light from the windows illuminated the large, wooden round table at the room's center. Covered with old books, manuscripts and maps, it was here that Grayson Kirby would spend hours pouring over crumbling tomes, translating manuscripts and searching for forgotten knowledge. He had written a number of books on a wide range of subjects from ancient civilizations to theology, but his main quest was to preserve the legacies and messages from the past. The overwhelming scents of old paper and parchment, and musty books, soon went unnoticed as it engulfed the visitors.

Kyra didn't hesitate long before looking through the dusty, leather-bound volumes that laid where Grayson had left them. Few had been here since his passing.

Kane looked around the room. "Weren't Grayson's journals in a small chest somewhere?"

Already distracted by a book he pulled from a shelf, Ethan pointed at the northern window. "I think it was below that window, on the bottom shelf."

Kane pulled out a chest that had sat there undisturbed for years by the looks of the dust covering it. He set the trunk on the table and Kyra immediately closed her book. She traced the leather trim edging, felt the age-darkened wood panels and the brass corner bumpers. The clasp was tarnished by years of touch. There was no lock on the chest. Kyra asked her father, "Are we going to open it?"

"Yes, we are, Kyra." Ethan lifted the clasp and slowly opened the lid, allowing the musty smell of the old papers to escape. Inside was a red-dyed, leather bound book. Ethan carefully lifted the book out of the trunk. "This is the *Red Book of Westmarch*. It's priceless. I don't know how Grayson acquired this, but there are only three known original copies."

"Let me see that," Kyra said with her arms raised.

Ethan handed her the book. "Be very careful."

"I will, Daddy." Kyra brought the book to the other

side of the table and sat down in one of the wooden chairs. She raised her fingers over the cover and the book opened. Ethan gave her a look. Kane hadn't seen what she had done, not that it would have mattered, but she knew better. He didn't want her to get into the habit.

Kane found a leather-covered metal tube in the chest. The end cap came off easily revealing a roll of parchment. He let it slide out onto to the table and carefully unrolled it, placing books on its corners to hold it flat. "I don't remember ever seeing this up here."

Ethan began examining the map. "Me neither. Look, here's the Valnastoi River and these squares are buildings in Haydburg."

There wasn't any lettering on the map other than a "N" next to an arrow establishing the orientation. Kane followed the Valnastoi down the valley with his finger above the map. "Here's the stream going through the Misty Valley and the cave is on the map. There's the Oak Grove above it." A circle of trees was drawn on the yellowed paper. "If this map is as old as it looks, how could those oaks be on it? They don't live that long."

Kyra looked up when he mentioned the Oak Grove, but no one noticed. Ethan pointed at another square on the map. "Our house would be right about here, where this square is." When he and Milena had built their house, they had left the remains of an old stone foundation under the southern wall. "A memorial to the past," Ethan called it. At the center of the wall was an archway that had been filled in with stone. Old iron hinges were still embedded in the stones. "Unfortunately, there's no date on the map. This town was founded during the early colonial days."

"So says the plaque at the center of town." Kane pointed at the squares at Haydburg. "These squares are the oldest structures in town. This church and those foundations look older than any other architecture in this area. Perhaps 1706 was carved later? Some of the old-timers always said this town was older than the history books claim. Maybe they were right.

"Here is the stream that flows over the cave, but this shows it starting at the center of Oak Grove. The stream comes out of the hillside, not down over it. And is this some sort of pathway going from about where your house is to the Oak Grove?"

"That's interesting," Ethan said. "Right on the side where the blocked-up archway would be." He followed the path to the top of the hill to an old well where a windmill once stood. Long ago it succumbed to the elements. A small circle on the map marked where it had been. Not far beyond the well grew the Oak Grove.

Ethan looked at Kane. "We need to bring this with us tomorrow. This appears far older than any of the maps we have used exploring the Old Wood. I want to start up here by the well like we did on our first trip out there."

Kane carefully rolled up the map and slid it into the tube. "Something is under that hill," he said to himself. "I know it."

Ethan went back over to the chest and pulled out a book. "Here's what we wanted. Grayson's last journal." He flipped to the last entry in the journal. It was written the day before Grayson had died.

"*Omnium finis imminent.*"

"If I remember my Latin correctly, that translates to 'the end of all things is near,'" Kane said.

"Not an encouraging start." Ethan continued to read, picking up the journal and pacing the room as he spoke.

CHAPTER SIX

Has the end come? Hopefully it has not, but if you are reading this, then I am no longer with you. I have little doubt of who will first read this. You are to be my successor, if you so choose. Nonetheless, let me be succinct: We are clearly at the edge of a new darkness that could soon blot out what light and hope remains in the world.

Please realize that the fate of mankind has often hung in the balance as most others have slumbered. We have reset the scales each time, though there were times where descent into the abyss was deeper than we would dare admit. I wish I could write with assurance that we will continue to succeed. Never has there been so few of us and at no time since the Great Cataclysm has life been so taken for granted. No matter what horrors unfold in the world, most quickly forget their fear or disgust and return to their carefree lives. Little do they realize that there are far more terrible evils awaiting us.

It is not that we have had no warning. The shadows of

what surely will transpire, if we do nothing, are all around us and always have been. Whatever schemes are simmering have no doubt been many years in the gathering. There are few that pay attention to the signs afforded to all. Some shadows are tinged with the Darkness, others are companions of the Light. Surely you know much of this. I know where your life has led you, but you must understand this fully.

They follow our every move. Shadows lurking among the trees, over the next hill and around the next bend they wait. They masquerade along the creek lying among the stones and fallen branches. They are concealed in the dusty corners of this old building. Beyond the attic door and at the bottom of the cellar stairs they hide. We often avoid them for no tangible reason until a candle is burned or a bulb lit. Even then we carefully proceed. On sunny days they follow us around quiet and unnoticed. At night, in the dim light of the Moon and stars, they are there tracking our footsteps. Many of these shadows are simply the temporary refuges from sunlight, but another kind have purpose. They remember our past.

The ancient tree standing in the young forest, towering over its children. The crumbling foundations of an abandoned home sleeping in an untraveled wood. A piece of flint or cave painting that reaches back into antiquity to nameless peoples. The musty book, ready to return to dust with every turn of the page. The forgotten cemetery in a quiet glen, where the faded inscriptions are the last remains of people whom long ago passed from the world's memory. These are shadows of the past, but there are many places like these where the shadows of events yet to unfold rest patiently. Waiting for the right time to emerge into the world, some want to inform and help it progress forward and survive. Others seethe for the day they can conquer and spread far-reaching terror across all of mankind's lands.

Every so often in the history of man these darkest of shadows have almost succeeded. Plagues and wars arise that kill millions and leave their detritus scattered far and wide. Fields and forests in every nation release remnants of the hordes and armies that churned the land with their destruction. More disturbing than these memories are the whispers of forgotten peoples and lost cities destroyed in cataclysms and by malice. Strange beings that litter the histories of man. Myths full of the fantastic and the terrible. Many have written on what other men became in the darkest of times. Do not be quick to dismiss all of these mysteries from the past as man's imagination. I suspect that not all of this is unknown to you and your companions.

In the seemingly endless ages since man first began moving around the globe, there are those who decided to live among these shadows. Some chose to become like what they discovered there. They listened to the deceiving spirits they found in the murkiness, whispering and conspiring to spread their darkness among others. Opportunities to exploit are never passed by lightly. This is their day-to-day existence, but they hope for something greater. An event like those in history where the Darkness crept over the land, this time not stopped at the eleventh hour. Even more than that, they hope and plan for those times only talked about in myth and legend. A time where man had yet to lose his connections to an existence far deeper than any can fathom.

Everyone encounters shadows of this existence and not all of these are shrouded in darkness. Consider the stranger that approaches you and starts talking as if he were an old friend. Or feelings of déjà vu that are consigned to coincidence and lost memories. Dreams that haunt the memory because they detail people and places that never have been seen, but are familiar. Locations where impressions of the past weigh heavy. These are the thin places where the veil between this world and the next are nearly transparent.

We all experience these, but by most they go unobserved or are promptly forgotten. It rarely crosses the mind that maybe a shadow of something that once existed or occurred was encountered. Or perhaps it is there just beyond the senses. Minds are too cluttered and busy to consider such thoughts. For every instance that modern technology saves time — as if time could be saved like coins in a bank — people fill that space with more busyness and work. No one stops to perceive what is around them. The smells, the sounds, the stars, and the shadows become invisible to the mind's eye. Where we came from and who we are is forgotten. Time, though, tries to remind us.

It leaves shadows of its own as messages in history and ancient relics. Others are more subtle connections threading through our culture, language and traditions. History is full of fragments of the eras before man began his chronicles. Faint echoes are often all that's left of the past, but sometimes from these come glimpses of our misted origins.

As I sit here writing this, the children run in the streets as the Sun sets over the valley. The whole town is out celebrating Midsummer's Eve, a day that reaches into history. No longer known by most, it once marked the first days of summer and the eve of the birth of the one who prepared the way. But here in this town, in a month named after a forgotten Roman god, the shadows of history are honored. They are, in a way, remembered.

These are not like the sinister shadows beyond our borders that have been ignored. I know my tone is dire, but hearing the children reminds me that there is reason for hope. This I have never lost.

In the midst of all these shades of Sun, darkness, existence, and time are those shadows created by radiant light. Here is where the Light will dawn in the face of gathering darkness. As some men love the darkness, others search out the lights shining in the night. There, in the borderlands of existence as most people remain unaware, is where the conflict will play out. Since the dawn of man, we have fought this war against beings that most people mistakenly believe to be nothing more than fantasy.

Make no mistake, this is a war. One of the worst sort.

I have been a part of this conflict longer than anyone now alive can remember. Along with other Watchers I have fought back the probing incursions of the Followers of the Dark One. We have endeavored to uncover and thwart their plans, but not always without loss. Since time immemorial we have been the remnant standing guard over humanity and sealing the rifts caused by dark conspiracies. While we walked hidden among the population, those that will replace us have been observed and protected. I only hope that you will be ready before the next devices are set in motion that could precipitate the twilight of man. I am certain that the hour is near. Darkness grows in places where it was long dormant. Masters of these realms, long thought to be dead and buried, are now rumored to be gathering servants for a campaign of which we have been unable to unmask.

My role in this drama will soon end as the curtain has already raised on my last scene. Evil has grown like a cancer in the world and all but a few have ignored the signs. The dam may break at any moment and what this terror may bring, I do not know. The Dark One certainly does. I have fought the war too long not to know this.

Never before have I felt the rooting of dread and worry inside me. Yet this is held at bay by the Light I have seen burning in those that are called to rise in my stead. The strength and power that can flow from your gifts has not been known since forgotten times. Realize this: Unless the next generation of Watchers comes forth and succeeds in their ageless duty, I do fear that when the outcome is known, it will be the End for all that remain. This is what is before you.

-Grayson Kirby, 30 September 1999

Ethan closed Grayson's journal. No one spoke. *Make no mistake, this is a war. One of the worst sort.* There were those words again. Grayson had often given out bits of wisdom. Here it was all together, telling them they weren't simply destined to dabble here and there in a world that needed so much help. He wrote that not only did he also know of this, but that he was one of them. What was going on, hidden from most eyes, involved more darkness than they had realized existed, and Ethan had seen a lot.

"Are we Watchers like Grayson?" Kyra asked.

It was the question they all had. Ethan knew the answer, but was still about to say 'no' when he looked into the chest again. At the bottom was a small leather pouch. He put the journal down on the table and picked up the pouch. He opened it and pulled out a silver Celtic cross. The amethyst at the center of the circle sparkled. It was the cross he had given to Grayson years ago. He looked at Kyra.

"It would seem that we're all about to find out."

CHAPTER SEVEN

When night fell, fog crept up the Valnastoi River, but it didn't enter the White City. Like an army stopped at a castle moat, the fog swirled at the city's edge, but went no farther.

Ethan stood in the doorway of Kyra's room. A small light sat on her desk, keeping complete darkness at bay. She lay in the bed under her sheets where she had fallen fast asleep after they had returned home, but it wasn't a deep rest. Her mind was focused on Grayson's old map and it had dominated their talking on the way home. Pieces were coming together for both of them. They had been given a key to a door that could be opened. No guarantees that everything found on the other side would be pleasant. Perhaps it was time to have a look at what lay to the south.

In his room, Ethan entered the walk-in closet. It was more like the size of a small room and, of course, packed mainly with Milena's clothes, with his taking up but a small section. At the rear wall was a door, and he paused for a moment after opening it. A light turned on, chasing the shadows up the short stairs and into the far corners of the attic. Along one of the walls was a dormer, but instead of a window, it framed a door that led onto the roof. Ethan had built a platform outside for setting up his telescope. It had been quite a while since he had walked out to observe the heavens. This night he left the telescope inside. He wanted to look at the darkening southern sky with his own eyes.

Kane was right, the light from the next town was missing, along with the muted stars along the southern horizon. The darkness in the valley below reached into the night sky, absorbing the light of the town and stars. There had been an urban legend that claimed a shadow had hung over the New England town of Immsmouth over a century ago, shortly before terrible events had happened there. What he saw above him wasn't a folktale. The plague in the sky was only a few miles from where Ethan stood. Tomorrow he would head south into the Old Wood, the forest that stood watch between him and what existed in the Dark Hollow.

He stared into the distance for a few minutes before he sensed it. A faint change out there in the darkness. He couldn't quite hone in on it, but it was like a new presence had arrived. Maybe it was nothing.

When driving through the Misty Valley, most people paid no attention to the narrow road that branched off through a break in the ridge that rose above the southern side of the valley. Lazti drove the circuitous route up and around hills before steeply declining through the darkening woods. By the time he emerged on the other side of the Dark Hollow, among the thick woods, nothing could be heard among the trees. No chirping birds or insects and their rhythmic sounds. No breeze through the leaves. On rare occasion, a sound would escape from an acorn falling or water flowing over a rock, like calls for help that would never come. The woods were overgrown with trees so twisted and old that few could be identified. They reached out and captured errant sounds out of the air and devoured them. Latzi missed the dead silence, much preferred over the incessant noise of people he had endured during his travels.

As the road snaked to the bottom of the Hollow, where a murky stream had carved out a path, a broken iron gate hid silently in the brush and trees. He parked his rental at the entrance, not bothering to lock it. Beyond the gate, remains of a driveway tunneled through the gnarled willows lining its sides. No end could be seen. In the age long past, when the home was built in the lowland at the end of the drive, perhaps it wasn't quite as dark. Maybe there was still hope that the land's past would remain lost to history. That hope had long since faded.

Eventually the people who moved into the Hollow sought out its dark secrets that were hinted at in the legends. *Battles. Wars. Beasts.* A conflict in native stories that sounded fanciful to the modern ear. Perhaps they didn't want to believe what they read in old tales. When his family, the Gerbchons, came to the Hollow, they studied what most others avoided. Rarely did they leave the valley, nor did the generations of those who had preceded them in the Hollow. The children didn't go to the schools; the parents never left for work. In the valley they labored, producing their own food and wares. They left society in order to achieve their dreams. To draw out the Darkness and serve it. In the Dark Hollow they could work protected and out of sight of prying eyes.

Latzi walked through the tunnel of willows to the crumbling family home. He knew the way through the dark, but he had a small flashlight. It forced the shadows to dance among the trees, trying to hide from the light. Here the trees had lost their leaves and the smell of decay enveloped Latzi. Not the normal fragrances of autumn, but the stench of death that would turn most noses away. He stopped in front of his home for only a moment. It had been ten years since he left, and there he had been abandoned.

No siblings, he alone buried his father in the family cemetery deep in the woods. His mother died when he was seven and his father had never left the Hollow to find another wife. Latzi would have left a year or two earlier to do just that, but his work kept him. Then he was the last. He would enter the world to learn and observe and seek out what the Dark Hollow couldn't provide. Then he would return home. His father had long ago told him these events would come to pass. Two days after his father died, Latzi walked out of the Dark Hollow into a world of light that he had never seen. He didn't even lock the door on the decaying Gerbchon homestead. No one entered the Hollow. Or, Latzi smirked to himself, was it no visitors ever left? Now its windows were broken and the front door was partially open, the smell of rotting timbers nearly overpowering. There was nothing in there he needed. He went straight for the gorge.

He followed a cloudy stream that his family once drank from. It disappeared into a rock-sided gorge where no light had tried to enter for many centuries. Much of what his family learned in there was unspeakable, but they did find the key to what they were seeking.

A doorway to the river of time.

Many faded writings had been carved in the limestone

at the entrance to the gorge. He paused at the entrance and ran his hand over the inscriptions as he and his family had always done. One still stood out, chiseled deeply in blockish letters:

NEC PLUS ULTRA   NON PROCEDES AMPLIUS
Nothing more beyond   Go no further

Below this, the single word:

MORTEM
Death

The light from his flashlight disappeared into the darkness in the gorge, so he shut it off, threw it aside and stepped into blackness. The mind relies so much on vision that most people begin to panic if there is no light. The eye could pick up nearly any light once it adjusted to the darkness, but in the gorge there was none. It was one of the few places complete darkness existed. Latzi didn't care. This was his home.

He walked quickly, his hands running over the smooth rock walls to guide himself. Then the walls ended and one side ran to the right, the other to the left. This was the Rift. Nearly circular, it was here the Gerbchon's had found a portal into spacetime. They were never able to use it fully, but now something had changed. The world was ready. The shadows were calling on their followers to begin a new campaign. One that would use armies long banished to myth. First, a weapon was needed to ensure the defeat of the enemy. Latzi would use the Rift to assist his master in assembling new legions and find the lost relic.

That was the plan. His family had spent decades trying

to uncover their purpose, and a few weeks ago, he began to feel the shadows creep ever nearer. Then the Dark One had summoned him from his studies in the ruins. The shadowmancer had tasked Latzi to return home and join him in finding the relic. Would the Rift work? The blackness in Latzi had never been stronger. Was that all he needed? There had been no secret processes or unholy words to utter uncovered in his research for activating the Rift. Not sure what to do, he closed his eyes and let the shadows envelope him. Then it began.

The ground shifted beneath his feet and rocks tumbled down the walls. The air rushed out of the passage behind him and he clutched his chest as his lungs emptied. He knew fear for the first time, if for only a moment, as he fell to his knees. Reddish light bubbled out of the ground at the center of the Rift. He began to catch his breath as the light formed a cylinder, rotating as it pushed outward, sucking air and leaves from the gorge. The Rift contained the cyclone as Latzi pushed his fear aside and walked toward the red whirlwind. Red reflected in his dark eyes and his black hair twisted in the wind as he looked skyward, holding out his arms among the flying debris. He screamed as the red molecules swirling around him tore at his body. Then the pain subsided, and before any more thoughts could enter Latzi's mind, everything went dark.

Latzi vanished from the Rift, into it.

The swirling debris fell instantly when the whirlwind abruptly ceased. The energy of the Rift collapsed back into itself, disappearing into a hovering point of light that quickly faded.

Ethan hadn't seen the red light projecting into the sky before he turned in for the night. Something strange did enter his mind, stopping him. A dark affliction pressed on it for a moment. He looked back to the southern sky, but saw nothing. It was disconcerting to have such evil so close to home. Too close. Something was awakening out there. No wonder the presence of unseen guardians in the Old Wood was so strong. They made sure the Dark Hollow was contained even if no others knew of its existence. Kyra said they were Servants of the Flame. For now, Ethan would try to sleep, but the Darkness would soon regret leaving its lair.

Kyra, too, had seen the reddish light, but she hadn't been at her window. In fact, she had been sleeping. She awoke instantly. The red sky was gone by the time she opened the window. The heavens were veiled, the stars hidden. Then a voice swept the fear from her mind.

I am here. Kyra started, but quickly recognized the source.

"Mother? Is that you?" She knew the answer. It wasn't the first time she'd heard the voice. It had kept her strong these past months. It was also one of the few things she ever kept from her father. This time it wasn't faint. No longer a whisper or a feeling. No uncertainty of its truth.

The time has come for you to go, my daughter. Then the presence was gone.

"Don't go!" It was too late. Tears welled up in Kyra's eyes, along with resolve building inside her. She had wanted to go to the trees for months. There was a doorway there, she knew it. The courage to leave had been out of reach. Now this. Everything was in its proper place, she knew that for sure, and now the time had come to go where she had heard the whispers before. Out the window, in the distance, the shadow of a single tree waited on the hilltop across the road and above the old farm.

Beyond there, under the the trees of the Oak Grove, she knew her journey would begin.

CHAPTER EIGHT

The welcoming yellow Sun of the previous day was muted, hidden behind gray clouds. A chilling wind swept through the hollows and around the hilltops. It would have been a good day to stay in, but Ethan had no intention of losing this day to winter's attempt to chase away autumn. If only this was to be an average walk through the woods. The previous day's discoveries in the White City assured this. As did the night sky over the Dark Hollow.

Voices carried through the house. A few minutes after eight and everyone was arriving, no doubt congregating in the kitchen. He would join them in a few moments, but not before watching the day begin for a little while longer.

Downstairs, Kane watched Anna tie back her shoulder-length, curly red hair to keep it from getting coated in grease as they began making the traditional pre-adventure breakfast. Every trip into the woods began with a soup pot full of bacon, sausage, eggs, and corn beef hash that would chase away the cold. Not exactly the healthiest meal, but it would fuel their bodies and quickly burn. He didn't care much for cooking — not that this simple meal required any great skill — but Anna was quite the chef. Only one of many reasons he had won the jackpot by meeting her. Anna didn't know of dark skies and lost maps, and perhaps she would never need to. He'd rather she didn't.

"Don't forget the chilli pepper. I want it spicy this time." Kane looked over her shoulder as she started with the eggs before tossing the other ingredients into the soup pot.

"You just worry about not getting yourself hurt out there with your friends." He always did come back in one piece. It was her nature to worry. A trait from her mother, no doubt.

"I'll be fine, Red." He tickled her side, making her jump.

"Get out of here!" She tried hitting him with the wooden spoon and laughed as he blew her a kiss and went to find Ethan. "Goofball, it's hard to believe you're a doctor." He was gifted at helping people, but some thought him crazy for setting up practice in a small town. He could be making a fortune back home. Sometimes Anna missed city life, but she still worked there as director of the museums. A recent exhibit on Irish history had her researching where her family had immigrated from generations ago, the Viking city of Dublin. Maybe Ethan had some books in his library on her ancestors. Funny how she always thought about those things here. Of course, Milena had known so much about history. They had become such close friends. Tears welled in her eyes. Where had she gone? Conrad and Christina Wojtek walked in, bringing a smile back to Anna's mouth.

"You look incredible, Anna." Christina hugged her after looking Anna over. She hardly looked pregnant.

"Well, maybe, but this food is making me nauseous. You mind if I borrow your girl, Conrad?"

"No, take her away. To the kitchen with you!"

"Watch it there, buster," Christina said, pointing her finger at him. "We control what goes in your food." Conrad eyed her as she followed Anna into the kitchen, giving him a laugh over her shoulder before Anna pulled her away. He followed, not about to have her being creative with his breakfast. This meal was the tradition he had started. Stopping for a moment, he watched her.

Christina's subtle Asian features came from her grandmother, the blue eyes were her father's, and straight black hair ran down her back. Her grandparents had met during the occupation of Japan after the war. She could be stern like her grandmother and playful like her father. Very much independent and modern, but a lover of tradition and mystery.

"If your mother could see you now," Conrad said.

"Yeah, right. She wouldn't have been caught dead in here," Christina said. "She disdained anything remotely resembling domestic womanhood. The polar extreme of grandma. One steeped in old Japan, the other in modern America." Christina liked to think she only inherited each of their best traits, the best of both worlds. "Be useful and get the rest of the meat out of the fridge."

"Yes, ma'am." Conrad said with a salute.

"Do it quick!" Anna added.

Christina laughed and then smiled at her husband. He could handle being teamed up on by the girls. He always made her smile, but had strength and didn't take nonsense from anyone. She had quickly fallen in love with him after they met, but something else intangibly connected them.

He was hiding something which, ironically, first drew her to Conrad. She looked down at her hands and felt the charge in her fingertips. She had secrets of her own. The longer she had known his friends, the more she realized they were different, too, and for once didn't feel like an outsider, a *gaijin*. It was like they all knew something, but couldn't discuss what it was. Or was she being crazy and still the odd one out? She should tell Conrad. Whatever her man might be concealing, he never appeared to have doubts about his purpose.

He had grown up in the Riverlands south of the sprawling cities — the Motherland, as he called it — quietly exploring and hunting with his old recurve bow. His mess of blonde hair made him look more like a medieval fighter instead of someone who spent his time hand-crafting rustic, off-the-grid homes for people. He had made a career of teaching people how to be self-sufficient.

"Here you go, ladies. This is the last of it."

"Thanks," said Anna. "You'd better check who's behind you."

"I suppose you want something, Scout?" he asked the cat that had been silently watching them. Scout made an affirmative growl and Conrad threw him a piece of bacon. Scout caught it in his mouth and ran into the living room and sat in front of the fireplace, quickly devouring his snack. "That's one cat I wouldn't mind having around," he mused. Scout could take the place of a hunting dog.

"That will be the day you have cats in the house." Christina laughed.

"Maybe a mountain lion. Though, do you know what they say about house cats?"

"No? What do 'they' say?"

"When they look at you, they are thinking, 'If I were

bigger, I would be eating you.'"

"Probably true," she said shaking her head. "Hi, Duncan." He entered from the living room and gave her a hug.

"How are you guys? It's been too long." Duncan shook hands with Conrad.

"It sure has. Ready for some man time, that's for sure, Mr. Duff," Conrad said.

"Well, you two work on that, we'll get back to cooking," Anna said.

"Whip up a truckload of hog wild; it's a cold one out there," Duncan said.

"Sounds wonderful when you call it that." Anna rolled her eyes.

"And it looks even better," laughed Conrad.

"It's the taste that matters." Duncan was hungry, but he could wait a little longer. "I heard Ethan and Kane out back, let's go find them." Duncan's clothes were, as usual, in shades of tan and green and his black hair cut short for the desert climate in Sedona.

"So how's the job search? I haven't heard anything for a few weeks. Any progress?" Conrad asked Duncan.

"I decided to keep working for the National Park Service. Can't beat getting paid to be outside hiking all day."

"I always said there are fun jobs out there," Conrad said. "You just have to look hard."

"Sometimes *really* hard," Duncan laughed. His family wondered why he had taken the job. With their money he had traveled around the world. He needed not to work, but he didn't care much for the excesses of his parents. Desire burned in him. It wasn't only desert and ruins out there. He had discovered something far more important.

"What about that girl you were talking about?" Conrad

asked. Duncan was the only one unmarried, but there was this girl back home who had been intriguing him.

"Oh, she's still there."

"Going that well?"

"Trust me, the time is coming." He would see her again when he returned home. He hoped so. She was another force keeping him in Sedona.

Breakfast was a raucous affair with everyone catching up on current events at home and work. Barely a scrap of food remained after an hour and a half, but they couldn't sit in one place for too long. The men retreated to the library while Christina, Anna, and Kyra made plans for the day in the living room. Not before the guys helped clean up, somewhat. Scout slipped outside for a mid-morning patrol for chipmunks in the gardens, not having been too impressed with the table scraps.

The library was brightly lit compared to the gray day outside. The shelf-lined room with its antique maps created another dimension isolated from the rest of the world. A sanctuary of light and wisdom. Ethan shared with Conrad and Duncan what Grayson had written in his journal and of dark skies and mysterious old men. Silence followed as they let it sink in before Conrad spoke first.

"So what's the plan?"

"Check this out." Ethan unrolled Grayson Kirby's map on the table. "We found this in Grayson's Tower yesterday."

Conrad examined the map. "This has all of the places we've been exploring for years. There's the cave and the Oak Grove. Weren't these houses on those old maps you found in the college library years ago?"

"Yes, all of those homes disappeared before any of us

were born." Ethan pointed at the map. "This one is where this house sits. That's the old foundation in the basement."

"We found some of these other foundations on our first adventure in the Old Wood." Duncan looked at Conrad and pointed behind him. "Get that album off the shelf."

Their first weekend trip after meeting in college had been spent exploring. The photos documented not only the old foundations, but underground structures and tunnels. Most had collapsed into the ground, not leaving any clues to their purpose. The remains of a driveway wound through the woods, past an old orchard and a murky pond that undoubtedly hid more secrets. Much of what they had found was on Grayson's secret map.

Ethan had spent most of his younger years in the woods closer to his home. Once, when he was six or so, his father brought him on his first visit to the cave. He had only been back a few times since then, but he had never forgotten that quiet, misty day in the Valley of the Old Wood. He had explored the cave, digging for lost artifacts and wondered where the passage at the rear of the cave led. His father had said it ran into the hillside, but was no longer passable. Years later, he and the guys had set out to find what secrets the cave held, following the stream until the bottom turned to limestone. There they found themselves at the ledge where the water fell over the cave's mouth.

Nothing was found in the cave that day and their attempt to explore the narrow passage deep into the hillside was limited by fallen rocks. They had continued to explore the caves and hollows above the Misty Valley for years, looking for what secrets it may give up. A history was there among the trees, but the woods were slow to release answers to its mysteries. The cave under the creek was a place isolated from the world. A forgotten hideaway that people speeding by on the road in the valley below didn't know existed. It no doubt had sat there for centuries as the forest went through its cycles of life. Nearby was the Oak Grove, a living Stonehenge that always had been out of place. What else was out there?

Ethan looked up at the bleached deer skull hanging on the wall. Its empty eye sockets tracked their every move. "Remember when we found that on the first hike out on the hill overlooking the cave? Already feels like a lifetime ago. Little did we know where our paths would lead. I don't think this will be another walk in the forest." Why did he feel like the future of man could be decided there? Maybe he was over-thinking it all, burdened by too many strange dreams and the anxiety over Milena. Perhaps the map was nothing but an old curiosity. No, he knew that wasn't true.

"Would I be mistaken to say we've all sensed something as autumn dawned?" Kane asked.

"Something is definitely afoot, but I can't put my finger on it." Conrad, like the rest, had never completely shared the stories of how and when he discovered his abilities. What they did know of each other came slowly and sometimes by accident. He had always been a bit more secretive. Well, not as much as Ethan.

"And now that you've seen this?" asked Duncan.

"I'm still not sure what we'll find out there, but I think we all know we will discover something," Conrad said. "We are all little more separated from this world than we like to admit. I think what Grayson wrote in his journal finally brings everything into focus."

"I agree. This is where it all begins or ends." Duncan paused. "Sorry, but there is something evil across that valley and it's not your everyday criminal variety." He had learned back home in the desert that it was here his future would be decided.

"So what are you thinking?" Kane asked Ethan. Kane hadn't seen that shimmer in his eyes in awhile, not since Milena had been at his side. Inseparable those two were. It had been years since his days of disappearing with her during the summers exploring the world, mostly concerning Milena's job — supposedly anyway — though the details were sometimes sparse. There was always the clear feeling they were doing something else. No one ever questioned it. Why would they?

"See this?" Ethan pointed to the map where a path led from the foundation under his home to the top of the hill above the old farm across the road. "That old oak stands here next to the well on the hill. From the well to the Oak Grove there's an old path made of stone. Remember how some places looked like the whole path had been stone at one point? Whatever path existed between my house and the hill was destroyed by farmers years ago."

"Unless it was underground and started from that old doorway in the basement," Kane said.

"There was another doorway like that in the ruins of the old house." Conrad turned to another photo in the album. "Behind it there's a depression where the ground caved in. It heads directly to the other old foundations."

Ethan looked at the photos and the map, tracing out paths with his fingers. "There could have been a network of tunnels through here. Those rocks in the path may have been the top of the tunnel. No, that couldn't be, the tunnels wouldn't be that shallow or someone would have found them by now. But who would build these tunnels? They would have had to dig them by hand."

Duncan pointed to the ridge overlooking Misty Valley. "There are old coal mines dug into the hillsides along here. It can be done. The other maps show many of these old foundations, so maybe the tunnels date to the same era, assuming the tunnels exist."

"We have every map that we know exists of this area," said Kane, "and none of them show tunnels or paths like this. Nor do they show the stream starting at the Oak Grove. They do show an old stream passing right by where this house stands."

Conrad looked again at the map. "It sounds like someone made a mistake on the old maps or maybe...maybe they altered those maps on purpose. Earlier homesteaders in this area would have found the tunnels when they began clearing the land. Someone made sure it stayed a secret. No new houses have been built around here in decades." In fact, there were only a handful of homes in the area. "Another coincidence?"

"There is the spring out back," added Ethan. "I always assumed it fed the creek shown on some maps before the well in our yard was dug. Maybe it didn't. This pathway and the creek on the other maps are in identical locations."

Kane turned the pages of the photo album. "What about the little pond at the center of the Oak Grove? It's fed by a spring beneath the hill. The streams that go over and under the cave come from this direction. So this old map must be right. The cave could have been an entrance to the tunnels."

"But the passage in the cave is blocked. We could dig where the map shows the paths are located," Conrad suggested.

"Even if we found part of the tunnel, it would be deep and who knows how much of it would be passable. If we do dig, we could start up on this hilltop where it looks like it has remained undisturbed," Duncan said.

"Better yet, let's start here and forget about digging." Kane was pointing to the circle on the map where the old well sat on the top of the hill. "Our suspected tunnel runs right beneath the old well. Who wants to bet it had something to do with the tunnel long before someone put a windmill there?"

Everyone looked at each other and Duncan said, "It's time to find out what has been hiding in plain sight."

Conrad nodded in agreement and shot a look at Kane.

"Of course, I'm in. There's no good reason to stay back with evil brooding across the valley," Kane added with a smile. He had once been leery of their forest hikes and camping trips with blazing bonfires and truck races in the woods. Not so much now. This was different in any case; nor would it be the only moment of decision. This was the easy one.

"Get your stuff, the day isn't growing longer," Ethan said.

They each grabbed their gear-laden backpacks. Flashlights, collapsible shovels and a metal detector were among the supplies. Ample first aid in case Conrad slid down a hillside again. Some food so they wouldn't have to return for lunch. They didn't wear heavy coats against the cold because the hike would keep them warm, as long as they kept moving. Conrad had his trademark camouflage jacket which partly hid his machete hanging at his side. Duncan's dark green coat hid the array of knives he liked to carry. Kane wore his brown leather jacket and set his smartphone to document their adventure. Hopefully, he wouldn't break it like last time. Ethan pulled on his green flannel and readied his walking stick, continuing a tradition he learned as a boy from his father many years earlier.

One of the woodworkers in town had carved a wizardly-looking face into the grip of the hardwood.

After saying goodbye to the girls and agreeing to their cautions to be careful, the men headed outside. Ethan could see Kyra wanted to go, too. *Not this time. When it's warmer.* He tried to avoid stock parent reasons like that. It wasn't the reason, but the breeze did send a chill right through their clothes when they stood still. Crossing the road, they followed an old farm lane that circled to the hilltop. It wasn't a hard incline, and in barely fifteen minutes they arrived under the old oak, the only tree standing near the edge of the hill.

From that vantage point, looking north toward Ethan's house, fields and a few homes were visible further down the road. The fields were empty, stripped of their corn weeks ago. To their right, a decaying barn sat near a fence row of trees, long ago abandoned. When the leaves would fall, the Northern City could be seen and, on a perfect day, some said they could faintly see the White City. Ethan thought it impossible, the ridges and trees hiding what lay beyond. Today nothing was visible as the cold air whipped around the exposed hilltop.

A few feet from the solitary oak, which had stood there alone as long as any living person could remember, the old well lay hidden in the brush. Rotting wood planks covered the deep hole and some of the boards were broken or missing. The rusted metal bands that held it together looked like they could be easily busted by hand. Oddly, the guys had never removed the cover to look inside. No reason to. Just an old well after all, and what parent hadn't instilled fear into children of being gobbled up by these holes in the earth? Even as adults, those warnings still spoke subliminal. Today they were no longer strong enough to overcome the desire to learn what was below.

Conrad stood over the well cover. "Let's see if we can get this off. It looks like we can break it apart." Conrad and Duncan tore the wood to pieces as Kane tied a rope around the old oak.

"Are you actually going down there?" Ethan asked Kane.

"No, someone has to stay up here," Kane said. "In case this adventure goes south." Granted, knowing his friends, it would have to go extremely bad for them to need help. For posterity's sake, Kane began recording the opening of the well.

"Now begins the journey where no ordinary men can go," he said. The line earned a few chuckles since it had been used on every one of their adventures. Here at its boundaries, they were about to go underneath the woods where, as far as they knew, no one had set foot for decades. Perhaps longer.

"The well is lined with cut rocks. It looks intact. I can feel air rising. It's a little warmer than up here." Duncan shined his bluish, LED flashlight into the hole, as did Conrad.

"I hear running water." Conrad peered harder into the well. "This can't be very deep, maybe fifty feet or so. A little stronger light and we might be able to see the bottom."

"We need to go down and take a look." Ethan stood near the well's edge. "But first I want to walk over to the Oak Grove for a second. I haven't been up here in a while. I want to see if anyone else has."

"Okay, let's go check it out," Kane said. He knew — they all knew — that the oaks had been one of Milena's favorite places.

The path to the Oak Grove began a few feet past the

empty hilltop where the solitary oak stood watch, like a doorway into the side of the Old Wood. Only a few feet into the woods they felt warmer, the towering trees blocked the cold wind. In a few places, the path revealed stones that had been fitted together. Most had been long ago removed for whatever reason. Then they saw the trees. No oaks grew this large.

They entered the Oak Grove — or the Circle as some called it — through an opening in the wall of branches. A cathedral of towering pin oaks loomed above. None of them knew of any other examples of this oak species so wide and reaching. Each nearly four feet in diameter, but their size wasn't the most peculiar of their features. The trees formed a perfect circle some sixty feet across, with their ancient, thick branches forming a dome of leaves far above the ground.

Ethan had heard locals try to explain the trees away claiming industrious squirrels must have planted them or a bizarre series of events happened to occur, though no one quite knew what those events might be. Oddly, even the old-timers who had farmed these lands for generations remembered the oaks being as lofty in their youth and some said in the youth of their fathers. Once they leaned back in their chairs, put their hands behind their heads and looked toward the sky, their tales could be as tall as the trees. Perhaps it was the distance of time clouding memory or maybe some truth existed in their stories, passed from their fathers.

Soft, green moss carpeted the clearing under the oaks. At the center, rocks cut by unknown hands circled a small spring-fed pond. Benches fashioned of stone sat around the pond. The branches of the dome's high canopy let in just enough light to illuminate the forest room. The clear water shimmered slightly as water bubbled up from its subterranean source. It had taken on a slight blue hue in the past year, yet had always been free of debris, and tasted pure. Ethan knelt down to cup some of the water in his hand. For a fleeting instant, at the touch of the cool liquid, images flashed through his mind.

Milena. She had been here.

This is where she had disappeared, but how? He had been here dozens of times, so why was this happening only now? The Grove had always felt like a gateway of sorts, but those thoughts were always chalked up to the mysterious nature of the oaks. He looked around the forest room at the other guys. They had spoken nothing since entering and had not noticed his look of confusion. Now the day's venture had a whole new level of urgency. He stood and recorded a few moments with his camera.

"Okay, let's go find out what's at the bottom of the well." Ethan put the camera back in its case on his belt. Once back around the well, everyone took their two-way radios out of their packs and turned them on. "I doubt these will work from underground so stay near the opening," Ethan told Kane. They would still work better than cell phones with the tree cover and hilly terrain. "All right, who's first?"

Conrad was already connecting his climbing harness to the rope. "I guess that would be me." He checked all of his connections one last time, turned on a light attached to his hat and went over the edge.

About a dozen feet down, he found rusted iron bars embedded in the stone-lined walls. A ladder of sorts. He grabbed one and it crumbled from decades of corrosion. Conrad continued his descent to the bottom, where the shaft ended about twelve feet above a solid surface. A small stream passed under the opening. He reached underneath his jacket and retrieved a compact Ruger 9 mm handgun with a LED light mounted under its barrel. *Just in case.* With one hand he let himself down the rest of the way, touching down on the edge of the shallow stream. He flooded the room with the first light it had seen in an age. He tapped the talk button on the radio hanging on his pack's shoulder strap.

"I'm at the bottom and you better get down here and see this."

CHAPTER NINE

than went down the rope last and paused for a moment taking in the cavern that Duncan had illuminated with his electric lantern. Being at least a hundred feet across with a twelve foot ceiling didn't eliminate the claustrophobic sense of being underground. Eons of mineral deposits on the limestone walls sparkled like stars as the light moved around the cave. Cool air with a tinge of dampness surrounded them, though it was still warmer than the windy autumn day they left above. Rusted pipes and the remains of a steel bucket sat near the stream, lost when farmers once tapped the water source. A few scattered bones of small animals stuck in the soft lime soil of the cave floor. They had fallen to their death down the shaft.

Ethan tossed a stone into the crystal stream and watched it sink nearly two feet to the bottom. The water source emerged from an opening four feet above the cavern floor, splashing in a small waterfall. The tiny opening could barely fit an adult crawling into it, assuming they didn't drown. The water flowed through a channel at the center of the cave and exited along a passage through the rock. Many quiet centuries had undoubtedly passed as the water sculpted in the darkness beneath the Earth.

"Come back here. Look at this tunnel." Ethan turned around and walked to where Duncan was shining his lantern. A small set of stairs had been carved out of the limestone and at the top hung a rotted wooden door bound by iron bands. It swung inward, hanging by one hinge. "This might lead back to your house. It's pointed in the right direction."

Ethan walked into the passage and his light found a cave-in about six feet in, formed by mammoth limestone slabs. "Look up there on the wall." Ethan pointed his flashlight near the ceiling. "Someone cut ledges in the wall."

"Maybe these slabs were placed here to support the ceiling." Duncan ran his hands over the ledges. They had been cut in place with tools, something he had done himself when he had designed his home to blend in with the landscape using local stone. He planned similar homes for others, built into hillsides where the ground eliminated the need for expensive cooling in the desert heat. Not a bad side job for a park ranger. "The edges of the slabs don't look broken and the ceiling above looks intact. These could have been pulled down on purpose to block the way."

Ethan documented everything with the camera then stepped back down into the main cavern where Conrad was looking closely at the walls.

"Conrad, did you find something?" Ethan asked.

"See this erosion on the walls? It's a lot smoother up to about where the stream enters the room. It looks like this place flooded in the past, but that would predate that passage or it was much smaller."

Duncan stepped down from the old doorway and looked up the well shaft. The stones that circled the walls ended halfway down the well. The rest was smooth limestone. "It would be tough to cut this shaft out by hand. Not impossible, but it could have been an existing shaft. Maybe a sinkhole. This cavern could have collected water like a cistern for centuries before the passage opened up completely."

"Whoever found these caves added their own improvements," Conrad said. "Surprisingly, I don't see any other signs of people being down here. At least not in recent memory."

"Maybe the stream will lead us to more rooms." Ethan nodded towards the passage into where the stream disappeared. "Ready to go take a look?"

"Hold on," Conrad pulled the radio off his belt and walked under the well shaft. "Kane, you there?"

"I'm here. Scout showed up. What's going on down there?" Scout stared wide-eyed into the well at the flickering lights.

"We're in a large cavern with a stream flowing through it. A passage to the north is blocked, but one to the southwest is open. It follows the stream and may be the one that flows underneath the cave. We're going to follow it and see where it goes."

"All right, be careful. I'm going to go down over the hill to the cave. It's too cold up here, but if I can't reach you on the radio I'll come back."

"Sounds good. We'll see you on the other side." Conrad looked at Ethan and Duncan. "Let's go."

Ethan led the way through the narrow passage, barely as wide as two people, including the stream than ran along the path. Over the millennia, the water had patiently cut through fissures in the soft limestone eroding the tunnel in the darkness. The ceiling was much lower than in the cavern, scraping the top of their heads. It wasn't as smooth as the lower walls; perhaps someone had enlarged the tunnel by hand. Whoever had done so probably suspected their work would never be seen.

A hundred feet in, a faint light appeared at the end of the passage. The stream disappeared under the rocks near the light. Conrad walked over and looked through the opening. There was a small room, barely enough space for two people. Water dripped from small stalactites on the ceiling, probably taking months, if not years, to filter through cracks in the limestone from the stream above.

"This is that little room at the end of the tunnel from the cave." Conrad tried to squeeze through the opening, but could only fit the top of his body through. A cramped passage led to the cave opening, light filtering in from the hollow. During their first explorations of the cave, they had all crawled on their stomachs to get to the small cavern. They could never get past that point, its exit blocked by large rocks. Now they were on the other side. "Wait a second," Conrad pulled himself out of the opening and started looking around at the ground. "We threw something in here one time."

"Here it is." Duncan picked up a small piece of wood. All of their names had been burned in the wood before it was thickly varnished to prevent it from rotting in the dampness. "It's still legible." He handed it to Ethan.

"Our first artifact of the day." Ethan passed it to Duncan after looking it over. "See if you can get Kane on the radio." As Conrad was about to talk into the radio, they heard noise coming through the cave in the valley. Rocks were falling. Duncan went over to the opening.

"Someone is in the cave." Duncan called into his radio,

"Kane, is that you? Are you in one piece?"

"Yes, after nearly rolling down the hillside, I'm here. Where are you at?"

"The passage led us to the other side of the cave. This opening is too small to get through. We could probably move these rocks, but it would take time and some tools."

Kane knelt down and shined his light into the tunnel. There was no use of him crawling back there. Scout stood beside him and sniffed the air in the tunnel. "You can make it back there. If you don't mind the dampness." Scout had avoided the small waterfall flowing over the cave roof when he drank from the pond it formed below. A little water wasn't going to stop him from entering the dim space. As quickly as he entered, Kane wondered if he had been there before.

"Scout is coming back," he called into the tunnel.

"Here comes the cat," Conrad said.

Scout jumped through the dripping cavern quickly and scrambled into the corridor where the guys waited. He shook his fur and surveyed his surroundings.

"Come here Scout," Ethan called.

Scout walked over to his master and Ethan rubbed his furry face between his hands. Scout purred loudly but was soon distracted by Conrad and Duncan looking around the passage with their lights.

"I think this is what we've been looking for," Duncan said.

His light revealed where the wall went inward a few feet, almost hidden by the surrounding rocks. It wasn't a wall at all, but a door carved from a slab of rock. The right side was tight against the smooth limestone wall. The other side entered the wall at least a few inches. A large Celtic cross had been carved in the center of the door.

"What do we have here?" Ethan asked. The surprises

kept on coming. Duncan brushed the dirt and limestone dust off the door.

"This is solid granite. Someone had to bring it down here." Duncan scraped away dirt from where the beams of the cross intersected. Carved out in the center was a small replica of the larger cross. No details, just a cavity. No, a space for a puzzle piece. "Something goes in here."

"That's interesting." Ethan took off his backpack and pulled out a small leather pouch. He removed the Celtic cross and held it up, comparing its size to the empty shape in the door. The silver cross reflected the light of their flashlights and lantern, and the purple gemstone at its center sparkled. They all knew what Ethan was about to do.

"I'm not sure if this will do anything. I don't know how it could, but all things considered..." Ethan walked over to the door and pressed the cross into the cavity. It fit perfectly. For a moment nothing happened. Ethan reached out his hand and pulled back as the gemstone radiated like a torch, lighting every corner of the cave. Behind the blinding light, the door shuddered and rock ground against rock. Metal mechanisms somewhere in the walls broke free from their rusted sleep. The cave groaned on the verge of collapse and threatened to bury them for eternity. They covered their heads as dust and small stones fell around them as the granite door awakened and slowly slid back behind the cave wall.

Ethan rubbed his eyes as they recovered from the blinding light. "Are you guys all right?"

"Yeah, I think so," Duncan said. "Looks like your cross burned out." There was enough space between the door and the rock to reach the cross.

"I'm fine, but what's in there?" Conrad asked. "What is this place beneath the Earth?"

As their sight returned, instead of darkness, a misty, turquoise light engulfed them from beyond the door. No evil lurked near — a complete absence of the Darkness in fact — but Conrad still unholstered his gun. Duncan retrieved the two large blades sheathed on the bottom of his pack. Ethan grasped the handle of one of his survival knives. It was habit, even the calming mist couldn't change that. As they hesitated, Scout walked silently into the lighted room unafraid.

Ethan approached the door slowly. Light shimmered as a cavern ten times as large as the one below the well emerged from the mist. A small pool, lined with rocks, not unlike the one in the Oak Grove sat directly ahead in the center. Scout was tapping his paw on the water, creating the shimmer throughout the room. The pool was the light source.

Ethan turned to Conrad. "Let's grab some of those large rocks and wedge them in front of this door. We don't want to be trapped for eternity down here." He put his hand on the silver cross in the door, expecting it to be warm. It was not, so he pulled it from the cavity. After the rocks were in place, they entered the room. The light slowly brightened, clearing away the mist of the cave. They laid their eyes on what no one had seen in an age.

The floor had been inlaid with cut stone, with paths outlined in polished quartz radiating from the pool to the door and unseen passages. Caverns weren't natural domes, yet this one was precisely that. Many people must have spent years reshaping the limestone. The domed ceiling had been plastered and painted with frescoes. Scenes of battles between armies of men. Armies with hideous beasts fighting among them. In some places, time, and water had damaged the images, but amazingly much of it had survived. There were also scenes similar to those in the old church. Indeed, they were nearly identical.

Along the walls chests stacked high, some of them simple wood and iron boxes. Others were ornate, decorated with gold and jewels. On iron racks hung swords, battle axes, and bows. The steel of the longswords still mirrored the light after a multitude of decades in the cave. Flails and daggers filled open crates. Armor had been draped on stands by unknown hands; chain mail and helms piled high upon chests. Shields with the red cross painted against a white background hung on the cave walls.

Tapestries depicting scenes of knights preparing to ride off on quests or into battle also decorated the damp walls. Many showed signs of decay, but were surprisingly intact after lifetimes in the cavern. A faded map burned into leather hung among them. Duncan traced the lines on the map — identical to Grayson Kirby's old parchment — with his fingers hovering over its surface.

"We need to be recording this."

"I don't know that we should." Ethan touched the camera hanging on his belt. "I don't know how this place remained hidden for so long as it is. We shouldn't risk leaving any clues." Ethan began deleting pictures.

"Amazing. How long has this place been underneath everyone's feet?" Conrad was examining the crossbows and longbows in one corner of the room. "I wonder who owns the land above us? They probably don't have a clue."

"It has changed hands a number of times over the years." Ethan walked over to the glistening pool. "I'm not sure who owns it now. No one's ever been interested in developing it. Most of it you couldn't build on anyway."

"Are you serious? What is this place?"

The men turned around and found Kane standing in

the cavern, mouth a bit agape and staring at the ceiling.

"How did you get in here?" Conrad asked.

"For some stupid reason I decided to crawl back through the tunnel the moment before everything started shaking. I thought I was going to get crushed by a limestone slab, but the rocks blocking the way shifted just enough."

"Glad you didn't get flattened, that would have been a hard one to explain. Though this place isn't any easier. This could be the key to all of our mysteries," Conrad said, "or the source of new ones."

"All of this was only a few feet into the cave. Barely beyond our reach the whole time." Ethan knelt down on one knee on the rocks circling the pool. He reached in the water and cleared away some sediment at the bottom. "Guys, come look at this." A space for a cross, identical to the one on the granite door.

"I'm afraid to ask, what does that mean?" Kane asked.

"Grayson's cross opened the door and nearly brought the place down. Not sure what it would do in this one." Ethan wondered if he should even try.

"Well, let's not get ourselves trapped down here." Kane walked to the maps, finding the twin of the one in the old church. Or was this the original?

"What was the purpose here?" Duncan thought out loud. "It looks like a cathedral and an armory." Above the pool, a small opening had been cut in the ceiling. The frescos stopped in a circle a few inches around the cavity. "Maybe that's where the water comes from."

"If my bearings are right, we're right under the Oak Grove." Conrad was examining an arrow he pulled from a barrel. "Take a look at this arrowhead." The flint was coated in blue film. He ran it across a rock. "No sparks and it made a cut like this rock is butter. It has been hardened or altered somehow." It reminded him of something he found years ago in the Riverlands.

Ethan looked again into the sparkling pool. It was crystal clear, yet light emanated from the pool, from the water itself. He dipped his hand in the water, cupping water in his palm. The water sparkled with tiny minerals barely perceptible to the eye. As the water ran down his arm, it slowed before falling off. Each drop vanished without a trace when it landed on the stone floor. He didn't hear Conrad and Duncan discussing the weapons as he pulled the cross from its pouch. He turned it, watching the light travel over the intricate scroll work. Slowly submerging it in the pool, he snapped it into place. In an instant, the gemstone began to glow and the water churned. A shockwave of energy reached out from the pool, sending Ethan flying backwards to the ground. Before the men could reach Ethan, the pool spun like a whirlpool and its bluish light brightened. Scout, who had been climbing over the crates, arched his back, raising his hair on end. The light shot up to the ceiling, narrowing in the form of a cone, its tip entering the hole in the ceiling. It looked like it was rotating, but the water moved within the cone of light, suspended against gravity, bound by the confines of the light.

As Ethan stood up and approached the illuminated water, he heard a voice.

"Welcome, my friends. I was beginning to wonder when you were going to arrive. The time for expediency is upon us."

Out of the shadows at the rear of the cavern appeared the last man they expected to see.

Grayson Kirby.

CHAPTER TEN

Deserts were full of life, you simply had to know where to look for it.

Duncan scanned the high desert around Sedona. Visitors were always surprised it wasn't barren. Not all deserts were like the Sahara or the Yuma dunes. He had spent years exploring the hills and valleys around Sedona, its reddish monoliths of rock rising around the town. Almost alive, they blazed like fire in the morning and setting Sun. His parents had been born in the Northwest, but they had moved to what his friends would later name the Western Heat. It was the only home he had known and he could scarcely imagine living anywhere else. Neither the first or the last to settle among the red rocks, many had walked the same paths. Their history was as old as the trails were long and Duncan knew their stories well. He dusted off his brown park ranger uniform and turned to address the tourist group.

"Before the Twentieth Century began, the Sinagua Indians had come here nearly two millennia earlier and lived throughout the Verde Valley. It wasn't only the scenic beauty that attracted them. The valleys provided shelters for their cliff dwellings and centuries of volcanic eruptions made the soil rich for farming."

"What about the energy here? The vortexes? Did they know about that?" interrupted an older woman wearing a sparkling red hat.

Someone always asked about the vortexes. Sedona had become a mecca for modern pilgrims seeking spiritual enlightenment. Most of them left empty-handed. The natives felt the red lands were sacred, but what they had found was much more complex than the seekers understood.

"They were drawn by the energy they believed enveloped this place. The volcanoes, wooded valleys and water that rose out of the desert were a sign of a focal point of Earth's energy, what some now claim to be vortexes. Perhaps the violent geologic eruptions and uplift have created natural anomalies." Duncan tended to think it was more the miracle of an oasis in the desert that drew people for centuries to the red rocks. All simply a sign of an ingenious creator who had many reasons for what was crafted. Still, he could sense the past strongly imprinted around him.

"In any case, the natives were closer to the Earth if for no other reason than they had to rely on it daily to survive. Maybe that is why they claimed they could sense something here that would someday be lost as people ignored the land."

"What did they sense here?" the woman asked.

"Not really sure. A lot of their history is lost. Some is kept secret from outsiders. They would tell you that the world doesn't end at the tip of our nose. Is there something more here or is there a more mundane answer?"

"Perhaps we have forgotten."

"Perhaps." Duncan had reflected on those mysteries for many years while exploring in the shadows of the red rock mountains and their sun-baked faces. He didn't have all the answers, but something teased at his mind. And there was one man in particular that had encouraged his search. Usually Ahote would be here with these tour groups. It was unlike him to be unseen for days. "Okay, unless there are more questions, let's head out to our next stop."

The Sun was beginning to set over Duncan's home as he finished packing gear into his backpack. Located five miles outside town where development had yet to intrude, his stone house blended into the landscape. The ever-growing tourist business created friction between the desires of the town and the need to preserve the area's history and timeless vistas. He loved the town, but preferred hiking through the hills to the west when he wasn't working. That is where the Palatki and Honanki ruins stood. At the Palatki site, two large sandstone dwellings sat at the base of sheer cliffs and it was there he had met the old Indian man Ahote. He claimed to be directly descended from the Sinagua and the Hopi. For some unknown reason, the aged native had taken a special interest in Duncan.

They would walk among the ruins, hiking to ones not readily accessible to the tourists. He had taught Duncan the history of the land, the *tutskwa*. Every rock, every tree had a story. He spoke of the people who lived there for centuries, building homes and farming the lands. Duncan learned which plants healed and which were poison. Where to find water in the desert and how to survive with little else but a knife. Ahote had abandoned the mysticism of the natives, but he felt his homeland was a beacon to the creator. A creator his people didn't fully know until some visitors arrived in the twilight of their history. He never did explain who those visitors were, only that "they knew what we should have known all along. Or maybe we had forgotten what the Old Ones once taught."

When the mood struck him, usually under a clear night sky, he would speak of the myths of his ancestors. The time of the *Kushurza* when the underworld emptied into the lands and the *powakas* plied their evil sorcery in a battle against the Light. Only a great cataclysm ended their terror. A great deluge. For someone who didn't believe in the ancient myths, Duncan sensed fear in Ahote. His father and his before him had passed on a sense of dread. Ahote would often remind Duncan, "Not all in myth is fable." He was a restless spirit that didn't want his people's past to disappear without bestowing it on someone else. He had no children and no family. Ahote was the last of his line.

As dusk faded into night, Duncan hiked into the valley with his pack of gear and his walking stick. The two inch thick, five foot tall piece of oak was more like a quarterstaff. He had cut it the previous winter when he was in the Northwest visiting cousins. Heading into the night with some sort of protection was simple common sense. It would only take about thirty minutes to reach a campsite he often used. He had told Ahote a few days earlier that he would be there, which was the norm. He always let someone know where he was going. It was unlikely he of all people would become another statistic lost in the desert, but why take chances?

The half-moon lit the way enough to walk without a flashlight, but there were other animals that could see better in the moonlight. Arriving at the campsite to start the fire before the coyotes decided to pay a visit was always best. He paused, watching the brighter stars twinkling into existence. The heat of the day would quickly escape into the cloudless sky, and by early morning, the heavens would be in full display, though the Moon would dampen them somewhat until it set. Duncan's eyes were adjusted to the dim light as well as they could be, but it wasn't enough to quickly identify the form that ran out of the shadows toward him.

At the last second Duncan realized it was a man and raised his staff in time to take a blow from the shadow that knocked him to the ground. After the momentary shock passed, he jumped up and this time was ready for the next blow. The shadow had his own staff, similar in size to Duncan's, and he managed to block every thrust and cut he made.

"Who are you?" Duncan demanded, catching his breath.

His assailant made no response, not a sound. He only continued to attack. They circled each other, trying to wear each other down with strike after strike. Their blows sounded across the desert. Finally, as exhaustion began to overtake Duncan, the shadow hit his shin, falling him to the ground. Duncan fought through the pain and lunged toward the shadow almost taking a blow to the head, catching it with his staff at the last instant. Then the shadow landed a blow against Duncan's side, crumpling him into the dirt. Instead of attacking again, he backed off and spoke.

"You're looking at the staff! Anticipate where it is coming from before it moves! Look at me!" The shadow stepped forward with his staff raised. Duncan's body ached from the blows and his arms were weak, but the anger rose in him. It was enough to unleash his remaining adrenaline and energy. He struck at the shadow's staff over and over in a furious rage. The man was wavering. Then, with a scream that echoed through the valley, Duncan brought his staff down on his adversary, splintered the enemy's weapon, and sent him crashing into the ground.

Duncan held the end of his wooden weapon over the man, intending to bring it down on whoever he was. The light of the Moon revealed he was an Indian, clothed only in the hides of some animal. He didn't look much older than Duncan and didn't appear afraid at all. Oddly, he looked pleased when he began to speak.

"You have reached the end of what we can teach you. Soon you will know why you were instructed all these years. You will leave, but in one of your returns you will reclaim these lands from darkness. It hides here somewhere. I have not found it, but someday you will. An evil of the Fallen."

Out of breath, Duncan said to the shadow man, "Did Ahote send you? Wait until I find him. I'll teach him the lesson this time. You're out of your mind, we could have killed each other!"

The man sat up and laughed, "Ahote was my son! I'm Hania, a warrior who has waited many moons for our replacement. You will defend and preserve these lands from the Darkness that will seek to conquer it. You will soon learn much in the East. That is where you will choose to continue forward. Or you will decide to abandon what you have learned."

Before Duncan could say a word, Hania vanished, merging not into the darkness, but into the moonlight that surrounded him.

***

After that night, Duncan never saw Ahote again. The feeling he had when Hania vanished returned when Grayson Kirby walked out of the shadows. Dead men don't speak. They don't fight either. Only a few weeks later, there had been an incident in the gulch. He had wanted to tell someone. Why hadn't he told the friends he now stood with? These men who were different too, but in what ways he didn't entirely know. It was crazy, the water, only that one time.

Now water before him defied gravity.

He had been hiking a dry creek bed that cut through a wooded valley. Thunder rumbled in the distance, but the skies above Duncan remained clear. The storms could move in quick, but he had time to get out of the valley. He had never been caught before. The thought barely left his mind when the roar came from behind. A wave of water swept toward him, a wall of debris and certain death. Instinctively, as the first spray of water reached him, Duncan drew the water around him, spinning it into a hurricane with himself at the eye. He threw it back as a shockwave of energy and water that reached out and collided with the torrential wave, obliterating all traces of it.

For the longest time he stood there staring, his hands shaking. The creek bed had been scoured of the slightest remnant of water or vegetation. He vaguely recalled a story Ahote had told him about natives who could interact with specific parts of nature. Duncan had thought they were just myths.

Then, he had to wonder, was he a water-wielder?

He had been thinking about Hania ever since Ethan mentioned his encounter with the old man on the street corner. Shadows and light, like his meeting with the Indian. After years of going back and forth wondering if something was wrong with him, and what was missing, he thought the answers were nearer then ever. Nevertheless, certainty remained elusive.

"Grayson?" Duncan asked cautiously. "It can't be, you died years ago."

"In a manner of speaking." Grayson's rough voice hadn't lost its deep tone. "But death is only a door. One can walk through doors both ways, you know." Nor had he lost his humor. He was still the stately, graying old man. Someone who belonged in an older era. He was more vibrant, not the tired, hurried man he had been during his last days, so Ethan thought. Maybe it was the water's illumination or maybe it was in spite of the bluish light. He easily noticed Ethan analyzing him. "You seem the least surprised to see me here."

Ethan smiled. "We're hundreds of feet underground in an ancient..." Ethan paused and looked around the cavern, "...stronghold, a keep of some sort, with energy emanating from the rocks; whom else would we expect to walk out of the shadows?"

"Maybe he's here to give us answers. Are you?" Kane asked.

"Yes, there is much we must discuss. But answers? I don't have all the answers. If the enemies we face didn't have minds of their own, we would know what their intentions are and we could have stopped them at the dawn of time. To allow some people freedom to act and not others wouldn't make sense. So all are given that opportunity. Many waste it on darkness. Without the free will we are born with, we would be as mindless as these rocks."

"The Watchers, who are they? What does this have to

do with us?" Conrad asked.

"To the point as usual, I see." Grayson knelt down to rub Scout's face. He had sat in front of Grayson, gazing up at him like an attentive student. "A fine animal. Cats are like us Watchers. Always moving in the shadows, noticing the slightest gathering of light. Quiet and in the background, but fierce defenders when they need be."

"'*Us* Watchers?' So we are what you...were?"

"You know the answer, Conrad, you knew since you stood against the shadow walkers at the rockshelter not so long ago. Granted, you all can choose to walk away from what I am to ask of you. Life conspires to bring you to particular points in time — it prepares you for what is coming — and there you make a choice. Once on the new path, more choices will be encountered. Destiny is for you to define."

"I can't imagine people not walking away from all of this and you haven't told us much of anything yet." Kane was trying to work things out in his mind. In spite of what he was, dread still crept inside. The creatures in the murals stared at him.

"Yes, some events occur with or without us, but our lives are not planned for us. Everything we encounter requires from us a reaction. A few have walked away from this life. They weren't condemned for it. They served well. Since men have always had a choice, and many choose to enter the blackness, there has been a need for those willing to stand against their schemes. Everyone makes that decision. Every person in this world. Some are needed to go further, because beneath the surface of our world, there is much hidden."

Ethan smiled. Grayson's humor was still subtle, yet clear, but he wanted concrete answers. "We were given the gifts to do what you did. Defend this world against the unseen. We know we can do more than we have, but it's clear there is much we don't know. For starters, what is this place? What happened in the Dark Hollow? And what exactly walks in the shadows?" He looked at Conrad who knew the answer to the last question.

"Good questions. Who are these enemies who stalk us?" Kane asked.

Grayson walked toward the water. "This place is where a rift in time exists. For many millennia, most who walked through these woods sensed nothing. A few, such as yourselves, did make note. Some were the early explorers of these lands." Grayson knelt down and reached through the pillar of light and cupped water in his hands. As he stood, he let it go in the light where it swirled and grew into a six foot cylindrical wall. Then the wall of water spread through the room, surrounding them, immersing their bodies and minds, yet not so much of a drop of wetness appeared on them. "See the past as it happened." As the images unfolded on the suspended water, first showing a fleet of ships moving along a forested coastline, Grayson walked among them.

"If these ships remind you of Vikings, you are correct. No longer invading coastlines hoping to be honored in Valhalla if they died in battle, these Norse had abandoned their beliefs in the old northern gods. Odin and Thor ceased putting fear in their hearts, but they still believed in the monsters that sometimes roamed dark lands. One of the reasons they found truth in the new religion from the East is that one of its apostles had written an apocalypse not unlike their own *Völuspá*, where good and evil meet in a final cataclysm.

"Nearly three hundred years after Norse settlements in North America had failed to prosper, most in Europe had forgotten the rumors of a new land. Some did remember, and not all were from the North." Scenes of knights shimmered into view. First at war, then in the Holy City before journeying home by sea. "They had been charged with protecting what had been found in Jerusalem and the rest of Outremer, before it had again fallen to Muslim armies. Now many of these knights were no longer safe at home. Persecuted because of their wealth and power, even though most of them truly weren't interested in money or position. They wanted to continue to defend the world from the shadows, the shadows their ancestors had feared so much.

"Many of the founders of their orders were descended from generations of defenders. In an age of prehistory long forgotten by humanity, they were called Watchers. None of the modern fraternities and orders are true Watchers. All of the conspiracies and speculations about these societies are amusing, but only serve to hide the authentic. The knights' predecessors had taken their name from their first enemy, the Watchers of Heaven. This first affliction on humanity was destroyed when history was still young. These were the Fallen."

The specters of men fused with beast, demonspawn and twisted monstrosities floated among them.

"It took centuries for the last of these and their terrible creations to be eradicated, but not before they instructed those that would succeed them. Over time, they became nearly as powerful as their ancestors."

The horrors were replaced with the vast forests and rolling mountains of the New World.

"The knights went far inland, trying to avoid any conflict with the natives along the way. They searched for a place to build a refuge. Somewhere they could hide the true relics found in the Crusades and the knowledge they had preserved for ages. There were refuges around the world, but Europe was unsafe and unstable during those times. After traveling up the Valnastoi River and exploring the Misty Valley, they found the cave and the spring above it. They knew the energy in this place, there were such places in Europe which could be used as portals to travel between gateways. They planted the Oak Grove to shield the spring and dug the well over a crevice that they named the Well of Knowledge. The Oaks grew into monolithic sentinels in only a few year's time. In the caverns they built this repository for relics, scrolls and weapons to defend their keep. Nearby they laid the first stones of the White City. When the first settlers of the Old World arrived decades later, the residents simply told them they had arrived a few years prior. The town hid its secrets in plain sight ever since, even from its own residents."

The images of the early building of the White City disappeared and the water pulled back into the column of light and fell into the spring. The men silently processed what they had witnessed. Grayson didn't have time left to waste.

"What you have seen is recorded in the books at the church in the White City. The histories of the Watchers and the Fallen in prehistory, before the Great Cataclysm, are recorded in the *Book of the Wars*. Supposedly, no original copies exist, but I suspect at least one Cache of Knowledge may have one."

After a few more moments, Ethan asked Grayson something their little history lesson didn't cover. "How are these portals created?"

"You would probably understand that better than I," Grayson said. "The forces that created and occasionally reshape this world can be violent and the physical structure here changed in such a way that a rift in time formed. When matter and energy are twisted and combined at levels we can barely understand, time itself can become accessible. Once someone aware of the greater existence discovers a place like this, it becomes tainted with their intentions. If a resident of the dark recesses finds one, the portal absorbs darkness. Once tainted with good or evil, they rarely change. Few can use both. Not only can they be used to travel to other portals in the present, but into the past as well."

"Time travel? Are you kidding?" said Kane. "Anyone can use this place to go through time and change history?"

"Not anyone can walk through the looking glass." Pointing to the ceiling, he added, "The doorway is aboveground in the Oak Grove. This is more of a window into time, a place to view history past. Kind of the innards of the machine, so to speak. One who senses the energy – no it's more than just sensing it – someone who can control the space and energy around and within them could simply walk into the portal and activate it by their own will. There are few such people and the portals are unusable to most. Fatal in fact. The body would be torn apart without the gifts we have. There are those skilled enough that they can bring others through with them. And even some who have no need for portals to travel the river of time. In any case they are valuable tools that we protect closely."

"These portals sound like wormholes," said Ethan. "They're tunnels through space-time, but to remain stable they need exotic material."

"Like this blue material covering all of these weapons? Or the cross in the water?" Conrad asked.

"Yes, that material is essentially infused with the energy

that was released in the creation of this place. Its dissolved form in the water bonds to rock and metals." Grayson went to Conrad, took the arrowhead, examined it, and said, "Weapons coated in the minerals found here can react with — or help destroy — beings not fully of this world. Or life of this world for that matter. Over time it can dissipate, but when energy clashes with energy, the result is deadly. These minerals cannot impart any power to the bearer, though they may enhance or channel what the person already has within them. Nor are they the energizing gems of conjurers, some of which only radiate radioactive energy harmful to life. The few minerals that can be used to magnify other energies, or are imbued with it like this blue material, are few and far between. Only energy channeled through man's true self can be used without destroying the body. Even then it can be dangerous."

"Our 'true self'?" Conrad asked.

"Your fundamental essence. The part of you that transcends worlds. Your soul." Grayson's words hung for a moment. Humans had often dreamed of immortality. They already had it living within them.

"What of the Dark Hollow?" Duncan asked. "Exactly what are we facing?"

"There lies the Rift, a Dark Portal. It's unusual for two portals to be so close, but there the shadows have remained dormant for many decades. Until last night." Grayson related the history of the Gerbchon family. "We monitored them as much as we could. Little ever came from the Hollow, but now the last of their family, Latzi, has returned and entered the Rift."

"Where did he go?" Kane asked.

"The Darkness that lingers across the valley emanates to us through time." Grayson pointed up at one of the faded murals on the ceiling. "After this place was established, but long before the Europeans had begun to explore and settle this region, a battle was fought in the Misty Valley. Evil had followed our ancestors here and assembled an army of Followers to take the portal and what lay beneath. If I were to guess, I would say that is where Latzi has gone. The evil originally amassed there and if they are doing so again, this would explain what now overflows in the Dark Hollow through the veil. He and his allies have entered the past to find a way to alter the present. They lost the first battle, but if that outcome is altered, what horrors we would awake to? Why fight this battle again, though? What has changed?" He shook his head. "We knew something was coming."

Ethan had been looking at the mural as Grayson spoke. One of the knights carried a jeweled white reliquary with the red *croix pattée*, the red cross of the Crusaders, on its cover. "I've seen this before," Ethan pointed at the jeweled box. "At the church, one of the windows and..." Ethan paused.

"What is it? What's wrong?" asked Conrad.

Ethan looked at Conrad and then at Grayson. "In my dreams. I have seen that box in my dreams. Was it here? Is it here now?"

"That box contained one of the last remnants of the True Cross. It was brought to Britain and then later hidden here by your predecessors for safekeeping with other relics found in the Crusades. After the Army of Shadows failed to take it, the reliquary was returned to Europe where I suspect it remains," explained Grayson.

"What good would an ancient relic do for the enemy?" Kane asked. "Surely they couldn't use something like that even if it had some sort of inherent power. Darkness abhors light."

"You're right, the relics are inherently dangerous to them, but that hasn't stopped centuries of trying. Those relics had their fundamental structure changed during the transcendent events they were exposed to. They are not unlike the minerals in this place, but far more powerful. At the very least, the capture of such relics would have tremendous propaganda value for the Followers. It would be strange for them to be trying again, if that is what they are doing, having failed so often."

"What if they were to find a way to use these relics? Or maybe they have?" Duncan asked. "What then? What would we be facing?"

"Look here, my friends, and see what could happen." Grayson walked over to one of the walls and traced the faded mural with his finger. "This depicts the battle of the Horns of Hattin, but it adds something that the standard histories omit. We know the Crusaders carried a fragment of the True Cross into the battle, but according to this the Saracens had the Spear of Destiny which their spies had stolen from Jerusalem. Mystics among them, probably not true Muslims, had learned to use the Spear as a weapon, or thought they did. The Crusaders may have very well lost that battle regardless, but the Spear was used against them."

Grayson stopped his hand over a skeleton holding the Spear of Destiny surrounded by a blackness radiating around him. "But the Spear also horribly destroyed the wielder and all those near him. It was never used again. It was recovered in a later Crusade, but the Followers never stopped trying to discover methods to use these relics without bringing ruin to themselves. Many would not think twice about using them in a suicidal fashion like at Hattin."

Kane looked at the skeleton, blackened and with

unspeakable terror on its skull. "What's to stop this Latzi or any other Follower from simply stepping through the rift and stealing a relic?"

"You asked the question," Grayson turned from the mural, "and you are the answer. We all are. It is people like us who stand against Followers of the Dark One. We have spent centuries hiding and obscuring history, so finding a relic or other tool for conquer is not a simple task. The relics themselves are closely guarded with many decoys planted throughout the world. Some no longer exist. Do you think that all the cities in Europe which claim to have the same relic actually have the genuine article?"

"Let me guess, the Watchers had a hand in that too," Conrad said. "Maybe this won't be so hard after all. We need to assure the outcome of the battle that occurred here centuries ago doesn't change."

"Perhaps, but never assume ease in defeating the enemy. We had thought the Followers had given up on these schemes, and maybe they have, though why else would the Misty Valley be in their sights? Maybe a reverse in the conflict's outcome is what they seek. The fates of many Watchers would be altered. In the end, the Darkness needs not be rational in its ways, it only seeks to envelop all in its death. Lucky for us..." Grayson laughed, luck had nothing to do with it, "...dark followers have never been gifted at traveling through time. Those who can are far and few between, even less than our own people, but now it would seem they have conquered that problem." Grayson pointed to some hideous creatures in the mural.

"There is one other thing, my friends. You all must be prepared to face evils from beyond this world that few have encountered and far fewer have survived."

CHAPTER ELEVEN

The white-tail deer didn't hear the arrow's imperceptible whisper until a moment before the broadhead
cut through its heart. Reflexively, the animal jumped
up and forward, crashing into a towering tulip poplar only
to die before it fell into a heap.

Unaffected by this brief moment of violence, the early
morning mist still lingered in the Riverlands as the Sun
lazily climbed above the woods. In the quiet, where the
day's sounds were beginning to emerge, one could nearly
see between the veil that separated one realm of existence from the other. Few would likely notice this, nor
would they likely see Conrad sitting camouflaged next to
an old hickory. From there he had often hunted since he
was a little boy. Overlooking the hollow below, he
glimpsed where his quarry fell next to the creek. The moment before he loosed the arrow, everything in the forest
had frozen for an instant. At least to him it had.

His mind could step outside of time, unfettered from

its boundaries, seeing what others could not.

Conrad stepped from the hickory's shadow and found the narrow path that descended below. Every autumn he would slip into these woods with his wooden recurve bow that his grandfather had crafted for him. He hunted like the natives who had done so for generations before the Europeans had ever thought to cross the ocean. These were ancient forests where the original inhabitants had followed the creek to the Great River a few miles to the north. There, into and over the eastern hills, to its mouth at the Great Forks. No one called it that anymore, but Conrad thought it more creative than Three Rivers. At the Great Forks, the cities built of wood, and later steel, had been constructed over the ruins of native villages. Near Conrad's home, away from the cities and towns, the land remained much as it had always been. Even what had been farmed had long ago been reclaimed by trees. It was where he had spent his youth, living off the land with nothing more than a bow and knife.

Dragging the deer home was never what he considered an enjoyable activity, but Conrad did it in record time. The early kill left the rest of the day wide open, so he returned to the woods in the early afternoon. This time he wasn't hunting even though he still brought his bow. He rarely entered his forest without it, hunting regulations to the contrary, and this time was no different. Moving silently over the soft forest floor, avoiding the smallest branch, he followed the creek toward a rockshelter. Generations of travelers and explorers had used it as a resting place. Now, local kids had a habit of fooling around in the cave. He couldn't stand any garbage being strewn about. They hadn't returned since his little "talk" with them, but one of the local farmers had heard a commotion coming from the woods last night. What he had described didn't sound like teenagers having a party, though the woods at night had a habit of distorting sounds. The farmer had heard screaming, not the normal carrying on of kids, but terrified screams. "Maybe it was a bobcat," Conrad had suggested. He had heard the otherworldly sounds of the bobcat during overnights in the woods up north.

"No, they're rare this far south. This didn't sound like an animal or a human." *Not human?* What bothered him was the fact that he had never seen the old farmer so rattled. Maybe — hopefully — it was nothing but imagination.

The early October Sun brought out the color of the leaves that had recently begun to change. The Sun managed to penetrate the leaves and warmed Conrad.

Then nothing. He stopped and looked to the sky.

The Sun had abruptly disappeared, smothered by a gray, overcast sky. A cold wind swept along the creek bed. The water ran wider and swifter. The trees he had known were gone and replaced by unfamiliar giants. The trails he had long ago memorized followed different routes. As a child, Conrad had seen glimpses into unseen worlds around him. Impressions of the past or windows that allowed him to watch history as it had existed. On occasion, since those early days, he would still perceive something. Entering one of those worlds was a different matter. That had never happened. Not to him. There were stories of others and their time-slips — all dismissed by the skeptics. They wouldn't believe him either if he told his stories. He looked around again. The leaves were gone. It was the dead of winter and tiny snowflakes wafted out of the gray sky.

It wasn't a question of where he was, but when?

He quickly pushed fear aside and chose survival as the

first concern. Figuring exactly what happened was a close second. The chilling wind brought with it a strange chatter of low mutterings in an unknown language. Conrad had never heard the dark tongue, something unspoken among people for ages. These weren't people. The sounds were guttural, almost animal. Dread crept into his chest, then determination. Who was in his woods?

Conrad walked slowly, careful not to step on any branch or move any stone. This would be the wrong time for a misstep. These weren't deer he was stalking. Carrying the longbow slowed his already measured pace, but he would never leave his weapon behind. The hollow began to narrow as it approached the cave. He stayed close to the hillside, crouching low among the brush, moving a branch at a time. After nearly an hour of deliberate movement, the rockshelter came into view. He barely suppressed a gasp at what stood in the cave. His heart dropped hard.

Dead animals hung from the rock ledge above the opening. Unrecognizable, they had been skinned and torn and now three abominations fed on the remains. A massive primate, covered in black, shaggy hair, tore a limb from the kills. It had the face of an ape and hands as large as its head. Some terrible vision of bigfoot, it stood upright over six feet tall. Next to it stood a black hound the size of a small bear. Its canine teeth protruded from its mouth, stained with the blood of its victim, matching its unearthly red eyes. Dried blood matted the fur, signs of the recent hunt. As large as the primate, the third monstrosity had no hair, its skin withered and stretched thin over its bones. A walking corpse from the netherworld, surrounded by the stench of rotting death spreading through the woods. It appeared to be the leader, exchanging disturbed grumblings with the primate beast.

It wasn't fear so much that overcame Conrad, but revulsion at the twisted horrors before him. Were these dark creatures en route to some place, feasting in these woods before continuing? Or had they made this their home? For some reason he had entered this long forgotten timescape. Their presence must have made a rift in the veil. He had walked these woods hundreds of times. Why pulled here now with no control over it? True, his abilities had never felt fully mature. That didn't matter now; something was wrong. The corpse looked out along the creek and sniffed the air. It roared twisted words, yet Conrad understood the meaning in his mind. *A human is here!* He moved backwards when the abomination spotted his hiding place.

"There he is! Almas, bring him to us so we can feed on human flesh!" The corpse pointed toward Conrad and the ape creature pounded its chest and leapt from the cave and turned to look back.

"Come Barguest, a fresh meal awaits us." Almas tore through the underbrush. The hound growled rabidly and chased after him. Conrad had barely enough time to turn and dash up the hillside using trees to propel himself forward. He reached the summit, but not before the demon hound made it halfway up the hillside snarling and barking, spitting foaming saliva everywhere.

Conrad pulled an arrow from its quiver on the bow, notched the arrow, and pulled back the bowstring. A moving target was always the most difficult kind, but time was on his side. For an instant, the bounds of time broke and the hound's movements froze in his mind's eye. He aimed at the hound's head and loosed the arrow in one fluid motion. The arrow flew between its teeth, the razor-edged broadhead breaking through the roof of its mouth, and sliced deep into its brain. The impact spun it backward, and by the time it landed at the foot of the hill, the black hound was dead. Conrad took off toward a clearing above the rockshelter.

Almas reached the hill as Barquest landed at his feet, its mouth propped open by the arrow. The primate's scream echoed through the forest. Barquest had been one of the most feared black hounds and now this man had killed him. He looked up the hill, but the man was gone. "You will die slowly for this, human!" He tore a small maple tree from the ground to use as a weapon and clambered up the hill to exact his revenge.

Only a few trees stood in the rocky soil, giving Conrad a clear shot at anything pursuing him. One problem: Too close to the edge of the overhang. Not a corner he should have let himself be pushed into. He drew an arrow as the ape came crashing out of the woods. Almas swung the tree over his head, baring his jagged teeth and letting out a thundering roar. Conrad aimed for its chest, controlled his breath, and began to release. The arrow flew wild as a sharp pain exploded out of his side, dropping him to the ground. Coming to his knees and holding his ribs, the living corpse stood at the other side of the clearing where it had hurled the rock like a cannonball.

"Now you will die, fleshling. These are our lands." It looked at Almas, Conrad's arrow had flown wide, and the hairy beast ran to where he had fallen.

"Not today, demons." Conrad fought through the pain and wielded his bow, waited until the last possible instant, and leaped over the side of the cliff hoping the spot wasn't too steep. As he slid, he caught a rock with his bow and stopped his fall in time to see the primate fly over the edge, landing on the rocks below. The beast didn't have time to scream as its body broke. "One more to go,"

Conrad muttered under his breath. He unhooked his bow from the rock and let himself down the rock face carefully. With each move, his side radiated with pain. Once at the bottom, he winced as he felt at least two cracked ribs. The bow, at least, had managed to stay intact, though the bowstring was frayed and would not last.

The rockshelter was empty other than the half-eaten animals. Their stench didn't compare to the reek emanating from the dead primate, broken open nearby on the rocks. A glint of light caught Conrad's eye from the back of the cave. A short sword. It had a blue coating on its blade. "This might be useful." Conrad weighed the heavy blade in his hand and slid it in his belt. Rocks fell behind him and the corpse climbed into the cave.

"You are very lucky, human, but that luck has ended," seethed the creature.

"I don't believe in luck. And by the way, these are my woods. So maybe you should move on before you join your friends." Conrad had too much adrenaline running through his body to fear the horror standing in front of him. The pain of his broken ribs had faded.

"So you can understand me? Very well, understand this: The people in these lands call me Kiwahkw and from the North I was summoned to destroy your kind. A new dark age is upon us and humanity's end is near. You can have the honor of being the first to fall."

Kiwahkw raised its hands, roared, and frigid wind whirled around him. The temperature plummeted and dark snow whipped through the cave. The creature's molted skin solidified into ice and the dead animals froze and cracked. The cold enveloped Conrad, but not before he loosed an arrow. It passed through the dark polar cloud only to shatter against the horror's skin. He pulled another arrow back on the bowstring and the sinew snapped, brittle from the cold.

"You lose, human. I will freeze you within a moment of death and I will call more of my kind to this place to feast on you before you die." He rushed at Conrad, who, with the last of his strength, fought through the cold and pulled the short sword from his belt. He thrust it into Kiwahkw's neck, shock spreading over its face. Conrad pulled the blue blade free, and before the corpse fell backwards, he ran the sword through its chest. The frozen corpse hit the ground, shattering in an explosion of detritus and white light, throwing Conrad from the cave. As he stood to his feet he opened his own eyes to a bright Sun. He had returned to his own time. In the center of the cave, stuck in the ground, the sword glinted in the sunlight.

"What evils might that be?" Conrad asked even though he knew. In a timeslip he had met horrors that he wished to forget. Unfortunately, it was not the only time. "Who or what would we face? What we see in these murals? In your history vision? What I saw?"

"The battle was brought to this valley by an army raised by the shadowmancer, an army of men and dark beings." Grayson looked at Conrad. "You have seen the beasts. They may have been on their way to the Misty Valley for this battle before you intercepted them. Perhaps you helped the battle to be won. But consider what would happen if the portal was used to summon creatures from other realms and other times to change history. Or they could be brought here. Many are no doubt hiding in our world right now, waiting for the Dark One to call them out. The first Watchers had thought they had killed them all, but history has shown otherwise. A portal can be a doorway to different points on Earth, or in history, but a Time-walker could be used by a shadowmancer to summon even more Death Bringers."

"Who are these shadowmancers?" Kane asked. "And what beasts did you see, Conrad?"

"Shadowmancers are lieutenants of the Dark One," Grayson explained. "Some are completely of the shadow realm and can only be killed by those of the Realm of Light, like the Watchers. Other shadowmancers are chimeras of man and beast, forged in dark places. For all their power, strangely enough, few are Timewalkers." He stopped and all looked at Conrad.

"Years ago, I encountered three foul creatures of the shadows in the Riverlands." He looked at Ethan, the only one he had told this story to before. "I killed them, but if I hadn't been...whatever we are, they would have easily killed me. It's been a long time since anyone has fought these creatures in open battle. If they can influence people with modern weapons, we'll be in a bit of trouble, to say the least.

"I also found a sword, coated with this blue mineral. I don't know where they got it. I used it to kill a beast that called itself Kiwahkw. It was a walking corpse that could control ice and cold to kill."

"So we wouldn't only be fighting strength. Some of these creatures can access the unseen around them," Ethan said. "Like us, but evil." He knew some of what hid in the shadows, they had avoided him, because they knew what he was. There would be no such luck now. These creatures were far worse as physical manifestations. What he had encountered before were often not. They had oppressed him, but ultimately had failed. To take on physical form was a far deeper evil.

"Yes, but many of these do nothing but perfect their

terrible skills," Grayson said. "No second is left to waste."

"Question?" Kane asked. "Where did this Latzi go when he left the Dark Hollow? "

"He traveled to Mexico to the Mayan ruins." Grayson shook his head slightly. "Jungles thrive where peoples once flourished. Whole civilizations oppressed by wicked men. There he studied the dark arts. What he learned in the temples we don't know, but what he did find apparently helped him enter the Rift."

Duncan walked over to the pool; he had a hunch. He dipped one of his knives in the bluish water and pulled it out slowly. It sparkled in the light, and as it dried in the air, a blue film remained on the steel blade. "This will help us?"

"Yes," Grayson answered. "Only a thin coating is needed and is nearly indestructible. Not all shadows can be killed instantly by it, but it does give an advantage. The dark beings have similar minerals, black metals fatal as poison."

"Are there others?" Kane asked. "Or are we the only ones left to defend the planet? There are only four of us. The world is a big place."

"There are others that have joined the Watchers. The Triquetra defend holy sites and Caches of Knowledge around the globe. The Arc Maidens are a sisterhood who have often fought alongside us and are masters of subterfuge. There are more of us, but few are ready and many are unknown. We have always been at the center of the struggle. We were the first. We are also the last line of defense. You four, whether you realize it or not, have within you powers far beyond any Watcher I have seen in an age." Grayson paused and walked towards the swirling column of water and gazed into it.

"I must leave you now. I don't know if we'll meet

again. If you so choose, you could be among the strongest Watchers ever to stand against the powers of desolation that emanate from the dark realms. That you have arrived in this time, tells me that these days will be in need of Watchers with the caliber of those who came first. You will face the vilest abominations unseen in the world for generations.

"Do not underestimate Latzi, but he's ultimately only a minor pawn. There are far worse foes behind him. What they are using him for, time will tell. I am sorry I cannot be of more help. I am still too connected to this world to see into the minds of men and creature. Soon my passage will be complete, the gift given to me of this last goodbye, ended. Our struggle is not simply against other men, but against the schemes of the Dark One and the rulers of his realm. Decisions should not be made lightly, but they must be made. I wish we would have destroyed the Rift and all that lived in the Dark Hollow long ago." Grayson walked toward the water, then faced his successors. "The world forgets evil exists even as it creeps over the land. You must stand firm. You do not have to wait for the day evil is to come. That day has already passed.

"All await for the next Sons and Daughters of the Light to be revealed. Go well my friends and let the Light be your guide."

Grayson stepped into the water and disappeared into the shimmering blue.

CHAPTER TWELVE

Before anyone could say a word, the column of light slowly retracted into the pool. The pool rippled, then quickly calmed as the soothing blue light dimmed. Quiet descended as the men stood thinking on the words of Grayson. Ethan stared at the water into which the Tower Keeper had disappeared. All of this would be very confusing, if not unbelievable, to most people. For him and his friends it was almost expected. Still, in spite of all they had experienced in their lives, what they had witnessed was the final stamp of reality. If any iota of uncertainty of what they were or what they could do remained, it too had vanished into the mist. The journey to this point had taken many years, and for Ethan, it all started when his dreams ceased being dreams.

⧗ ⧗ ⧗

He was sixteen when it finally happened.

When his eyes opened in the dreamworld, he found himself at the edge of an unfamiliar lake, crystal clear, and surrounded by forested hills with small summer cottages situated near the shores. Completely foreign, yet it felt too real to be fantasy. If there was part of him beyond his physical body, like mankind had long believed, this was it. Where, though, and when? Perhaps right now or some time in the past. Or maybe a glimpse of a future. He had often been able to think and act in his dreams as if he were awake. Always searching for something or someone, though the dreams still remained blurred or disconnected. He wanted to take the next step, but didn't know how.

The human soul could only be imprisoned for so long.

This dream was different.

Near one of the cottages, a family sat along the shore, and a young girl waded in the shallows looking in the water before taking a swim. Ethan watched from a distance away, then found himself on a small dock near the girl. He didn't remember walking; he simply was there and her family had vanished.

Now an adult, the girl looked up at him with large brown eyes and he knew this was who he had spent thousands of dreams looking for. He knew her from the past and from the future, or from beyond the universe itself. There was no mistaking it, Ethan had never met her in his waking world but he knew the woman before him. He tried to talk; no words escaped his mouth. The dark haired woman swam toward the dock, reached up, and handed Ethan a small purple gemstone. The moment she placed it in his hand, he awoke.

His heart fluttered. Light from the Moon filtered through the open window and the summer breeze silently entered slight and cool. He felt something in his tightly closed hand. Ethan opened it and held the small, faceted object in the dim light. All tiredness had left him, so when dawn came, he still sat awake thinking about the woman he had always known but had only just met.

As the Sun burned away the morning mist, he went into the woods to a favorite place where the trail passed a cluster of three giant oaks that looked like they had sprouted when time began. Near the trail, remains of an old farm hid in the underbrush. Crumbled rock walls and knotted fruit trees from a forgotten orchard had been absorbed by nature's growth. An easy place to forget time; it could stand still in this place, if it hadn't already. That night Ethan had crossed a threshold he had long hoped to breach and awakened from an ancient slumber, new and reborn. An energy coursed through him. He had discovered — or rediscovered — a long forgotten part of himself. Something he knew was there, but could never quite control, always beyond his fingertips. Was it the soul hitting the barriers of physical existence?

He felt the gemstone in his hand. The dream was no hallucination. Did the path through time and space that had opened remain so while awake? Or was it limited to the night? A shadow of doubt — or maybe it was the anxiety of the possibility that the night's events would never happen again — clouded in his mind like a growing storm. Maybe in the timeless forest he could find the answer.

Ethan stood on the trail near the oaks and closed his eyes. The sounds of the forest dimmed as he tensed every part of his body. He reached deep into his being, his essence, the sum of himself that wasn't of the world, and felt every particle of his being pulse with their energy. The air around him charged and the forest stood by in quiet anticipation. It had not seen something like this since before the trees had been born out of the ground.

Then he ran.

Down the trail as fast as he could with his eyes shut,

but he could still see, at a speed no human should be able to achieve. Sight or memory would have helped him from stumbling, but he didn't need it. Ahead of him a small ravine divided the path, but not so small that it could be jumped. When Ethan reached its edge, he didn't hesitate. Nor did he stop. He landed on the other side and fell on his hands. Opening his eyes, he turned and looked across the ravine to the trail that ran to its edge. As he regained his breath he smiled. Ethan had crossed the barrier. There would be no turning back.

He spent hours in the woods that day learning many new revelations about himself, but when he returned home, only a few minutes had passed since he had left the house that morning.

⌛   ⌛   ⌛

Ethan snapped out of his daydream. Voices. He looked around and remembered where he was. Even though they had seen and experienced events in their lives that few others could understand, this all took time to sink in. Their humanity still didn't want to fully let go. It would always be there in some large measure. Duncan was speaking.

"It appears our weekend has become a bit more than we were expecting." Duncan knew it to be an understatement, but where should they begin? They had prepared — and had been prepared — for this moment since birth, but now they had to choose whether to continue or hope others would take their place. "What are we supposed to do next? Use the portal? Find others?"

Ethan thought about that day in the woods, not all that far from the cave. That day he knew he had the ability to make a difference. The day he met his future wife in a dream.

"Ethan?" Duncan asked.

"There aren't any others," Ethan said. "At least not enough people who are ready. Who knows where they are? We have inherited a historic legacy from our ancestors."

"We can walk away from it." Kane accepted and used his abilities. They were part of himself, but this was too much. Battles? Dark beasts? He wasn't so sure about this. He was a healer, not a warrior.

"Is that what you want?" Ethan answered. "All our lives we made decisions that led us here. This wasn't forced on us. Not all in our families had the gifts or the insight for this life. We all knew we were on the edge of something greater than ourselves. Always wanting to do more for the world." Ethan stopped, he had become angry.

He had often faced evil. Not monsters, but human darkness, though he had no doubt they had allies far more heinous pulling their strings. They couldn't hide from him, though they kept their distance, at least until the encounter in the library. He had walked away from that life so his family could live normally. He'd nearly blocked out all of what he had found he was capable of doing. After Milena had disappeared, it was all he could do to keep from self-destructing. The anger and fear inside him had wanted to consume him and prevented Ethan from reclaiming his suppressed abilities. Darkness oppressed those it feared the most and it assaulted him like it never had before and eroded his power. One night, on the verge of losing the battle, he rediscovered his compass. Actually, it had found him. He could again notice the thin places and manipulate the energy within him and around him.

Not like he once did, but every passing day brought improvement. He took a breath and relaxed.

Ethan knelt on one knee, picked up a small rock, and placed it in his hand. "I often started to tell you guys stories. Stories of where I've been and what I've done, but I've never quite told you everything." He looked at the rock, his eyes narrowed slightly, and then burned blue. The rock floated out of his hand five feet into the air and exploded into a fine mist of dust.

"I think now is a good time to fill in the details." He stood and walked around the room, looking at the murals and the tapestries. "I once told Conrad how I met Milena in a dream, but never about the gemstone she gave me in that dream. It was in my hand when I woke up. That was the day I jumped the ravine that I told you about, Kane, after I watched you heal that disabled girl in at the amusement park. When Duncan told me of the thin places in the desert, I told him what I thought the Oak Grove might be. You have all confided to myself and Milena some of your experiences and abilities, but never fully to us or to each other." He looked into the sparkling water. "Funny how we fear rejection or misunderstanding from those closest to us. I've been no better." Now he told them all of that day in the woods, and why he and Milena had been traveling around the world. And then he spoke of the dreams that were a link to the unseen, perhaps a path to the soul that straddled their world and what lay beyond it.

Kane had always been fascinated by dreams. There seemed much more to them than random images. Certainly all people had pondered this at least once in their life. How could they ignore what happened to them every single night? "Are we not told that we may be spoken to in our visions of the night?" he mused.

"Yet more messages we all tend to ignore. Dreams allow us to break the bonds of time." Ethan glanced at the ceiling. "What stands above us appears to be more proof that time need not be an obstacle." He hoped they weren't the only ones who could see what was to come. "It felt like Milena and I were alone all those years, even though we knew some, like yourselves, to be like us. There are others out there, but we never found many. Even after we left that life, something was left undone. There was more that we were meant to do. Milena had known it, too, but we had to move on for a time. Now it all looks like it led right to this moment, to prepare us. Somehow Milena's disappearance figures into all of this. I don't know how, but it does." He turned from the men, his eyes had teared.

⧖   ⧖   ⧖

Exactly a year before, his life had crashed to a halt on that day Milena had taken a walk in the autumn woods. Since fall began, she said that the woods were subdued, like it was trying to tell her something. A warning perhaps, but not a danger. A message from the trees and animals that normally weren't bothered with the concerns of humans.

"I don't know what it is, but I feel like the world we left behind to live a normal life has returned, though not completely the same. Did you ever think maybe we never fully realized what we were to do? What everything was about? Was that all? It's like something will soon change. I can't see it all, but we never could. We are still too attached to our physical bodies. There is one more leap we must make. Soon it will come."

Soon after, Milena went into the woods she loved so

much and disappeared.

Ethan experienced crippling anxiety when his connection to Milena severed in an instant. At first she was there, barely out of reach. Then even that began to fade. Soon, nothing. "Where did mommy go?" Kyra had asked.

"To the woods, where the oaks are." Ethan said it reflexively, knowing something wasn't right.

"She's not there anymore. I can't find her." Kyra had never left the house, but she had looked for her mother. She began to cry. Never before had Ethan seen fear in his daughter, the young girl who could see and feel the unseen that could terrify the strongest of men. He tried to bury the fear from his confusion, and absorb what he felt from Kyra as he held her tightly in his arms. In the end he couldn't hold back his own tears.

It became worse, much worse, before the pain would subside. Two sides of Ethan's being fought a bitter battle. One that knew everything was going as it should and the other full of distraught and fear. He searched. Others searched. There was no sign in the woods. None at all. No one could figure out what had happened. There were investigations and rumors. Ethan couldn't work; he was losing the battle, torn from the inside over Milena. His beautiful wife had disappeared and all that he had accomplished in life — all that he once done, his abilities, his intelligence — crumbled into darkness. He could sense nothing in the woods. He ceased dreaming for the first time in his life. The essence of life leached from his body, from his soul. He knew he had to stop it or it would kill him as nights went by without sleep. The fear of Kyra losing both parents pounded in his head. The man that had once walked among the shadows striking fear in evil now stood at the edge of a bottomless cliff. Hopelessly alone, Ethan didn't know if he could prevail, but he did, if by a thread. Then, one evening, the thread nearly broke.

Distressed in mind, weak in body, he laid in the darkness and gloom of his shuttered bedroom. The half-empty bed had never felt normal and it only accelerated the thoughts that came quick and terrible. *How long must this go on? Will death come next? Why can't I sleep? Where is my Milena? Please, help me.* Never had he imagined he would be at such a place. To other people maybe, but not him. He could focus on nothing else as emptiness and anxiety churned his insides. The Light seemed so distant as the hours passed. The mind fought off the body's need for sleep. Suffocating oppression surrounded him. Then, at the remotest edge of perception, rose a glimmer. Or maybe it was a force pushing away the fog. So faint he didn't take note of it at first, but the presence grew and the Darkness shrunk from it in fear. His mind cleared, refreshed like first light at birth, and his soul emptied of anguish. This power came from beyond any part of himself. Something had touched his soul and a voice came to him.

"Long ago, before this world existed, you chose the Light over evil. You have refused to turn your back on it no matter how close the abyss came. Because of those choices, darkness will not overtake you. The last bonds between this existence and your soul had to be broken because you soon will choose to lead. To the edge you went, but you did not go over. The world is full of deadened hearts who chose darkness over the Light. They made their choice and grew cold. They will soon unleash new assaults on this world. You must stand against them. You will not stand alone. You are not *alone."*

Ethan fell asleep and dreamed for the first time in weeks.

When he awoke, midmorning sunlight lit the house,

sneaking in the windows. A cool summer breeze wandered through the halls, cleansing every room, every hidden space. It reminded him of summer days long ago at his grandmother's home. The broad, thick maples had shaded the old farm house from the heat of summer. The breeze that blew there felt like a presence from ages past guarding the homestead. Back then he hardly noticed, but he did notice.

That morning, in his home, Ethan noticed again and realized the worst had past. They would somehow get through this. Kyra walked into his room smiling again.

Nearly everything was as it should be.

⏳ ⏳ ⏳

"Sorry." Ethan shook his head. He had been staring at a point across the room. The memories vivid like they had come to life once more. "The day everything came back, I could see through the veil again. I still couldn't hear Milena, but I had a stronger sense she was just on the other side. Alive, but not here. This isn't only about saving the world for me. It's about finding her. That might sound selfish, but she's part of me. I can't do this without her. Whatever is to come, I need her to make our stand." Ethan looked around the cavern at his friends. They were the people he knew better than anyone in the world. "She's out there somewhere and every passing moment I feel like I am getting closer."

"I'm in," Conrad said with no hesitation. "All of our families deserve to grow old and not face the evil that is coming." He held the arrowhead in front him and the blue coating began to glow.

Duncan stepped toward the water and knelt. He unsheathed one of his knives, pricked his finger, and let it fall into the water where the drops created a gentle whirlpool. On reaching the center they vanished in a faint sparkle. "As long as my blood flows, we will stand together."

Kane touched Duncan's hand. It healed before their eyes. "If I didn't come, who would keep you guys from getting hurt?" With a smile, he added, "Besides, when else will I get to use all those survival techniques you taught me? And I would like to learn that neat trick with the rock."

"It doesn't always come easily anymore. Not like your little skill, but I have been improving." Ethan pulled the cross from its underwater cavity. It glistened in the blue light as water rolled off the polished silver. "In any case, it's settled."

"Today is the day the Dark One has long feared. The Watchers of old have returned."

CHAPTER THIRTEEN

A journey of thousand miles begins with a single step," Kane mused. "Here we are beginning that journey in a place where no person may have walked for centuries. Who knows where will we will end up? Where do we begin?" Kane's trepidation about where recent events were leading them was subsiding. More or less. "Should we try to access the portal above ground or should we wait?"

"Wait for what?" Duncan was ready. He knew they were all about to get into something way over their heads, but the years of wondering where life was leading him were over. So was the waiting.

"I mean, do we need to prepare? Is there nothing else we need to do?" Kane wanted to be sure, doctors didn't like making mistakes.

"I don't know what else we can do. We have the knowledge and the abilities we need. Our lives were the preparation." Ethan pulled a broadsword from a rack along the cave wall and felt its weight. "We'll probably be tested to our limits, no doubt. We can go back to the house first, but we can't delay any longer. We're not even sure what we're jumping into or what the Darkness is planning, but this evil is on our doorstep. Literally."

Then he stopped himself for a moment. Kyra. What about her? What if they didn't succeed? He turned the sword slowly in the light, reflections shimmering down the blade. Leaving Kyra was unthinkable, yet at the same time he knew he needed to go. It was a paradox that the Darkness was trying to exploit. Anguish tried to twist his stomach. None of them would be entirely free from oppression. That part of life would never change no matter how proficient they became in piercing the veil. "Gather what you need." They all had stood quiet as Ethan had paused. Certainty had returned to his eyes.

Conrad gathered some arrows from a rusted iron crate. "I might need some of these. I'll have to get my bow from the truck."

Duncan chose two matching short swords he had spotted earlier, along with well-preserved sheaths on a leather cross belt that would hold them on his back. Even Kane found two daggers and contemplated taking a mace. It would be prudent to bring a little back-up. "You never know," he said as he felt the weight of the weapon.

"Let's get out of here," Ethan said once he saw his friends had all the gear they could handle. He exited the cavern last, carrying the sword in its scabbard on his shoulder, but not before giving the room one last look. The blue light shimmered and afforded hope that the Watchers would succeed. In stark contrast, the ceiling mural reminded him of the horrors that the knights were fighting. He was determined that he would prevail no matter what the cost was against those dark armies. They would fight to the end and so would he.

Ethan positioned the cross in its place on the granite door. After the door rumbled shut, and the room disappeared from view, they left the hidden underground sanctuary through the passage Kane had entered, not sure when, or if, they would ever return.

"Where do we tell the women we are going?" Conrad asked.

"If I understand how these portals work, we can return only a few moments after we left. Perhaps at the same time," Ethan said.

"And suppose we don't come back?" Duncan asked.

"If we don't come back we will have failed. At that point all hope would be lost." Or would it? Ethan had tried to suppress all emotion since leaving the cave, mentally preparing for what was to come. Man had overcome evil over and over, but could he fail? Could they? Fear could kill where they were headed, so he tried to block it from his mind.

It didn't take long to make their way back to the house. Before they opened the front door, Krya thought, *Why are they home already? Dad?*

When Ethan saw his daughter he said, "We needed a couple more things. Come with me for a second, Kyra." He led Kyra into the library and sat on the couch. "I need to talk to you for a moment."

"You're leaving. Going to the oaks, aren't you?" Kyra knew there was more to the circle of oaks than a natural oddity. She always had.

"Yes, we must go and find your mother. And we must stop some very bad people." He paused, not knowing quite what to say. "If something were to happen...if we don't make it back...if I don't come back, take Scout and go to your grandparents. Tell them there is a metal box in the attic above my old room. Inside it will tell them what to do. Okay?"

Her bright blue eyes teared. She hugged him.

"You'll be back. I know it." She tried not to cry. "Mommy is there. I've felt her. I've heard her."

"I'll bring her back to you." Ethan hugged Kyra harder. *Heard her.* Was Milena that close? "I love you, Kyra. Always remember that."

"I love you, too."

Ethan wiped the tears from Kyra's face. Did she truly know that they would be back? That Milena was safe? Could her vision see that far? "Let's go see if the guys are ready. Anna and Christina are going to be taking you out for dinner soon. Hungry?"

"Not really, not now. Well, maybe a hamburger." Ethan laughed, she was definitely his girl. Her smile was a welcome sight and her presence gave him strength. For a moment she looked into him, and then said, "It's time to go."

Once the men left the house and were walking up the road, Ethan looked back and saw Kyra in the window holding Scout, keeping him from running after Ethan. She would be fine, but would he? *I'll see you later.*

Bye, Daddy. Sad, but eager, Kyra didn't want to stay behind.

The Sun had finally broken through the clouds as they climbed the hill to the well. Conrad stopped and covered the well with the remains of the old wooden planks and brush. Sunlight filtered through the leaves, lighting the trail to the Oak Grove. They entered the circle and stood around the small pond. Rays of light penetrated the towering sentinels, illuminating the natural cathedral. The pond sparkled and rippled slightly from the current of its hidden source. Enough clouds scattered overhead to allow small snowflakes to fall glittering like tiny diamonds.

"This is the moment of truth. Are we sure we know what we are doing?" Conrad asked, not looking for an answer.

They all knew.

"We must return to the time before the battle for these woods took place and make sure it is won and any relics stored here stay secure." Ethan didn't have to say it, but he did anyway as he walked closer to the water. "And somehow, find Milena."

"She could be anywhere. How will we know where to look?" questioned Duncan.

"I'm not sure." No, that wasn't true. *Mommy is there. I've felt her. I've heard her.* Had he known that all along, too? Ethan touched the water. "She felt close to these woods, like she knew its history. She went through this portal. Where we must go is where its history is the strongest. The time when its memory was forged. The history that calls on us." Ethan stepped back.

"Ready?"

They all nodded. Ethan wasn't sure how easy, or how hard this would be, so he closed his eyes and simply began to think about the past. He found images of the history he knew, trying to cross the barriers that separated man's two essences. Then the veil thinned like it had the day in the woods at the ravine. The energy enveloped him and the connection was like in his dreams, only these were windows into the past. The climate changed and he witnessed the land shaped by creeping mountains of ice. Generations passed through the lands he now stood on. Natives came and went; forests and fields grew and receded. He searched through the histories, and among all of these visions in time, he found the knights from the Old World arriving in the land and tunneling under the Earth.

That's where we need to go.

The energy in Ethan burned like a star and reached out to the air, charging it. Blue illumination filled the pond and a column of light emerged from the water. It rotated slowly, rose to the treetops, pulling the air around Oak Grove with it. The towering oaks creaked and groaned as they awakened from their slumber. Leaves were grabbed by the blue vortex and vanished. Ethan opened his eyes. *It is time.*

He took a deep breath and ran into the light.

He didn't remember falling out of the vortex and for a moment Ethan saw the world through a haze. The passage had been instantaneous, no tunnel or lights warping by. He tried to rub the fog from his eyes and heard the muffled voices of his friends. Their undefined shapes moved in front of him. Oddly, his brain didn't register any breathing or heartbeat. A horn echoed through the woods and startled the confusion out of Ethan's mind. He gasped for breath like he had surfaced from the deep of the sea. "That will take some getting used to." He looked around. "Is everyone okay?"

"We're fine." Conrad had his longbow at his side.

They had followed Ethan into the vortex of light as soon as he vanished. Ethan was about to ask if he was imagining the horn when it blasted again through the woods. Shouting came from the Misty Valley. The wind carried the snorting and whining of horses to their ears.

"We're not alone," Duncan said. "The question is who is down there?"

Ethan stepped out of the Oak Grove into the woods he had known since childhood. Thicker and darker, the trees stood ancient and untouched. The contours of the land curved the same, but the paths leading south and north out of the Oak Grove had not yet lost their pavement of stone. "Let's go out to the Ledge."

A few hundred yards to the south of the Oak Grove, where the hill began its decent downward, a natural formation of rock protruded from the ground along the hilltop. At least that's what it looked like in their time. It had always appeared a bit like the remains of something man-made and now they knew why. At the Ledge, they found a four foot rock wall, hewn from limestone slabs that circled the hill's crest through the woods. At the center stood an iron gate bolted shut with a rusting iron lock. A limestone slab sat behind the wall near the gate with what looked like iron eye bolts embedded in its side, probably used to pull the stone behind the gate to block it.

"We can't see into the Valley from here." Duncan scanned over the wall into the thick woods below. "There are some trails below that circle the hill."

"That will take too long; we can go straight down." Conrad jumped over the wall and slid down the incline, grabbing trees as he went.

"Some things never change. Once crazy, always crazy." Kane went over the Ledge muttering.

Ethan looked at Duncan. "Well let's go, desert fox." At the bottom, they came to a trail along the stream, much swifter than they remembered. They didn't have time to sight-see. Conrad was already unleashing arrows into a frenzied mass of charging, horse-mounted warriors.

Wild-eyed with skin darkened by filth and Sun, they shouted in an unknown tongue, covered in animal skins and furs. Yellowed bones from kills hung around their necks and from their horses. One had been swinging a flail around his head before Conrad's arrow hit him the chest, throwing him off his horse into the stream. A second arrow buried itself into another horse, sending it into the hillside. Its rider jumped before being crushed by the horse. Rising from the ground he pulled his sword clear of his dying horse and ran toward Kane. He struggled to free his mace, its chain tangled on the frame of his backpack. Ethan unsheathed his own sword and ran to meet the warrior's blade before it came down on Kane. The blue blade nearly cut through the other's steel, sending him backwards. Ethan didn't hesitate in advancing and brought his blade down and across his foe. The screaming warrior dropped his sword and turned, clutching his chest. Ethan finished him by running him through. When he pulled the sword free, the man crumpled to the ground.

Duncan turned to face an attacker charging at him, catching the blow of the sword aimed at his head with one of his own blades. With the other, he sliced into the wild man's leg. It wasn't enough to dismount the screaming fiery-eyed fighter, but when he turned to rush Duncan again, Kane's hurled mace struck him in the head. The warrior toppled lifeless over the side of his horse. Kane retrieved the mace and readied for another fight, but the last two warriors fled. Before Conrad could send two arrows after them, the attackers fell from their horses, hit by arrows from another source. From out of the woods west of the cave, six knights clad in chainmail rode out on armored war horses. Battered shields hung on the sides, painted with the crosses of Crusaders and the Celts.

"Don't shoot!" Ethan was addressing both Conrad and the knights. Turning to the latter, looking for who may be the leader, "We have come to help you." He wondered if they could understand him. The knights kept their swords drawn and circled around the small battleground surveying the damage. One of the knights rode up to Ethan. He wore a steel breastplate over his chainmail with a small black *crux ordis* of the Teutonic Knights painted over the left side of his chest. He sheathed his sword and pulled the mail coif back over his head, revealing short brown hair and a chiseled face. After dismounting his horse, he removed his heavy leather gloves and looked at Ethan who still held his sword in front of him. The knight's blue eyes were piercing, but Ethan didn't flinch.

"So who do we have here? New recruits? I don't know of anyone who is supposed to be arriving." He circled Ethan as he talked, his accent thick Germanic. "You speak in some dialect of Britannia. Strange clothes, too. You are a skilled fighter at any rate, but the question that I have is where did you get that sword?"

"From the cavern under the Oak Grove," Ethan answered.

The knight jerked back and gave Ethan an incredulous look.

"Do not insult me with such nonsense. I know all who enter the Citadel. I have been here since the first and I have never seen you before."

Ethan drove the sword in the ground in front of him. "Let me show you something from my pack." He held his hands to his sides.

"Slowly. Very slowly." The knight gripped the pommel of his sword while staring at Ethan. His men had their bows at ready. *Have I met this man before this day? He looks so much like...no it cannot be.*

Ethan pulled off his pack and found the leather pouch as the knights watched him carefully. He removed the silver cross, its purple gemstone sparkling from what sunlight filtered through the thick trees. Then it glowed on its own accord and he held it upright in front of him.

"I am Ethan Dietrich and we are Watchers, like you. We came through the Oak Grove from another time in history."

The knight's expression briefly revealed surprise,

quickly replaced with knowing. A smile came across his face as he dismounted his horse.

"I am Theodoric of Malbork, Captain of the Citadel. Welcome to the New World my brothers."

Ethan clasped the knight's hand firmly like they were long lost friends. The other knights slowly relaxed. Ethan's friends did the same.

"Ethan, you and your men may regret arriving at the present time." Theodoric nodded his head to the south. "Dark forces gather beyond the Valley. We expect them to launch their attack soon. We are not sure if they know of the Citadel, but they come for relics that they believe we brought with us."

"The True Cross?" Ethan asked.

"Perhaps. There are many they seek, but they won't succeed. We have nearly a thousand men here and we hold the high ground."

"The reason we came is to assure this battle is won and that the relics remain secure. A man, a Timewalker named Latzi, has come from our time to help them. He knows of the portal and perhaps the Citadel below it." Ethan paused, then, "We aren't many, but we are skilled and we suspect that the Dark One has been calling Followers from throughout time to this battle. Beasts and dark shadows."

"Indeed, we have seen strange beings approach our sentries at night, but we are not without our own help." Theodoric nodded to his left. From behind a cluster of ancient oaks along the trail emerged a giant. Eight feet tall and muscular, the warrior wielded a sword and shield that together weighed as much as the average human. Perhaps more surprising was that the warrior's long brown hair framed the face of a beautiful woman. Near where the creek crossed the path, a rock outcropping shuffled out of the ground. Before their eyes, a being, nearly as tall as the woman, but more massive, morphed out of the rock. The creature moved like a human, yet it was fashioned of stone; its arms and powerful hands looked like they could shatter any object. The outlines of a face formed on its squat head. It stood silently in the center of the creek. As the Watchers from the future stood in awe, from a hidden perch high above in the trees, an eagle flew to the ground. When it stood, it's golden head drew eye-level with the knights. Its talons the size of a lion's paws and a wing span twelve feet tip to tip, it eyed the newcomers inquisitively.

"This is Aoifa, warrior princess from the Otherworld Kingdom." Theodoric introduced the woman casually to the speechless men.

Aoifa nodded and said, "Welcome to the Misty Valley." Her feminine voice softened her daunting size.

Theodoric continued. "Here we have an Earth elemental." The rock creature shifted slightly, rocks grinding, and uttered some unintelligible sound. "His name is un-pronounceable so we call him Stonecor. And there are not any 'hims' or 'hers' among the elementals." He walked over and stroked the eagle's head, "And this is Øyvind, a young roc from the Far East deserts." The eagle made a few high chirps.

"Young?" Kane asked. "How big will he get?"

Theodoric laughed. "He is nearly grown. As you can see, we are not without allies from the Otherworlds and Earth itself. Humans aren't the only creatures of the Light. At any rate, the Sun will begin setting soon; let us return to camp."

Øyvind flew back to his perch while Stonecor sank into the creekbed, completely camouflaged. The knights led the way up a narrow path that twisted up the hollow next to the creek that flowed over the cave. Aoifa followed them.

Here too the forest was thicker than they remembered, but the lay of the land remained the same. They passed the cave, knights guarding its entrance. Along the ridges above the hollow many unseen eyes watched them. Where the path exited the hollow, they turned left past the area that in their time held the ruins of forgotten homes. Scents of burning hardwoods and cooking food hung in the air. Chattering voices and the clanking of steel traveled through the trees.

Soon they came to a clearing where an encampment of hundreds of knights greeted them. Acres of tents filled the clearing and above most of them hung banners and flags flying the seals and emblems of distant kingdoms and various orders of knights. Near the center of the encampment, where a grassy opening served as a gathering place, Theodoric's tent stood larger than the rest. From the center of the tent flying higher than all others, a flag with the Celtic cross fluttered in the breeze. Below it hung flags bearing the *crux ordis* and the *croix pattée*.

The voices in the camp lowered as the newcomers entered the camp. Many eyes watched as they walked by. Theodoric stopped at a clearing near his tent.

"What you see here is our primary force of infantry, cavalry, and archers. The rearguard is encamped to the north beyond those woods. Some of our families are there. Most have not arrived as of yet." Theodoric pointed to the trees. "And a legion of our best warriors arc garrisoned near Oak Grove, though the fact that you came through there unnoticed is most troubling. Some were in the valley hunting those vile men when you arrived." He looked at his men. "Nevertheless, there should have been men at the wall." As he dismounted his horse, a young knight, only a squire, took it and tied it near the tent. All the knights kept their horses close at hand. Theodoric dismissed the other knights and turned to the Watchers. "Join me in my tent. There is much to discuss."

The tent had an outer room with a wooden round table covered with maps at its center. "Water or wine?" Theodoric asked and handed goblets to the men in which they poured from bottles on the table. He flattened one of the maps and pointed. "We are here at the high edge of a plateau. The Norsemen found this place years ago and established an outpost here. We are planning a town where the river cuts through the hills from the west. A frontal attack on our present location would be difficult with only this hollow near the cave and another one to our right flank as potential approaches. Both are covered heavily from the surrounding ridges. The shadow army could send forces east or west through the Misty Valley and take these valleys north and enter from the rear, but that long march would give them away immediately."

"The frontal attack would definitely be suicide," Conrad commented. "But it would be the only surprise they have. What are their numbers?"

"Nearly twice us." Theodoric wasn't worried. "They have been recruiting from the native peoples all over this continent, convincing them that we are here to conquer them. We have sent for more people from the home-lands, but they are not likely to arrive before this battle begins. We had hoped to be building a settlement by now, not fighting a war. We left that life behind. God willing, this will be the last war we will have to wage." He looked to Ethan. "If you are from a future time, how does the battle end?"

"From our place in time the battle was won and the

shadow army driven off. Now it may be that more shadows are being summoned to alter the outcome. Or there is something here they wish to obtain."

"What if its outcome does change?" Duncan asked. "As of right here and right now the battle hasn't happened. In our time the battle had been decided without us and without Latzi bringing more shadows to this place."

"Then changes would ripple throughout history, a change in the river of time, so to speak," Ethan answered. "From our perspective that wouldn't seem possible, but if we were outside of time, the change would look instantaneous. On the other hand, many think time itself would prevent changes from happening. Some sort of safeguard. Or the battle may have always been won with us; we just don't know it yet."

"If history does change, what happens to us?" Conrad asked.

"Since we are here, we would be isolated from those future changes. We could return to a very different world." *A world that was already riddled with evil*, Ethan added silently.

"In the last days all who cling to darkness will face the second death." Theodoric drank from his goblet. "Until that time the Dark One and his armies will attempt to stave off the inevitable; many will die and lands will be scorched in attempts to stop the shadows. The more evil fails, the harder it will try. Some of my men have asked me, 'Why fight then? Why not let history run its course?' Because this is our world given to us, and whenever an enemy invades, we take back our land and protect our people. It is in this world that we prepare for the next. "

Theodoric paused and looked over the map again.

Kane swirled his wine, thinking. "You know, some

people find it odd that humans have arrived in history only after eons came and went before us. Think about it though, the pinnacle is always built last so it's no accident that we are here. No matter how long humans exist, it will be an eye blink in time, but that's why we fight. We fight because the end is always near and it is here in this world where the enemy will be defeated." Kane had been the most cautious and leery of all of them only a short time earlier, now he understood what needed to be done. Their brief battle with the wild men had awakened him.

Ethan raised his goblet.

"I'll drink to that."

Theodoric held up his wine. "To the destruction of the darkness arrayed against us." They raised their drinks and finished them. "Now let me show where you can retire for the night." He led them to a large tent appointed with small beds and chairs and racks to hang their weapons. "I will send my armorer to take measurements. Those clothes simply will not suffice here. Good evening."

With that, the leader of the first kingdom in the New World left the tent, and the armorer arrived a few minutes later. He was another reminder that they were far from home on the verge of a battle whose likes hadn't been fought in centuries.

A battle fought against creatures from the abyss.

CHAPTER FOURTEEN

As the Sun slipped beneath the horizon, the early October air began to chill. Ethan had asked the armorer what month they were in. Interestingly enough, they had traveled centuries to find themselves within a few days of when they left their own time. Perhaps it was coincidence. No, he had a hard time believing that. Time and history were intertwined and conspired to remain that way. A lifetime of study had yet to reveal all of the universe's mysteries. It was unlikely that another hundred years would be enough.

Ethan walked through the camp where the earlier activity was now subdued. Lights flickered in tents and knights sat around fires in silence. The crackling fires were the sole sounds penetrating the night air. The perimeter of the camp was well guarded with many unseen sentries beyond the tree line. Ethan assumed some of them were probably not human. In fact, he could sense that they were not all members of mankind. There was one person he knew for certain wasn't among them. Surely if Milena had been here, he would have known her presence; he was sure of it. Yet she tugged at his mind, and the awareness grew with each passing moment. Not here in the Misty Valley, but she was somewhere in this age.

In the dying light, bands of stratus clouds had begun moving across the sky, not thick enough to completely hide the emerging stars. A faint ring circled the full Moon. Both were signs of coming rain. A storm was coming, rain or not. At the southern perimeter he stopped near a low stone wall and let his mind wander. A nervous peacefulness, the strange feeling generations of soldiers had the night before a looming battle, surrounded his thoughts. Ethan had experienced it many times before under similar stars in places thousands of miles, and years, away. It was a life that, in some ways, now felt like a distant dream. Like the last mission that had always haunted him.

He encountered an evil more insidious than the everyday variety. One that didn't fear him or those like him. It had also been one of the few times when he was sure that he found another. There had always been encounters with other people in which he would sense their true nature. How does one broach the subject with a stranger? Perhaps they hadn't completely realized what they were. Uncertainty kept the truth hidden, just out of reach. He had surmised that dark forces in the world colluded to keep the Watchers apart, and destroy and trap them like they tried with Solana. Or was it him they were after? Maybe anyone they could get. He never saw her again, but now everything was changing. The Darkness would no longer hide from the eyes of men.

It was here, out in the shadows across the valley, growing since they had arrived. The army itself, and the shadowmancer had come to lead his Followers. His oppression clenched stronger than anything Ethan had ever encountered and he was not even within sight. What was this shadowmancer? Ethan could not gather any more knowledge of his foe from afar. Footsteps approached. Theodoric walked to the stone wall next to Ethan. "This is not your first time in battle, is it? You know it is coming."

"Yes, and with it many will die in a few hours." Ethan looked to the sky. Would such hatred among men ever disappear? He knew the answer all to well.

"Most here are not new to war. They spent years in Outremer fighting the Saracens." The knight paused. "That experience does not make them eager, but it does give them the knowledge to win. They want to cease being soldiers and return to being farmers. This will be their last battle. Most of the enemy have never seen a war horse, let alone how it tramples dozens of men at a time. Armored knights will strike terror in their hearts. Their shadowmancer will rely on what dark warriors they can conjure, but that will not be enough for victory over us."

"Maybe they aren't concerned with winning the battle," Ethan said. "They're sacrificing natives to buy time, maybe to steal relics. Or maybe change the outcome here just enough to alter the future and give victory to whatever scheme they have planned." He wondered what it was that they had set in motion. "Certainly they were behind the persecutions of the knights returning from Outremer, if not also the corruption of the Crusades themselves."

"We wanted to reclaim the lands that had once been populated by so many of our people. Our cause fell apart as the Dark One turned his hounds loose on us and manipulated our people," Theodoric said. "Some say war was the wrong path, but they threatened to move farther into our lands. I often asked then, and now ask again, 'Will there ever be peace?'"

Part of him believed there would be peace, yet he knew evil would never cease raising its ugly head until the End of Days.

"If we win this battle you will see peace for a time. These lands will be largely free of war, at least compared to the Old World," Ethan said. "But the century I was born into saw unprecedented destruction. Conflicts on a scale that no one here could possibly imagine. Terrible darkness.

"We succeeded in conquering many evil movements, but the conflicts to stop them had dead counted in the millions. Wars started by men driven by evil and nothing else. Cities destroyed in a few hours or in an instant flash of light. Historians once referred to your era as the Dark Ages. That's what they will call us someday. It's partly our fault. Every time we defeat some scourge of humanity we become complacent. We forget the evil in the world and then something horrible will happen and take everyone by surprise. Then, for a time, we see the danger again, maybe even try to conquer whatever darkness has come for us. Then we forget all over again." Ethan didn't understand how so many could pretend the world was free of malice. Just ignore it and maybe it would go away. Let someone else deal with it. It happens to other people. He had seen too much to believe such clichés. "And yet the worst evil isn't the kind that shows itself, but that which works quietly and hidden from sight."

"I am afraid that only the dead have seen the end of war. The evil that propagates it will never go away," Theodoric said. "It hides, it changes shape, but it is always there waiting for the right time to return. It only negotiates when it needs time. To give up emboldens it. I have been to those places too, Ethan. I have fought because I had to, not because I wanted to go to war. There will always be people who think we should turn our backs or give in. I refuse to become that slave to evil."

"So do I," Ethan said.

"Good evening then." Theodoric grasped Ethan's hand tightly. "Soon we defend the New World together."

"And together we will win," Ethan said. But what would the price be? Theodoric returned to his tent leaving Ethan to his thoughts. *Only the dead have seen the end of war.* A long-dead philosopher had written those words. How right he was.

Even when the killing of men was a necessary enterprise, it was a terrible one. No one walked away from it unchanged. The years didn't erase memories, and now, standing on the edge of a new battlefield, those locked away images came flooding back. The fact that he could deal with it reasonably well, frightened him at times, but Ethan had no regrets of his service. Blending into foreign cultures like he was one of them, hiding in plain sight or venturing into the darkness, using it to make himself disappear. He had earned the name Shadow from allies and enemies. This shadow didn't bring evil with him. Instead, justice. Not darkness, but light into the dark places. The enemy never knew who he was, but learned the inevitability of the Shadow finding them no matter where they hid. Nor whom they surrounded themselves with afforded any deliverance from their fate.

"And here we are at it once again, Milena." Ethan looked to the stars. She had said once, on a night like this, *People are needed in this world who can experience what we do without eroding their soul. We have to take care, but we are gifted in many ways.* "Maybe, but this gift sometimes feels like a burden." Who would understand what they had done? It didn't matter, because from the depths of his soul he knew standing against the Darkness had to be done. They must succeed and any other outcome was unconscionable.

Now, barely a few miles from where he grew up in a future era, Ethan would look inside himself for the Shadow and release it once again.

And he would again understand why so few had his gifts or wanted them if they were given the choice.

Not three miles from where Ethan stood, Latzi also looked to the sky. He didn't care about rain or talk about the weather. Only the relics across the valley deep in the Earth behind the cave ruled his mind. He could conjure in the darkness and scheme where no one could see him, but in the end he was only a human. Frail and mortal, he had no real powers beyond what he could teach himself. Sure, he used the portal, but he barely was able to control it. If he was a Timewalker, he wasn't a very good one. There, under the mountain, was what could change that. His father had read the ancient histories and taught him, tantalized him, with bits of lost lore.

Natives had populated the region with grand villages. For most of their existence they were peaceful, until someone found the Dark Hollow. Those who were corrupted fought to enslave every nation up and down the rivers. Evil legions of men and giants. Ultimately they failed, but not before most of the villages laid destroyed and thousands of natives dead over hundreds of square miles. The Corrupted were driven away, but the survivors knew they would never be the same as they buried their dead in towering mounds.

Eventually the Great War was misted in legend and

new rumors arose. Runners from the distant sea told of white faces exploring the coast. For centuries, small bands would arrive and live, affecting the natives little. They traded and fought, mostly keeping to themselves. And one day, the legends wrote, a large group of white men arrived at the Misty Valley and never left. The descriptions told of armored men on terrible beasts. Knights on war horses, Latzi was sure. They settled at the bend in the river and on the land overlooking the Misty Valley, gaurding the cave closely. The natives had never hunted there; a sanctuary where even the most dire enemies would not fight. It was where the Sparkling Water bubbled from the ground.

Vague legends and incomplete histories had long suggested that the New World was visited by more people than often thought. Inviting hints of lost relics hidden there, out of the reach of corrupt kings of the Old World. Latzi knew he hadn't entered the world at this location by accident. If ancient secrets were buried here, he could use them to cross into the world populated by nether beasts and shadowmancers. He would become one of them, their equal and not their slave. What his father had taught him and what he later studied in the temples rang with truth. He knew this because once, when he was a child, he had left the Dark Hollow and climbed out of the Misty Valley.

Too scared to crawl through the passage at the rear of the cave, Latzi squinted to see anything. Odd, he had never feared the crevices of the Dark Hollow. Somewhere beyond the tunnel, light flourished, not darkness. The piercing power of the Light repelled him as it called to him.

He ran, scrambling up over the hill as fast as he could. Stumbling over rocks and logs, he fell into a clearing. His knee throbbed from a rock and he held it for a minute before looking up. Towering over him rose thick oaks, ancient beyond anything his young mind could comprehend. He stood, forgetting his pain and walked around the circle, speechless. There at the center glittered a pond, ringed by rocks. It bubbled ever so slightly, calling to him. He cautiously approached and stopped at the sight of a glistening object at the bottom. Without thinking, he knelt and reached for it through the water.

Latzi opened his hand and beheld a tiny golden pendant sparkling with diamonds. It had three interlaced loops with a circle through them. A triquetra. He had never seen something so beautiful or precious. Nothing like this existed in the Dark Hollow. His family owned no such treasures. He stared into the diamonds and, for a few moments, he knew that there was good in the world and all was not dark. Time ceased in the circle as Latzi stared, entranced by the jewels. His eyes burned; he couldn't look away. It was there for him to take and no one would stop him. His hands tremored. He had to decide. Bring light to the Dark Hollow or run from it. No more hesitation. He threw the pendant back into water and ran from that place, never to return.

⏳ ⏳ ⏳

There were greater treasures under the oaks, and now Latzi stood ready to claim them. He would make sure no one else would ever again have to choose between darkness and light.

CHAPTER FIFTEEN

Rain fell as Alexander's army left. The city had been destroyed again and Tyre lay in ruins. Scraped into the sea like the prophet had predicted. Centuries before, Nebuchadnezzar had laid siege to the Old Town, leaving it in ashes. The prophet had foreseen that as well. The town had been cursed because it wouldn't acknowledge the Light. It was also where Ahriman had been born. Many centuries had passed since that day and here he was, standing once more on the shore.

He looked down at the sand and listened to the water. It was where he had played as a boy when Tyre was still a small settlement. In another age, during the campaign of the Second Scourge, he returned with the Sea Peoples and took Tyre. It had become the gateway to the civilized world. A perfect stronghold from which to spread infections among the weak-minded people that thought they controlled their destinies. The main city had been built on an island off the coast, a fortress that even the

Babylonian king couldn't destroy. Alexander had used the rubble of the mainland town to lay a causeway to the island. His navy attacked the ancient city from the sea. "The Great" they had called him. Indeed. Tyre hadn't stood a chance.

Ahriman looked at the ruined city one last time. The rain rolled down his face and he screamed into the thunder as the waves crashed. The great campaigns had failed. Two Scourges that nearly brought mankind to its knees. These frontal assaults on their empires with armies of men brought chaos and collapse, but victory was fleeting. Without the evil of old — the gods that had once roamed freely — the Light in men would rally and push the darkness back into its caves. During the invasion of Egypt with the Sea Peoples, he had intended to awaken ancient evils in that land. That old fool Ramses had managed to drive them back to the sea. The Light had taken hold there.

It was time to be patient. Work in secret and influence the wills of men. The day would come for a new campaign. A time when men weren't the primary weapon. If it took decade upon decade to summon what had been lost, then so be it.

He turned to leave and for a brief moment felt sorrow. A memory of a little boy on the beach. When had that boy made his choice? Perhaps when his parents were killed by sea raiders. Or when his sister had disappeared. The Light had allowed it all to happen. That's what the shadows had whispered to him day and night. None of that mattered now and one thing was certain.

Never would he return to his birthplace again. It was dead to him.

As the first light of dawn tried to break through the

clouds, the rain came. The rain always reminded Ahriman of Tyre, and the many conflicts he had fought. Battles always seemed to bring the rain, but usually after the bloodshed. Fog swirled through the Misty Valley, as did the energy of both realms that would soon clash. *Very soon.*

Watching Latzi look out over the Misty Valley, Ahriman sat on his horse, pelted by raindrops. His blackened steel armor and cloak kept him dry, but the cold penetrated deep to his core. A dragon forged on the helmet masked his entire face. Only shadows could be seen through the slit openings over the eyes; metallic sinews formed a screen over the mouth. Few had looked upon what was beneath. For decades he had been one of the grand puppet masters, a shadowmancer, pulling the strings of subversion around the globe. Evil had grown rapidly in the Twentieth Century, too fast at times. When it became so obvious, no matter how horrible it was, the enemy could find and destroy it. Better to work quietly and silently while the world slumbered blissfully unaware. More damage could be done through patience than through frontal assaults. He had learned that long ago. At times he still longed for the mayhem of battle. Now he was about to fulfill that desire. That simpleton Latzi had made it possible. By pure chance, no doubt.

⧗   ⧗   ⧗

When Latzi had arrived in the Yucatán, trying to unlock the secrets of the dark religions that hid in the ruins, Ahriman's underlings had informed him at once. "Do not bother me with such trivial manners." His deep, gravelly voice was agitated. "Another fool looking for gold. Leave me before I end your life." Months later, another pestered him with more news from the dead city.

"Your Darkness, Latzi comes from the Dark Hollow, where a battle once raged. He claims relics are still buried there and another portal lies waiting." Ahriman's spy was a spindly, black-cloaked druid, or at least he fancied himself one. He was also the Caretaker at Uxmal.

The battle near the Dark Hollow. Ahriman knew of it and had been to the Hollow once, years ago on some apparently unproductive venture. He didn't know anything about relics there. None of this would he tell the spy. "So? Relics are unpredictable, uncontrollable." He had spent many fruitless years using the Third Reich to track down relics that were never found. Few could wield them, most died trying. "We have enough portals; who cares if there is another?" He knew of this portal, the Rift. No one was ever able to use it. It was dead.

The druid pulled an old book from underneath his cloak. He had taken it from Latzi. It had been written by Latzi's father — though Latzi hadn't recognized the handwriting — who had spent a lifetime uncovering and recording the tales that arose out of the Misty Valley. Whispers of the past had been recorded in dusty volumes that only existed in Hayden. Apparently Latzi's father had visited there often as a child and perhaps as an adult. The book was familiar to Ahriman. He had taken it from the old man while he still lived. There was nothing of importance in its pages, so he sent it to the Caretaker. Had something been overlooked? Unlikely.

"The legends speak of something else. Something of far greater consequence that may be hidden in the Misty Valley."

Ahriman read the page the druid had opened for him. Had he not been wearing his mask, the Caretaker would have seen the surprise on his face. He had missed something. "Indeed, this is quite the find. Well done, minion. Now where can I find this fool? This Latzi?"

⏳　　　　　⏳　　　　　⏳

It had been months since the Caretaker had brought his revelation. Now Ahriman was ready for war. The former leader of this campaign, the one that failed the first time, had an unfortunate encounter with a cliff. There would be no such failure this time. He turned to one of his hooded lieutenants, his skeletal face barely visible. "Bone Lord, it is time to send those knights to the underworld. Make them regret leaving their homes across the sea. Ready the natives. Let them die first and send the wild horsemen with them." *Stupid humans. To think I was once one of them.*

"Yes, your Darkness." He spurred his horse and rode off into the rain. Ahriman turned and looked behind him among the trees and saw hundreds of natives and wild men encamped, preparing their weapons and horses. At the rear, among the thickest trees waited the Fomorii. *Disgusting creatures.* He raised his blackened sword of twisted metal into the air.

"War has come!"

Across the valley, Ethan and Duncan had finished eating breakfast. Roasted deer meat and a brew of sassafrases tea that Kane had concocted. Not true tea, just boiled leaves, but flavorful in any case. Kane also produced a supply of cheese he had packed in his supplies. An old hiker's secret, some hard cheeses could last days without going bad as long as they were kept dry. They talked little, and Kane could tell where Ethan's mind lay.

"She's here, isn't she?" Kane asked.

Ethan broke his quiet and spoke after a moment.

"Yes, in this time, but not with these people." The question was where? Once the battle was over, nothing would stop him from finding her.

The roar of the enemy's chants and screams from across the valley reached his ears and Duncan looked up from his meal. "They're coming."

He stood immediately and went to a horse tied nearby. Conrad had gone to the forward positions early in the morning. A horn blew a signal. They were readying to cross the valley for a frontal assault. Ethan mounted another horse as Theodoric exited his tent. He raised his sword and Ethan returned the sign. Earlier, at dawn, they had finalized the plan of battle. Theodoric would hold the high ground along the ridges. He would direct the defense from near the Oak Grove. The small hollow that led directly to the cave followed the rocky and narrow streambed. Defenders overlooked it from all sides; a perfect place for the enemy to die. Ethan and Duncan would join a group of knights riding from the west into the Misty Valley. There they would strike the army of Followers from behind and keep them from out-flanking the knights.

There would be no rallying speeches. No rousing of the troops. Most had been to war and knew what was to come. From somewhere in the trees bagpipes played an uplifting tune. It swept among the troops, through the mist, touched every ear, reminding everyone of home, regardless of where home was. Ethan had heard those same sounds in another time, in these same woods, yet no one else had been there. How many other times had there been brief glimpses into the past without him realizing? No time for that now. He looked at Kane. He was staying with the camp's defense and would heal the wounded.

"We'll be back about noon for lunch," Ethan smiled.

"You better be. I'm making mushroom stew." Then Kane said to his friend, "Go well."

"To the ends of the Earth, if need be." Ethan rode off.

Duncan gave a silent nod and followed.

Along the western front, as Duncan took to calling it, a cavalry of two-hundred mounted knights waited behind barriers of stone and trees ready to engage the forces of darkness. Calm veterans, their faces betrayed little emotion, but the coming danger was not lost to them. Even the ground could reach out and pull them down. The slope in front of them was gradual, yet still thick with trees and rocks. The soil wet and muddy. All dangerous to charging horses. The rain had lightened into a faint drizzle, but it didn't take much to make riding and wielding weapons more hazardous than it already was.

"Open the gate," Ethan told the soldiers manning the wall. It took six of them to move the massive timber gate. Another horn sounded from the embattlements at the forward lines. "That's our signal; the enemy is crossing the valley."

Owain, the commander of the cavalry shouted his orders. "Forward men!"

The gate closed behind them. War horses pulled large boulders in place to block it. On the outer side, Stonecor piled more rocks in front of the gate. No one would get in or out. The elemental, satisfied with its work, shuffled into the woods toward the battle about to begin.

Overlooking the Misty Valley, Conrad stood at a rock wall built along the ridge. Knights armed with bows and crossbows manned the barrier. There were too many trees for catapults or trebuchets, but a large sling-shot device positioned between two soaring maples could launch rocks and some primitive exploding cannonballs, though with not much accuracy. A couple of the alchemists among them had been experimenting with gunpowder, but had little time to create large quantities. The dampness offered no help either. Conrad's pistol wouldn't do much good without considerably more ammo. *Automatic weapons would be useful right now.*

Aoifa stood ready near Conrad. She would operate the sling-shot and was probably the only one who could do so with any affect. Clad in thick leather armor, the giantess' brown hair fell braided down her back. Her brown eyes radiated friendliness and caring. *A princess, yes, but a warrior?* Then Conrad looked at her sword and her crossbow, which probably each weighed five times more than anyone else's.

"Have you been to war before?" Aoifa asked, almost in a whisper.

"No, but I have faced these dark creatures before. They die like humans."

"My people were human once." Aoifa scanned the valley through the trees. "We lived peacefully among the green forests of the Emerald Isle. Then the fomorii came and laid waste to our lands, killed and enslaved our people. The only way we could fight them was to enter the Otherworld Kingdom and alter our humanity. We became the giants of old, unable to live among men, but we could fight off the terrors spawned in the oceans. Few of us remain."

"Is there a way to reverse the change?" Conrad sensed a longing in Aoifa.

"We have not found a way to return. What method or

conjuring that made us has been lost. There are rumors of those with regenerating powers. For now, I must live with both a curse and a blessing."

The cries of the natives increased as they ran across the valley. They reached the edge of the woods and began climbing the steep hillside. The slick ground didn't slow them.

"Today it is a blessing." Aoifa loaded her over-sized crossbow with little effort and fired over the wall. The bolt passed through one of the natives, killing him and the unlucky person behind him. Most were still out of range of the other archers.

"There are hundreds of them!" Conrad could hardly see any empty ground.

"Steady! Wait until they reach the markers!" The commander of the wall stood among his men maintaining order. They had carved daggers into the trees to indicate when the enemy was in range of the archers. Wasting arrows was not an option. Some of the natives slid in the loose soil and rocks, but most scaled fast. They had spent generations in this terrain; some stopped to fire arrows, but none yet found their mark.

"Fire!"

Clouds of arrows descended down on the natives like locusts. They tried to hide behind trees and debris, but that didn't save them all. Warriors tumbled to their death. Some took others with them, crashing onto rocks on the hillside. The less fortunate were impaled, still alive, to trees. Aoifa used the sling shot to rapid fire rocks into crowds of warriors. Screams filled the air as limbs broke and bodies were crushed. A few lost their heads.

Conrad fired steadily and calmly, finding his mark each time. The sounds of battle became mute. Arrows flew near him, but as time slowed for him, he could see them coming, and avoided their sharpened tips. To the right he caught a glimpse of mounted warriors, the wild men they had encountered the day prior, attempting to climb a narrow trail up the hill. Aoifa launched a cannonball toward them, but the damp powder didn't ignite. The second did explode, sending shrapnel through the air and killing a horse from underneath a fur-clad man, hurling him to the bottom in a heap. Another horseman met his end from Aoifa's crossbow. The natives kept coming, using their own dead as cover. Some of their arrows met their mark and a few knights were sent back to the camp. Still, the defenders held the upper hand, but for how long?

These people are on a suicide mission. We'll run out of arrows if these waves don't cease. Conrad kept finding targets. The chaos before him was much like the stories Anna's grandfather had told him of the Pacific War. The Japanese didn't stop coming until they were all dead. Then a crashing and breaking of trees came from below. A half-dozen giant men clad in rusted iron plate from head to toe, plowed up the hillside. They equaled the size of Stonecor, but moved with surprising speed and agility. Arrows bounced off their chests as they broke into a run. They didn't care if they stepped on the dead or dying of their allies.

Aoifa noted the surprise in Conrad's eyes. "Those are not men, they are golems! Conjured from earth and metal." Whatever they were, two were running straight at Conrad and Aoifa.

Ethan and Duncan rode with the heavy cavalry through the woods. They had spent little time here in their own time in which the land had been emptied of trees and farmed. Now, centuries before, trees towered to the clouds. In spite of natives clear-cutting large swaths of land with fire, these forests were still nearly primeval. If left alone, would they again look like this? There was no time to speculate. At the bottom of the slope, two monstrous black cats appeared out of the thick forest.

"Cat siths." Duncan breathed. He had read about them in fairy tales, never thinking he would actually meet one. Of course, he could say the same of rock creatures and giant birds.

"They are ours," Owain said. One of the cats approached him and murmured some sort of cat-speak. Apparently he could understand it. "The legions of evil haven't approached this way. They are concentrating all of their forces at the center." The chaos of the battle rumbled through the valley. Screams and thrashing among the trees. "They have emptied out of the Dark Hollow. We will cross the stream near here and strike them from behind."

"Their only escape would be to the east. The ridges flanking the cave are more rugged there. No hope for a siege." Ethan asked, "So what are they trying to accomplish? Why aren't they trying to outflank us here?"

"If they want the Citadel, what better way to tie the bulk of our forces elsewhere? They have to know that an attack at the center would fail," Duncan said. "They can send warriors to the south and around into the eastern end of Misty Valley. Or a small force into the hollow below the cave while the main armies have at it."

"Indeed." Owain was disturbed. "Our forces are the thinnest to the east. We are relying on the terrain and embattlements."

One of the cat siths hissed under its breath.

"What did it say?" Duncan asked.

"The cats sensed something terrible arrive in the Dark

Hollow before dawn. It could have been their shadow-mancer or their corrupted allies." Owain paused. "Or it could have been something far worse. When one of the great cats appears rattled, we must assume the worst."

"Whatever they have, we still must attack their rear, decimate their numbers, and take up position below the Citadel."   Ethan was tired of waiting. The battle was already underway.

"Well, my friend from the beyond, there is no reason to wait any longer." Owain looked to his men. "For our families! For the New World! Let us send them back to the underworld to burn in hell's flames!"

Shouts rose up and the knights set out into the Misty Valley.

From behind Conrad came a crashing. Stonecor, or at least that's who it looked like, vaulted over the wall and down the hillside. It launched itself into one of the golems, breaking it in half and sending iron and clay into the air. A fireball exploded around another. From the left came another elemental, this one awash in flame. The golem jumped back to its feet only to have a fireball slam it against a tree. Stonecor tore the head from the stunned golem and it collapsed into a steaming heap. The fire elemental turned its attention to human foes and began firing its flames at natives. The lucky ones had already retreated; the unlucky stood scorched into statues of ash that melted in the rain.

One of the golems charged Conrad's position and Aoifa leaped over the rock wall, sword in hand. The golem caught her first blow with its forearm, but the sword cut deep into the rusted metal. Aoifa swung the heavy sword around, its blue tinge aglow, and her braids flew in the air as she took the golem's head at the base of the neck. There was no living thing inside, only clay. Some sort of insidious horror raised by dark magic. The golem's body stood stuck in the deep mud, and with a yell, she kicked it down the hill.

Conrad leaped on top of the wall. He strung a blue-tipped arrow and took aim at the golem bearing down on Aoifa. Before she finished raising her sword, the arrow embedded into the ironman's ear. It spun around, flailed its arms, only to pull its own head off and crash into the mud.

"Nice shot, Timewalker!" And with that, Aoifa ran to silence the mounted wild men.

As Conrad jumped from the wall, dark hounds came running through the retreating natives. Red eyes and foaming from the mouth, they stood nearly as large as horses, more massive than the one he killed in the Riverlands. Other knights had joined the fight, driving the remaining warriors from the hill, or killing them where they stood. One dark hound tried to reach the wall with arrows all through its body. A knight's sword ended its misery. Conrad made it to a small ledge halfway down the slope. He again tuned out the sounds of battle. Swordsman fought against the wild men. Balls of fire shot through the trees looking for targets. Stonecor used the last golem to club hounds. Conrad notched an arrow and found a target. Aoifa had just dismounted a wild man, not seeing a hound bounding toward her. As it leaped to attack her from behind, Conrad's arrow sliced through it's heart, knocking it from the air. A second hound followed, but fell to Aoifa's sword. A quick scan of the hillside found no dark beings left to kill. The natives were fleeing, leaving piles of dead and wounded behind. Cries of victory rose from the wall. Conrad went to Aoifa. There was some blood on her face. Not her own. "That was too easy."

"If you say so. There's more of them out there," Aoifa said. "They may be reforming for another attack. We must go into the Misty Valley and end this." Swordsman, infantry and archers took formation at the foot of the hill. Their commander mounted a horse that once belonged to a wild man, now dead, torched by the fire elemental.

"Into the Misty Valley!"

CHAPTER SIXTEEN

The battle unfolded as Ahriman and his lieutenants watched from the edge of the woods where the trails led into the Dark Hollow. The assault on the center had been driven back sooner than he had hoped. The natives crumbled in the face of real warriors. Now it was time to send true terror into the fray. This battle was far from over.

"Bone Lord, send your cavalry forward. They will lead the rest of the natives we have in reserve. Kill all those who try to flee."

"Yes, your Darkness. Victory is at hand!" The Bone Lord went to his warriors and Ahriman turned to a hooded figure by his side.

"It is time for your friends to begin their siege. Do not fail me."

"We will not disappoint you."

Under its hood, Ahriman could see a disfigured green face, one eye at its center. It headed east into the woods.

He wondered how, or if, such foul creatures had ever been human. What the Darkness could corrupt surprised even him at times. No matter, they would serve their purpose. The Bone Lord's charging horsemen thundered through the narrow valley, the natives close behind. Emerging from the trees to the west he saw movement. Knights. Their threat would be short-lived.

"Go after that filthy wretch and tell him to send Balor to crush those knights." One of the lieutenants rode off after the hooded creature. "The end of men shall begin in this valley of death."

As the knights rode forward, with cat siths leading the charge, natives fled from their failed assault. Chaos quickly engulfed the valley. Balls of flame shot from the woods, incinerating targets in an instant of fire and screams. Dismounted knights gathered at forest edge in an unbroken line. Ethan saw a giant at the end. Aoifa no doubt. He thought he could see Conrad near her. Stonecor moved ahead of the knights in a steady gait like a linebacker, his fire-wielding brother close behind.

From the Dark Hollow, a storm front of mounted warriors galloped forward with abandon. They didn't slow for retreating natives, trampling anyone who didn't move out of their path. They weren't the wild men, these were hooded in black robes, holding darkened blades at their side. Some turned to face the cavalry; the remainder sped to the line of knights marching at them.

Ethan raised his sword and rode hard into the oncoming thunder. He had never rode into battle like this. Nor remotely experienced in fighting with a sword, mounted or otherwise, as compared to those around him. He and Duncan did have something they didn't. An uprising of power flowed inside him, stronger than it had since before Milena had vanished. Each oncoming foe was in his mind. Their every move anticipated before it would happen. His reach through the veil approached its former strength. The enemy of the shadows, who had walked among them without fear, would make them face the Light.

Along the stream the land opened with less trees. Other obstacles took their place and more than one knight lost his horse to the terrain. The hooded figure leading the charge from the Dark Hollow never saw the stone fall from the sky that knocked it from its horse. Those that followed didn't slow, trampling their leader. Duncan allowed himself a smirk, seeing more stones plunging to Earth. Rocs circled above. Apparently the one they met wasn't alone. Natives tried to shoot them, but the birds were far out of range. One swooped and snatched one of the hooded warriors, flew into the sky, and dropped it to its death, its scream cut short by the ground.

Nearly a dozen cat siths at the leading edge launched themselves at riders and horses alike. The bloody remains of a dark hound, that survived the earlier assault, scattered through the air, ripped to shreds by two giant cats. An instant later the two mounted forces collided in an explosion of clashing steel. The shouts of men and shrieks of horses overwhelmed their ears like colliding freight trains. Those who could not ignore the sensory overload and focus on their attackers would not survive long. The knight's horses, raised for such a battle, had no problem entering the storm. They could endure more damage than the enemy's, but they weren't invincible. And friend or foe alike were in grave danger of being crushed if thrown to the ground.

Ethan clashed with a hooded figure, its face hidden in

darkness. The skilled fighter surprised Ethan by meeting every blow with ease. His mind raced to find and use anything it had on sword fighting. Anyone else would have already been dead. In spite of his surging strength, his endurance was being tested. From behind, Duncan stabbed the dark warrior in the back and slashed at its neck. Out of the hood fell not a head, but a skull. It rolled to a stop, its empty eye sockets and gaping mouth frozen in terror. These weren't men.

They were the dead.

Conrad ran ahead of the wall of knights and knelt behind a fallen tree. Aoifa joined him, firing her crossbow into the coming horde. Some of the hoods had come off of the riders.

"Skeletons!" Conrad shouted.

"Bone men!" Aoifa laughed and looked to Conrad. "We are making all kinds of new friends today."

"Not the kind of friends I need." Conrad took down the closest bone men with arrows shot through their skulls. Apparently whatever raised these dead from the Earth didn't prevent them from dying again.

A bone man that had been dismounted by a cat sith ran toward Stonecor only to be shattered by its fist. Four bone men rode towards the fire elemental, the first two knowing they were about to be incinerated. Those that followed hurled dark steel lances into the stone and fire creature. The flame that whipped around him withered and his joints stiffened. A bone man raised its horse on its hind legs and kicked the elemental, shattering it into a pile of rubble.

The mounted knights had overwhelmed most of the bone men; then the foot soldiers charged. Many of the natives panicked at the sight of cat siths flinging their brethren through the air. Those that made it to the charging knights were killed quickly. Clubs and axes had little chance against the experienced swordsmen. Some did get lucky shots off with spears and bows. Rocs grabbed bone men from their mounts, hurling them to their death. One roc was too slow and had its wing clipped by a sword. The natives launched a barrage of arrows at the great bird, felling it to the ground among the maelstrom of men and horses.

Knowing now what he faced, Ethan surged like a whirlwind and struck down one assailant after another. The dead men had lost their advantage. They weren't the only ones that could fight beyond the plane of humanity. Some did manage to reach Ethan's horse. Its wounds were too great; blood drenched its sides. It was dying. With most of the bone men defeated, Ethan dismounted and fought among the other knights. Most of the natives had lost their will to fight and fled at the sight of his sword, but they were not alone. Another bone man materialized out of the chaos directly in Ethan's path. Two feet taller than the rest, with a sword that reached out a mile, its blackened skull pulsed with red eyes. Through the confusion someone called out, "The Bone Lord!"

Duncan killed the last mounted bone man in time to see the Bone Lord run for Ethan. Duncan turned his horse to find a half-dozen or so wild men standing in his way. The shadow-eyed, corrupted men didn't scare as easy as the natives. Two attacked Duncan's horse with stained swords, bringing it to its knees. Duncan jumped clear and faced the men and one of the skeletons that had been tossed from its horse. They circled around him and began to close in slowly, even cautious in their numbers. Duncan readied his swords and was about to engage and fight until either they were all dead or he laid among the bodies. In a moment of clarity, he realized he stood next to the small creek that flowed through the center of the valley. The battle had polluted the water, turning it into a slurry of mud and blood. The water was his only hope.

The energy of the battle bottled inside Duncan. He had yet to tap into it fully. Even as he moved his swords, a moment of doubt flashed through his mind. *Will this work?* That thought existed so briefly, it might have well have never occurred. Duncan thrust his swords into the stream and poured his energy through it at the evil before him. The water boiled and swirled around him into a hurricane before it shot out against the foes. It met them with such force that they vanished into a cloud of mist, denying them even an opportunity to scream. Vaporized. After a brief second of bemusement, Duncan set off to find his friend.

Ethan stood firm before the giant terror, awash in adrenaline, covered in the filth and stains of battle. As he raised the sword in front of him, the blue energy cleansed the blade of blood. The Bone Lord hesitated for but a moment, enough time for Duncan to launch one of his short swords through the air. It swiped the Bone Lord along the shoulder, but the demon spawn didn't falter. Conrad who had watched the situation unfold, embedded two arrows into the Bone Lord's back. It stumbled, but didn't fall. It knew what Ethan was, and when it was finished with him, it would take care of his friends.

Aoifa, fighting in a throng of natives and knights, couldn't break free. Duncan inched closer. The Bone Lord ran, its followers in crumbled heaps all around. The battle slowed around Ethan. Natives fled, trees were ablaze, arrows sliced through the thick air. He ran towards the skeletal horror. As the Bone Lord nearly reached him and raised its sword, Ethan propelled himself to the side and as he hit the ground, he swung around and cut through the Bone Lord's legs. It fell backward, screaming an unintelligible curse, crashing hard onto its back. Ethan leaped up, spun around, and drove his sword through the skull. It twitched twice as the blue fire shot through its body. Ethan looked away as the bones exploded into a hailstorm of fragments. He opened his eyes, the stench of charred bones burning his nose, and saw Duncan and Conrad running to him.

Duncan raised his sword. "Victory, my friends!"

"Are you all right?" Conrad said, out of breath.

"I'm fine. Good to see you're in one piece," Duncan said. "You, too, Ethan."

"Yeah, well, I hope this is over." His body tingled from the energy that had been expended. He didn't feel weak, the energy had been instantly replaced. Something still wasn't right. Darkness still weighed heavy on his mind. He looked over the battlefield as cheers rose above the melee, drowning out the screams of dying men and beast. The Evil One's army laid broken. The survivors ran to escape capture. As the knights regrouped, ready to pursue the enemy into the Dark Hollow, an earth-shattering roar rose up through the valley and silenced them all. Then, to the east, out of the forest came a beast of such enormity that even Stonecor and Aoifa were but specks. Another of the creatures that had haunted Ethan's dreams, the giant stood as high as the towering trees. It broke them like twigs and threw the wooden missiles at the weary soldiers.

"They have raised Balor!" Owain had come to join the fight against the Bone Lord. Now something more deadly had arrived. "Do not let the Fomorii's king capture you lest you become its meal. We must kill him through his eye quickly!" Balor had one massive eye in the center of its forehead. It was in no hurry, plodding slowly to its enemies. Its brownish skin rippled with muscle as it clubbed a roc that had come too close. Effortlessly lifting a boulder from the valley floor, it hurled the projectile into the knights, crushing many.

"Look, over there!" Conrad pointed to the hollow that led to the cave.

A group of misshapen creatures, some mounted and others on foot, were charging into the hollow. Deformities of multiple arms and legs didn't slow their approach. Like insects, the gray and bluish beings swarmed into the woods. With them were the last of the natives and a handful of bone men.

"Cavalry, to the Citadel!" Owain turned to Ethan. "You must stop Balor at all costs. He cannot be allowed to reach the cave."

"Easier said than done." Aoifa joined them. The last of her crossbow bolts had been emptied into Balor. Archers fired in futility. The arrows sailed through the sky, many falling short.

Ethan had an idea.

"Call in the rocs."

"You're not serious?" Duncan asked.

"Better idea? Now's the time."

Aoifa called out to the birds circling overhead. Two swooped down and landed among them. One was Øyvind. "This man needs a ride," Aoifa pointed at Ethan. Øyvind, speaking like a hawk, turned its head and pointed to its back with its beak. Then Aoifa called out to the soldiers. "Take the ropes from those horses and harness the rocs."

"Who else is coming?" Ethan asked.

Duncan was the first to answer.

"I'll do it."

"Okay, Conrad, you and Aoifa lead the knights and try to distract that thing. We'll try to kill it from above." Ethan went to Øyvind where Aoifa was rigging some straps from a horse mount so Ethan could hold on. Owain did the same with the other roc.

After Ethan mounted Øyvind, Aoifa handed him his sword. "Aim for the eye." Ethan smiled, and said to the great bird, "To the sky my friend." The rocs launched swiftly into the sky like rockets. Ethan wasn't terribly fond of heights, but that was the last thing on his mind as he gripped the straps.

"How many blue arrows do you have left?" Aoifa asked Conrad.

"Five." Not nearly enough and his gun was somewhere on the battlefield.

"Shoot them as close to his chest as possible. Aim for his vitals."

"Where's a rocket launcher when you need one?" Conrad mused. Aoifa rumpled her brow at him. "Never mind, let's go."

Kane was helping with the injured as fast as he could. Some would run off to battle as soon as they were healed. Others were too far gone for even Kane to help. A knight ran into Kane's tent where he was mending the wounded.

"We have crushed the Dark Army in the Misty Valley, but they have released Balor!"

That didn't sound good. "Who is Balor?" Kane asked.

"The king of the Fomorians. Dark creatures, once-men from the netherworlds. More are heading for the Citadel." The knight left and Kane walked outside. Knights were rushing towards the Citadel. Theodoric led the defense during the initial assault, which had been light. Apparently this battle wasn't over yet. Kane went back in the tent, finished with the injured, grabbed his mace and sword, and ran to the cave.

Ethan and Duncan flew far out of Balor's reach as it threw debris at the oncoming knights. The wounds that it sustained from arrows, bombings from the rocs, and whatever Stonecor could hurl at it, had only injured it slightly. "Let's go down," Duncan told the bird, controlling it with the harness much like a horse. The rocs didn't speak any human tongue, but appeared to understand their allies. As he swooped in from behind, he slashed the back of the massive head. The sword drew blood and Balor belched a horrifying scream. "So it does bleed. Maybe a bit easier with this sword."

Balor couldn't decide which attackers to attend to first. He went to swipe at the rocs when another barrage of arrows struck him. Duncan used the distraction to swoop low again for another attack. Hanging from the roc, rope coiled around one hand, with the other he drove a short sword into the side of Balor's head. Balor instinctively swatted at the sword, driving it further into his skull. He grabbed for the birds and their riders, far out of reach. Below, Conrad closed in with his bow ready. Balor faced the advancing knights and Conrad unleashed the first arrow, impaling Balor below the neck. Stonecor drove part of a tree in Balor's foot, narrowly missing being kicked by it. Another blue tipped arrow struck Balor, this time in his throat. A third in its stomach. The last two in the chest.

Balor flailed about. He was losing focus, but still

managed to crush under his foot a knight that came too close.

"Give it the death blow!" Aoifa yelled to the sky. Conrad unsheathed his sword and Aoifa followed suit. "Attack the tendons in its feet," she said before taking off in a run.

Attacking from behind, Conrad drove his sword into its left foot. Aoifa cut hers across the right, slicing deep in the flesh. Balor roared and looked into the sky in time to see Øyvind diving at him. Ethan hurled his sword at the grotesque eye, bursting it into a spray of fluid.

As the roc flew upward, Balor stumbled and begin to fall. The knights below scattered, Conrad and Aoifa ran in different directions. Balor fell face first, driving the sword into its brain. Death came quickly.

"Take us down," Ethan told Øyvind. Duncan and his roc followed close behind, landing near the fallen giant.

Duncan wrestled with the sword — driven deep into the dead creature's head — finally pulling it free and wiped the gore off the blade in the grass. Aoifa turned Balor's head and removed Ethan's sword from its ruined eye and handed it to Ethan. The knights that had been fighting Balor were already running toward the Citadel when an explosion came from the hollow. Smoke billowed from among the trees.

"To the cave!" called Conrad. The battle for the Misty Valley still had not been won.

CHAPTER SEVENTEEN

When Kane arrived near the Oak Grove, soldiers were everywhere. The last surge of natives had nearly reached the stone wall when mounted bone men led another group into the hollow. Kane looked over the wall as one of the last bone men and its horse were flattened by a boulder released from the top of the ridge. Kane had a strong stomach, but it almost turned inside out.

The natives storming the hollow were hit from both sides with volleys of arrows. They refused to go back. Something more sinister than undead skeletons drove them forward. A mass of disturbed, twisted creatures that had crawled out of the deepest pits of Sheol lumbered up through the stream. The more agile scurried over the slick rocks with multiple arms and legs. Those with a single probing eye showed no emotion as they sought victims. Some had greenish, slime-coated skin. Others were gray with their dry skin stretched tight over their skeletal frames. All reeked of death, and no semblance of humanity remained if it had ever existed in these demon spawn. Behind them rode black-clad men on horseback that made sure that no one fled, using arrows to send some fomorii back to the dead once and for all. One of the black knights was feared by all.

"The shadowmancer!" Theodoric was surprised to see him enter the battle. From the wall overlooking the cave he shouted, "You and your fallen devils will die here today!"

Ahriman laughed. He turned to his lieutenants and Latzi. "Go with these putrid degenerates and retrieve what I want!"

Kane ran through the forest to the well and climbed down into the cave. Knights guarded the entrances at both ends. Too many people stood in the way to see through the small passage that led out into hollow. Then he caught a glimpse of a grayish, one-eyed fomorii. Between its four arms, a ball of white light spun in a cloud of green fog. A shout of "They have a sorcerer!" was cut short by the beam of light that shot through the cave seeking out any life. Kane hit the ground and rolled into the stream as dark magic suffocated the cavern. The shallow water was deep enough to protect him. Those in the direct path of the beam weren't so lucky as their bodies first illuminated from within before bursting into a cloud of ash.

Kane surfaced and choked on the human remains hanging in the air. He waded to the edge and slowly tried to climb out. His body ached briefly from the impact before the wave of healing cleansed him. Screams and clashes of steel came from the Citadel. Infiltrators had followed the magic in. Kane's mace had been thrown in the explosion, but he found his sword laying in the passage and he charged down the tunnel, dimly lit from the few torches not snuffed out by the sorcerer's destruction. As the fighting still raged in the hollow, the noise in the Citadel ceased. He hid near the doorway, listening.

"Here it is, in this chest, Latzi." The greenish fomorii held a scroll in its bony hand. Latzi walked to it and snatched the scroll from its hand.

"That is no relic; that is not what we are here for." Latzi hadn't come for some crumbling parchment.

The fomorii backhanded Latzi, sending him to the ground. "No, human, your usefulness has come to an end. The relics we need are not here. This is what we have come for." He turned to the lieutenant of Ahriman. "Kill him." The man clad in black armor walked over to Latzi and raised his sword.

"No! What are you doing? We must find the relics!" Pain radiated through his chest and surged throughout his body. His eyes focused on the image of a terrible creature on the ceiling's mural. Then the world faded.

"Come, you wretch, retrieve the scroll." The lieutenant could barely stand the sight of the grotesque fomorii. Hopefully, they would all be killed once their usefulness had ended. "His Darkness is waiting."

Kane didn't have time to wait for more knights to arrive. He stepped toward the Citadel; a noise came from behind. Before he turned he knew it wasn't a friend. A dead-looking horror stood in the dim light. Bleeding, but still alive, it rushed at Kane reaching and grabbing with multiple arms. Kane crippled one with his sword, but it used another arm to throw him against the rock wall. He stood, ignoring the pain, and the fomorii stared at him for a moment. It had no weapons and would attempt to kill Kane with brute strength.

Even a healer could die; he needed to end this quickly.

The cramped passage was a coffin. He ran into the

larger cavern under the well. The monstrosity came after him, and at the center of the room, Kane spun and slashed at another arm and then another. Each hit brought forth bloodcurdling shrieks before it finally fell to the ground. The dying creature used the last of its strength and came to its feet. It had to know that it was going to die, yet it still attacked Kane who didn't flinch as he drove his sword through the fomorii's chest. Only inches from his face, Kane could see the evil in its eyes quickly replaced by shock. It hadn't known its own mortality. Kane pushed it away and let the corpse fall to the ground as he removed his sword. He looked at it for only a moment, felt no sorrow for what he did, but instead pitied what lay before him.

Kane ran into the Citadel. The only people there were the dead. Behind him the knights entered. "It's too late! They're gone. Out through the passage into the cave." The knights ran out, some trying to fit through the tight tunnel. Kane sat on a chest staring at Latzi's lifeless form.

What had his comrades taken?

Above the cave, Theodoric's men launched the last of their primitive cannonballs into the hollow. One exploded killing two of the fomorii, including the sorcerer. "Into the hollow! Do not allow them to escape! They were in the Citadel!" Theodoric went over the wall first and slid down the hillside into the stream. Owain's knights from the valley had arrived to join the mayhem in the hollow. Few enemy remained and they had nowhere to go. Theodoric joined the fight against the last of the natives and the hideous fomorii. They had little chance against the veteran knight. His heavy broadsword cut through the air as if weightless. Most fled before it. Those who failed to, did not survive. Through the smoke and fighting bodies, he saw Ahriman on his armored horse. A pale green creature handed him a scroll and Ahriman put it under his cloak. He kicked the ghastly beast, knocking it to the ground. The shadowmancer turned to leave, but not before locking Theodoric's gaze for an instant. He rode off, his horse running as if possessed. The shadowmancer wasn't the one Theodoric and his men had encountered before in the Old World. Who was he? The Evil One had many subjects. This one must not be allowed to escape.

Before he could order the chase, he saw Stonecor about to kill a fomorii. "No!" Theodoric ran to where Stonecor stood. "I want it alive. I want to know what it gave the shadowmancer." No emotion showed on the rock creature's face, but Theodoric thought he saw an imperceptible flash of disappointment. Natives were already being bound and led to a stockade. There were few prisoners. By the time Ethan and the others reached the hollow, the battle was all but over.

"The Citadel, is it safe?" Ethan asked. The shadowmancer had been near. His depravity left a wake of ripples in the veil.

"There was a breech," Theodoric said. "The entrance had been guarded by the fire elemental, but we sent him to the center lines. Some fomorri made it inside. They had some sort of sorcerer who conjured balefire. These once-men do not die easily." He watched as the bound green survivor was led up the path through the hollow to be interrogated. For a moment he looked over the field of battle. The beast, Balor, lay still. Bodies littered the valley below and polluted the creeks. His men walked among them looking for survivors. Horses ran free. Smoke hung in the air. The destruction and death pressed heavy upon his mind as the adrenaline drained away. Theodoric drifted in a fog. He had won, hadn't he?

"Let's go into the Citadel and see what happened

before we jump to conclusions." Ethan put his hand on Theodoric's shoulder. He nodded silently. They climbed out of the hollow and entered the caverns through the well entrance. Men were already inside tending to the wounded and removing bodies.

"Kane!" Duncan went to his old friend who stood over Latzi's body.

"I believe this is Latzi. They killed him before leaving."

"Did they take anything?" Conrad looked around the room. It was torn apart from the struggle between the knights and the Dark Army minions. Bodies were among the debris. Theodoric and the other knights searched through chests and crates.

"The relics are intact, Captain," one of the knights said.

"The True Cross?" Ethan asked.

"I never said the True Cross was here," Theodoric said. "It is still in Britain awaiting transport to their portal. There are other relics here. They are safe."

"What did they take then? What was this all about?" Ethan wanted to know if the battle they had fought, or re-fought in a sense, had been for naught.

"I heard them say they found something, but didn't see what it was. I was detained before I could confront them." Kane looked out the doorway. "That thing over in the cavern was nearly the end of me."

"Looks like you were the end of it, tough guy." Conrad smiled.

"It wasn't enough to stop them in here."

"We all gave more than we thought possible today," Ethan said. "Theodoric, is anything missing?"

"I saw the fomorii give the shadowmancer what looked like a scroll. Search the chests again."

The knights privileged with maintaining the inventory were brought in. They could recite every last item in the

Citadel from memory. Right down to every last arrow. It wasn't long before the discovery was made.

"Over here a scroll is missing." A knight searched through an open chest near where Latzi lay.

"Which?" Theodoric asked.

"One that catalogs the dark tomes at a Cache of Knowledge."

"The what?" Conrad asked before remembering something Grayson had said.

"The Caches of Knowledge are where all the histories, wisdom, and knowledge of civilization is kept." Theodoric had the privilege to see one of them. "Certain volumes are hidden to protect man. They are moved to different locations as needed. Evil, dark books like the *Necronomicon* and the *Ildatch*. This scroll held the location of the most evil of these books. The *Book of the Second Death*."

"Sounds fun." Kane was ready for this day and all of its death to end.

"The servants of the Dark One have repeatedly used disease to assault mankind." Theodoric had seen sinister sicknesses wipe out entire villages. "This book was written long ago by those who studied and used these plagues. Millions have died because of its knowledge, but under the cover of a crusade we found it and hid it. The secret remained secure, until now. Mankind may not survive another epidemic conjured from its pages. Or it may weaken us so we can no longer stand against the Darkness. Some fear it could be used to raise the demons of Resheph and Qetab who destroyed thousands with their weapons of pestilence."

"That sounds like something we'd like to avoid. Where is this book?" Ethan asked. "And can it be destroyed? Better yet, why wasn't it destroyed?"

"It is secure in St. Catherine's Monastery at the foot of

Mt. Sinai. These black testaments were not destroyed so we could use them to understand and defeat the evil of the Dark One."

"In our own time we preserve strains of deadly diseases to maintain vaccines." Kane also knew their potential as biological weapons. "It's a double-edged sword."

"Indeed." Theodoric paused, looking at Latzi's lifeless body. "Can we be certain the relics were not another goal of these evil ones?"

Then Kane remembered. "They said the relic they needed wasn't here. It was vague but sounded like they were going after relics elsewhere."

"Wait a second," Duncan said. "Grayson told us the True Cross had been brought here and that may have been why the battle was waged. You're saying it wasn't here yet something far more dangerous was found in its place. Is that correct?"

"It is," Theodoric answered.

"Latzi," Conrad said as Latzi's body was removed from the cavern, "is the new variable. Something he did, I'm not sure what, changed the intentions of this Dark Army. History was changed just a little, not enough to destroy the future, but enough to set more potential danger in motion."

"So where are the relics? And are they actually looking for the True Cross?" Duncan asked.

"They still look for the True Cross." Ethan looked at Theodoric. "I've seen it in a dream. No, not a dream, a view of the future. Maybe it's not their only goal, but someone wants it. They're not putting all their bets on one horse. At least not now."

"There are two known genuine fragments of the True Cross and thus two places in history where they can be found," Theodoric said. "The shadows will know as we do where they are. At the Horns of Hattin the Crusaders carried a fragment into battle with them. The Saracens captured the Cross and hid it away, losing it. Empress Helena, mother of Emperor Constantine, had recovered another fragment in Jerusalem. This relic she brought to Britain, which has been one of our strongholds since before the time of Constantine. We had hidden it in the lands to the north, but with the rumors of darkness growing, we moved it to Glastonbury Tor."

"Is there a portal near Glastonbury?" Kane asked.

"Yes, Stonehenge is a day's ride from Glastonbury Tor. Centuries ago, we believe our ancestors were the first to recognize the region's many doorways through the veil, though those times are lost. The pagans had built temples and monuments over most of the sites. They used Stonehenge for worship and watching the skies, never fully understanding why they were drawn there. For centuries the shadows tried to use it as a portal, but they failed. We took control over it. We have kept the shadows at bay, but it is not the only place in Britain that they can use to bring darkness into the land. It is, though, one of the most powerful portals in existence. "

"This battle was only the beginning," Ethan said. "The Dark Army never wanted a foothold in the New World."

"What they seek now is far worse. Wielding a relic successfully by evil is uncertain and they know that," Duncan said. A plague conjured from the Darkness would kill millions long before medicine could stop it. If it could. "This book is as dark as evil gets. There will be no problem using it. Yet they still search for the cross. We can't let it fall in their hands and risk them using it in any way, to say nothing of the possibility, as slim as we think it may be, of controlling it. We have to cover all the bases. We have to go to Britain and St. Catherine's and to Hattin."

"If we do that, we'll have to split up." Conrad thought it may be easiest for one to go where he planned on traveling to. "I'll go to Hattin."

"Do not be so eager. We are not entirely certain that it was a true relic," Theodoric said. "There's no portal there. Only death. If the relic is a genuine, it can be used to slip through time."

"If I don't come back, someone will have to come find me." Conrad knew someone had to do this. "I slipped through time, once before, without a portal." He didn't add that it was against his will. His control was far more advanced now, though he didn't open new rifts in time. He perceived ones that already existed.

"It is possible, if you have the gift," Theodoric said. "If the relic is real, it may guide you there like a beacon. Some Watchers can travel without portals or relics, but failing to control that power can also destroy you. The abilities you all have can protect and renew your physical self, but you are not immortal. Once your soul and body are completely separated, they cannot be rejoined. You cannot be completely of both worlds at the same time. As humans, we straddle that line, but ultimately we are limited. Only the Christ was without limits, though he chose to control them."

Theodoric's caution gave pause to the men. The adrenaline of the day had softened the mortal dangers they had faced in battle. There was no time for fear or worry. In some ways, they were superhuman, but they were still human. Ethan didn't want to stop and contemplate these concerns and give fear a chance to establish a foothold in their minds. Time would quickly cease being their ally.

"Ducan, Kane, someone needs to lead the monastery's

defense. Destroy the book if you must." Ethan turned to Theodoric. "Can you ready men to reinforce them?"

"Once we take an accounting of our casualties, some men can be sent. It will take time to send a force through the portal and stage them in the desert. You may also be able to gather men in Britain."

"We will go," Duncan looked at Kane. "Both of us."

Kane waited a moment before speaking.

"Okay, but don't be late. I don't suppose there are many soldiers at the monastery."

They all turned as a knight ran into the Citadel.

"Captain, we need the Healer! Aoifa has been wounded by a dark spear of the bone men!"

CHAPTER EIGHTEEN

Aoifa was carried to the encampment and into the tent where Kane had been healing the wounded. It took some of the strongest knights to carry her from the valley below. Too big for the makeshift cots, she was laid on the ground. After they ran much of the way, Kane and Ethan entered the tent out of breath, Theodoric right behind them. Conrad stood in the opening. The brave warrior he had fought with, side by side, was nearing death. Duncan waited outside, looking in.

"What happened to her? She was unhurt when we left the valley," Ethan said. Aoifa's unblinking eyes stared upwards.

"She's barely breathing." Kane examined the wound on her leg, tearing away the fabric of her clothes. Black lines radiated from the gash; her skin turning gray.

"When they were rounding up the last of the natives, one of them threw a blackened spear at her," said the knight who had alerted them of Aoifa's condition. The sight of her falling to the ground had shocked him as much as the battle itself. She was stronger than all of them. He looked at Kane, "Can you heal her?"

Kane didn't answer, only looked at Ethan and then to Conrad with uncertainty. Conrad stood silently as worry washed over his face. Kane put his hands on either side of the wound. Her body spasmed and she gasped; her head fell back to the ground, mouth open.

"She's dying!" a knight called out.

Kane concentrated all of his self into Aoifa. The energy flowed from his body and his soul. His eyes closed and he clenched his teeth as he fought against the darkness in Aoifa. It wasn't enough. Life faltered as evil crept throughout her body faster than he could turn it back. Kane trembled, barely able to hold her leg and was about to pull away when he felt another stream of energy. Then another. He opened his eyes and Ethan had his hands on Aoifa. So did Conrad. Duncan came in the tent and held her head. They weren't healers, but the energy that flowed through them boosted Kane's threads of life that struggled to repair the damage. A blue glow started to shimmer over her body, erasing the grayness and the spidering black lines. Her head jerked up, her eyes opened wide, and she gasped for air. A surge forced through her body. The energy shocked the Watchers, pushing them away from Aoifa.

The giantess began to change. Her body shrank, smoothly and silently. When the transformation ceased, she drew in a breath and her body shuddered. For a few moments she laid still, breathing slowly. No one made a sound. Aoifa looked around the room and tried to sit up. Conrad helped her. She looked over herself. No longer a giant, the large clothes and leather armor sat over and around her in a pile. Her long hair, having come unbraided during the battle, hid what the clothes no longer covered.

She looked up at the men around her.

"Looks like I'll need a new wardrobe," she said as if she had not just been at death's door. The tent erupted into cheers. Theodoric was smiling at her. Aoifa smiled back. She was going to like being human again.

Later, Ethan stood at the rock wall near the Oak Grove. A misty and quiet rain had come, slowly washing away the horrors of the day from the land. Now it was nearly dusk and the clouds had parted. A red glow from sunset filtered through the valley. Not the red of death, but the warm light of life. His friends readied their gear near the towering oaks. The remainder of the day had been spent helping the injured, collecting the dead. The dead would be buried under the church to be built where the White City would soon take shape. Theodoric had said that the area had been considered for a settlement and now, after this battle, it would be the most defensible location. Fortifications would remain here though, guarding the Citadel.

Theodoric, Captain of the Citadel approached Ethan. "It is best that you leave soon, but not without a night's rest."

Captured natives were led down into the valley. "What will happen to them?" Ethan asked.

"They will be allowed to return home. They were under the spell of the Dark One and this Ahriman that led them, but most have seen their folly in the chaos of this battle. We have no quarrel with them. We do not seek to conquer their lands."

Ethan thought of the time where disease would wipe out nearly all of the natives in the New World. Untold generations of civilization would end. Some settlers would live in peace with them. Others would not, using them as pawns in wars or engaging in eradicating their culture. The history of those who first came to the New World when it was truly new would soon come to an end. It would be a sad, and truly unfortunate, part of all their history.

"In Britain you will find allies at Glastonbury. They may be able to send men to the Sinai. Britain is an ancient and holy land, full of sacred sites. We are strong there, but where we are drawn, so are the Dark One's servants seeking to subvert us. But you know this. The True Cross is not the only thing you seek. What lies beyond the great ocean in the Old World?"

"You perceive correctly. Milena, my wife, is somewhere through that portal. Quite possibly right on the other side. If she is not here, then it must be across the waters." Ethan looked at the oaks, unwavering, untouched by battle. "I don't know how it happened or why, but she went through there. I sense her here, not at this place, but in this time."

"The last family who came here told of a raven haired beauty, a princess from the Hinder Sea they called her. She wore a strange double cross, the Cross of Lorraine she said it was, a symbol of the Arc Maidens. She could understand the animals and they would obey her. She revealed little about herself to the people, but she was waiting for someone. Watchers, she said."

"That has to be Milena." There was no doubt. It was her. Perhaps he shouldn't wait until morning to leave.

"Go now and find her. Together you will stop this madness."

"How can you be so sure?"

"Why else would she already be there waiting for you?"

Ethan didn't know how to answer that. He knew that the Light intended for them to be here at this moment because they were the best equipped to make this stand. That didn't guarantee their success. They were still making choices. Were their decisions the correct ones? He held out his hand to Theodoric.

"You did well today, my friend. It will be a long time before Darkness comes here again."

"Go well, Ethan. Your path now leads elsewhere." Theodoric grasped Ethan's hand. Again, he sensed some recognition as he did when he first met Ethan.

Ethan was nearly the identical twin of Theodoric's father.

The night had passed quickly. Duncan had slept deeply, the exhaustion making sleep come uninhibited, but the visions of battle didn't fade with his dreams. He left the camp and made his way down into the Misty Valley in the faint twilight. Full of the mist that was its namesake, the valley was quiet. It would have felt more serene had he not been a participant of the storm that raged where he stood only a few hours previous. The horror of the ordeal would be with him forever. The dead. The dying. The blood. The screams. Why would man insist on repeating this scenario over and over? Generations of writers and artists tried to imagine what hell was like. Here it was for all to see. At least this had ended, for a while. And yet it bothered him much less than he would have expected.

The sunlight began to push back the mist. Duncan looked towards the light as it slowly bathed the surrounding hills. It was as if something obscured the experience just enough to allow him to bare it. Was this part of his gifts and that of his friends? Would they be here if they couldn't handle this?

In some ways a gift. In other ways, a curse.

Ethan made his way to the edge of the Oak Grove where his friends already waited. Not much was said. There would be no more time to recover from what had passed. Time was critical, and the only hope for success would be to split up and attack each goal at the same time. When you fight a war to win, you attack all points at once. Ethan did not know what to say. What could he?

"This is it; we need to go now. Conrad and I will meet you at the monastery once we are finished." *If we are successful.* No matter how confident, doubt tried to enter the mind. Just a little, but if it was allowed to grow, it could be fatal.

"We won't fail." Duncan knew, as they all did, there was unknown darkness arrayed against them. They had won the Battle of the Misty Valley, but what they experienced here was only a glimpse of what may come.

"It will be done; somehow we will prevail." Kane's confidence had been strengthened again after witnessing Aoifa's transformation after his unnerving encounter in the Cidatel. A few hours ago he had been a doctor in a small town. Now he was in a forgotten time, warring with forgotten evil. If he sat down to think about it, he feared he might believe he was trapped in a dream. Or was it a nightmare? Maybe he would know when this was over.

"Let's stop talking about it and show these Followers the quickest route to their death." Conrad was certain, but death had been a hairbreadth away from all of them. If Aoifa could be brought down and an elemental destroyed, what of him? He was — they all were — still learning to transcend their humanity the best they could. There were limits to what they could do.

Ethan looked at his friends, hopefully not for the last time. He grasped their hands. "Go well my friends. Let the Light burn in us, from us." They nodded silently and he turned, walked among the Oaks and looked to the sky. Fear tried to flood his eyes, but he thought of Milena. *No, they will not win this time.*

His friends watched him become engulfed in blue light that swirled around the Oak Grove. The light rose out of the ground and spiraled into the canopy overhead. When the light vanished, all was quiet and any evidence of Ethan was gone. The travel was nearly instantaneous and Ethan barely registered what was happening to his body. This time he remained in control and didn't stumble out of the vortex, but as the haze cleared from his mind and he rubbed his eyes, he saw mounted shapes riding toward him in the early morning light. He reached for his sword.

"Wait!" The knight that called out approached Ethan. He did not have a weapon in his hand, but he did have the red cross on his surcoat. "Are you the one that we have been waiting for?"

"Perhaps." Ethan didn't like being quizzed, but thought it better to answer nicely. "My name is Ethan and I come from the New World where I defended the Misty Valley with Theodoric of Malbork, Captain of the Citadel. The Followers of the Dark One failed to take any relics, but they learned the location of the *Book of the Second Death.* I believe they also seek the True Cross, so I come here to secure the relic." *And to find Milena.*

The knight was intrigued, but not entirely convinced.

"The Maiden said you would most likely bring the symbol of our order." The blond knight was stout and strong, a veteran of many conflicts.

Ethan removed the leather pouch from his belt and removed the silver cross.

"Is this what you are looking for?"

The knight turned to his men. "Bring the horse, this is Ethan the Watcher from Beyond Time."

Ethan was about to ask who this Maiden was, when he noticed the massive stone monoliths encircling him. The knight again addressed Ethan, seeing his look of amazement.

"This is Stonehenge, portal between lands. Welcome to the land of the Britons. We now ride to Glastonbury where the holy relic is held and where your Arc Maiden awaits."

Milena.

CHAPTER NINETEEN

The autumn morning had awakened under a crystal clear sky. Already nine on the clock that ticked the minutes away on the mantle. Milena opened the windows throughout the first floor, the temperature perfect in its fall coolness, allowing the fresh air to cleanse the rooms. Scout would make sure nothing would scurry through the French doors she left open in the living room. She sat on a patio chair, letting the Sun warm her body, energizing her. Her and Ethan had slept little, but she felt most alive on this beautiful day. Extravagant beauty. Could chance create this?

The light of the day raised memories of a little girl spending countless hours outside in the dirt playing and gardening with her parents. The native artifacts she had found in their garden would inspire her passion of archaeology as she grew older. A blanket of peace surrounded her. She was back there, a little girl, in those days. *When the light is just right, and you let the calm surround you, see into the past, on a day like this.* Kyra ran outside and hugged her, ending the calm.

"Morning, Mommy." Kyra had been awake for hours, watching the day begin outside her window. "What are we going to do today?"

No school for Kyra on Saturday. Nor any classes for Ethan or Milena to teach. "I'm not sure yet," Milena said. "Maybe we can start by having breakfast in the garden. Go get dressed and I'll get the food started."

"I want dip eggs and toast!" Kyra ran back inside. "And let's go to the White City!" she called back before heading upstairs to change out of her Supergirl pajamas.

Yes, Saturdays often included a trip into Hayden. The old village reminded Milena of the Old World town where her parents had been born. The shops would be busiest today with people crowding the sidewalks and filling small restaurants. General stores like Hayden Mercantile sold everything from cider to herbs, brought in by local growers. Craftspeople offered their rustic wares. Then there was that cozy bookshop in which they all spent prodigious amounts of time. The old-fashioned nature of the town where everyone supported each other appealed to her. Strong communities could thrive no other way.

She loved the people and activity, but here among farms and forests that were once farms, Milena bathed in the quiet. It was the same countryside where Ethan had grown up. In some ways it was like the farmlands her family had originally settled in the East, nestled among the rolling mountains. Here the mountains weren't so high, but the forests were just as old and full of history.

She went to the garden and cleaned off the furniture on the stone patio. The plants had begun their autumn die-off and soon all would be bare except the few evergreens among them. The garden circled around a small spring that had bubbled there for ages. The water was ringed by cut stone four feet in diameter and about two feet high which gave it the look of a small well. Buried pipes carried water from the spring throughout the garden. A cast iron grate sat on top of the stone well, in the shape of the *vesica piscis* — two interlocking circles — the symbol of purity. Hidden in the foliage design around the circles were two vexing numbers: 717 and 2111. She had asked the iron worker, whose shop was also in the White City, what they meant and he had replied cryptically, "An artist never gives up all of his secrets." Strange man he was.

Scout appeared out of the flowers and shrubs. "Where have you been?" Scout answered Milena's question with a sniff and a loud purr. Kyra appeared at the back door shaking a canister of food and he dashed off for his snack. It was more habit than anything because he probably had spent the night hunting critters in the garden. She didn't care so long as Scout kept the rabbits and other rodents from destroying her herbs and vegetables growing among the other plants of the garden. Most were already finished for the season, but she picked a few peppermint leaves and let their sweet scent tantalize her senses.

The woods to the south caught her eyes. It had been midsummer since she had walked among the paths and ancient trees. Something was different this year. A peculiar silence blanketed the woods weeks ago. Not threatening, but he normal sounds of wildlife had become muted. She had always been drawn to wooden sanctuaries; now the call resounded stronger than ever. She would take a walk later and put this to rest. Seriously, what was there that she should fear?

"What is it?" Ethan startled Milena. She had felt him come outside, but stayed lost in her thoughts.

"I was just thinking I haven't been out there for a while. Been so busy at the college."

"There's something else, isn't there?" Ethan wrapped his arms around Milena and held her close, breathing the flowery scent of her hair.

She savored the feeling of his desire. "I don't know what it is, but I feel like the world we left behind to live a normal life has returned, though not completely the same." She paused. "Did you ever think maybe we never fully realized what we were to do? What everything was about? Was that all? It's like something will soon change. I can't see it all, but we never could. We are still too attached to our physical bodies. There is one more leap we must make." She looked to the forest. "Soon it will come."

"You're probably right. I've become so busy with work and life that I don't see very far anymore. Weren't we trying to avoid that? We hurried to change our lives. Did we leave something behind?" Before Milena could answer, Kyra called from the house.

"Come on guys, I'm hungry!"

During breakfast, the phone rang. Kyra quickly answered. "Moira wants to know if I can go over to her house today."

"What are you two going to do?" Milena asked.

"Stuff." Kyra's blue eyes sparkled and she smiled as she gave her favorite answer.

Milena looked at her husband. *She gets that from you.*

"They're going to do whatever girls their age do," Ethan replied. "I can take her over."

Moira lived in downtown Hayden, over the businesses her family had owned for generations.

Before leaving, Milena kissed Kyra goodbye. "I'll see you later, behave yourself." She wasn't worried, but moms were required to say that.

"I will. Love ya."

"Love you, too. Don't be gone too long, Ethan." *This could be a great day for relaxing, don't you think?* Their nights never erased their love, or want, for each other.

"Oh, brother." Kyra saw the look between her parents.

Ethan kissed Milena. "I'll be back soon."

Milena watched Kyra climb into her father's 4x4. As they drove away and Kyra waved, an uninvited foreboding washed over Milena. Something barely perceptible had changed. Where had the peace of the morning gone? She shook off the sensation and went inside.

In the library, on one of the higher shelves, sat a small replica of the Khufu pyramid, the largest of the Giza wonders. Milena had bought it in Cairo years ago on a trip with Ethan. The top of the replica opened, revealing a hollow for storing collectibles. Among the items inside, she chose a necklace made from a simple leather strand. From it hung a small golden cross, barely two inches high. The cross had an extra bar, a shorter one above the longer beam. The gold sparkled in the light from tiny, nearly imperceptible gemstones embedded in the gold. She had found it in a shop as a small child when visiting Reggio Calabria in southern Italy with her parents. They had been born there and returned every few years to visit family and friends.

When her parents had tried to buy the cross, the old woman who ran the shop insisted on giving it to the young Milena saying, "I'm only giving back what belongs to her." As Milena looked at it with big eyes, the shopkeeper told her its history. "It's the Cross of Lorraine, a symbol of resistance against tyranny and evil. One who resisted was

Joan of Arc, born in the Lorraine region of France. She claimed to have divine visions, and when not even twenty years old, she led armies during the Hundred Years War with England. The English got their hands on her, accused her of false heresy, and burned her at the stake!" Milena's mouth dropped open and her parents were about the say something to the woman, but she continued first. "She was later declared innocent, her visions genuine. Someday this will mean something to you. You will resist like she did." Her parents thanked the woman and tried not to rush too fast out the door.

Milena glanced at the clock on the wall. The bronzed timekeeper with exposed, over-sized gears had a steampunk vibe to it. A little something she picked up at an antique shop. There should be enough time for a quick hike up to the oaks before Ethan came home. No doubt he would stop somewhere in town after dropping Kyra off.

She put on the necklace like she often did before heading out, a tradition that started when she was a girl. After tying her hair back, she grabbed her backpack from the bedroom that was already filled with a few supplies. Ethan had taught her to always be prepared, ready to go in a few minutes, even if was only a short walk. Milena slung the pack over one shoulder after putting on her leather jacket. Black and worn, it fit well. She caught a glimpse of herself in the foyer mirror. "Practical yet stylish," she said to herself with a smile. "Not quite the stereotypical nature girl." She closed the heavy wooden door behind her and turned the key in the deadbolt. The bolt slid strongly and the key snapped when she went to pull it out. Milena stood there for a few seconds. Was she coming back? "Please, it's only a key."

She found herself walking quickly and it wasn't long before she was standing under the lone oak that stood on the hilltop. The natural watchtower marked the entrance to the path leading to the Oak Grove. Its leaves were only slightly tinged with dark red, they wouldn't fall until winter neared. Behind it, among the weeds, hid a covered well where a windmill once stood. A good place for one, but long ago abandoned. Ethan had talked about installing new ones around the property, not for water, but for electricity. Solar cells on the roof already provided most of the power. When building their house, Ethan had treated it like a science experiment, seeing if they could live off the grid. A couple more improvements and they would be doing just that.

No breeze swept around the hill on the nearly perfect fall day. Only a few rustles in the brush and a few brief calls of birds intruded on the quiet woods. Normally there would be much more activity among the trees under the sharp blue sky. Animals would be drawn to Milena almost like she was their master. Now they were wary of anyone. It was troubling, but there were no obvious signs of distress. No new predators or diseases. Nothing to upset the balance. Maybe that was the problem, something that couldn't be seen. She took a breath and continued down the trail.

At the edge of the Oak Grove, the sight of the soaring trees took Milena's breath away. To some people the sight might take them aback; to her the trees were a haven, no matter what was going on in her life. Walking between two of the trees, she entered the Circle illuminated by rays of sunlight. She had been here countless times, yet the branches and their near-perfect dome rivaled human architecture.

Milena knelt down near the sparkling pond; its soft light made the normally unseen green specks in her eyes glitter. The minerals in the water left a shine on her skin, yet it was pure and clean. She drank from her cupped hands. Never so much as a speck of dirt had ever been seen floating in the pond. Drinking the water always was like awakening from a perfect sleep. Taking a purple stainless steel water bottle from her pack, she filled it with the pure liquid. Then the sensation was clear.

She was not alone.

Milena stood and turned. From the shadows of one of the oaks, a person walked into the light. No, not a human, but surely a female of her race. Color radiated from the autumn leaves that clothed her. They formed to her body, but there were places where the tree behind her remained visible. Her young face, nearly translucent, had the color of the sparkling spring water. Shimmering red hair fell around her face and flowed down her back to her waist.

"Who are you?" Milena sensed no danger from the tree girl, but couldn't help tensing from caution.

"I'm Elah, a spirit who has long watched over these trees. I was once as you are, a Maiden of this world. When my walk on this world was over, I chose to protect this place for a time. I walked with you once as a girl. You do not remember."

"No, I don't."

"Perhaps you will someday. That is not important. What is now at hand is a decision. You know that you are different among others of this world. You know that there is more. But are you ready to continue? Are you the one to gather the Arc Maidens? They have been without a leader for some time. You, over all others, have shown unique strengths and gifts. Being paired with a husband and daughter with similar gifts seems beyond chance. Yet alike souls do find each other. Do you know of this which I speak?"

"I know we have been given opportunities others

haven't. We've felt there were others in the world like us, but have found so few of them."

"Milena, it may not seem this way, but all are born with the gifts. All have a soul not of this Earth. You chose at some point not to ignore those truths, to not allow them to be drowned out in the noise of civilization. You and your family and those you have gathered around you have made the choice to embrace who you are. Now, as evil strengthens its grip on man, do you wish to complete this journey? Do you wish to become what few have before you?"

"I am ready, but what is it that I must do? And what of my family?" Milena was unsure of what was being asked of her. Here she was, alone with a supernatural entity, without those she loved the most. That same being standing in front of her made her confusion and doubts soften. There was a complete absence of darkness in Elah. A pure being of the Light. A servant of the Creator.

"Your family will face their own trials. You are to be the first. You now stand in a gateway to other places, other times. It is to one of these times that is only history to you that you must go. In the land of the Britons darkness grows when we expected none. The Followers of death seek the power of a sacred relic of the Light. They once gave up the quest, but now seek it again to wield its power against men. It was hidden by our people on the great Tor overlooking the Somerset Moors. There you must protect it until others can join you."

"Must I do this alone? Now? Is there no one there who can do this?" The idea of leaving her family scared Milena. *Ethan, where are you?* Anxiety pushed away her stalwart calm. Her connection to Ethan had never been blocked.

"You are never truly alone. The Light is always with

you. The choice, though, is yours and yours alone. The time of that decision is now at hand. This place is a doorway to where you must go if you so choose. You have come this far, but need to go no farther." Elah stepped back into the shadow of the oak, her face and hair disappearing. Then a breeze blew apart the leaves that had formed her body and carried them high into the trees.

Milena stood conflicted by awe, and then fear and sadness, not knowing how many minutes passed. The Light was strong with her, it always had been, but this would be the toughest decision she had ever made.

And yet there was no doubt left clouding what she had to do.

Milena picked up her pack and stood over the water. A tear dropped, giving the water a subtle blue glow as it rippled. The light brought comfort, but the pain inside her wouldn't be completely suppressed. How could it? She cared for them so much. Looking back through the woods to where her home was, she knew this was it. Why now, why not wait? One last test before she could become fully what she was born to be. No, it wasn't a test, because she knew the answer. This was a choice, the most difficult one that could be made even though she had often told Ethan they were still missing something. Their part in the Story was not complete. Now, at this moment, she would be the first to change that. *I love you both.*

Not quite knowing what to do to initiate the portal, she closed her eyes and began to search for the place Elah had spoken of. There were images of a place far away. A church on a hill overlooking a small town. Air swirled around the trees and a blast of energy snapped her eyes open. A rotating column of blue light emanated from the water, reaching above the trees. Leaves were sucked into the vortex. The light drew her closer.

She stepped into it and disappeared.

CHAPTER TWENTY

than had never ridden horses for any significant
duration. Now, after recent events, he was easily
keeping up with the more experienced knights. One
tended to learn quickly in a time of crisis.

There had been six of them. Two stayed behind at
Stonehenge. Ethan now knew why the site had such a
mystique surrounding it. Not aliens or mysterious cults,
but a portal not unlike the one ringed by oaks across the
ocean. One of the world's greatest mysteries solved. Too
bad he couldn't publish a book about it without being
labeled as a nut. Maybe he could disguise it as fiction. The
knights around him seemed unfazed by such wonders.
When they slowed to ford a small stream and allow the
horses to drink, Ethan questioned the one who had first
approached him at Stonehenge about Milena's arrival. He
had said his name was Cináed.

"About six months ago," Cináed answered. Milena
had been gone a year from Ethan's perspective. "Once she

arrived in Glastonbury the knights would not let her near St. Michael's church on the Tor. After a few weeks she demanded to speak with the monks. They refused, but once she relieved the guards of their horses, the monks intervened, having realized she was the one they were expecting."

"They could have warned us ahead of time," a young knight with a tangled mass of brown hair said under his breath.

"I take it you were one of the knights that tried to stop her?" Ethan asked, almost laughing.

"More like she assailed us. Lucky for us she is on our side."

Cináed laughed. "Indeed. She could be a ruler in these lands. We could use some that are not mad for power."

"Our visit here is only temporary," Ethan said. "Unless we fail."

"It is my great hope that we shall not," Cináed said. "Now let us continue. We are only a few miles from town."

By the time they neared the outskirts of Glastonbury at the River Brue, evening had turned to night. The Moon watched from high in the eastern sky. Overlooking the town, and the Summerland Meadows around it, loomed Glastonbury Tor. The Tor dwarfed all the nearby hills and at the summit, Ethan saw St. Michael's church and monastery standing among the shadows. The village below was quiet, its people asleep. It was an island of peace and calm, a welcome change to the battle that had swirled around him a few hours ago.

And for the first time in months, he felt as if Milena was only a few feet away.

⧗   ⧗   ⧗

When Milena first arrived at Stonehenge, after the haze wore off, the location didn't surprise her. She almost expected it. What was annoying was the realization she didn't have any weapons. Leaving her katana blades home wasn't the smartest choice, but how often did she ever carry them into the woods? She hadn't set out the front door expecting to be swept into the past. Not many people were a threat to her, but that didn't mean no one was. A woman alone in the middle of nowhere made for a perfect target. If she had her geography right, she knew the general direction of Glastonbury. Still, it would be an awfully long walk over thirty miles through unfamiliar lands. "Might as well take a look around for a bit."

The towering monoliths circled her. It had been part of a larger complex of causeways and henges used to celebrate the passing seasons and cycles of life and death. The site had always fascinated Milena and, in another age, she had been a visitor on more than one occasion. The last time, she convinced Ethan to sneak out to the stones one night. That could have landed them in hot water, but wasn't she an archaeologist and not just another tourist? In any case, they spent hours looking at the stars. That night had felt like they had traveled back in time. Now she had done precisely that. If her understanding was right, her actions were meant to prevent more of the world becoming similar ruins.

She walked among the stones, running her hands over their surfaces. Many stones were standing, nearly unmovable against nature and man. Of course, the latter had left parts of the site in disarray. Already a shadow of its former self, the fallen stones that weren't hauled off would someday be raised to their original places. The outer stones formed a circle of gates that separated the inner monoliths from encircling earthworks. These standing sandstones, the sarsens, rose taller than two men and most were capped with lintels that ran continuously around the stones. Someone could walk around the site up there and never touch the ground when all the lintels had been in place. A few feet inside laid a circle of smaller bluestones, barely taller than the tallest men. Much larger sarsens — trilithons — formed a horseshoe within that circle, standing twenty or more feet high. "So why all the stones? To mark this place? To contain it? Or to control it? Who went through all this effort to bring you guys here?"

She looked for carvings on the stones, most of which had eroded long before her first visit to the sacred henge. "Lost in the mists of time, your creators are. Long before the Celts and Druids someone discovered this place." The myth of the ancients being mere cavemen had given rise to silly claims of the stones being erected by Merlin or visitors from another galaxy. Such stupidity bothered her. The real history was far more fascinating. Obviously far more so than anyone realized. Apparently the first people here had at least recognized something unique even if they knew nothing of portals. Or did they? Most of their descendants quickly forgot those realities as they worked to expand their sacred landscape. Someone eventually remembered.

Milena walked out of the circle of stones through an opening in the earthworks. Standing there was the Heel Stone that marked the rising Sun on summer solstice. Well, it was at least a close approximation. Whatever the ancients had intended, the stone actually marked the June sunrise better in her time than when it was first set In place. From it she could see out over the rolling Salisbury plain. Copses of trees dotted the landscape. Even now there were few of them, the forests of England being used for the growing population. Nearby there was a path, a road of sorts, well-worn by travelers and wagons that ran in the general direction of her destination. The Sun was not high overhead, but she needed to stop wasting time and start the long trek.

Barely a mile down the road, she stopped. Someone was coming. The clomping of a horse and the noise of its cart met her ears a few moments before she saw it in the distance. Milena waited as the cart came nearer. Not something she would normally do in a strange place, but she sensed no danger. She waved as it drew closer and could see an older couple driving the cart. Simply dressed with a cart-full of crated and covered goods, perhaps they were merchants. Was she in the Middle Ages?

"Whoa there." The old man called to the brown horse. The the sight of Milena surprised him. Short and stout, with silver hair, perhaps he was in his fifties. "She usually doesn't listen that well."

Milena walked to the horse and held out her hand. The horse sniffed it and she began to run her hand over its mane. "She's tired. She doesn't like being a work horse."

"Alice never has, but she's reliable." The man looked at Milena closely. "What are you doing out here, miss? Are you alone?" He eyed her carefully, her clothes were a bit odd. Her hair dark like a raven. Was she one of the strange folk that liked to lurk among the ruins?

"Yes, I'm heading to Glastonbury. I have...friends there." At least she thought she did.

The man's wife spoke up.

"Our home is in the town you seek. We can give you a ride if you'd like." The woman didn't hesitate in offering the ride; her husband cast her a look of dismay. "It's fine, Samuel. She is no stranger. She is a traveler from afar.

What is your name, dear?"

"Milena." She answered after listening carefully to their words. English had changed over generations, but not so much that Milena couldn't understand.

"Never heard that before," said the man.

"It is from a land distant from here." She paused, looking for some truth to tell, but veiled. "The birthplace of my parents. Near the great Hinder Sea."

"A long way you have come." The woman smiled. Taller than her husband, with gray-streaked, long red hair tied behind her, she was in charge. "My name is Bernadette. Please, get in. We have much ground to cover before nightfall."

"Thank you. You are kind to help me." Milena climbed into the back of the wagon, finding a place to sit between sacks of flour.

"That is a beautiful cross you wear."

"Thank you," Milena said.

She zipped her coat to hide the cross when Samuel gave it a hateful look. Anger and sadness burned in him, but his wife was different. The Light burned strongly in her. Milena could almost see a connection through the veil. An unknown gift. Was this woman expecting her? She resisted the impulse to try to probe the woman's mind, an ability that had come far easier to Kyra. Instead, she watched Stonehenge disappear over the horizon and quickly shifted her thoughts elsewhere.

That night years ago under the stars had also been a romantic one. Had that been six or seven years ago already? Her eyes misted as she thought of Ethan and Kyra. Thankfully, her companions talked little during their journey, leaving Milena to spend the time in thought. Her family felt so far away and she was drained. Was it the portal or the anxiety? Sleep came fitfully on the bumpy road, and the sudden stop jerked her awake when they arrived in Glastonbury, the Isle of Avalon. Evening was falling across the town and its residents were closing up shops, preparing their dinners. Such normalcy for a place so wrapped in legend. Why did it become so sacred? Just chance or a remnant of something lost in antiquity? Maybe it was founded by those like her and Ethan. She had always felt that way about the White City, too. There was no doubt that the veil was thin around both towns.

"We are home, my dear. Our home is there by Wearyall Hill," Bernadette said. "Looks like you could use a good night's sleep."

"Yes, that would be nice." Milena didn't know if sleep would come easily in the strange bed, but it did. She awoke to a soft light entering the window. A mist hung in the air, moving slowly through the village. *A perfect morning to take a look around.* Her hosts were still asleep, and she was careful not to wake them. Outside, the water droplets swirled around her as she followed a path to the hill's summit above. About a mile or so away, stood St. Michael's on Glastonbury Tor, standing watch over the town.

Under a hawthorn tree, as the morning Sun slowly rolled back the blanket of mist from the town, the quiet beauty relaxed her heart and mind. A bird chirped in the tree above. She looked for it and walked around the thick and reaching tree. Was this the Glastonbury Thorn? She knew the legend that spoke of Joseph of Arimathea traveling to Glastonbury as a tin merchant prior to the death of Christ. After the crucifixion, Joseph returned to these lands, and planted his staff into the ground, causing leaves to burst forth from it. A sign to live here and build a church in the town. His staff grew into the tree that would stand for centuries. So it was said.

Milena touched the bark of the tree for a moment before walking down the hill and heading to the Tor. It was a short trip and the destination disappointing. The knights at the base of the Tor denied her access. No one was allowed to access the church. There were other churches to pray and make offerings. Milena returned to the house trying her best to suppress her irritation.

"The people I had hoped to meet have not yet arrived," she told Bernadette. Nor did she know when they would. In all honesty, she didn't know what to do or where to go. Why wouldn't they let her in the church? Shouldn't they know who, or what, she was? No, they had no reason to. She didn't quite know who to trust, but her perception was strong and would root out any impure intentions. "I may be here longer than I had planned."

"Do not worry yourself about that. You may stay here as long as you need," Bernadette said.

"You're too kind, but I do not wish to intrude in your home."

"It is not an intrusion at all. You can help us in our store."

The couple was one of the few tailors in the town, making and repairing clothes. When Bernadette saw Milena riding Alice later that day, like the two had known each other since birth, she spent the night making her two pairs of split-riding skirts. She had a town shoemaker craft for her boots that were ready a few days later.

"We've had Alice for five years and she's never taken to someone like this."

"She's a fine horse. She has a unique personality, almost like a person."

The days passed, sometimes quickly, other times they slowed like a wagon stuck in a pit of mud. When not minding the store, Milena rode Alice around the countryside, exploring and losing herself in her mind. Her family never left her thoughts. Did they have any idea where she was or what happened to her? She should have left a message. That was stupid not to do. She didn't have to leave without finding them. No, when with Elah she had felt overwhelming immediacy that the decision had to be made right then. It had to happen this way, a final test, one she chose to take. Still, such reasoning could not hide or suppress all of her sadness. Couldn't she go home through the portal?

Bernadette noticed, but said little. Her husband still scowled and paid close attention to all transactions Milena made in the shop. Every penny was accounted for, counted twice. Eventually he became a little less concerned, though still looked at her with disdain. She was good for business, he couldn't deny that. Word traveled fast in the town of a traveler from an exotic land staying among them. Many of the townsfolk went out of their way to stop in the shop.

On her fourth Friday in Glastonbury, Milena noticed they were not staring as much. Perhaps they had gotten used to her. She was no longer a stranger as she walked into town to Glastonbury Abby. Inside the grand sanctuary, she prayed and contemplated. The church was a ruin in the modern world; here some sections of it were still being built by craftsman who had dedicated their lives to its construction.

One old man, always seated in the church, and missing most of his hair and teeth, had made sure he related more stories every time he saw her. He said Joseph of Arimathea was the great-uncle of Christ who, as a youth, came to this town with his uncle. He constructed a wattle and daub hut to worship in while Joseph conducted business. Later, the hut was preserved by building a church over it, the remains of which were under the Mary Chapel at the western end of the Abby. Was there truth to the legends? Milena didn't know, but the wall between worlds was nearly nonexistent here. No wonder it was later destroyed. The Darkness didn't want such places to exist. Even after shedding tears for her family, she felt peace before leaving the Abby. But she was still cautious. She was in a land where she truly knew no one. No, it was she that was the unknown. And there, as she left the church, Samuel stood watching her. This had to stop.

"Have I offended you in some manner?" Milena addressed him calmly.

There had been a time that her fiery side was not so controlled. Always one to speak her mind, and still never one to stumble over truth, but her approach had changed. Being emotional made her like those confronting her. *Choose to be the adult,* her mother had said on many occasions. *Control shows strength.*

"Did you find answers in there? You are just like Bernadette, always looking to Him for help. Where was He when our daughter was taken?"

"I am sorry; I didn't know." The source of his sadness and anger was now clear.

"Your sorrow will not help me. He allowed it. He could have kept her from becoming sick."

"True, He could have stopped it. Why He did not I do not know. I do know we were given a choice on what this world was to become long ago. We have suffered ever since." Milena paused, the grief in this man was great. She couldn't imagine the loss of a child. Of Kyra. "I don't go in there simply for comfort," she said, nodding to the Abbey. "I can get that anywhere and it's fleeting. Nor do I need to be in there. Yes, it's important, but too many people treat it as another thing to do. Our creator is not limited to our buildings. He is not the small god so many make Him into."

"By why my little girl? What did she do?" Others had stopped on hearing Samuel's loud cries and watched his confrontation with Milena. "I am no bad man, no criminal. Why am I being punished? Did I not pray hard enough? She hurt no one, she was a good girl!"

"I have no doubt she was and neither you nor she were being punished. I wish being good was the solution. It sounds so easy, and while we weren't created to embrace evil, our free will is a power too great for us to wield alone. Someone always chooses corruption. This world will never be completely free of it, but what if we had no choice? No minds of our own?" She watched his eyes tear. The pain ran deep and she alone could not heal it. "The Darkness wants us to forget about the conflict that has raged since the Fallen declared their war. For us to pretend it's all a myth and accept that we are just another animal doomed to a brief, useless existence in the universe." Milena walked to Samuel and placed her hands on his arms. "We are so much more."

"But why did it happen to her?" Tears ran down his face.

"The answer is both easy and hard. The universe created for us is infected and our very essence exists here and beyond at the same time. That is the paradox we live in. We are torn. We have proven we cannot seal the rift on our own. Every one of us struggles because we are born knowing there is something better than all of this, whether we accept it or not." Milena's own eyes began to water as she felt Samuel's anguish. Few went through life without facing a loss they could hardly endure. She had lost her parents when she was seventeen. "As long as we live like this, not everything will be right. How could it?

Our soul was created in the Light, and here we are in this existence for a brief time, oppressed by the Dark One. But look past the shadows and at the glimpses of greatness, and the pleasure and beauty we do experience. See the intricate universe and how man stands above all other life. If there is no purpose, then what of all this? Even the Darkness can only hide for so long what is plain to see."

She could sense Samuel searching for words. Somewhere inside he didn't want to continue to suffer.

"My anger has torn at my soul for so long, it is easy not to see." Samuel looked into Milena's brown eyes. They were tinged with green, illuminated from within. "It is easier to hold on to anger than it is to see the answers."

"No one expects sorrow and anger to vanish overnight. Your daughter doesn't have to be forgotten. Do not stop speaking of her, remembering her. She will live on in the Light long after this world passes. What was her name?"

"Nicola."

"A beautiful name."

"She was beautiful," Samuel said, looking away. Then he looked at Milena. "She still is."

Milena smiled. "I better go, I have much to do today. See you later?" Samuel nodded and watched her as she walked away. She had peered into his soul and found a glimmer of light buried in the blackness. He looked toward the church as she left.

The time had come to release his anger.

Milena found one of the town's blacksmith shops and browsed the swords hanging from the walls. She picked up a short sword from a rack and tested its balance.

"That's not a toy, my lady," the blacksmith said, approaching Milena from behind. She spun around, handling the sword with ease. The blade tip stopped only inches from the blacksmith's nose.

"Can you make me two of these? Perhaps slightly shorter?" After overcoming his state of shock, the man, dirty and sweaty from his trade, shook his head.

"Yes, but how will you pay?"

"I have some coin." Her hosts had insisted on paying her a small wage. "I also noticed your children could use some new clothes." He had seven kids by her count, only one son barely old enough to help his father in the shop.

"Well?" She asked, raising an eyebrow.

The man had been staring at her, thinking. He hesitated, then finally spoke.

"I agree to your terms." He was a bit nervous with Milena still holding the sword.

"Sorry." She handed the sword to the blacksmith.

"When will they be ready?"

"Come back at next week's end." He returned the sword to its rack. "May I ask what your name is, my lady?"

When he turned, she was already gone and some of his children ran out after her, watching her walk down the street. She looked back and waved at them. Such beautiful little ones, who knew nothing of their uncertain future. They would rely on each other to survive and move the world forward, never giving up. Simple, yet strong. There were times, like in Samuel's loss, where all was clouded, but these people still had largely not forgotten the true nature of both man and the unseen. Her own people could learn something here. They had killed more in only a few years than had ever died in this supposed primitive past. Who would history judge as the barbarians and the civilized? At least she could help this family. Every person met was an opportunity to send a ripple through history and cause dramatic change without any chance of knowing the results in this lifetime. But the Darkness could plant seeds, too, and that was one reason she was here, to exterminate noxious weeds.

Six days passed before the swords were finished. Samuel made Milena two leather sheaths and a belt that would hold one at each side as she had insisted. She didn't plan to always carry them around town, unless it was late. Crime was rare, but she wasn't about to let her guard down. On this morning, like most, she went to the Chalice Well, west of the Tor, at the bottom of the aptly named Chalice Hill.

Through a grove of yew trees, the spring that never dried bubbled out of the ground. It still did so in her own time. Someday a wrought iron cover that looked like a round hatch would be placed over it. It was the design that was copied for the lid for their spring-fed well. Odd, though, they had bypassed Glastonbury on their travels. They had explored the British Isles, but here, perhaps the most sacred of all the ancient sites, they had never been. She drank from the well and filled containers to bring the water back to Samuel and Bernadette. Many claimed the water could heal or bring long life. Others wouldn't drink it because of its reddish hue. The Blood Spring, they called it. Probably caused by iron deposits, but local lore insisted the red appeared after Joseph of Arimathea buried the Holy Grail under the hill. Or was it the nails from the cross some said had been thrown in the water?

Milena sat near the waters listening to the stream carving a small path through the trees. Glastonbury Tor towered nearby and St. Michael's church was visible at the summit. The hill's terraced sides were once thought to be natural formations or the remains of farming. There wasn't much in the way of crops on the hill. Perhaps it was a labyrinth, as some had theorized, crafted through the great toil of forgotten souls. Maybe a processional path to the summit or a decent into the Celtic underworld of Annwm. So much lore and legend to muse over.

A monk approached her on the path that led from the Tor, interrupting her thoughts.

"My lady, I have come to gather water from the well." The man wore a simple brown habit and carried an earthen jar.

"Go ahead, I am finished here." She stood, but he didn't move, and stared at Milena with curiosity.

"You are the one who wishes to go to St. Michael's?"

"Yes." She paused, wondering if this man had answers. "That hill overlooks these lands like a guardian. It's a perfect place for a church. It's unworldly up there, looking over this village. Especially when we are blanketed by the morning mists. This entire region feels like it was created as a beacon from the next life."

"It has indeed been recognized as a great spiritual place for many generations." The monk's green eyes opened wide in recounting the history. "Why certain places on this Earth seem to straddle both worlds, I do not know. Something transpired here when man was still young. Before us, the pagans came and sensed it as well. They had forgotten some of the truths of their ancestors, but a sliver remained. When we first came, we brought what they had lost."

"Long ago, man began in one place," Milena said. She knew this history as well. "When he spread out across the world, beliefs changed, but tidbits of the first truths remained." Archaeology and genetics would affirm this history, once only codified in legend and the ancient religious texts. But this monk had no need of this knowledge from the future. "All are free to choose a path."

"Yes, but do all lead to the same place? Of course not, do all roads lead to the same town?" The monk became more serious. "One can always find a truth here and there, but the nature of people attracts them to beliefs that put them at ease. The One that created us came to us in a way we could comprehend and to uproot the Darkness from our hearts, but did not promise an easy life free of turmoil. What men would write this for themselves to follow? Certainly they could come up with something easier.

"Our power to choose forbids this world from ever reaching perfection. And yet, in all our failures, we were not abandoned. If we give over our weakness and join the rebellion against the Fall, we are promised something far greater when this life ends" He paused and held the Celtic cross that hung around his neck.

"We have shown the Celts where the truths that they know fit into the larger reality. It was not forced upon them; the fit was natural. It was expected. They knew something was behind the veil. Most people do. Soon Christ's Mass will be upon us and we will celebrate the birth with their evergreens and those of Germania. They respected the creation, as do we, seeing the designs of the Truth Maker. Like most others, they never felt complete. Even we do not, being of two worlds. Even those who do not search nor care about their place in the universe are haunted by a voice quietly asking one question:

"'Why do you run from me?'"

Milena had never run. Why was this man speaking to her this way? Her soul was drawn to the Light from an early age. Perhaps that made it easier in some regards, but she was never afraid to test and question — the Creator demanded it — even though part of her never doubted. Her intellect and ability to connect with all around her were equally strong. To read the emotions of others was as natural as breathing, as was an innate link to all created life. Passion that drew so fiercely from within that the results had nearly been uncontrollable in her youth. There were rumors of those who could control this element or that. Talk of healers and timewalkers and shapeshifters. Her other gifts, like Ethan's, were mostly more tactile. Strength and speed. Object manipulation had never been an easy one for her, but Kyra had shown early inklings of it. In spite of it all, they were still human and it wasn't always easy to choose the correct path. Darkness was always attacking the perimeters, causing misstep and loss. Even if one could not be turned, it brought great joy to the Dark One to make people stumble and forget.

To forget that everyone has a part in the Story, a purpose, and a choice to accept or turn away.

She once committed to never ceasing until hers was found. Nor was she ignorant to the games of the Serpent and his shadows. Keep people guessing and confused. Happy for a little bit at a time. Pretend truths could change like the wind or that everything was equally true. She knew even belief had to be rooted in fact. Realizations like that made her a target, as if she wasn't already for other obvious reasons. So here she was after a lifetime of journeys about to turn the page. The time for discussion was over.

"Listen, I have come here to protect a relic you have on the Tor." She approached the monk, who hesitated again.

"Who sent you?" He couldn't hide his surprise and took a step back. No one knew the relic was here. Impossible.

"I am an Arc Maiden, from a time and place distant from here." Milena pulled the cross from underneath her leather jacket, but remembered that the Cross of Lorraine would not be known. "I come preceding others who know the Light and will come through the portal among the stones. Together we will turn back the shadows that seek to take this land."

The monk only looked at her, not knowing what to say. She knew of the portal and a relic, but which relic?

"What relic do you seek?"

"I was not told which relic was here, only that it is."

She was as smart as a scholar, but her look and accent foreign, her dialect difficult to follow. Was she who she said or a deceiver from the enemy?

"I must return to the church and consult with the others. This is strange indeed. I know of none who are coming to our aid." In fact, he wasn't aware of any immediate threats. If something was pressing, the Watchers would send knights instead of a lone woman.

"Have you already forgotten to pay attention to those signs that those before you also neglected?"

The monk didn't answer, turned, and started back up the path. Milena watched him until he was a speck at the gate of the church. Tomorrow she would follow and no one was going to stop her.

⏳   ⏳   ⏳

The peace did not last. Ethan saw a flash of light from the hilltop, quickly followed by shuddering ground. The horses reared and screams came from the village. Shouts came from the hill.

"What was that?" Ethan yelled over the noise. The ground continued to rumble and homes in the village collapsed. People ran in the streets. Fires broke out in homes where the candles had toppled. Something catastrophic had happened at the church. Was Milena there?

"To the Tor! It is under siege!" Cináed turned his horse to the hill and took off down the lane through the town. What could have caused such a massive tremor? It didn't matter, Ethan needed to find Milena and was right behind Cináed. As they approached the hill, knights were fighting the intruders around the now ruined church. In the dimming light it was hard to make out who they were, but it was enough to see most of them weren't humans. They towered nearly twice over the tallest men, rippling with muscle. Surprisingly human-like faces roared under bald heads and brownish, dirty skin.

"Land trows!" Cináed yelled as he unsheathed his sword and drove his horse into a frenzied flight up the hill.

He gasped for air, only to choke on the stench of death. Latzi looked around and realized he was laying among the dead in the Misty Valley. The deceased Followers and natives had been piled in one area until they could be buried, or burned. Presumably it was the latter. A massive funeral pyre had been built near the other side of the narrow valley.

"What the..." Latzi tried to piece together his memories. Ahriman's lieutenant had come at him and slashed across his chest with a dark sword. Latzi had fallen backwards and lost consciousness. He was sure he had died. Everyone else also thought he was dead. In their haste, his evil comrades had been careless. They assumed the dark sword, forged in some evil place, would have killed him quickly. But his assailant wasn't terribly skilled and the wound wasn't deep. And what about that place under the Earth? Did evil lose some of its power there? That blue light had felt soothing. It didn't matter. That chaos was over.

What mattered is that he had been betrayed.

What else had been in the book the Keeper had taken from him? Ahriman had used him to find some map or scroll and then tossed him aside to die. He would pay for that arrogance. Latzi felt the anger course through his body. Dark lines slithered across his body, crawling from the black scar sliced from the sword. The corrupted energy fed on his rage as he embraced the darkness. The Sun would soon be below the hills and he could sneak across to the entrance to the Dark Hollow. He would enter the Rift and seek the relic for himself. Nothing could stop him.

Now that he was no longer entirely human.

CHAPTER
TWENTY-ONE

Kyra petted Scout, who had curled up next to her on the bed, not on his usual nighttime excursion. Three hours had passed since everyone had turned in for the night, but Kyra couldn't sleep. After returning from dinner, she had spent the evening trying to play games by the fireplace with Anna and Christina. She couldn't focus for long, her attention distracted by the flames dancing over the logs. Thoughts lost in the orange and red tendrils as faces of people flickered in and out of existence. Animals leaped among the light and, in the dark voids between flames, nameless creatures sought to escape.

Now the clouds that had filled the sky earlier had cleared and moonlight filled the room with soft light. The darkness in the southern sky was no more. Something had changed. Did it have something to do with wherever her father had gone? Had they succeeded? Why then hadn't they returned? Her father's friends had told Anna and Christina that they were going to camp that night in the woods. Kyra knew better, she knew that the great oaks held some sort of secret. She had felt presences watching her there. Beings of the Light. Her father had found where her mother had gone and was looking for her. Kyra wanted to help. She needed to.

She jumped off the bed, opened her closet, and found her backpack. It still had some snacks and gear from her previous walk in the woods with her father. She opened the door to the hall quietly and called back to Scout.

"Are you coming?"

Scout leaped off the bed silently and followed Kyra to her parents' darkened room. They never had nightlights around the house. The night hid nothing that could frighten any of them. She knelt before the bed and reached around underneath until she found the cherry-wood case. The polished surface reflected the moonlight and she hesitated. She knew not to ever touch what was inside and never had done so without her mother. This time she flipped open the small brass latch and opened the cover.

Two objects wrapped in white silk lay inside upon a red cushion. She held one and unwrapped it slowly. The light slid down the mirrored steel of the slender blade as Kyra turned it. The two-foot blade was a *katana*, a traditional sword from feudal Japan. Technically, her mother had explained, this shorter style was the *wakizashi,* but katana always sounded more fierce, not to mention easier to pronounce. The handle was wrapped in red leather and as Kyra held it, she felt the weight of the steel, a gift from an exchange student that stayed with her mom in high school.

Kyra had watched her mother practice with the blades for hours in the woods. She told Kyra that when she was older, she could learn how to wield them. They were perfect for those preferring stealth and speed over open combat.

"They're not something you would normally carry around with you," Milena had told Kyra. "Learning to use them is more about discipline and control." What Milena hadn't realized was that her daughter had memorized every move and technique just from watching. Her only problem would be that she was still too young and lacked the strength and size to use the blades against a competitor. Or an enemy.

Kyra removed two leather sheaths from the case and placed a blade in one. She did the same with the other after unwrapping if from its silk. There were some straps that attached to the sheaths so they could be worn on her back or waist. She put them in her backpack as best she could, leaving them sticking out the top, closed the case, and slid it back under the bed.

Sneaking downstairs on the wooden stairs had taken years of practice. In the kitchen she rummaged through the snack cabinet for more food, including some for Scout, not that he ever had a problem finding his own. After grabbing her heavy jacket in the foyer closet, she stopped for a moment and listened to the quiet of the house. There was movement in one of the bedrooms, then silence. No one had heard her. Unlocking and opening the front door without making any noise took a few minutes of slow movement. Kyra had never done anything like this before. There had never been any reason to.

Entering the calm night, the cold began to chill her legs quickly. Pajamas weren't the best cold weather gear; what was she thinking? *Haste clouds judgment,* her dad would have said. It didn't matter, her destination wasn't far, so she pulled her hood up and tried to make out the tree that stood on the hill. Not quite visible, even with the moonlight. She took her flashlight off her backpack and scanned the area ahead. The shadows, and what roamed in them, didn't frighten her, but she was still a young girl. Her gifts had never convinced her that becoming an adult needed to come sooner. Quite the opposite. This time she would make an exception. She had to help her parents and nothing, or no one, was going to stop her. It wasn't like she would be alone on her journey. Scout stood next to her.

"Are you going to help me find the oaks?"

The cat made a sound that was a cross between a meow and a growl which Kyra took to be a sign of agreement.

"Okay then. Here we go." She aimed the light forward and walked toward the darkened hill.

At the edge of the oaks, Kyra checked her watch. A little over a half an hour had passed, twice as long as the trek in daylight. She had gone slow, careful not to make noise. No one, or no thing, appeared to be out this night, but she kept looking behind her. Just nerves, no one could sneak up on her. Then she saw it, a light back at the house. She had to get to the oaks quickly.

She barely stepped between the trunks when a glow began to emanate from the water at the center of the circle. She clicked off her flashlight and put it back on her pack. The bluish light intensified and lit the trees as she entered underneath the towering canopy. It was an unearthly, yet comforting, feeling that was warm, washing away the frigid night. The water rippled making the light shimmer and chase all the shadows away from her.

Standing there, near the water, looking into it as it bathed her in light, Kyra could sense her parents. They were alive somewhere and not very far apart. Maybe they were together. She smiled and didn't even hesitate in what she did next. She stepped into the water, not feeling the wetness seep through her clothes. Scout paused, unsure if he should follow, and jumped back when the water swirled around Kyra, engulfing her as it formed a column of light that rose up into the trees and vanished from the bottom up, taking her with it. Scout jumped in after her.

When the light dimmed, there was movement among the trees.

Gasping for breath, Kyra landed on her hands and knees. Her long, messy hair covered her face. She flipped her head back and cleared the hair from her eyes. As they adjusted, she could see the stone monoliths around her, bathed in the Moon's glow as the remnants of the blue mist lingered around her. Her body ached as she stood and her clothes felt tight. She held her throbbing head and at first she thought she imagined the growl. The second time it woke her from her stupor. She turned and froze.

A mountain lion stared back at her.

"Wait a second." There was no projection of aggression as she looked closer at the lion and its stubby tail. "Scout?" The cat walked toward her and sniffed. Then it rubbed its massive head on her legs, moving them. Kyra petted Scout on his head, scratching him around the ears. "Uh, what's going on?" She held her hands in front of her face. They were no longer the hands of a child. She switched on her flashlight and shined it over her body.

"I don't think I'm eight years old anymore." Now taller with a body that had matured. "Maybe a twenty-year-old, give or take?" Her clothes threatened to split apart with every move, her pajama bottoms now more like shorts.

"Good thing my pj's were baggy." Scout cocked his head at the sound of her deeper voice. "Why did our little voyage age us, my little kitty?"

Scout offered no reply, still a bit bewildered. Trying to figure out what happened would serve no purpose. She needed to find her family. Dawn threatened in the eastern sky, so she soon would get a better look at her surroundings and go from there. "This place is spooky. It looks familiar, from a book or something." Scout didn't care one way or another. "Wait, mom has a model of it in the library. Stonehenge, wasn't it?" One of the few things she must not have paid attention to. It didn't matter; she was basically lost. Maybe she had been a little hasty in all of this after all.

"Not quite what we were expecting, Scout, is it?"

Then something entered her mind.

Why wait?

Mother is that you?

You can do far more than you know. Time and space are no obstacle to you.

The voice stopped. It was her mother. Where was she and what was she talking about? As Kyra tried to hear the voice again, a town appeared in her mind. A town that had been terrorized by evil. *So, that is where we must go.* She felt the Light surge through her body. She smiled at Scout. He wasn't going to like this.

"Are you ready?"

A moment later they vanished into the moonlight.

A short time earlier, Ethan had been riding hard after Cináed up the Tor. Knights fought the land trows — trollish monstrosities uttering a grating, unintelligible language — as remnants of the church burned around them. At the top of the hill, Cináed leaped from his horse and cut down a trow about to hurl a monk through the air. The trow roared as Cináed's sword slashed across its lower back and thrust deep into the beast's side. He pulled it free as the trow flailed madly; its last mistake was placing its head within Cináed's reach. He took it off with one powerful swing of his steel blade. As the evilspawn crumpled to the ground, another came running out of the fire, its clothes ablaze. It did not seem to care about its predicament, and Ethan rode to it and reared his horse. The kick of the horse crushed its chest and it flew backwards, falling into a burning heap. The knights finished off the last of the trows; there hadn't been many. Ethan dismounted his horse and ran into the ruins of the church.

In what was once the sanctuary, thick with smoke, the monks tried to get the fires under control with water from a nearby well. A trow lay among charred and shattered pews. Monks and knights attended the bodies of their fallen brothers. The altar and the wall behind it had been completely destroyed, leaving an open view of the fires that burned in the courtyard beyond.

Ethan went to one of the monks.

"What happened here?"

The monk finished tending to a knight who had died of his wounds.

"One of the sentries saw a dark shape approach the wall out of the darkness. It raised an object above its head and in an instant all before it lay in ruins. Whatever weapon was conjured destroyed that which used it. From below, hidden in the wood beneath the Tor, trows and frost giants rushed in killing any that stood against them. They took the sacred relic. In their hands it will be far more dangerous than whatever weapon they used here."

"Was there a woman here? Milena...was she here?"
No female bodies lay among the carnage.

"Yes, the Maiden Milena had come to us months ago and we would not let her in. We were guarding the relic, the True Cross that had been brought to us by the Empress Helena. As more Followers of the Dark One came to these lands, we secured it here. Or so we thought. We turned the Maiden away, not knowing her, but one day she revealed to me who she was. She knew of the relic and claimed she was preceding more like her. Watchers no doubt.

"We had been watching the Gate waiting to hear from those across the endless waters. We wanted to send the relic to their Citadel, but had been told to wait. Armies of the Evil One were gathering to strike them. The morning after I spoke to Milena, she came to the church and the knights tried to stop her from entering. They did not succeed; I intervened and allowed her to pass. The night prior I had inquired with the wife of the tailor where Milena was staying. Bernadette confirmed the truth of what Milena had told me. Since her youth she has had the Gift of Dreams. Few have knowledge of it, but I have known her since we were children. She foresaw Milena's coming and had found her near the Gate. Your maiden told us that you would soon follow."

"Where is she now?"

"See the corpse of the beast laying beyond the wall?" The monk pointed through the gaping hole to a dead frost giant, its white fur matted by blood. "The Maiden killed it as it tried to escape with the relic. Another frost giant captured her and the relic. They headed east, in the direction of Saken Castle. Darkness has been hovering over that place for months. Cináed wanted to lay siege, but too many men had gone to defend the Citadel."

Ethan left the monk and went outside to look for answers. The frost giant was larger than the trows and covered in dirty-white fur. It had a mouthful of sharpened teeth, now stained crimson. Its massive hands tipped with claws. What could create such monstrosities? Near the corpse lie two short swords. Ethan picked one up and wiped away the creature's blood. On the blade near each handle was etched the Cross of Lorraine. These belonged to Milena. The monk came up to Ethan, seeing his despair.

"She was unharmed and is likely a prisoner in the castle. She will surely stay that way since they most certainly recognized her as a unique prize. These shadows are led by a confused fool, a man in league with Dark One. He will not move the relic until a shadowmancer sends for him. We have not yet seen him in these lands."

"Nor did you see this attack coming."

"You are right; we did not." The monk put his hand on Ethan's shoulder. "It is up to you now to retrieve the relic. The others here have little chance to stand against the evil at the castle. You must lead this fight."

"How do you know that?" Ethan asked the green-eyed monk.

"Many years ago, the Dreamer was shown that a Watcher named Theodoric would someday come to these lands. He would be followed in a time of great darkness by one of his kin from a faraway land across the seas." The monk looked at Ethan for a moment and walked away.

Confused, Ethan watched him leave. Anger rose quickly. He had been a few minutes too late. Milena had been right here. Dawn's first light flickered in the eastern sky. He would not wait, he would leave now. He would not lose her again. Then from behind came a shuffling and the sound of rocks grinding.

A strange tongue began to speak.

***

At the edge of Glastonbury, Kyra wisped into existence. Scout, wild-eyed, stood next to her and hissed, not appreciative of the mode of transportation she had taken.

"You'll get used to it."

The town before them was in chaos. People ran every which way. Fires burned. People screamed. They didn't notice the strange girl and her frightening pet as she entered the town. Nor did her flashlight arouse curiosity as she walked the narrow streets. Not far into town she stopped in front of a relatively unscathed building. It was a tailor's shop.

"Wait here, I need some clothes." She wasn't quite sure how she would pay for them. There were probably a couple coins in her pack. Not enough. Maybe they would take the flashlight. Inside a woman attempted to return order to the shop. Clothes and tools were strewn everywhere.

"What happened here?"

Bernadette didn't look up. "Something happened up at the church. The whole land was shaken to its foundations." Then she turned around and stared.

"What is it? Yes, I know I look odd. I see this is a bad time, but I need clothes."

"Wait here." The woman went into another room and returned with a pile of clothes and a pair of boots. "These are yours."

"Mine?"

"I mean they should fit perfectly. I was making them for —"

"For me? You knew I was coming, didn't you? Was my mother here? Milena?"

"Indeed she was. It does appear little can be hidden

from you." Bernadette smiled and continued, "Woe to any man who courts you. Take these in the back and try them on."

"Thank you. My name is Kyra, by the way."

"I know." Milena hadn't spoken much of her family, though Bernadette had eventually managed to draw a little from her. She had left her family behind, including her young daughter. She struggled with the decision even though she planned on returning to them. "I can see your mother in you, Kyra." A striking young woman, though her long dark hair was curled, unlike her mother's. Nor was her skin tanned, but her piercing blue eyes were a window to another existence. Or was the power of the Light swirling in them? She had a sense of youth about her. "I do not recall how old she said you were."

"Well...that's a little bit complicated right now. I know, that doesn't make sense, but trust me, I'm a bit confused, too."

"I see. I am sure you will figure it out." Bernadette sensed truth, even if she didn't understand.

Kyra took the clothes into the room and removed her jacket and her pajamas. "Wow, you did look silly walking around looking like that." The riding skirt and the boots fit perfectly. As she buttoned her top, she stopped for a moment to look in a mirror. "Definitely not a little girl anymore. Taking after Mom, I see."

The necklace that hung around her neck caught her gaze. The gold triquetra was a symbol of the unity of the three Lights — the Trinity. Her father had given it to her a few years ago. A treasure found long ago in the woods. The white riding cloak that Bernadette made fit over her clothes. *White over black. Interesting. Like some sort of angel.* Underneath she attached the katanas to her belt. One last look in the mirror earned a "very nice, a perfect

fit" from herself. Back in the shop she found Bernadette.
"Where is my mother?" Kyra asked.

Before Bernadette could reply, Kyra collapsed on the floor.

CHAPTER
TWENTY-TWO

As the Sun rose on the troubled morning, its rays reached into the dungeon through the tiniest of windows and awakened Milena. She sat on the damp dirt floor of the tiny cell deep under Saken Castle. The iron manacles around her wrists weighed heavy and she tugged on the thick chain bolted into the wall with no avail. She had dreamed of Kyra. No, it wasn't a dream, she was here. They had spoken. Then she remembered killing a terrible beast and only a moment later being frozen by the touch of one of those hideous giants.

Her core still shivered, but light had found her even in this dark place. The weakness would pass and her captors would regret taking her. Exhausted, she fell asleep again. Then she dreamed.

A primeval rainforest surrounded her in every direction. Moss draped over the branches of sprawling Bigleaf Maples and Black Cottonwoods, dwarfed by towering Sitka

Spruce and Hemlocks. The ground, thick with centuries of decaying debris, silenced her footsteps. The sunlight flirted among the leaves from its distant source, just enough to keep the forest inviting for visitors to its realm. Peaceful sounds came from birds flying tree to tree and squirrels chirping from branches above. Solitude and quiet. A wooded paradise untouched by man. Milena knew this place, but when was she here last? Was it real or just an image conjured by the mind? As she walked along a path, a river splashed nearby and a hushed rumble hid in the distance.

As the trees thinned, she came upon the river, perhaps forty feet wide. Swift and clear and not terribly deep, Milena knelt at its edge and drank pure water. The minerals fed her tired body. Her ears caught the rumble again, louder now. As she looked up and down the river, a cloud of mist hovered over where the water dropped over an unseen edge.

She followed the path, worn by the animals who came to drink. Standing near the edge of the waterfall, the mist from the falling water surrounded her. Only a few feet further the water quieted and formed a deep, calm pool before flowing downstream through the forest. Milena then remembered her last visit to the hidden paradise.

She and Ethan had backpacked into the untouched forests of the Pacific Northwest on the Olympic Peninsula. For two weeks they intended to relax and completely leave everything and everyone behind. Here there were no people. No cars. No jobs. No clocks. The busyness that people often created for unclear reasons didn't exist here. Nor did their malice and hate. Ethan's profession —

if it could be considered a profession — was taking its toll. Like most jobs, it eventually gained control over most of life, but this did so in a different, darker, manner. Milena joined him on many of the missions. She too was worn by the endless struggle against evil men. It didn't matter that they had Gifts of the Light. They were still human. She wanted to step back from it all. Perhaps there would be another time and place for them to bring light to the shadows.

The time away from home weighed on her mind. Agents of the government for only a few years, yet the danger of being lost forever in the tangled web of global machinations threatened. True, they were not on any official payroll, but someday that could raise another issue. If the people in power could not control them, would they be considered a threat? The empty suits didn't frighten them; becoming numb to the world in which they fought evil did. Neither wanted that. Both knew this wasn't the last stop for them, but for now, it was time to move on. Especially if they wanted to start a family.

Looking up at the falls from below, Ethan caught himself being surprised that such a wonder still existed. An Eden hidden from the knowledge of most men. A reminder of a lost past. "When did we forget about places like this? It's like we have gone so far forward that we have started moving backwards."

"We forget that we don't belong here on this world." Milena had sat her pack down and removed her boots and socks. She sat on a rock at the river's edge and dangled her feet in the cool water. "Or at least in what it has become. This was for all of us, but we — I mean people — aren't like anything else in this world. Everyone is too busy to stop and wonder 'Why are we so different?'"

Ethan sat down next to his wife.

"I don't want to be busy anymore," Milena said as the water moved slowly around the pool. "What did people do before they complained about not having enough time? In some ways our lives are better, but what did we lose in the process? I can't remember a time before computers and cell phones and when having friends meant hanging out with people in person. Isn't that sad?"

"We've forgotten what is important. Our families, our friends and places like this." Ethan paused before turning to Milena. "And we have reached an end. The people we work for don't get it either. Most of them are lost in their schemes and power struggles. The government doesn't care about people. There's more for us, but it's not with them. We need to get back to finding our life before it's lost forever."

"It's settled then." Milena smiled and kissed Ethan quickly. "How about a swim?"

"Let's see, I'm in this beautiful paradise with a gorgeous woman hundreds of miles from humanity...I'm not sure..."

"Hey, pal!" Milena punched Ethan in the side and then he grabbed her.

"I'm not sure if I could ever leave this place." He kissed Milena, enjoying it for a few moments before she playfully pushed him away.

"You have to come catch me first." She stood and quickly peeled off her clothes and dived into the water, quickly surfacing at the center.

"And they claim mermaids are myth." Ethan followed his wife into the water. They would spend the next couple days camping near the falls. Time, here at least, had no meaning.

⧗   ⧗   ⧗

Those days were some of Milena's fondest memories. Here she was again years later in a dream, or was it? Her dreams had become real doorways long ago. Though, of late, she and Ethan had little utilized that gift. She found the rock she had swam from during those days in the lost Eden. Real or not, she dived into the cool waters. Refreshing and invigorating, she could spend hours in the living waters, washed pure, almost reborn. She had no sense of how much time passed.

Then something from the other world tore her back to reality.

Her eyes readjusted to the dim dungeon cell. Sounds came from the corridor. Then a twisted, ugly voice, wheezed.

"The master would like to see his prize!"

CHAPTER
TWENTY-THREE

Duncan watched as Ethan and then Conrad disappeared into the blue light. Now it was his and Kane's turn. Their destination would be quite different from Northern Europe or where they now stood. A harsher environment than where he made his home, but what had risen and fallen in the eastern Sahara for centuries, beckoned like a cryptic mystery from the past. Or was it a memorial full of warning from a dead civilization?

"So to Egypt?" Kane asked. "A little heat won't be so bad right now."

"No, it wouldn't," Duncan said. "It's hard to believe North Africa was once lush and beautiful. One wonders what is buried under the sands."

"It is a land of timeless mystery." Theodoric had been watching from the trees. "Where the sands have long fought against the water. Sometimes the desert loses, but it always returns stronger. The Nile it never did conquer, and its waters have preserved many peoples for centuries on a precarious edge. History upon history. City over city. Much had passed through there, most of it forgotten.

"It is also the land of the Oppression and the Exodus. And there the prophet said an altar would be built in their midst and a pillar near the border, and one day the Christ would go there as a child. Our history is embedded along the Great River, but as at every such crossroads of humanity, so do shadows of darkness simmer under its surface."

Duncan knew Egypt's mythos was littered with fusions of man and beast that he hoped were nothing more than fantasy. "Maybe the sands buried the darkness they once battled, forever."

"If only we were that lucky," Kane mused. "Odd, though, considering where we are going."

"What do you mean?" asked Duncan.

"Out there in the desert, between Egypt and Israel, a fortified monastery has a library with thousands of manuscripts. Probably relics, too. Yet it has remained un-scathed for centuries."

"And now it is known that it is the home of the *Book of the Second Death.*" Theodoric looked at them both. "I will now leave you. Go well and stand fast." With that, he disappeared through the oaks.

"Are you ready?" Kane looked at Duncan

"Yeah, let's go. Egypt, here we come." He managed a bit of a smile.

Moments later he and Kane nearly tumbled down the mountain as they blinked into existence. A rocky trail led down the dusty slope to the monastery, protected by massive adobe brown stone walls that blended into the surrounding soil.

"There it is," Duncan said, and realizing that he wasn't on just any mountain, continued, "and this must be Mount

Sinai." It felt good to be in the dry desert air again after the damp, rain-drenched forests.

"But there is no portal here." Kane observed as he rubbed his hand where a jagged rock had cut it. It was already healing, but even a Healer felt pain.

"Remember what Theodoric said about relics being a beacon?" Duncan asked. "A place like that is bound to have more than a couple."

"And a couple that could destroy mankind," Kane added as they began the descent down the narrow trail.

As they approached the gate of the fortress monastery, a monk returning from some place outside the walls stopped. It took a moment for Kane to comprehend why the monk was staring at them.

"We look like knights. He probably thinks we are ghosts from the Crusades."

"Brother monk," began Duncan, not sure if the man would understand, "we need to speak to your abbot. An urgent matter is pressing and there is little time."

"When two men appear on the mountain, either Moses and Elijah have returned, or two of our kind. In either case it would be an urgent time." The monk approached them. "From the looks of you, neither are Moses or the prophet. Just as well, the place is a bit of a mess. I am Archbishop Tychicus, abbot of St. Catharine's. You speak some language of the Britons? I journeyed there an age ago, is that from where you have come?"

"I'm Duncan." He held out his hand not knowing if it was proper manners with a monk or if the greeting was known in these times. "And this is Kane." Tychicus hesitated, then cautiously took their hands, still not completely sure of the strangers. "We come from the New World, across the ocean, where we have defeated an army of the Dark One. They stole a scroll describing this place."

"This place is no secret, what would they want that we have?" Tychicus was disturbed. He knew what was hidden within the towering walls. Few others did.

"The scroll detailed what is hidden here," Kane said. "Of particular interest to the shadowmancer is the *Book of the Second Death*."

The abbot said nothing, he didn't have to. Despair fell over his face.

"Follow me." Tychicus led them through a door high on the wall and through a maze of alleys and courtyards to a well. "Drink. Your journey has been long and appears to be distant from its conclusion." Both drank the water and were surprised by its coolness in the desert.

"You seek to destroy the book, do you not?"

"If it is such a danger to men, why not?" Duncan asked. "What benefit can it be?"

He had heard Theodoric's reasons, and as rational as they were, he would gladly make an exception in this case. The danger was now too great. The abbot hesitated for but a moment before he began.

"The book is written in cryptic dark languages, difficult to decipher. Occasionally we have gleaned useful information from its pages. Locations of dark places, their secret conjurings that can kill thousands. Few, though, are brave enough to study it for long. Its pages are heavy with malice and hate, oppressing even the most faithful with darkness." Tychicus paused. He was troubled simply speaking of it. Few others than him had ever opened its covers. "It is the last copy known and has proven to be a valuable weapon against the Dark One. His minions had long forgotten about it and use lesser tomes. Those pages are deadly, very much so, but they are tiny shadows of this one. Some have wanted to destroy it from the beginning. We will commit it to the flame only when no other option remains."

"We don't know when the shadowmancer or his forces will arrive. Soon though, I expect." Kane asked Duncan, "How can we know when in time they will arrive?"

"We went through the portal to the same era that we left. That is the only time they can be absolutely sure that the book is here. They are too close to take any risks. I don't know if they expected to win in the Misty Valley, but I do know they got more than they bargained for." He didn't like the uncertainty. Hopefully, as Watchers, their souls could see a little further than their physical eyes and minds.

"I realize Watchers are skilled, but that will not be enough to stop whatever horde the Dark One throws at these walls —" The sound of horses running through the gorge interrupted Tychicus. Duncan and Kane ran to the stairs that climbed the wall. About two-hundred knights rode toward them. Among their ranks were the cat siths of the Misty Valley. Above flew a pair of rocs.

"That should be a good start," Duncan said to the abbot who had reached the top of the stairs last.

"Hopefully, this will be enough," Tychicus said.

As dawn broke the day after the battle, even with the defeat of so much evil, the sunlight still didn't penetrate the Dark Hollow. Ahriman and his remnant had gathered near the entrance of the Rift. After securing the scroll, he and his lieutenants had ridden east through the Misty Valley and followed a hollow to the south. A rearguard of warriors waited for them in a hidden valley that led back to the Dark Hollow.

The fomorii were left to defend the retreat. Their stand would be their last. Theodoric, caught up in the aftermath of the battle, had quickly forgone assembling a force to follow the fleeing survivors. By the time he realized his error, it would be too late. The folly was to Ahriman's advantage, as his incompetent sorcerers had yet to open the portal. Latzi had been a pawn, but at least he could open the Rift. Those who could do so easily were far too rare. Nonetheless.

"Rajnai, you will go to Britain and see if that dimwit Saken has found the relic. Then dispose of him." Ahriman looked at her Indian face, partly hidden by her long hair, black as night. Many generations had passed since Rajnai had left the Indus Valley, yet she had aged little. She held her black cloak around her, but he knew very well what was hidden beneath. He could see her collar studded with rubies, cut with the faces of demons. It had been his gift to her after Rajnai had submitted to him and he had guided her to levels of depredation she could have scarcely imagined. Obsidian eyes matched a dark beauty that few others than her master dared to look upon. She was also a vicious warrior. Her skill at combat and stealth was legendary, few could challenge her power, but she stayed behind during the assault to protect the Rift.

"Nothing would please me more, my master." Ahriman thought he caught the barest hint of a smile. Perhaps not.

"Meet us in the desert when you are finished. There we will call forth the undead armies of the Nile. Man will regret dismissing so much to myth. Nothing is left to interfere with our taking of the *Book of the Second Death.*" He had promised to make Rajnai his queen once they ruled the remnants of man. Maybe he would find another. Was she not already his slave and was not that position enough?

"What of the relic the Crusaders carried at Hattin?"

Rajnai would have sent Latzi after the relic, had he survived the battle. Such a shame, he would have made a nice pet.

"The relic did not help the Crusaders. A worthless scrap of wood they worshiped; it brought them death, nothing more. Time to forget it and ready ourselves for the new reign of the Dark One that is at hand. The world will soon tremble as death cuts them down before us!" He turned to one of his sorcerers. "You had better be ready to open the portal."

"Yes, your darkness, we are ready," said the cloaked man, his eyes hidden. If this didn't work, the Dark Hollow would be his grave. Rajnai had always had some skill as a Timewalker, but her control was imperfect, unstable. He wouldn't allow her to open it on her own for all of them.

"Then let us leave this place. We have waited long enough."

Rajnai had more questions, but thought better of asking in front of the others. Hadn't the Followers used another relic at Hattin? Maybe just another legend. Ahriman's focus had abandoned the objects of power in favor of this other plan. Odd, though, he hadn't discussed it with her in private. They had spent little time in the darkness together as of late. Soon this would all be over, but first one more task for her master.

One by one they entered the gorge and soon wind howled through the rocks and reddish light filled the hollow. Latzi hid behind a cluster of twisted maples watching as the shadowmancer and his death wielders vanished into the gorge. Was Ahriman right? Was the relic used at the Horns of Hattin a fake? The Crusaders had lost that battle. Badly, in fact. But wasn't the power of a relic contingent on who wielded it? They never sought to use it as an actual weapon. And would the holy army bring a relic they didn't believe authentic? Or did someone purposely lead them astray?

There were too many dark Followers, and Watchers, in Britain. Arriving before the battle in Hattin ended was his best hope. If the holy relic was a fraud, he could be stuck there. He would be killed with the rest of them. Or would he? Latzi ran his hand over the darkened skin of his arm, changed by the black blade. No, he would no longer easily die. He had learned much in the forgotten labyrinths beneath the Mayan ruins in Uxmal, more than he had dreamed possible. The immortality he had been promised under the temples no longer alluded him.

⌛   ⌛   ⌛

Latzi had traveled throughout the Western Hemisphere seeking esoteric knowledge, but Mesoamerica kept calling to him. He quickly surmised from his studies that those civilizations must have appeared a contradiction to the Spanish. The Aztecs and Mayans built towering temples and stone cities with precision that rivaled Giza. Vast markets and palaces on par with the best in Europe. Mayan astronomers calculated calendars based on the movements of Venus that were accurate to a day over five centuries. The *Books of Chilam Balam* eerily, and accurately, predicted the end of the Mayan world at the hands of "men of the east."

They were also the people that sacrificed thousands to placate their gods.

It was too bad, Latzi thought, that by the time the Spanish encountered them, the Mayan peoples had already largely destroyed themselves. Conflict and their populations strained the lands. Terrible droughts had hastened their demise. Most of their sprawling cities had already been abandoned, their people disappearing into the jungle and absorbed by other peoples. An empire that had rivaled those of the Old World had lay dying long before Columbus was born. Not that it would have mattered. The Spanish would still have conquered them, sooner or later, but why the haste to destroy what remained of the Mayan culture?

Greed and the belief that the natives were inferior primitives drove the Conquest. Wealth and property had alluded the Conquistadors in the Old World, but nothing would stop them in the New. Directives from the crown to convert natives in religion and allegiance were laughed at and used as an excuse to torture and enslave. The destruction of countless Mayan writings was instigated by a fear of what their astrologers and priests were conjuring. Perhaps the Conquistadors and their friars did find the horrible and unspeakable that were far worse than the Mayan nobles and priests who ate the flesh of the sacrificed victims. Still, invaluable history was lost in the purges, and many died. What most intrigued Latzi in the histories that he read was a simple suggestion.

Not all of the Mayan codices had been burned. Not all had been found.

The day he arrived at what was once Uxmal in the western Yucatán of Mexico, not far from the coast, was a dreary affair. Stepping off the tourist bus into a deep puddle left from the remnants of a hurricane, Latzi stared at the ruins of the Palace of the Governor towering above. Facing the southeast, it watched for the rising of the Eveningstar. On the summit of one pyramid was the Dwarf's House, a building too small for humans, so what had lived there? At the Pyramid of the Magician, said to have been built in one night by a Mayan god, many chosen were sacrificed. Darkness still lingered after all those centuries, pulling at his soul. It was time to ditch the tourists and their cameras and incessant jabber.

He hid among the ruins until nightfall, waiting for the last tours to leave. Then he would enter the Magician's realm. The myths described multiple levels in the under-world, entered through caverns and cenotes over which the temples had been built. Were there undiscovered cat-acombs under the temple? Latzi was sure *Xibalba*, the Place of Fright, lay beneath Middleworld.

Early morning came before he found it. One of the temple rooms had been roped off from tourists. The room absorbed the rays from Latzi's flashlight like a black hole. He walked around the stone walls, curiously absent of decoration and carvings. No doors, no windows, but a small pile of dirt in a corner caught his eye. The room was clean except for that one corner. Why? He brushed the dirt away to reveal a glyph of a grotesque skull carved into the base of the wall. Someone had tried to hide it. Its mouth hung open creating a small gap into which the light disappeared. He put his hand in the skull's mouth, felt around and pulled a lever. The stone shifted forward, and after a pause, the wall shuddered.

Latzi moved back as an outline of a door appeared in the wall. He approached it with caution and excitement, pushed, and the door swung slowly inward. He entered the dark hall and when the door closed behind him, fear tried to conquer his mind.

The hall led to stairs descending to rooms deep under-neath the pyramid. Few had stepped foot in the dark abyss for centuries, because virtually none knew of its ex-istence. But someone did. Unlit candles and torches scented of recent fire. Neatly organized rooms full of lost scrolls and forgotten books oppressed the mind; Mayan codices long thought destroyed. Others came from older times and some more recent; a repository of black thoughts. Who watched over the place? Latzi looked behind him. No one was there. Now he would begin his education.

Days passed before Latzi left the ruins to return to a local town for supplies. Before reentering the pyramid, he tried to imagine what it would have been like living there during the height of the empire. Sometimes in the twilight, strange lights flickered out among the ruins; a greenish glow hovering over the rocks. To the south, in Inca lands, it was known as the *la luz del dinero*. The money light. Signs of treasure, some thought. Or something emitting from the rumored hundreds of miles of subterranean tunnels and caverns. It reminded him of why he was here. If only he could have lived here when the Mayans ruled at their pinnacle. Perhaps he could use the Rift to travel back before they collapsed. If his own world couldn't be conquered, maybe he would leave.

By lanterns and candlelight, he learned about the portals, like the Rift near his home, which his family had not been able to use. Only a Follower hardened from all light could travel through the darkness. There were some Timewalkers of such ability who could use any portal or need none at all. He also learned of the creatures of myth that weren't so mythical. Some still roamed hidden, waiting. Others could be called on or reached through time and space. Faded pages told of hideous experiments to create man-beasts and alter men into giants and immortals. One book, not so ancient as the others, but still quite old, shocked him.

It told of the legends of the Misty Valley.

Latzi sat in the flickering light, absorbed by what he read. He had heard some of these accounts from his father. Stories and tidbits of truth gleaned from native tales.

Something under the mountain. Relics of great power. Secrets and scrolls. Maps of misplaced objects and hidden realms. Not all of it was certain, but it was more knowledge than he had been taught. He looked up. An overwhelmingly dark presence had entered the room. Latzi turned. A hooded man stood behind him.

"Who are you?"

"I am the Caretaker of this place. A servant of Ahriman, one of the Dark One's unchallenged shadowmancers. We have been watching you since you arrived." The man's face was hidden from the dim candle lights scattered around the room. Latzi somehow knew it was better that way. "You are from the Dark Hollow. Have you found what you are looking for?"

"Yes, I have." Latzi picked up the book. The Caretaker didn't seem to be any danger to him. "This book tells of the Misty Valley. Powerful relics may still lie hidden under the hills beyond the cave. I have felt power there. Something that the Dark One surely would want."

"Relics you say?" The Caretaker stepped forward and took the book from Latzi. He skimmed the fragile pages with his skeletal fingers and stopped for a moment, a brief moment, over one section. "This is interesting indeed."

"Can this be of use to the Dark One?"

"I must consult with Ahriman. Remain here and continue your search. I will return." He closed the book and left the room.

"Wait!" Latzi ran into the hall.

Too late, the Caretaker had vanished with his book. Annoying, but he knew something for certain now. Whatever vestiges of fear from the place that surrounded him, and of the dark world that he had fashioned for himself, were now gone. He knew his time to return into the world would soon come.

⧗   ⧗   ⧗

Now, infected with the evil he had craved for so long, Latzi felt no fear. He entered the gorge. The Rift, *his* Rift, awaited him.

CHAPTER
TWENTY-FOUR

Kyra awoke with a start. Scout sat in the corner watching her, where he had waited for her to stir. She had forgotten how large the feline had become. Her back ached from the stiff bed in a backroom of the tailor's shop. She sat up rubbing her eyes at the sunlight streaming through the window, then felt the sore lump on the side of her head.

"What happened?" Scout walked over and Kyra scratched his chin. It was more of a rhetorical question. She knew what happened. Transporting herself through time had drained her body. In a way, the whole experience was mind-boggling. On the other hand, she grew up knowing she could do what other kids could not. She could see into the minds of people. Know their thoughts. See right into their souls. It was something she had to learn to control. Invading someone's mind without profound cause was wrong. And those beings who weren't human, or not entirely so, couldn't hide from her. They feared that she would become another like her parents, but stronger. She looked over herself again. No, coming through the portal as a grown woman was more shocking to her than hurtling through time, or place to place. "We won't be doing that again for awhile." Scout let out a growl of agreement.

Bernadette walked into the room. She nearly dropped the pitcher of water she was carrying.

"Oh dear! A friend of yours?" She didn't move a muscle.

"It's okay. Scout is my pet cat." She scratched him between his ears. "Maybe 'pet' isn't a good description anymore. Long story. Don't worry, he won't hurt you. Sit down, Scout."

He sat and watched Bernadette as she filled a cup with water and then a bowl. She cautiously set the bowl in front of Scout and he lapped it up. In a few seconds the bowl was empty so Bernadette refilled it.

"See, he's just a big kitty."

"If you say so. How are you feeling? You took a nasty fall."

"The side of my head is a bit sore. A little weak, but we have to be going." Kyra drank the water and stood, still a bit wobbly on her feet. Bernadette helped her stand.

"Are you sure you must go so soon?"

"My family needs me. I've been here too long already."

"I know. I had to ask." Bernadette looked out the window. It had become a clear day. A good sign perhaps? The town was full of activity with people running about to fix the damage. "The knights rode to Castle Saken. Milena, I mean your mother, was taken there. My husband is readying a horse for you."

"Thank you. I appreciate all that you have done for me."

"Here, you will need these." Bernadette handed Kyra the katanas.

"Thanks. Hopefully, I won't need them." She tied them to her belt and put on her riding cloak. "Ready Scout?" Scout stood and followed them out to the street. Samuel had the horse waiting for them.

"This is Alice. Ever ride one of these?" he asked.

"Well, once when I was younger, at a fair." Kyra laughed, then mounted Alice like the horse was her own. Taking the reins, Kyra walked Alice around and faced Bernadette and Samuel.

"Follow the northeastern road. It will take you straight to the castle," Samuel said. "Saken is a despicable lord who has long had his eyes on our town. It appears he has aligned himself with the Dark One. He has whatever was hidden in the church." Samuel wondered what was so valuable as to incite last night's catastrophe. Some relic no doubt. Most were fakes. What good would they be if they were not?

"He also has my mother. That will be his last mistake. Thank you again for your kindness." Kyra turned and rode through town, breaking into a run after she cleared the last buildings. Scout followed her with ease, attracting many gasps from the townsfolk.

"May the Light go with you, my child." Bernadette took Samuel's arm in hers as Kyra rode out of sight.

The twisted old dungeon master opened Milena's cell and his filthy, stench-drenched ogre of an assistant unchained her from the wall and pulled her to her feet. "Don't fight, princess. Our master would hate for us to damage you."

"Careful with her, slime-wretch!" The dungeon master, hunched from his years in the labyrinths beneath the castle, ruled his domain among the rats and decay. King beneath the abhorred lighted world above. Little light existed here, other than the dim torch he carried. Many decades had passed since he took the name Undertaker for himself, serving under many rulers. He led Milena through the damp catacombs past many cells. Some held the remains of withered dead. Others were occupied by those who prayed for death to come soon. Milena didn't say a word, but soon she would sweep away the evil in this place. The frigid darkness of the frost giants had left her. The water. The Light. Her energy was restored. She could easily overcome her captors. Patience.

They climbed a narrow stone stair to a wooden door, which the lord of the dungeon pounded. "I have the king's mistress. Open!"

The door opened and he cringed backwards at the light. Two guards in black armor entered; one grabbed Milena and pulled her into the hallway. The other closed the door behind him leaving the other two to their kingdom of hopelessness and gloom.

Milena found the castle surprisingly well lit. Apparently the king didn't want the complete darkness his monstrous allies enjoyed. That would change. This kind of alliance only led down a road of ever faster hardening to the world. The king may had already passed the point of no return. From the looks of the skulls mounted in little coves along the walls, this was certain. The skulls had the names of who they once were etched on metal plates beneath them. These were conquered enemies of the king. Their blackened bones looked like they had been scorched by flames. At the end of the grotesque hall of trophies, they entered a stairwell and ascended two floors. Entering a large hall, they led Milena to a double oak door at the far end. This hall was stark and dim. The shadows tried to run from what little candlelight lit the hall. At the end, two guards opened the doors and her captors led her inside.

Stolen treasures from people of the kingdom filled the expansive ornate chamber. Exquisite Persian carpets covered the cold stone floors. Hand-carved furniture made from oaks older than the castle lined the walls. A timber-framed, curtained canopy bed pressed against the furthest wall, situated between two closed windows that overlooked the courtyard below. Emerging from a small door to Milena's right, at the center of the room, a man appeared. Presumably this was the king.

"My Lord King, here is the maiden as you requested."

"Leave us." The king looked Milena over. Her hands were still shackled. "First, remove those irons." The soldiers did so without question then promptly left. The doors shut behind them.

"I am Lord Saken. This is my home. Welcome." Saken was a tall man for his era. Red hair to his shoulders and a short, triangular beard. Clothed in dull silver chain mail with a sword at his side and a purple cape, he was ready for battle even in his chambers. At least he tried to project that perception. He looked her over again, luridly. "I hope you were not treated badly, they put you in the dungeon before first consulting me."

Milena didn't answer. She wasn't impressed with the grandiose Saken. More than a bit infatuated with himself, to say the least. Now, how was she going to extract herself from this situation? A battle sword was mounted above a bureau to her left. On a table at the center of the room sat the jeweled reliquary that held the relic. The white box was inlaid with jewels of many colors, primarily red, that formed an eight-pointed red cross on its lid. It was the same box that the monks had shown her before the frost giants and their disgusting allies had attacked the church.

"Yes, it is here. It is undamaged. I was surprised to learn that such a beautiful creature was found defending it. The frost giant claimed you killed one of his kind. I do not believe it."

"Perhaps you should."

"Ah, tough and brash. You will soon learn that attitude will not work here, precious. You will submit quickly or suffer at the hands of the Undertaker in the cells of his nightmare until you do."

Milena didn't sense any black magic from this man. Nor the slightest ability to cross the veil. He was no conjurer, only a power hungry man bent on subjugating men and building an empire to suit his delusions of grandeur. He did have that long sword, though. It wouldn't be enough. "You will get nothing from me. Soon others will arrive and tear down the little fantasy you have built here."

"Fantasy?" Saken laughed. "Dear one, here is where all peoples across the Isles will send tribute. I will then conquer those across the waters if they do not bow to me. History will forget Alexander and call me Saken the Great!"

He was mad, and madmen were dangerous. She had to be careful. "That relic is a fake. I opened it myself. I came to steal it, but it's a fraud." Milena hoped her bluff would distract Saken from his exhortations.

"Please, do not lie to me, dark-haired one. But if you are correct, your fate is still the same. You shall soon wear a collar of iron etched with my name. All will know to whom you belong, and you will learn obedience. Guards!" The doors opened. "Watch her while I change into something more comfortable." Saken went back into the side room and closed the door.

Vile man. There was only one man who touched her, and he wasn't him. Outside of the windows birds called. Ravens. Milena closed her eyes. Would they come? Or were they enslaved to this evil place?

"I see you are preparing yourself. Good." Saken had changed out of his armor into a golden robe made from Oriental silks. "Guards, leave us and do not enter unless I call on you." The flapping wings grew louder, their shrieks piercing. "Cursed birds." As Saken stepped to the windows, the glass shattered and knocked him to the ground. A black wave of feathers poured through the opening, filling the room; some swirled into a protective cyclone around Milena, while others attacked the guards. More soldiers entered and hacked at ravens with their swords. Some were felled, but the rest overwhelmed the men, attacking with their beaks and talons, quickly drawing blood.

Milena opened her eyes and they burned fiery green.

She ran to the sword, grabbed it and the reliquary. More men charged up the stairs. She didn't know how many and didn't want to find out. Even she could be overcome, though not easily. Fight only when necessary. The windows were her only exit. As she leaped through, the ravens swept around her forming a funnel of air that let her fall safely to the ground below. Landing on her feet, Milena nearly dropped the relic. The birds left as an overwhelming presence of evil came over her. Thunder cracked overhead and she looked to the sky. Clear except for the ravens that flew above. From atop a wall to her left, a cloaked figure stood and called out an evil incantation. Swarms of crows burst from outside the castle and attacked the ravens, engaging them in a vicious death match. Birds fell all around the courtyard and a black snow of feathers floated through the air.

"Ahriman was right. Saken is a weakling. He could not handle you, but I shall." Her hood had fallen, revealing her face of Indian decent to Milena. It was unusual to encounter that race in Britain in these times. The sorceress jumped from the wall, her black cloak floating in the air. "Give the relic to me and I will not be as harsh in your death."

Milena raised the sword and backed into the courtyard as the woman slowly approached her. This was no local thug. The evil surrounding her was unmistakable. There was no where to run. The gate was closed, knights gathered on the walls and they would soon be streaming from the keep. A frost giant guarded the gate, no doubt unhappy about what she did to its friend. A well was near the center of the stone courtyard. She would have to run. The witch chased after her, but Milena reached the well, dropped the relic in the bucket, and unlatched it sending it crashing to the bottom. She spun around and raised the sword with both hands above her head. Rajnai stopped short and drew her *talwar*. The long, curved saber was etched with charred symbols that memorialized her many kills. From the pommel protruded sharpened spikes tarnished by those deadly encounters.

The blade came down hard at Milena, but she knocked it away. Again and again she attacked the sorceress. Rajnai deflected the strikes, but didn't stay on the defensive as they circled each other. The women traded blows fiercely with inhuman speed, swords twirling through the air and clashing in a grinding of steel. Knights who had entered the courtyard could only stand and watch as the two dark-haired warriors tried to disarm each other. Milena grew weary. Her opponent obviously did this much more than she. The sword wasn't her normal weapon. Heavy and cumbersome, holding it two-handed slowed her movements. They locked blades again and Milena landed a blow with her boot to Rajnai's chest. She spun backwards and nearly fell to the ground.

"That is the last time you will touch me. Once I bring you to the edge of death, I will offer you to the *vetala*. They will feed upon you before you become one of them." Rajnai, though, was surprised at Milena's ability. She too was tiring. Who was this woman? It had been ages since someone had challenged her so. "Do you think you can defeat all of us?" Rajnai said as she motioned to the knights. Then she spoke one of her incantations; her sword darkened more.

"Your evil will not harm me, wench." Milena stood her ground as Rajnai charged her.

As their swords clashed, Rajnai saw the light burning in Milena's eyes. A fear she had never felt before swept through her. This woman was one of them, a Watcher of the Light. Ahriman claimed any that remained were such a shadow of their ancestors, that they would be of no consequence, and yet here was the woman. A horn sounded from beyond the castle walls, breaking Rajnai's concentration for a second. It was all the time Milena needed to spin away and slash her side. Rajnai doubled over and grabbed her ribs, blood seeping over her hands. Milena kicked her under the chin, slamming her into the stone courtyard. The *talwar* skidded across the ground and Rajnai didn't move.

Milena ducked as the gate behind her exploded into a mass of splinters. Through the cloud of debris, a stone creature launched itself at the frost giant knocking it to the ground. The two inhuman brutes wrestled and pummeled each other, destroying anything that was unfortunate to be in the way. The arctic monstrosity smashed a wagon over the head of his foe. It had no effect on him, nor did the horse that the giant broke over him, other than making the stone man more angry. After one crushing blow to the frost giant's head, he grabbed its leg and launched it through the air. It landed among Saken's knights, flattening nearly a dozen of them. The stone elemental roared as knights led by Cináed and Ethan entered the courtyard through the dust and debris.

"Ethan!" Milena saw her husband and almost didn't believe her eyes.

"Behind you!" Ethan drove his horse and the other knights followed his charge. Milena turned and saw Saken's knights raising bows, and others running toward her. She was caught in the middle; there was no time to think. She ran to the well, ducking behind its stones as arrows flew around her. Ethan jumped from his horse and barely stopped the momentum that propelled him towards the first wave of foot soldiers. They came at him with swords drawn, but no one was going to stop him from reaching Milena.

His sword was tinged with blue as he swung it at his attackers, cutting through swords and bodies. As the next swarm came, more experienced fighters engaged him. None could match his speed as the energy flowed through him. He moved as if nothing but air stood in his way. What he lacked in technique was more than compensated by brute force. Bodies piled around him as he finally reached Milena. He started to breathe again as he saw her by the well. The dead lay at her feet. The woman who could find such peace among the trees and their inhabitants was as lethal as a jaguar in a fight.

"Are you all right?" He held Milena by the arms.

"I'm fine, but there's no time for this now."

The fighting stormed around them as their allies clashed with the enemy.

"You think so?" He turned and took down one of the black armored knights. They went back to back. "Reminds me of that time in Mexico."

"Great vacation that turned into." Milena disarmed another attacker and used him as a shield against incoming arrows.

Ethan slashed another and grabbed his head and bounced it off the stones of the well.

"Where's the relic?"

"Down there." Milena nodded at the well as she fended off another attacker. The arrows had begun to die, but one more flew past. The stone creature was making quick work of Saken's finest. Most were now retreating into the keep.

"What is that thing?"

"Stonecor. Theodoric sent him after me to help until they can send more people through. They're cleaning up a mess in the Misty Valley. We just lived through a battle there."

"Explain later, we need that relic." She began to pull the rope up and Ethan helped her. "Where's Kyra?"

"She's back home."

"No." Milena grabbed Ethan's arm. "I felt her. She is here." Milena caught the bucket and pulled out the reliquary.

Ethan looked at her.

"Are you sure?"

"She came through the portal at Stonehenge, right before Glastonbury was attacked. I know it. I tried to talk to her. I don't know if she heard me. I thought she did." Milena's eyes filled with tears. Now she was unsure of her daughter's fate.

"We'll find her. She must be near. Someone would have seen her." Milena calmed. Why hadn't he sensed

Kyra's presence? He looked around; the battle was ending. He managed fairly well, twice in two days, he had thought his gifts had fully returned. Had he fallen that far? No matter, something else was looming. This battle was over; the knights and Stonecor had silenced Saken's warriors. The last of them barricaded themselves in the keep. He turned to Milena again.

"Okay. We'll find her." Milena whispered. She finally had a moment to relax. Her husband had found her. Ethan had come. She hugged him tightly and kissed him, letting it linger. It would have been a nice prelude to when they were back home to normalcy, had it not been interrupted by Saken's booming voice.

"You have not won yet, my friends! Searbhan, rise from your slumber! It is time to feed on the flesh of our enemies!" From beyond the castle walls, in the moors to the north, an Olympian roar caused all to shudder.

"Great. Sounds like another Balor," Ethan said.

"Who?" Milena asked.

"Later."

"We need to go now!" Cináed gathered his men and the injured. "Ethan, we must leave before this beast arrives."

"I know, I met his friend back home. Though he is no longer with us."

"What do we do with the relic? Do we use it?" Cináed asked.

"No, it's power is too great. We need to get it away from here and back through the portal. Then Milena and I must find our daughter."

"Your daughter is here?"

"Yes, somewhere." The roar came again, and then screams. Searban was passing through a village, destroying as he went. His footfalls could be felt through the ground. "Let's go now."

"Others are coming! Wild men! There are —" One of their knights that had climbed to the top of the wall called out and was cut short by an arrow and fell to the court-yard.

Ethan found his horse and another for Milena. Ethan took the relic with him and then pulled Milena's short swords from his saddle.

"I believe you lost these."

"Thank you. You're always picking up after me." She smiled, taking the swords, tossing the one she had bor-rowed from Saken's room.

"I don't mind, miss."

"Fleeing will not save you!" Saken yelled from the castle wall.

Cináed's men had broken into the keep, but had not reached Saken.

"Lend me your bow," Milena said to one of the knights.

"Yes, my lady."

Milena took the bow and aimed for Saken as he prepared to taunt them again. Only a few syllables left his mouth before the arrow reached him. He fell over the wall and plummeted to the courtyard.

"Thanks for the stay. The dungeon was lovely." She tossed the bow to its master. Ethan shook his head. It had been some time since he had seen that side of Milena. The green fire in her eyes. The hatred of all things evil.

They rode through the gate first. Cináed and his knights followed. Some stayed behind to secure the castle to slow the wild men and their giant leader. Ethan wondered if it was a suicide mission against the beast, but the relic couldn't fall into the hands of the Dark One's minions.

No matter the cost.

CHAPTER
TWENTY-FIVE

History would remember the day as the 4th of July of the year 1187 A.D.

Saladin, king of the Saracens, looked across the battlefield littered with bodies. He had encamped his army near the village of Hattin in northern Palestine. The water and pasture was more than enough to replenish his army that, in a few weeks, would be at the gates of Jerusalem. The Christian army, coming from Sephoria, had marched through miles of parched land to reach them. It was ludicrous to drive thousands of soldiers through the sands before a battle, and yet they came. His legions stood between them and the nearby Sea of Galilee.

His archers had attacked the Franks as they approached, forcing them to fortify at the base of the Horns of Hattin for the night. The ancient well at the rocky, double hill was dry. Throughout the night, his Saracen army encircled them and set fire to the sun-baked, summer grasses around the hills. By morning, the lack of water had driven the Crusaders mad and some were convinced to charge the Moslem lines to reach the life-giving shores of the sea beyond. They hadn't survived.

There would be no victory for the once powerful and nearly unstoppable Army of God. Saladin had taken heavy losses, but the obliteration of those who remained against him was near. The lucky ones had retreated as the Crusaders made two charges and were driven back, enduring unbearable casualties each time. The last of the knights, mainly Templars and Hospitallers, were readying their last stand on the Horns of Hattin with the True Cross. There, some thought, was where Christ gave the Sermon on the Mount. Saladin looked over his men. The time had come.

Across the battlefield, no one noticed Conrad when he shimmered into existence, his armor blending in with the other knights. He probably could have been dressed like a Halloween pumpkin and they wouldn't have noticed. Surviving was their only concern and that was going poorly. The dead and dying lay everywhere on the hilltop. At the center, near the red royal tent, Conrad identified the Bishop of Acre by the vestments he wore. He was the barer of the True Cross. He was also dead. Conrad ran to him, unaware of the arrows flying into the Crusader's position. This battle would soon be over and many of the survivors would be executed. He didn't have much time.

Latzi appeared directly into the tent. The dead bishop lay outside the opening with a knight leaning over him. Latzi turned, and there it was: A jeweled cross on top of an ornately carved staff stood planted in the center of the tent. The cross held a hidden compartment and inside would be the True Cross. What luck. He tore the cross from the staff, but before he could open it, a blow to his head brought him to his knees. He screamed in pain as he clutched his head.

"Don't know who you are, but this doesn't belong to you." Conrad picked up the cross. He had seen the man materialize and immediately sensed evil. Now he could see into his dark eyes.

"You idiot, you do not know the power before you!" Latzi leaped to his feet and rushed his attacker, driving him into the ground. Conrad could barely fend off the rapid blows the thief landed on him; his arrows and longbow had been thrown from him. He reached for the staff, barely in reach, struck his assailant's head, and jumped to his feet. Conrad landed another strike on the man, stunning him, but he stood nonetheless.

"Weakling, you're no match for the power of the Dark One." Latzi approached Conrad so fast that he didn't have time to react. Conrad couldn't slow time as he tried to strike again with the staff. Latzi caught it and they struggled to gain control of the weapon. Conrad tried to overpower his foe, but Latzi wrestled the staff from his grip and brought it up against his head. Conrad went down, nearly unconscious, blood dripping from his face. Latzi tossed the staff and opened the cross. In it were slivers of wood.

"I will use this to take my rightful place. Those who betrayed me will live no longer on this world. I, Latzi, will take my place beside the Dark One." He drew on the power of the relic to cross the space-time barrier once more. As he did, he felt a sharp, burning pain in his foot.

Conrad had hurled a blue-tipped arrow at Latzi. His head was still spinning as he stood, but the thief was gone.

The Crusaders were making their final stand outside. It would be their last and he would suffer their fate as well if he didn't find a way home. Then he saw something on the ground where the evil Timewalker had last stood.

A small piece of wood.

When the Saracens reached the tent, all that they found was a dead bishop at its entrance. They took the cross, shut its compartment, and informed Saladin they had captured the True Cross.

Ahriman stood at the entrance of the gorge, mounted on his horse. The heat taxed the beast of war, but it knew any movement would earn a sharp kick from its master. Shimmering in the desert at the base of the mountain loomed the fortified monastery. Two hundred or so knights had taken up positions outside of the walls. Archers stood behind the parapets. Where was Rajnai? She should have been back by now. He had waited for her and now the monastery had been reinforced. No matter, these knights would be no match for what he was about to conjure. Ahriman looked down at the hooded Caretaker standing next to him.

"Soon the one text that has long alluded you will be in our hands."

"But how do we get through them?" He motioned to where the knights had encircled the monastery. Ahriman's warriors weren't as numerous as what stood before them. More had been lost in the Misty Valley than he had anticipated. He didn't need them.

"Have you lost your faith in me? Have years hiding in your pyramids like a rat made you fearful?"

"No, my master." The Caretaker stared at the ground, avoiding Ahriman's gaze. A distant bird cry reached their ears. A roc circled high above, far enough to be out of reach of their arrows. Where had it come from? They had been seen.

"We can wait no longer. Bring up the sarcophagus!" Four of Ahriman's armored warriors, faces hidden by their darkened steel helmets, brought forward an object covered by a black sheet and laid it on the ground next to the Caretaker. They removed the sheet and tossed it aside, revealing a rectangular cedarwood sarcophagus. Its sides were painted with images of people – if they could be called that. They had heads of jackals, scorpions, cobras, and other creatures of the desert. Not all were recognizable, but a woman with the head of a lion covered the lid. The goddess Sekhmet, who had been sent to punish Egypt during the Destruction of Mankind, stared back at Ahriman.

"Begin to unseal the sarcophagus, but do not open it completely," the Caretaker instructed the warriors.

They pried the lid open with their swords. No others moved, silenced from anticipation of the coming battle or fear of what would emerge from the ancient box. He had waited many years for an opportunity to release the power of this lost terror. He had discovered it decades ago, in a long-neglected, corner of the Museum of Egyptian Antiquities in Cairo. Forgotten and ignored, he had immediately recognized its importance. He removed a papyrus scroll from a leather case that hung on his belt and carefully unrolled it. Faded hieroglyphs, words that had never before been spoken aloud, would now receive life from the mouth of the shadowmancer.

"Demons of the netherworld, Messengers of Sekhmet, arise from the Sands of Time and bring forth destruction to those that oppose us. Unleash the Fire and the Scourge, and watch empires crumble and fall in terror. Awake now and throw off your chains!"

Quiet blanketed the gorge. For a moment, nothing happened, but then the air stilled and the box shuddered. Streams of sandy air emerged from underneath the lid and curled around the men like spirits before disappearing into the ground. Abruptly, sand shot up into the sky before raining down onto the desert floor. The entire gorge shook violently and shifted beneath their feet. All around them pillars of rock and sand pushed out of the ground, quickly morphing into Sekhmet's demons. Nightmares that had long ago faded became real once more. Men with the heads of jackals; ghastly, muscled men with the claws of scorpions for hands and heads of crocodiles. On others, where the faces of men should have been, cobras hissed. Eager for prey, many a sinister ibis snapped their long, down-curved bills. The chimeras of man and beast wielded crooked blades and twisted swords. Hundreds of the beasts emerged from the poisoned earth, growling and hissing and speaking dark tongues. They quieted once the entire horde had morphed out of the sands. Then some parted, allowing another to come to the front and approach the Caretaker and Ahriman.

Slowly the beautiful woman, arms and legs covered in golden armor, flexible like paint on her skin, came forward. She carried a silver scythe at her side and its sharpened edge glistened in the sunlight. Her head was that of a lioness and her golden hair flowed over her body. She stood before Ahriman and roared, showing her wicked teeth.

"Such beauty and evil. No wonder the ancients locked her away." Ahriman wasn't frightened by Sekhet and her servants. "Will you join us and lay siege to the fortress? The Watchers have the *Book of the Second Death* that will let us lay waste to this world. The bound horrors of Resheph and Qetab will be allowed to roam free once more. When we succeed, you and your demons will lead the army of the Dark One's new kingdom. The world will be at our mercy."

"I will follow you who summoned me." Her voice was

ethereal, hypnotizing. It also dripped with malice. Sekhet was never more eager to inflict pain and death. She had spent an eternity locked away and didn't intend on simply being this one's slave. He wouldn't be the first that she influenced. That would come later. "We will destroy and enslave all who stand against us." She paused, then added, "My master."

"Very good." Ahriman thought if Rajnai didn't return, this evil goddess could be his new mistress. "We wait no longer." He unsheathed his sword and raised it above him. "Breach the walls but do not destroy the buildings within. Leave no one alive!"

The Dark One's shadowmancer led his Army of Darkness through the gorge. The knights that guarded the monastery would soon face terror unlike any they had ever imagined. They would be shown no mercy and the Watchers would be put to the fire, if they survived. Perhaps he would give some of them to the demons. Ahriman laughed at how easy this had all been.

The Light would soon be extinguished once and for all.

Ethan and Milena rode hard for Stonehenge as the evening light began to falter. The knights that had stayed behind hadn't slowed Searbhan; his roars still echoed across the rolling hills. Cináed and the last of his men had turned back to stop the beast. What happened to Stonecor? A moment later, Ethan knew. He turned his head in time to see an object hurtling through the sky. Milena had pulled ahead and he tried to turn the horse with a violent pull on the reigns, but it only reared up on its legs, throwing Ethan into the grass. The projectile slammed into the horse, mangling it into a bloody mass of flesh.

Embedded in the ground was Stonecor, what was left of him.

Milena looked back and saw Ethan slowly coming to his feet. The landing had knocked the wind out of him. Nothing was broken and he still had the relic.

"Ethan!" Milena rode back and tried not to look at the flattened horse. Stonecor's death was a terrible loss. What face he had was frozen in an expression of shock. "Get on my horse."

"It will never carry us; it is injured." There were two arrows in its side. "Go ahead and get into the inner ring of Stonehenge. I'll follow, it's not far." Before Milena could object, Ethan added, "Go now, we don't have time to discuss it."

"Hurry!" She turned her horse and rode as fast as it would allow. The ground before Ethan was the same as it had been in his dream. He never knew how that dream ended. Now he would find out. Searbhan and the wild men approached.

Ethan ran toward the shadows looming on the crest of the hill as arrows cut through the air a few feet from his head. His feet barely touched the ground, the Light propelling him forward. The heavy footfalls and clanging of weapons of his pursuers came for him. Only a few more feet and he would be home. The monoliths of Stonehenge formed ahead in the moonlight.

An arrow clipped his boot, tripping Ethan into the dirt. He rolled over and tried to ignore the pain of another impact and saw that he had made it through the outer monoliths. Milena ran to him and helped him to his feet.

"Are you okay?"

"Yeah, I think so. If only I can stay on my feet." Milena hadn't been in his dream. The future wasn't written in stone. Or was this the past? The ground shuddered and air began to flow past them.

A bluish mist swirled at the center of the ancient monument. It grew upward as it rotated like a helix, hovering over the ground. Its height reached only slightly above the towering monoliths. At its edges the light blurred the surroundings, pulling at the fabric of space.

"Time to get out of here my love." Ethan grabbed Milena's hand and started for the portal. Searbhan's guttural roars grew closer. The other pursuers had stopped a few yards out, fearing to enter the sacred grounds. Searbhan would have no such fear. Ethan and Milena stepped toward the blue light. It was time to leave. They could get help and return for Kyra.

Before he reached the portals, two people separated from the mist, weapons in hands. Both raised their bows, aimed at Ethan and Milena, and let arrows loose.

Kyra and Scout had come upon Saken castle as a hideous gray-skinned giant crushed a knight under its foot. It roared a foul, foreign oath before lumbering off with at least a dozen wild men running ahead of it. Others stayed behind to fight the knights that held the castle. Two wild men flew screaming over her head into a cluster of trees. The impact broke their bodies instantly. Out of the chaos a creature of rock ran after the horrid beast. The situation did not appear to be improving, especially when the screaming, filth and blood-covered men came running for her. Some wore skins and furs of animals; others with nothing but war paints and mud.

Mythical beasts and battle. What had she gotten herself into? Hopefully she did know how to use her mother's weapons. With a deep breath she cleared her mind and let the Light fill her. The blue in her eyes swirled.

Kyra dismounted the horse with a spin and pulled the katanas from their sheaths that hung at either side of her belt. She headed directly into the approaching attackers.

The first never saw Scout launch at him. He only momentarily glimpsed the deadly white teeth before the jaw locked onto his face. The second missed the cat with his sword only to get swiped by its claw, spinning him around. Perfect position for Scout to pounce on him and bite into his neck, snapping it.

The wild men were too frenzied to notice or care that it was a woman who approached them at a steady pace. One, though, wondered why she didn't look the least bit afraid, and why her eyes radiated in the fading light. Unfortunately, his fear didn't overcome his momentum.

Kyra easily deflected the first blade and thrust a katana into the man's neck. She pulled it out and turned to block another attack. He at least made another swing before she wrestled the sword from him and slashed him with her second blade.

This all before the first attacker hit the ground.

Another ran at her, only to be pummeled into the ground by Scout. Two others were almost on him with their swords when they screamed in pain and hit the ground face first. Arrows stuck in their backs. Knights had chased the wildmen, wondering who fought them in the moonlight. A woman walked among the carnage.

"Are you another from the portal? Another Watcher?" They asked her, nervously eyeing the cat as it approached Kyra, its teeth and fur stained crimson.

"I suppose I am." She wiped the blades on the ground. "I came here looking for my mother. Saken took her, and I mean to take her back and show him my mother's blades."

"Saken is dead. Your mother saw to that. They left for the portal. That way, where the beast went. It is not far."

"Come, Scout, this isn't over." Alice hadn't strayed. Kyra mounted her and paused to catch her breath for but a moment. A terrible strength had been awakened in her. She liked it and she didn't.

The arrows flew past Ethan and Milena, and between the standing stones, before embedding themselves into Searbhan's chest. The blue-tipped arrows wouldn't be enough to stop him. They didn't have enough, but Theodoric and Aoifa let loose more arrows.

"You found them. You found them both." Theodoric looked at the relic and Milena. "Go through the portal. More of us are on the way, but it will take time."

"No, we can't leave. We need to find our daughter. Give the relic to him." Milena looked to Ethan. He tried to give it to Theodoric, but he wouldn't take it.

"No, we will not leave you here with this beast. It must be destroyed." Searbhan had reached the outer stone ring. He hesitated for a moment. He was nearly twice Balor's size. His thick grayish skin rippled with muscles. The foursome readied their weapons and Searbhan lifted one of the lintels from atop the sarsens like the massive stone weighed nothing. His intention was clear.

"Run!" Aoifa shouted.

They scattered among the rocks as the lintel embedded itself in the ground where they had just stood. She shot more arrows. Searbhan's skin blackened where they hit, but it wasn't enough. A hundred arrows, maybe. Even then it might take time for the fomorii giant to die. Another roar came from outside the sacred site, but this time it wasn't Searbhan. It came from behind him.

A battle cry of a lion roared again.

The cat leaped out of the moonshadows and landed

on Searbhan's back, digging its claws into thick skin and tearing flesh with its razor-sharp teeth. The giant tried to grab the cat and only succeeded in striking his own back. It flailed around in rage, unable to reach its attacker. Aoifa and Theodoric fired all of the arrows they had at Searbhan. Screams came from the wild men, and the last of them began to flee. Out of the moonlight walked a woman.

Ethan and Milena tried to run from the henge, but Searbhan's wild movements blocked them. "It's Kyra!" Milena knew it was her, but what had happened? She was older with familiar katanas in her hands, their blades bloodied. Had they not been in the middle of a battle against a monster in another time, seeing her daughter as she was would have been more shocking.

It's me. Kyra looked to her parents, then quickly to the beast. *How do we take down this monster?*

Ethan had the relic. Its power could destroy them all. Could he wield it? Milena was unsure. "Can we use it?"

"I don't know." He handed it to Milena. "But if what I'm about to do doesn't work, we'll have no choice."

"Wait!" It was too late.

Ethan was off in a sprint toward Searbhan whose anger was growing with every second. Scout couldn't hang on much longer. One wrong step and Ethan would be crushed under the beast's foot. It wasn't terribly fast or smart, and seconds were all Ethan needed. He didn't stop; he ran the distance in an eye-blink. As he came up to Searbhan's foot, he swung his sword with both hands as energy seethed through its steel; its blue coating glowed like a star. It sliced through the tendons of the giant's ankle, buckling its leg. Ethan swung around, cut the other leg, and the beast fell face first to the ground. Scout leaped clear before the impact, but Searbhan was not yet finished. He thrashed about and hollered in pain. Ethan drove the sword into the beast's back. It had little choice but to yield to death. Kyra approached the dying creature and it calmed.

She looked past his fearful eyes and into his mind. Long ago, once a man, his name had been Diggory. A woman had approached him, a radiant, tempting blond who said she could give him great strength. All his life he had been small and weak. Lilith, she said her name was, led him to a rotting cabin deep in the woods where no light reached. Fear overcame him, but it was too late. He awoke implanted with organs of beasts and awash in dark sorcery. Diggory transformed slowly, writhing in pain for days on the forest floor. Finally it passed once all recognizable humanity had fled. He no longer remembered his name. His people hunted him. Only in the shadows did he find friends. There Lilith returned to him and he worshiped her, becoming her slave. But there was still some humanity left in him that the Darkness had overlooked. The weapons of the Watchers and the Light that flowed through them had found it. There was sorrow in his heart. Kyra touched his forehead.

"What this world has done to you, the next will undo." With that, the last of Searbhan's life left him.

Milena reached Kyra first and hugged her. "I missed, you mommy." Tears formed in her eyes.

"Oh Kyra, what happened? Are you okay?"

"When I..." Scout came to her side. "When we came through the Oak Circle, it changed us. I don't know if it's permanent or not."

"We'll be finding out, I'm sure. I was worried about you — I couldn't stop thinking about you — but I should have known you'd be fine."

"You worry too much mom."

"Daddy!" She hugged and kissed Ethan.

"You shouldn't be scaring your mom like that, little one. Though you're not so little anymore."

"I'm not sure if I'm ready to be a big kid quite yet." Tears rolled down her face. What had she been doing? "It looks like you've managed." Ethan knew it wasn't that easy. He could see it in her eyes. He had hoped his daughter wouldn't have to become involved in something like this. Not at her age. No, not ever. She still had a childhood to live regardless if she could handle this. No child should have to see such horrors. Or kill someone. Had being his daughter made this all inevitable?

"You need to get to the monastery," Theodoric said. "I sent Owain ahead with his cavalry. With or without the relic, the shadowmancer will attack. I fear he will call on more forgotten horrors to his aid."

"Take the relic back to the citadel." Milena handed it to Theodoric. "We can't let it fall into the enemy's hands."

"We will try to send more help through the portal. We also need more men here to secure Britain and destroy whatever evil remains. Hold out as long as you can. All of this will soon be over."

"Theodoric, Stonecor is dead." Ethan felt like he had lost an old friend. "He fought to the end, but this beast destroyed him."

"Stonecor was a selfless warrior." Theodoric said, after searching for words. He wasn't sure when or how the elemental was created. In some distant age when his predecessors battled the horrors created by the Fallen. Those on the side of Light had created their own inhuman allies. Theirs, though, weren't the twisted perversions of nature of the Dark One. "We will return and gather his remains and bury him in the New World. He will not be forgotten."

"If we do not meet again, let me say it has been a

great honor." Ethan knew there was more between them. A connection of some sort. He had felt it before. What had the monk on the Tor been saying? "I feel as if I have known you before, in some other time perhaps."

"Maybe not another time or place, but through flesh and blood." Theodoric smiled and clasped Ethan's hand. Ethan wasn't sure, but anything was possible at this point.

"It has been a pleasure to meet you, Milena. Warrior women are rare in our time, though I suppose there would be more if we allowed it. You have taught your daughter well. I sense she will be a painful thorn to the Evil One."

"I wish Kyra only had to be a little girl and not follow her mother's life."

"It is not always a bad life, is it?" Ethan asked.

"No, I suppose not." Milena's life had been full of peace and love. "It looks like you have at least one person who can teach your women."

"Hopefully, I won't have to," Aoifa said. "War has become old to me. I would like to have a family away from it. I know evil will long knock at our door and we cannot forget or ignore it, but still, life must continue." Milena sensed that much of Aoifa's words were directed at Theodoric. She also knew their future was bright.

"Good-bye, Kyra, young princess." Theodoric took her by the arms. "Take care of that feline friend of yours."

"I will, sir." It was the voice of a woman, yet a girl was still very much in there, somewhere.

"Ready?" Theodoric asked Aoifa.

"Yes, we cannot hold them up any longer."

"Very well, then. Go well, my friends." Theodoric, holding the reliquary in one hand, took Aoifa's with the other, and walked toward the vortex of light.

A moment later, they were gone.

CHAPTER
TWENTY-SIX

After the ground shuddered, Duncan and Kane returned to the wall of the monastery where Owain kept watch. Most of his knights positioned on the outside, waiting for the attack that was certain to come.

"What happened?" Duncan asked.

"Down there, at the opening of the gorge, the shadowmancer is there." Kane pointed at the black-armored man mounted on his horse. "And not all of his Followers appear to be human." Blowing sand obscured their view. Funny, the wind was calm at the monastery, but a thick dread passed over them. Evil had been released and was coming their way.

A knight called up to Owain.

"Sir, look up there! Someone approaches from the mountain."

"It's Conrad." Kane could tell by his longbow.

"Let him pass." Owain called out.

Duncan and Kane went down to meet him.

"About time," Kane said. "Did you find it?"

"I did." Conrad opened his hand.

"That's it?" The splinter of wood didn't look like much to Duncan.

"This is only a piece. The shadows sent someone after the True Cross and stole most of it. I couldn't stop him. He claimed he was Latzi, but he was different, like he was infected or possessed."

"Latzi is dead. We saw him in the citadel," Kane said.

"I don't think Latzi being alive is out of the question, all things considered," Duncan said.

"Unfortunately, you're probably right," Kane replied.

A rumbling came from the gorge.

"They are coming!" Owain shouted orders to his men. What few archers they had took positions on the walls.

"It would seem I'm right in time for the action. I'll head up there." Conrad found a place on the wall and readied his bow. He didn't have an endless supply of arrows. No one did. Each one must count.

"Where do you want me?" Kane asked.

"Don't let anyone near that library. Destroy the book if we fail." Duncan mounted a horse left by one of the archers in an outer courtyard and rode off. Knights sealed off the entrance behind him. Built to withstand thieves and average desert marauders, the fortress architects had not anticipated hordes from the underworld. Hopefully, Ethan would arrive soon with reinforcements. The defenders might have a chance, but if they failed, there would be no retreat. Duncan readied his swords. The Evil One's army approached.

Latzi stumbled on the rocky slope as he materialized. In the distance a cloud of dust rose where Ahriman's army rode to assault the monastery. His foot throbbed from whatever the Watcher had stabbed him with. It had vanished coming through the veil, but the wound fought against the evil that the dark blade planted inside him. Maybe it was the relic as well. He hadn't thought about it at the time, but why hadn't it harmed him? Whatever happened, it wasn't just physical; the battle played out in his mind. His passage through time wasn't instantaneous this time. Images had flashed through his mind of his childhood. He couldn't remember them clearly, impressions mostly. No matter, the time to prove himself had arrived. He would find the book that they so desired. No one would doubt him then.

As Ahriman's army of horrors came closer, Duncan got a better look at the monstrosities running with the mounted warriors. Conjured from some evil long ago locked away. Even after the battle in the Misty Valley, he had a hard time believing such devilry existed. Volleys of arrows began to rain down on the approaching mass. Those unlucky enough to be hit were trampled by those behind them. There weren't enough archers. Not enough arrows. This would be fought man-to-man. Or man to monster.

Over half of the knights readied their lines; they would charge directly into the storm. The remainder would hold back and guard outside the walls. The arrows stopped. It was time.

Owain raised his sword.

"Send these devils back to the abyss!"

With that, he led the charge. What little ground remained between the two forces closed quickly. At breakneck speed, the armies clashed in an explosion of steel and thrown bodies. Some of Sekhmet's soldiers needed no weapons. A humanoid jackal jumped, pulling a horse and its knight to the ground. A scorpion-man crumpled horses with ease until one defender sliced off his tail and his head. This encounter would be better fought on foot.

Duncan jumped from his horse and drew his second sword, cutting down a reptilian monster. A dead-looking female lunged at him with twisted daggers. The corpse moved like the wind with intelligible shrieks, but her haste cost her a hand by Duncan's sword. Still, she came at him. He would have to take her a piece at a time. As their swords locked, a jackal pounced from the side. He had no time left; the demon had to die, then suddenly she went limp. A glimpse of the jackal as it hurtled through the air interrupted his surprise. A behemoth lion pounced on its prey, killing it with one bite of its powerful jaw.

"Must be on our side," Duncan said under his breath.

"Sure is." A woman pulled her blade from the corpse woman. She looked familiar, but Duncan wasn't sure, then in the maelstrom around them, Milena and Ethan were there, fighting like the unearthly beings trying to overrun them.

"Ethan! Milena!"

"Just in time for more fun, I see." Only Ethan could block out the death around him so easily.

"Who is she?"

"That's Kyra. She was bored playing with her dolls."

Duncan wasn't quite sure what to make of it, as he witnessed Kyra dispatch another horror from the ancient world. Its body torn by her blades.

"Okay then." Duncan went after a black knight that had been thrown from his horse.

Much of the enemy had swept right by them, reaching

the walls of the monastery. Conrad used the last of his arrows and went over the wall without a second thought. Time slowed and he landed squarely before a mutant of man and cobra. Before it could even think of striking, Conrad brought his sword through its head. Like a raging river, he engaged beast after beast, their blood drenched bodies piled around him; others still made it to the monastery walls. A gold clad woman with the head of a lion stood before the imposing fortress and uttered a dark incantation. Bricks exploded in a hail of fire and debris, ripping a gash in the wall nearly to the ground. The concussion threw Conrad into the air.

"They have breached the wall!" Milena yelled.

"Don't let them find the book. We'll stop Ahriman." Ethan had seen him at the rear of his troops, letting them die first. "Duncan, the shadowmancer!" Duncan followed Ethan as they fought their way through the chaos. Milena and Kyra hardly touched the ground as they raced to the monastery. All the Followers that tried to intercept them fell to their blades.

While guards ran to defend the breach, Kane sprinted into the library and took the book from a vault. Tychicus had shown them where it was hidden, poorly at that, for a book of such evil. Kane tried the doors on the nearby structures and all were barred shut. One of the buildings had to have a fireplace or oven, something. Around the corner in the path stood a terrifying, yet beautiful, agent of evil. Sekhmet roared.

"Give me the book and I will allow you to die quickly." Her voice was strangely feminine for such a fearsome creature

"Sorry, but this book isn't for casual reading." Kane went for his sword and saw a shimmer of light as Sekhmet's scythe hurled at him and embedded itself into his side. He dropped the book and fell trying to pull the blade from him. Sekhmet was on him in seconds, kicked him aside, and picked up the *Book of the Second Death*. She pulled the scythe from Kane and he groaned in pain, gasping for air. She smiled. He wouldn't live much longer, but she raised her weapon anyway, only to shudder as agonizing pain shot through her body. Kyra's katana had found its mark under her shoulder blade. Sekhmet faced her.

"You fool, I've been dead for centuries. Your little blade," she pulled it from her back and threw it to the ground, "will not kill me so easily."

"We have more where that came from." Milena joined her daughter and stood before the lioness. Sekhmet dropped the book in the sandy soil and drew a twisted dagger, nearly as long as a sword.

"I will kill you both with the bite of this dagger. It will slowly work through your body, inflicting decades of pain before you succumb and become one of my Messengers." She charged Milena, but her swords deflected the blows.

Kyra attacked from behind only to have Sekhmet anticipate her moves. She deftly blocked every attack as Milena and Kyra whirled around her. Steel clashed at imperceptible speed, but the lioness would not tire. Kyra dived as the scythe hurled by her face, and recovered from a roll to sweep the woman-beast's legs off the ground with her own. Milena slashed at Sekhmet's face as she fell. By the time Milena turned to attack again, the evil hybrid was already to her feet.

"So you do bleed." Milena flourished her swords. Black blood covered the tip of one. "You may be older, but you're not wiser, old hag."

Sekhmet roared and her anger exploded as she rushed Milena. Before she could conjure evil magic, Kyra's blade pierced her back, through the spine. She writhed in pain and Milena thrust her swords into both sides of the creature. The energy coursing through Milena poured into the ancient curse before her. Her burning green eyes peered into Sekhmet's bottomless black orbs as both screamed. Its body began to redden like hot coals, growing brighter with every passing second.

Milena had held on long enough. "Run!"

She and Kyra didn't get far when an explosion of energy and fire sent them tumbling.

As they tried to recover from the blast, the remnant of Sekhmet crawled towards the book. Her gold, what was left of it, scorched and her skin blackened. With her legs shredded and tar-like fluid oozing from her entrails, death was near, but the insidious evil that possessed her pushed her forward. If she reached the ancient pages, she would unleash a power far more horrible than she had ever been. As her bloodied hand reached for the evil tome, she heard a voice:

"You know, I'm not for censorship, but I'll make an exception in your case." She looked up as Kane plunged the katana into her head. Her last look was one of surprise and she could muster no final words of protest. Then her body fell still. "I don't die so easily, either. Should have used your special dagger."

"Are you girls okay?"

"We'll live," Milena said. "Kane, the warrior doctor. Who would have thought it?"

"Not me, that's for sure."

"Disgusting." Kyra pulled her sai from the dead lioness. She twitched, then dissolved into a mound of burnt sand. Her weapons glowed red before crumbling into dust. "Good riddance."

"This isn't over yet, ladies." Milena and Kyra turned to

see what Kane was looking at. Four of Ahriman's dark knights were coming for them.

"Follow me!" Kane had seen something from the wall. If it was what he hoped it was, maybe it would destroy the book. He crossed the courtyard, trying his best to avoid the fighting around him. Milena and Kyra neutralized a couple threats, but the black knights pursuing them attracted additional allies more than happy to join the chase.

"There it is!"

"What are you talking about?" Kyra asked. Only a dry, barely alive bush grew in front of them. Not to mention no escape routes. They were cornered.

"There is nowhere to run. You will die very slowly." The largest of the armor-clad warriors led his companions toward the threesome.

"You might want to get down," Kane said.

"What?" Milena asked.

"Get down, now!"

Kane tossed the *Book of the Second Death* into the bush. On contact, the entire bush erupted into fire and sent searing flames into Ahriman's men. The screams lasted but for a few seconds. Smoking piles of black cinders remained where they once stood.

Milena lay still on the ground where she had dived. "Uh, please explain?"

"Well, as the story goes, this is the burning bush. You know, the one of Old Testament fame?"

"How did you know that was really it?" Kyra asked, brushing dirt from herself.

"Truthfully, I didn't, but given everything that has played out so far, it seemed a plausible solution."

"Did you have a backup plan?" Milena asked.

"Nope."

***

Duncan and Ethan had been held up fighting perversions of man and beast. Before more abominations of the Dark One could assume the place of those he had killed, Duncan turned to Ethan.

"Go take down the shadowmancer. I'll finish off these beasts. Go now, I'll be fine."

"Okay, it's time to end this...look!" Smoke rose from within the monastery's walls. *Milena! Kyra!*

We're okay. The book is destroyed.

It was Kyra. Ethan turned to Duncan. "The book is destroyed, they're all fine. I'll go after Ahriman."

"Good, let's finish this." Duncan ran back into the fray.

Ahriman's plan was failing. His army was dying. He would never lay down and surrender no matter what the odds. If he survived this battle, he would return someday with another sinister plan. Darkness made Ethan shudder. Ahriman had come to him and stood only a few yards away.

"So you are the one who thinks he can destroy me? Look to your fortress and see it burning. My demons must have the book. Join me and the coming kingdom. Join me or face an unfathomable time of torture."

"The book is destroyed. It is your army that is burning. We will not let you leave this place."

"You lie! And you shall die for it. " Ahriman dismounted his horse. His black armor was intricately inscribed with symbols of a foul language. He stood nearly as tall as the Bone Lord Ethan had faced in the Misty Valley. His sword was wide and jagged, every edge sharpened perfectly and forged from Damascus steel. The shadowmancer had the strength and experience from centuries of fighting. He had long waited and prepared for the day he could rule the world for the Dark One. In the past, he had relied too much on humans and they had failed him. This time he relied on evils forged in darkness that even he couldn't imagine. If the book was destroyed, he would personally finish these Watchers. No one would ever stand in his way again.

The strength of his swing nearly caught Ethan off guard as he clashed with his sword. Ahriman hacked away without pause. Ethan drew from within himself and matched blow for blow, but the weakness ached in his arms. He needed all of the energy, the connection beyond the veil, the Light that made him human and a Watcher. The stakes were too high to fail. This servant of evil could not be allowed to continue his oppression. As he met Ahriman's every move, he could sense worry in his opponent. In that moment, Ethan swung around and slashed him across the chest with the glowing sword. Ahriman stumbled and fell, his helmet sent flying.

His chiseled face was scarred from endless war. A red sword with a black snake coiled around the blade had been inscribed on his forehead. The symbol of the Dark One. His golden hair reflected the sunlight, like a Fallen. This caught Latzi's eye as he searched for a way around the battle to the monastery. He knew Ahriman's face. The images that had come to him while crossing through time now coalesced into a memory.

⧗   ⧗   ⧗

He was five years old and out playing in the woods. Arguing voices came from the house. Hiding behind a tree, Latzi watched as a tall man argued with his father. He remembered what they were saying.

"I'm moving my family from the Hollow. I visited the White City. I cannot stay here any longer.

"Listen to me, you ignorant fool. You must continue your work here. You have no choice."

"I want no part of my ancestors legacy any longer. I will free my family."

"You leave this place and you will die."

When the man turned to walk down the lane, he looked right at Latzi. Now Latzi knew that the man had seen him. That man had been Ahriman. Three days later his father had told him they were moving and to start packing. The morning they were to leave, his mother had walked out to the car. There was a scream. Father went running. When he returned, he told Latzi they were staying in the Dark Hollow.

He also said his mother would not be returning home.

Latzi cried and tried to run out of the house, but his father wouldn't let him.

"She's gone. She isn't coming back."

"No! Where's mother? Let me go!"

"She's dead! She's dead!"

"No!" Latzi collapsed at his father's feet, crying uncontrollably.

⧗　　　　　⧗　　　　　⧗

Tears ran down Latzi's face again. The man that had killed his mother and imprisoned his father in the Dark Hollow stood before him. The man that had turned Latzi's heart black. He had deceived them, and when his father tried to save them, the shadowmancer took his mother. He pulled the remnants of the True Cross from his pocket and held it tightly as his body began to shake. His jaw tightened and he ran into the chaos of the battlefield

***

Ahriman leaped to his feet before the Watcher could strike the death blow, channeling his anger in every swing. Even when the Watcher's sword began to shine brighter and brighter blue, he fought on. He would not lose to the human. But the human was as fast as he and again slashed him. This time deeply through the armor like it wasn't there. For a moment Ahriman held his arm, blood flowing freely from the wound. It had been generations since anyone had drawn his blood. The evil surged in him. He charged the human. He would kill him and feed him to Sekhmet's undead army.

With each swing, with every move, Ethan's power multiplied. He was no longer hindered by pain and grief. All of the control returned and then exceeded what it had been. Some horror tried to attack him from the right and Ethan dispatched it without even looking. Now Ahriman rushed towards him leaping over the dead, wielding his blade. Ethan ran to meet him and the Dark One's servant tried to bring his sword down upon him by cutting across low. Ethan jumped over the sword and swung his blue blade down through Ahriman's arm and spun by him, the two warriors barely missing a collision. Ethan hit the ground hands first before jumping straight to his feet. He turned and saw his adversary standing there holding his mangled arm, his sword gone. Ahriman watched as Ethan raised his blade touched by the Light. Fear filled his heart and mind. It was not supposed to be like this. No one could destroy him.

He didn't move as the Watcher approached him, his eyes burning with blue fire. He watched the sword move toward his head, but it never made contact. Instead, a piercing fire ripped through his body. Every molecule began to break its bonds, releasing their energy in a flash, tearing apart the body until nothing remained of the shadowmancer. There had not been even an instant for Ahriman to have one final thought.

The shockwave of energy spread through the gorge, bringing with it a torrent of sand and debris, engulfing all in its path. Those who called the Dark One their master, met the same fate of their leader. The last of Sekhmet's demons were torn and vaporized into dust so quickly, their horror and pain barely registered, only to be replaced by far worse where they would awaken. Rocks and debris tumbled from the mountain in a way that they had not for many millennia. A time when the wrath of the Light was first seen in the valley.

Ethan crawled to his feet, wiping dirt from his eyes. Dust still filled the air. Where Ahriman had last stood, the sand had melted to glass. A few dozen yards away, knights gathered around a body laying on the ground.

"Over here! Come look at this." One of the knights called out.

Ethan ran over to the dying man they stood over. It was Latzi, it had to be. The darkness had vanished from his skin, though much of his body looked like it had been ravished by fire. Ethan faintly remembered a boy he had once seen in the Misty Valley in the man laying before him. It had been the day he found the triquetra while hiking with his father. Latzi was alive. Barely so. Milena, Kyra and Duncan came to Ethan's side.

"What happened?" Milena asked.

"I'm not sure." Ethan said.

Conrad worked his way through the crowd, holding his head.

"Where have you been?" Duncan asked.

"Resting. Knocked out by some golden-lion-lady or

something." Conrad looked at the dying man. "That's who I fought for the relic."

Ethan knelt by him. "Latzi..."

"I used...the relic. I...destroyed him..." Latzi's torn body was failing him. The hand that had held the relic was charred, most of it gone. None of the True Cross remained.

"Why? Why did you stop him?" Ethan asked.

"Because he killed my mother. He...led me down the path...of darkness."

Kyra held Latzi's other hand, and as she knelt near him, her golden triquetra that had been under her shirt fell out and hung above him; the same golden charm that he had found at the Oak Grove. Its diamonds sparkled in the light.

"If only I had followed that instead of darkness. I have caused so much...pain and death. I deserve to die...please don't save me..."

"What we deserve doesn't have to be. You can choose to be free from the Darkness and whatever you have done or whomever you harmed." Kyra held Latzi's hand tighter. Tears filled her eyes.

"It's too late for me."

"No, you may die here on this day, in this world, but it is not the end. The Light will still take you. No one has done anything so vile that they would be turned away. You only need to ask."

Latzi looked into Kyra's eyes. She was like an angel. He could see the Light calling to him like it did among the Oaks that day long ago. The pain left his body. He could see someone approach. No, he knew who it was. *Forgive me for what I have done. Cleanse my soul and reclaim it.*

The Darkness was gone.

Latzi died, but not before seeing the beautiful blue sky

above for the first time.

All stood quietly. Sand blew through the valley. Kyra felt the change first. The relic had altered, or awakened, the part of creation that only she and those with her normally could sense. She didn't completely understand, but time was short.

"We have to go and we have to go now."

"What is it?" Milena asked.

"Something has changed. The relic altered everything. The portals are fading. And there are none here."

"I didn't come here through a portal." Conrad held out his hand. "I used this." He had the remaining sliver of the True Cross. He couldn't believe he had forgotten he had it during the battle.

"Will that be enough for all of us?" Duncan asked.

"Kyra did it without a relic or a portal," Milena said. "Right?"

"Yes, but I almost died doing it. I don't know how to control it. It could kill everyone."

"But we all came here through a portal on the other side even though none are here," Kane said.

"You are wrong about one thing." It was Tychicus. He had come with Kane. Behind them, Scout had been sitting silently and unseen.

Kyra smiled seeing her cat still in one piece and then said, "Wrong about what?"

"There is a portal here. On the mountain top, where the Light once lived. There you will find the Circle of Moses. It had been erected near where the monastery now stands. Centuries ago my predecessors moved it to save it from vandals and pilgrims."

Ethan looked around at the destruction. Many of the knights wouldn't be able to return. Kane had healed only a few. Others he could not save.

"Do not worry, we will take care of this. You cannot wait. If you are stuck here, your own age will be in peril. We may be able to get some of these men through, but you must go now to be certain."

"All right, let's go home." Ethan looked at Latzi one more time.

"We will give him a proper burial, in the monastery." Tychicus sensed Ethan's concern. "Go well, my brave friends."

"Thank you," Milena said as she passed the monk. He nodded in reply.

As Ethan came near, Tychicus grabbed his arm.

"Listen, Watcher, I fear this is only the beginning. Evils like this have been scarce since the time our order was formed." There was fear in his eyes. Ethan didn't know what to say. "Yes, evil is always lurking about, but rarely are such horrors unleashed. The Dark One and his Fallen still long for the day when they once roamed this world unchecked. Only the near destruction of mankind and costly war erased their rule. Be vigilant, my friend. Do not allow those days to return. Whatever evil you know in your time pales in comparison to what once was." The monk let go of Ethan's arm and walked away.

Ethan stood still for a moment before following his friends who already were climbing. Then he stopped. The monk's voice. It had sounded like Grayson. He looked back, but Tychicus was already gone, tending to the injured.

"Ethan, come on," Milena called.

Ethan shook off the feeling and caught up to his wife. No one said a word and no one stopped to rest during the difficult climb to the top of the mountain. The battles had tested and spent them. Kyra saw it first. A simple altar, crafted centuries ago from stone, encircled by the time-worn remains of twelve stone pillars. They had paid it no attention when arriving on the mountain. Built for the twelve tribes of Israel that had ages ago been absorbed by the relentless movements and conflicts of the Near East, they weren't sure if it still existed in their day.

"We're here," Kyra said.

She held her parents' hands as they all stood around the altar. Bluish light sparkled around the stones and reached out between the pillars, connecting them. As a wall of light moved toward the altar and enveloped them, she looked around at her family and their friends one more time, closed her eyes and thought to herself:

Take us home.

CHAPTER
TWENTY-SEVEN

It was the day the fire came.

Mohenjo Daro. The greatest city of the Indus Valley, it was also Rajnai's birthplace. In the dim early morning light, she wandered the streets exploring, observing, and enjoying the quiet. Soon it would be transformed into a crowded mass of people. Some merchants were already preparing their goods and she lifted a mango as she passed the stands. The juicy pleasure awoke her tongue. The daily urban chaos fascinated her with its markets and hundreds of people buying their daily goods. The brick temples and those who sought to please the gods. The thieves who hid in the shadows. No one dared accost her. It was like they knew. Born with gifts of strength and heightened awareness, sneaking up on Rajnai didn't happen.

If they tried, they never did again.

But the city fell in decline. Trade with foreign nations was no longer reliable. The weather changed making water scarce. When the rain came again, relentless, catastrophic flooding engulfed many of the cities. Raiders constantly bit at the fringes of the outlying towns. Rumors arrived of a horde in the east sweeping through the land. All across their sprawling civilization people fled, including Rajnai's closest friends. She didn't want to abandon her homeland, but would she live to adulthood in this ruined world? Hatred grew inside her for the gods who let it happen. Why had they turned their backs on their people? Had they not shown their devotion for generations?

Two people up ahead pointed to the sky. Orange balls of flame silently arced through the sky. The fruit fell from her trembling hand. The first fireball hit a tower. Then another. She stood frozen as people ran by screaming; her mouth opened and tears ran down her face. This was it. Her people would not see another day. A building burst into an explosion of brick and dust, knocking her flat. Choking on debris, everything went black.

She wasn't sure how long she had been out and more than a little surprised that she was alive and only bruised. Sounds slowly filtered into her ears. Cries and moans. People dying. She pulled herself to her knees; shadowy figures moved about the wreckage and smoke. Dark warriors clad in black leather, wielding blades coated with the blood of her people. Only the strongest had remained in the city. Those like her who would not allow their city to die. Now they were being slaughtered. One invader walked up to her and raised his sword.

"Stop! Do not kill her!"

Out of the billowing smoke emerged another warrior. Taller than the others, and even in her youth, Rajnai could see his strength. This was their leader. He removed his helmet, forged from steel in the form of a dragon. His blonde hair contrasted dark eyes empty of any color. A red sword with a coiled snake imprinted its form on his forehead.

She knelt before him, moving the long hair from her face.

"How may I serve you, my lord?" Rajnai's voice trembled.

"Come with me, girl." He reached his hand to her. His deep voice resonated his strength, yet it did not scare her. In fact, she found it mesmerizing. She would do anything for this man. It was as if he was the one speaking inside her all these years. She took his hand and stood.

"I knew someone like you was here. If I destroyed this city, I knew that among the few survivors I would find you. The Darkness is in you, and with my guidance, all will fear you. Come now, I have set up my quarters in the citadel of your people." Rajnai followed him to the citadel sitting high on a mound overlooking the city. Halfway up the stairs she hesitated and looked back.

Fires burned and black smoke hung over the streets. Warriors rounded up slaves and others begged for their lives. Once the pride of her civilization, the ruins would someday become known as the Mound of the Dead.

My family!

It was too late. Something tried to push her darkness away. A tear ran down her cheek. She could either embrace what was inside her or die like them. She had wrestled with the shadows for too long. Sometimes winning, sometimes losing. The more she had lost, the darker her mind had become. She would embrace it. The guards prepared to close the doors in front of her. From within came a voice.

"Come, girl, my servants have prepared a bath for us. Let us wash away the day's death from ourselves and come to know each other. Do not dwell on what has happened here, much of the world is being cleansed by the chaos. A new age is upon us."

"Who are you, my lord?"

"I am Ahriman."

Rajnai resigned herself and made her decision. She stepped back into the room as the doors closed and were locked from the outside.

Rajnai arrived too late. Any earlier and she would have been dead as well. She looked into the gorge full of remnants of death, scoured of the evil hordes. Ahriman was dead. He had found her thousands of years earlier in Mohenjo Daro and had always been more than the one she called master. Everyone knew it, but none dared speak it. Now she was alone.

When she had regained consciousness at Saken castle, that fool and his army had been defeated. Searbhan lay dead at the portal. The relic was gone. She used the portal even though it was one used by the Watchers. Supposedly, passing through a portal infused with the Light by a Follower was unheard of, if not fatal. She had no choice but to take the chance. She had survived the passage through Stonehenge, but her body was beaten and exhausted.

She stumbled down rocky paths, grasping her side. The wound throbbed through the blood-stained bandages she had tied around her. No one had ever brought her so close to death and she had not known pain since her city had burned. She would have her vengeance, but now she had to find a way home. She stopped, her head spinning in the heat. Where was home? She had no place to go. Then Rajnai spotted the the sarcophagus.

The defenders of the monastery had not yet destroyed it. Burnt by a blast from some powerful source of the Light

— she could feel it even now — it had been at the far end of the gorge and escaped complete destruction. Wisps of evil still clung to its charred remains, but wouldn't be enough to allow her to leave before she was found. She had always been just short of the ability to travel the river of time on her own. A skill that none of her kind had mastered since the Beginning. She had been Ahriman's best hope to change that. She had failed him in that as well. Her only chance was to flee into the desert and hope to find some lost sanctuary of darkness. Or she would die in the sands. Perhaps that would be better.

The moment she meant to leave, a choking malice surrounded her, far worse than anything she felt in Ahriman's presence.

"And where do you think you are going?" The voice was sinister yet smooth, every syllable deliberate. Rajnai looked at the woman and fell to her knees. She couldn't breathe and clutched her throat and barely sputtered out the words.

"Lilith. Please..."

"Get a hold of yourself. Are you not, I mean were you not, Ahriman's most prized killer? Or were you only his plaything?" Lilith laughed at Rajnai, but released the oppression that she had laid upon her.

Rajnai looked up at the dark eyes that watched her, so out of place on a woman who looked as if she had been an exquisitely sculpted statute that the gods had breathed life into. She wore the clothes of a nomadic woman, yet also a blood red hijab from under which a few stray blonde hairs fell from. Her light skin was strange for someone who had been created among the four rivers of Eden. Or had she been something else?

Lilith was the cast out one. The mother of the night creatures, a master of demons. Her humanity all but an illusion. All of the Followers knew of her and Ahriman had claimed to have met her. Most thought she met death long ago in the ancient wars or was nothing more than a fable of the Hebrews. And yet here she stood.

"Please stand up. If I was here to kill you, the act would have already been completed." She walked around Rajnai as she spoke. "Ahriman had his final chance. I don't know why the Master gave him such a long leash. Sure, he had his victories and he was ruthless. I always liked his methods. Just bad luck, I suppose. I see you, on the other hand, did have a lucky day. Not being vaporized like your lover can't be a bad thing, can it?"

"What do you want from me? I failed Ahriman in my duties to him and the Dark One. This crusade has cost us many allies and raised new Watchers to oppose us. I do not deserve to live."

"That is true, but there are many more of us still hidden and waiting and this little debacle of yours will awaken many more. I had hoped this quest that your shadowmancer was pursuing would succeed, I truly did. It would have made my life easier. The humans are so clueless, they cannot smell the rot or see the decay of their world right before their eyes. So many of them are in our hands already. You see, I have been waiting for the right time to step back into the world. Waiting for a very, very long time."

"The right time for what?"

"That is what I am here to discuss. I have a small, little job for you back in the time present. There you will conjure revulsions long thought dead. Races bred for evil that escaped the ancient destruction. Legions to wield your hatred against all and those that fancy themselves Watchers. You can eclipse your former master in the death you will cause. It is time to raise Lemuria from the depths. The rumors of those who had escaped and hid in the mountains and the deserts are true. The ones who were created by the Fallen when the world was new. Seek them out. What was locked in shadow now stirs, and where darkness has laid dormant, evil awakes.

"And you," Lilith drew close, her eyes now a reddish-yellow, and ran her finger along Rajnai's face, "dark one, will be Queen of them all."

EPILOGUE

The late fall evening had an unusually comfortable warmth. Ethan sat in the garden as dusk gave way to night, Scout at his feet, resting before a night of hunting. He appeared content with having returned to normal size. Nearly a month had passed, yet Ethan couldn't help but to constantly run through his mind all that had come to pass. The past could finally sleep, perhaps for a time. With the veil so thin, though, how long would peace last?

One thing was certain: Darkness no longer hung over the southern sky beyond the Misty Valley. Autumn had returned, but as it always did, it would end too soon.

Traveling back through the portal, Kyra had returned to her younger self. Why had she changed? Was it because she had such a strong connection beyond the veil? Perhaps something in her mind or soul saw a glimpse of what was to come and allowed her transformation. The reasons were uncertain, but her ability to travel without a portal pointed to the great depth of her power. She hadn't tried since. Nor did she plan to for a long time. Scout's large size on the other hand, made a little more sense even though he would never be that big. Kyra had always wished he was large enough to ride.

With Duncan, he had placed the last sliver of the relic in the Citadel, along with all that Theodoric had left there. They sealed the passages to the cave and the well, making it difficult for anyone to find the way again. There probably wasn't anything of value to the Dark One, but the relics still surged with power, even if the portals did not. Those who sought them were dead. Even the Dark One's vision couldn't see inside the stronghold. Would someone seek the objects once more? Perhaps they learned their lesson. Relics infused with the Light would always be suicidal in their hands even under the best of circumstances. Even Latzi, who had cast off the darkness in his last moments, did not survive.

The Oak Grove was different. Not a leaf rustled. The water had lost its sparkle. The Circle still stood as a testament to antiquity and past forgotten, yet now it was almost just another part of the forest.

Almost.

The men had quickly returned with their families to their homes. Everyone needed to spend time with who mattered the most to them. They were changed, scarred in some ways. They had succeeded in the face of evil that they couldn't have imagined only a few weeks prior. They also knew that while their victory rolled back this assault, there would be more. Evil never slept, no matter how quiet it became.

Ethan wondered what became of Theodoric and Aoifa. He intended to search the old records of Hayden, but had not yet done so. Certainly they would have left some message for their friends in the future. If he had his dates right, the Black Death would have ravaged Europe not long after they left. Nothing in the native histories suggested that the plague made it to America, but the Viking excursions and those who traveled with them ceased during that era. Had the settlement at the White City been cut off? The speed at which the plague had traveled was suspicious. The book of pestilence had been destroyed, but had something else been unleashed into the world when the veil was torn?

The aberrations of creation they had faced haunted his mind. What normal person fought in battles against mythical creatures or traveled through time? On the other hand, if Kyra could wander about unconcerned, then so should he. Besides, Milena was home. They couldn't spend enough time with each other since they returned. Trying to explain her absence had been a challenge. Milena was extraordinary at deflecting the inevitable questions, often simply saying, "It's a long story, one I'm not ready to tell." Indeed it was quite the tale. Eventually people stopped asking.

The stars slowly appeared in the clear dusk sky, and Ethan's thoughts quieted. He never tired of seeing the nightly emergence of the heavens, no matter how many times he witnessed it. Mercury, low in the western sky, reflected the Sun's light brightly. Soon, one by one, the constellations would twinkle into existence. Long before man had done much else, he had looked upward and dared to dream of better futures. Now, hypnotized by ceaseless entertainment and busyness, few bothered to look anymore.

We think we are so much better than the ancients. But are we? The smarter we have become, the less we actually get it.

Soft footsteps from behind ended his mental

wanderings. Milena wrapped her arms around him.

"Thinking big thoughts?" she whispered before kissing him. "Remember how we always spent hours under the stars when we first started dating?" She sat next to him and then laid her head on his lap to view the sky.

Some of the brighter stars started to shine in the darkening sky. Deneb, at the head of Cygnus, the swan, twinkled into existence. As with most people, it would always be the Northern Cross to her. Soon the Big Dipper would point to the North Star.

"Some say this makes them feel small, lost in the cosmos. Not me." She knew what people throughout time had always known. They were part of something much bigger than themselves. And all of this, in one way, was for them. If the universe wasn't exactly how it was, Earth and its life wouldn't exist.

"Yeah, we don't do this enough. It's a reminder to slow down and take a breath. How can people miss something so incredible right over their heads?"

"I don't know, but I do know that we will be remedying that problem. I don't want to miss many more of these nights," Milena said. "There can't be many left this late in fall. I was hoping winter didn't come soon, but I felt it today. Snow is in the air."

"You like the snow. For the first few weeks anyway," Ethan said.

Milena waited for the kind that blanketed everything in quietness and for a moment transformed the world into what it could have been. She would go out into the winter wonderland like a little girl lost in a magical realm. The quiet snows were rare and brief. They had to be experienced. Perhaps these were truly phantoms of another time. Maybe the timeslips or tesseracts that Conrad had been telling them about.

"Just those snows. I run on sunlight, you know. I can't wait for Christmas, seeing how I missed it last year." It had always been a contemplative and restful time for her. No one ever asked her if she was ready for Christmas more than once. "You don't get ready for it," she would tell them, "you let it surround you."

"If we get too much snow we'll have to go out west for a few weeks. Duncan won't mind."

"Yeah, right. Nothing is taking me away from here for a long time." They sat in the quietness, then she said to him, "You know, we haven't talked much about what happened."

"Kind of a lot to take in. We all needed a bit of a break."

"No, I mean what we found. Who we actually are. It was always dreamlike before. Now it's, 'Okay, we are Watchers, defenders of the Light, standing against the Darkness.' In a way, I feel normal for the first time, not like an alien living hidden among another race."

"We found out what we were meant to be and chose it, embraced it." Ethan looked at Milena, never tiring of staring into those eyes. "We found our part in the Story."

"Yes, we have." Milena smiled. "And what a story it has become." She moved to accept the kiss Ethan was about to give her, stopping only when she heard the voice.

"Here are your drinks." Kyra bounded down the pathway, almost stepping on Scout.

"Sorry, kitty."

Scout, annoyed, left.

"Thanks, Kyra." Milena sat up. "Sit next to me and watch the sky with us." Milena couldn't believe how much she had grown in a year. Then again, she knew the woman that she would someday become.

"There isn't any romance going on here?"

"No, goof-pot, not right now," Ethan said.

"Okay." Kyra sat down next to her mother. "But 'not right now' means 'maybe later.'"

"That's what happens when —"

"Ethan!" Milena gave her husband a look. The one with the raised eyebrow.

"I wasn't going to say anything," Ethan said.

"I bet."

"It's a beautiful night. Maybe we'll see some meteors. Keep an eye out, Kyra."

"I will, daddy." Kyra made herself comfortable and laid her head down on her mother's lap.

"I think someone is sleepy anyway," Milena said.

"Maybe a pre-nighttime nap," Kyra said. Then she opened her eyes wide.

"Hey, mom?"

"What is it?"

"I think I'm going to have a brother." Both Ethan and Milena gaped at each other. "I guess 'not right now' means 'we already took care of that,'" Kyra said with a smile.

Christina had waited long enough. She stood in the kitchen holding the LED light-bulb that she was about to screw into the ceiling fan. It had been weeks since Conrad came back from his trip into the woods. She could feel the heaviness pressing on his mind and had tried to ask him for days what had happened. This was it. She marched into the living room where Conrad sat in his chair reading a book. Probably another one of those Dylan Hunter novels.

"Connie, we have to talk."

"This can't be good." He knew that tone and she had her arms crossed. "What about?"

"No, this is serious. You have been in a fog since your little hike. What happened?"

"What do you mean —"

"Don't try it!" Now her hands went to her hips. "Don't pretend you don't know what I'm talking about. I know what is under those giant oaks. I watched Kyra disappear."

Conrad was speechless. Then he started to grin. She had beat him to it, proving again how smart she was.

"There are some things I've been wanting to tell you for some time." He stood, approached Christina, and held her by the arms. "I just didn't know how. I'll explain every last detail. Just don't be angry with me." Strangely, though, she didn't look all that mad, or confused, when she looked up at him.

"I'm not." Now it was her turn to smile. She held the light-bulb in front of her. "I have a little secret of my own."

The bulb began to burn like the Sun.

Nearly at the other end of the country, Duncan looked at the late-evening sky. Dark clouds moved over the town. A storm. *Great.* He had walked into Sedona, as he often did in the evenings, and just happened by a certain clothing store. It wasn't the trendy, over-priced clothes that he found attractive — not his style at all — it was the brunette with the elusive smile who worked there. Never quite caught her name; she was always in a hurry. There was some connection between them, wasn't there? Or was he imagining it? No, he was sure. He hadn't seen her in weeks and there she was, running out of the store, her boots hitting the sidewalk hard.

"Get out of here!" She yelled at the sky and a wind blew across the town, sending the storm clouds away. She pulled a hair tie out of her skirt pocket and started to tie back her hair, now a mess from the wind. Turning to go into the store, she stopped. *It's him, did he see that?* "Hey, haven't seen you for weeks. How are you? Duncan, right?" She had made sure to get his name last time by asking to see his credit card.

"Yes, that's me. I'm getting some gear together for a trip up to the canyon."

"Sounds like fun. I haven't been there in years." She gave him a half-smile and started to walk away. Not this time. Duncan wasn't going to mess this up.

"Wait a second. I don't think I have ever got your name."

She stopped quickly like she had wanted him to say something more.

"Solana." She didn't move.

Here it goes, Duncan thought.

"What are you doing for dinner, Solana?"

"That depends on where you are taking me." She smiled, for real this time. "Maybe we can talk about this trip you are going on." She held out her hand. "Come inside while I close up early. Business has been slow tonight."

When Duncan took her hand, a breeze whirled around them. His hand tingled with a charge. Definitely something different about her. What had she been yelling at, and where did that storm go? He didn't know, but there was no doubt that the connection was real.

And something new was about to begin.

One of the tremors from the thinning of the veil shook dust and stone from the canyon walls. The tranquil river rippled and tried to awake from its lethargic sleep. Drought and a growing population with an unquenchable thirst had decades ago stole the Colorado's power. The ancient rock walls towering above the muddy water held the history of many epochs in its layers. There was one secret that had been carved by unknown hands. Beginning twenty feet above the water, the stairs rose steeply and stopped short of the precipice above. Hidden from the prying eyes of the few adventurers that ever wandered into the forbidden quadrant, a stone slab rumbled open. Something stirred in the darkness.

Their master was calling.

GLOSSARY
OF NAMES, PLACES AND EVENTS

Ankh Cross – In Egyptian hieroglyphs, the ankh means "life." A loop is in place of the top arm. The rounded form — the Coptic Cross used by Coptic Christians — is also known as the *crux ansata*, or "cross with a handle."

Black Death – A plague that swept across Europe (and much of the world) during the middle of the 14th Century. At least one-third of the population died, numbering in the tens of millions. Mainly caused by the bubonic plague, its virulence has led some to believe other factors or diseases were also at work. Black Death was a later term; originally known as the Great Pestilence, Great Plague, or Great Mortality.

Book of the Wars – Technically *Book of the Wars of the Lord*. A lost ancient book referenced in the *Book of Numbers*.

Celtic Cross – Has a circle centered on where arms intersect. Often decorated with scroll work. Legend has it that Saint Patrick introduced this cross during his missions in Ireland, though this is unlikely. Use seems to predate Christian times, but was not as widespread until that era.

Cross of Lorraine – A two-barred cross, the upper bar usually smaller. Often used in reference to Joan of Arc, but it didn't originate with her. Used as a symbol of those fighting against oppression.

Cross pattée – Often red, the "footed cross" best known for use by some knights in the Crusades, such as the Templars. The arms of the cross are even in length, narrowing at the center, and broad and concave at the ends, forming a total of eight points.

Crux ordis – The cross of the Teutonic Knights. Usually black and simple. Sometimes similar to the cross pattée, with a longer bottom stem.

Fallen – See Watchers of Heaven.

First Scourge – Approximately 1600 B.C., near the beginning of the Late Bronze Age, upheaval tore through the world. The Hyskos conquered Egypt, the Indus civilization completed its collapse, the volcano Thera explodes in the Mediterranean, and the Xia Dynasty in China falls, among other catastrophes.

Glastonbury Tor – A hill that rises over five-hundred feet next to the town of Glastonbury in Somerset, England. Tor is Celtic for "hill." The Celts called Glastonbury Tor *Ynys Wydryn*, the Isle of Glass. Evidence of occupation dates back to Neolithic times.

Great Cataclysm – The first and most destructive calamity to befall early man. Many ancient cultures recall a destructive flood, such as the Noah account recorded by the Hebrews in the *Book of Genesis*, the Sumerians in *Eridu Genesis,* and in the Babylonian *Epic of Gilgamesh.* Thought to have been brought on to destroy the extreme depravity of men and the Watchers of Heaven.

Hinder Sea – Mediterranean Sea. Also known as the Western Sea, Great Sea, and the Sea of the Philistines.

Horns of Hattin – Location of the Battle of Hattin during the Crusades in Lower Galilee of modern Israel. It derives its name from the twin peaks of an extinct volcano overlooking the plains of Hattin.

Lemuria – A lost continent rumored to have existed in the Pacific Ocean. There, the Fallen and other evils that had been driven from the world, built an empire. From there they had hoped to reconquer the world.

Mohenjo Daro – Once one of the great cities of the Indus Civilization, it collapsed during the First Scourge. Its ruins lay in southeastern Pakistan and is now known as the Mound of the Dead.

Sea Peoples – This large group of people emerged from somewhere across the Mediterranean in a mass migration and invasion into the Near East during the Second Scourge. Ramses III repulsed them from Egypt, but they would prosper in what is now Lebanon (see Tyre). It is unclear what drove them from their homes.

Second Scourge – Approximately 1200 B.C., the Late Bronze Age comes to an end during global turmoil. Volcanic and earthquake activity is rampant. The Sea Peoples attempt to conquer Egypt. Many empires like the Assyrians and Hittites go into decline. The causes of both Scourges are debated, but whatever they were, they drove people, or were used by others, to war and conquer.

Servants of the Flame – Angels, as referred to in the *Book of Hebrews*.

Spear of Destiny – Weapon used by a Roman soldier to spear the side of Christ. Apocryphal books name the Roman soldier as Longinus. Many relics in history have been claimed as the true spear. Known by many names, including the Holy Lance, Lance of Longinus, and Spear of Christ.

Triquetra – Symbol consisting of three interlaced, continuous elliptic shapes, often with a circle passing through the loops. Used by various cultures, mainly northern Europe and Germanic lands, as art or with religious significance. Christians use it to represent the Trinity.

Tyre – On the Mediterranean coast of modern Lebanon, the origins of this city reach back thousands of years, perhaps as early as 2750 BC. Invaded by the Sea Peoples around 1200 B.C., it would become a prosperous city of the Iron Age and the Phoenician people. Once on friendly terms with Israel, they later gloated over Jerusalem's destruction at the hands of Nebuchadnezzar. The prophet Ezekiel would foresee Nebuchadnezzar laying ruin to most of Tyre, and its destruction completed later by Alexander the Great.

Watchers of Heaven – Fallen angels cast out during the War in Heaven. The *Books of Enoch* detail both good and fallen Watchers and the *Book of Daniel* refers to holy Watchers. Some postulate that the Fallen became the gods in the myths of the ancient world and they fathered the Nephilim (mentioned in the *Book of Genesis*). The Great Cataclysm was intended to destroy them and what the Fallen had wrought.

AUTHOR'S NOTES

The history of this book is one that unfolded over many years, with many influences, but its final shaping benefited from a number of individuals. Editor Jaimie Engle has a great eye for rooting out problems and uncovering bad habits. I did violate her "no prologues" rule, but Jaimie's excellent work has made this a better story. Any odd writing habits or choices are undoubtedly my own. Readers can check out her outstanding books at jaimiengle.com.

One of the early readers of this book included my sister Kristy, who's colorful commentary would be perfect for a "special edition." She also created the map and did the digital work on the covers. She takes payments in the form of gift cards and food. John Millam, Nancy Reid, Martha Lopata and Daniel McCarthy were all test subjects, I mean beta readers, of an earlier draft. They all provided valuable input that was very much appreciated. Last, but certainly not least, my wife Annette was the first to bravely read the manuscript when it was finally in presentable form and I think she actually enjoyed it (she is even planning on reading it again).

The years of adventuring with a certain group of friends (you know who you are), may have inspired some elements of this story. Those adventures — both on and off the page — shall continue.

On a few other references: When Milena muses over the "extravagant beauty" of nature, this comes from writer John Eldredge. He also often writes in his books about "the Story" that we are in, which Ethan and Milena refer to. This is something also explored by C.S. Lewis, and the quote in the opening epigraph comes from his book *The Weight of Glory*. If you are wondering about the book Conrad was reading (Dylan Hunter), check out the Vigilante Author at bidinotto.com (full disclosure: Robert is my cousin).

I'm not one to reveal too many details "behind the curtain" of what I write, but here are a few tidbits:

The early scene with Ethan in a college library viewing the stained glass of *Paradise Lost*, is based on the real locale, McCartney Library, at Geneva College. The rockshelter at which Conrad encounters evil beings is inspired by the Meadowcroft Rockshelter, the site of oldest habitation in North America. Stonehenge and Glastonbury, like most places in this story, are real enough. If you would like to explore them further, try George Wingfield's little *Glastonbury: Isle of Avalon* and Christopher Chippindale's exhaustive *Stonehenge Complete*. And while the Battle of Hattin and the Templars eventually played a minor part in the tale, Stephen Howarth's *The Knights Templar* gives a conspiracy-free history of that order and those times.

The characters of Ethan and Milena are both educated in the sciences, and both question giving "chance" any miraculous power in creating the complex universe they live in. They also, obviously, don't see conflict between religion and science. In our own existence, many scientists have also doubted the probability of complexity arising randomly. A small sampling of this would include *The Privileged Planet* by astronomer Guillermo Gonzalez or *Why the Universe is the Way it Is* by astronomer Hugh Ross. The latter also shows that the "war" between religion and science is, at best, a myth. Oxford mathematician John C. Lennox addresses this as well in his excellent *God's Undertaker: Has Science Buried God?*

On the subject of science, there are glimpses of the nature of space-time, unseen energies, and related physics in the story — just enough to root the fantastic in fact. Astrophysicist Brian Greene provides more depth on the fantastic nature of the universe in his readable classic, *The Elegant Universe*. Hugh Ross outlines the implications of multidimensional physics for belief and existence in *Beyond the Cosmos*. Central to the story of the Watchers is a dual, but in ways separate, nature of humans (soul/body). Neuroscientist Mario Beauregard's *Brain Wars* and *The Spiritual Brain* explore this reality.

I could say more, but I don't want to risk spoiling the Easter eggs scattered throughout the story (many of which are in reference to things of a less serious nature). As Ethan wondered about what bits of truth may be hidden in myth and legend, I leave the reader to consider the same.

Dark Snowfall
A Lost Tale

"Are you ready for Christmas?" asked the cashier. The woman's grayish, curled hair still hinted red from her youth. It also sparkled with red and green glitter. Milena had never seen her before, but she didn't often venture to the chaotic department store. The lady was probably working through the Christmas season for some extra money. Something felt strangely familiar about her. She had the signature, perhaps? No, it was just one of those days when the veil was thin. There had to be a reason, one that could be wrapped in either light or darkness. Unfortunately, something pointed to the latter. Milena couldn't put her finger on it.

"You don't get ready for Christmas," Milena replied, "you let it surround you." She noticed the woman's name tag. "And how about you, Ashling, are you *ready*?"

"Yes, the family is coming over, which I love, but the days of cleaning and cooking aren't something I relish." Ashling scanned the winter boots that Milena was buying. Brown leather and fur-lined, with thick treads which would no doubt serve their purpose in the snow. "Very nice, these look warm."

"I hope so. I wore out my last pair." Then, with a laugh, she added, "A girl can never have too many boots, though my husband might disagree." Ethan said it was her one bad trait. Or was it two with the whole purse issue? Milena handed the woman cash for the boots.

"Here you go." The cashier gave the change and receipt to Milena. "Have a Merry Christmas." Milena noticed a faint accent. Irish. Now the origin of the woman's unusual name became clear.

"You, too, Ashling, have a Merry Christmas." Ashling handed Milena the box, and held it for a moment before letting go. Her eyes widened; her voice dropped.

"Be careful. An odd snow is falling. Strangeness is about," she said.

"Okay...I will," Milena said, not sure what to make of the woman's sudden change. "I didn't know it was suppose to snow." The cashier let go of the box and smiled, her demeanor reverting instantly. Her attention shifted to the next customer, avoiding Milena's troubled look. She shook it off and left the store.

The snow slowly drifted out of the sky, shimmering in the lights scattered around the parking lot. Milena pulled on her hood, her long, black hair falling along her face and over her coat. For a minute she let the world fade and watched the snow fall from above. Was this the kind of snow that blanketed everything in quietness, and for a moment, transformed the world?

No, this was something else entirely.

At the edge of perception, the veil shifted and snow dumped out of the dark clouds. Winds tore through the parking lot, engulfing Milena in a cauldron of whiteness. She covered her face and knelt to the ground. Then, after an impossibly long minute, the wind ceased. She opened her eyes as the last flakes floated by. She stood, leaving her box in the snow.

"Well, this can't be good." Only Milena could be so calm in seeing what lay before her. The cars had vanished; the land the store had occupied was thick with trees. She had crossed through the veil into the distant past, to the same location. A timeslip. But why?

Milena had used portals to travel through time, but never without one like Kyra had done. Nor was she overly sensitive to the tesseracts, the thin places, to the point she could see through them as her friend Conrad was so gifted. Milena had certainly experienced much as a Watcher, but this was new even for her.

Dreadful darkness lurked among the leafless trees and moonlit shadows tangled over the snow. The oppression weighed heavy on her mind. No doubt this darkness had caused the rift. Most people would have paid it no attention, if they perceived it at all, but she wasn't most people. Her soul sensed it for what it was and could pass through the window into the stream of time. She wished she would have recognized the rift earlier and not allowed it to pull her through.

A twig snapped. Chatterings of a foul language spread through the calm, winter air.

"Strengthen me with the Light," Milena whispered. She had no weapons. A small pile of rocks poked through the snow at the base of a tree. "Those will have to do."

Into the light, walking on its hands and feet, crept a spawn of the Dark One. Leathery, vaguely greenish skin, stretched tight over its skeletal frame. Black saliva oozed from fangs, leaving a dark spray on the snow as it hissed. Bulbous, unblinking, yellow eyes with dark slits stared at Milena.

Iyyim.

Milena remembered the ancient word for an ancient terror. Better known in modern myth as a goblin or orc. In her rapid train of thoughts, she wondered if this evil was on the way to the Misty Valley. Ethan had mentioned no goblins among the combatants there. Maybe that was to be decided here at this time, maybe it always had. Maybe this had nothing to do with that at all. No matter.

With the speed only a Watcher could attain, she ran to the rock pile, grabbing one in each hand, and spun to face the orc. It cried out, leaped through the air towards Milena. The first rock she threw smashed its left eye, obliterating the yellow orb in a spray of black fluid. The creature shrieked and fell to the ground, clawing at its face. The second rock hit it square in the forehead. The snap of its neck no doubt heard deep into the woods.

Milena found two more projectiles, but the goblin twitched twice and died. Her brown eyes swirled and glowed green, the energy of her soul and the Light cascaded through her body. An Arc Madien wasn't so easily defeated. She calmed and walked towards the corpse.

"'You throw like a girl,' my gym teacher used to say. So much for that theory." Disturbed screams emerged from within the forest. Her heart raced again. More orcs. Lots of them. "I'm going to need some help." She closed her eyes and controlled her breath.

Come to me.

In a few moments she heard soft padding on the snow. She opened her eyes. Twelve wolves crept slowly out of he underbrush towards her. She knelt down on one knee as they approached and allowed her to pet their faces. "Beautiful creatures, will you help me?" Tame as dogs in her hands, she had learned of her gift as a child. Few animals could ignore Milena's mind. They were creations born out of the Light, not the Darkness.

To her left, a cougar sat silently, and to the right, three stags came near. They snorted and shook their deadly antlers, far more massive than she had ever seen. "Now I have an army. See that disgusting horror? More are coming." The wolves circled the dead orc, howling into the sky. The orcs had killed many of their kind.

Interrupting their barks and howls, goblins crashed

through the woods, screeching in their obscene tongue. Seven of them skidded to a stop in the snow at the sight of the animals. The blood of their dead comrade blackened the snow. They hesitated; Milena stood.

"The fight you picked today will be your last." She looked around her.

"My friends, send these filth back to the Dark One." A unison of howls, the roar of the cougar, and the stamping of hooves, exploded into a stampede rushing into the orcs. Before any could move, the closest orc was impaled by a stag's antlers and hurled against a tree. Another flailed wildly as the cougar landed on its back and sunk its teeth into its neck. The wolves rabidly bit and tore into the vile creatures. Not all avoided the razor-edged claws and fangs of the orcs.

The forest didn't have to endure the maelstrom of screams and yelps, the fury of fang and claw, for very long. Quiet soon returned and Milena approached the carnage.

The orcs lay dead in crimson streaked and blackened snow. Four wolves had died and a stag had been torn open. As it breathed its last, Milena stroked its face.

"Thank you." Her eyes teared. The animals came to her. "I am sorry that this occurred, but the Darkness has fled. I no longer sense oppression in your land. You are all safe now."

As Milena walked among the dead, the snow began to brighten, the Moon chased away the shadows, and snow swirled around her. When it cleared, she stood in the parking lot once more. Her box lay on the ground. Hundreds hurriedly walked through the lot every day, completely oblivious of the horrors that had hunted in this land.

Unaware that once, long ago, in this very spot buried under the asphalt, the Darkness and Light clashed. Lost to history, buried in myth, the world had been a very different place. She knew the Darkness still conspired in the shadows to execute their return. It nearly had done so, and would try again.

When that day came, the Watchers would be ready, as they had for many millennia, to turn the spawn of the Dark One back to the Abyss.

ABOUT THE AUTHOR

Darrick Dean is an engineer by education, but always seemed to enjoy writing more than math. Stories have been simmering in his mind for years, but in the meantime he has written a newspaper column, nonfiction articles in a variety of magazines on topics ranging from space exploration to archaeology. Yet it was those stories from elsewhere that kept intruding.

Among the Shadows is the first of three *Watchers of the Light* novels. The *Servants of the Flame* duology, set in the same universe, will parallel the events in the trilogy.

Join the War Among the Shadows at **darrickdean.com** for updates, previews and much more on history, legend and imagination. Be sure to follow on Facebook, Amazon, Goodreads, and review *Among the Shadows* at these places or any of your favorite book haunts.

The war to save mankind has only just begun.

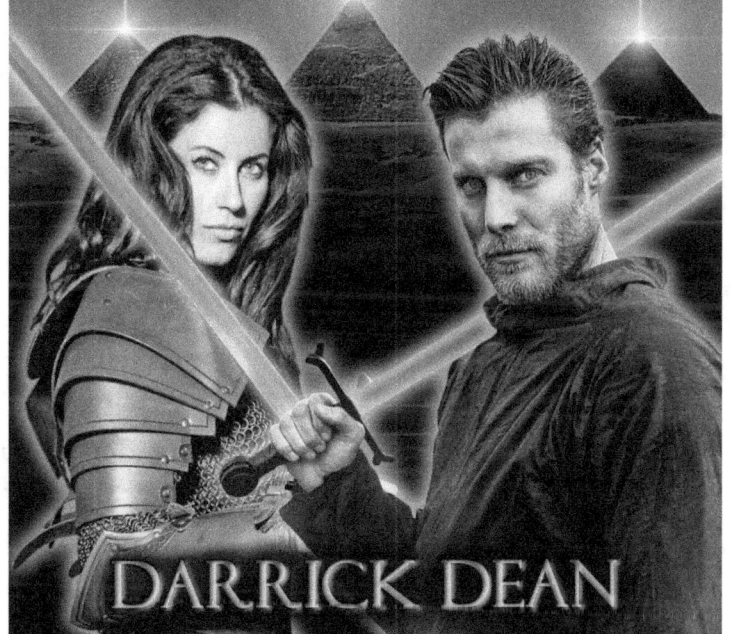